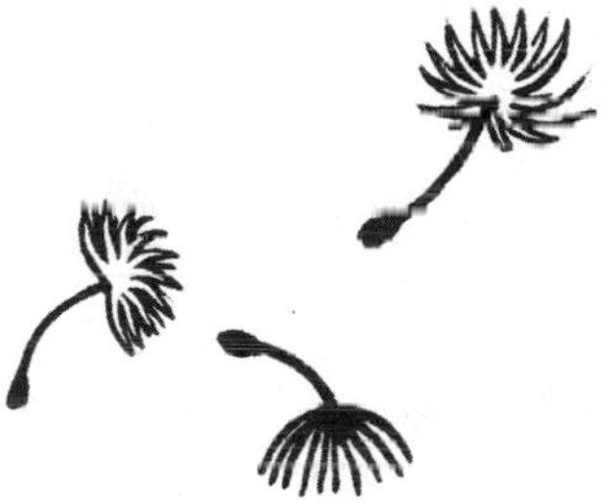

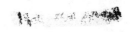

Oddity

ELI BROWN

illustrated by
KARIN RYTTER

WALKER BOOKS

The geography, events, and people of *Oddity* are invented, though sometimes inspired by reality. The Native groups included in the Sehanna Confederation are fictional, though inspired by the political organization of the Haudenosaunee/Iroquois of the Northeast. I chose to craft fictional groups rather than misrepresent the legitimate figures and history of Native groups by placing them in a magical, alternate history. I do not have the same reservation regarding Napoléon Bonaparte, the only historical figure featured, whose story and character I have manipulated to my own ends. Inventing Native cultures is problematic, especially as I am a white man, and my solution is not a perfect one. I am humbled by the complexity and import of our shared history and direct you to https://americanindian.si.edu/sites/1/files/pdf /education/HaudenosauneeGuide.pdf for information on the Haudenosaunee/Iroquois. Though I consulted with an expert on the Haudenosaunee/Iroquois while writing this novel, mistakes and missteps are mine alone.

Text copyright © 2021 by Eli Brown
Illustrations copyright © 2021 by Karin Rytter

First edition 2021

Library of Congress Catalog Card Number pending
ISBN 978-1-5362-0851-1

20 21 22 23 24 25 SHD 10 9 8 7 6 5 4 3 2 1

Printed in Chelsea, MI, USA

This book was typeset in Goudy Old Style.
The illustrations are linocut engravings.

Walker Books US
a division of
Candlewick Press
99 Dover Street
Somerville, Massachusetts 02144

www.walkerbooksus.com

A JUNIOR LIBRARY GUILD SELECTION

To Ben, my first word,

and Tony, who completed our set

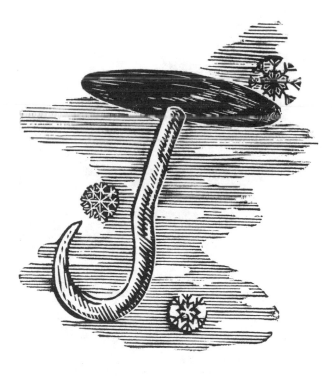

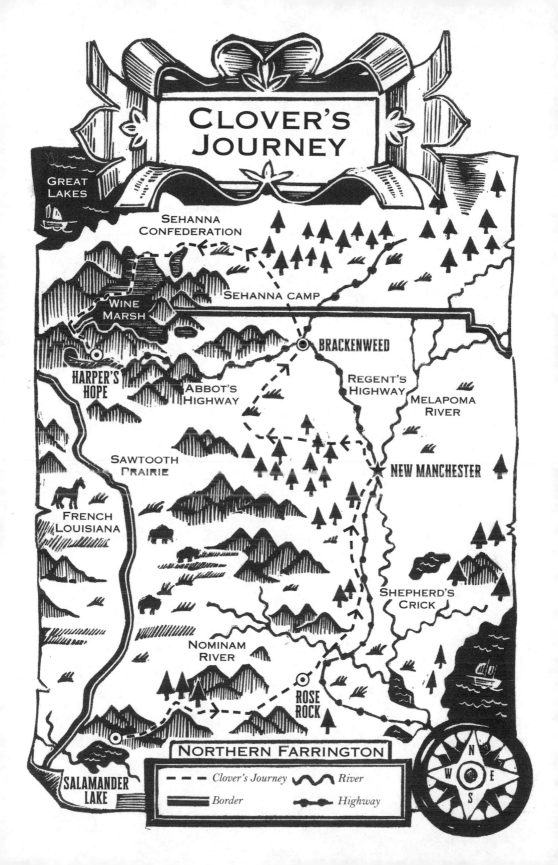

Mama, Mama, look at me;
found myself an oddity.

Beat the rug, wash the clothes,
put a ring in the red bull's nose.

Worry, worry, fly from me;
I don't want no oddity.

Fire's gone cold, bull is dead,
Mama's lying in her bed.

—TRADITIONAL NURSERY RHYME

PART I

CHAPTER 1

TROUBLE BREEDS TROUBLE

Are you keeping mice in your bag again?" Constantine asked, turning in his saddle to peer at his daughter. "You couldn't choose a filthier pet."

"I haven't kept mice since I was a little girl," Clover said, folding her haversack closed and pulling her hat down to hide her eyes. If her father knew what she *did* have in her bag, he would wish it were a whole litter of mice.

"I can hear you fiddling with something back there. When you turn fourteen, I'll be giving you your own medical bag, but not if you plan to keep buttered bread and rodents in it."

Clover held her tongue. In addition to remembering the portions that turned poison to medicine, never flinching from the horrors of pus or spilling organs, and keeping his tools clean and orderly, her father also wanted Clover herself to be *tidy*: useful and trouble free, like a porcelain spoon. She was too tired to argue anyway. For the past two days they'd been assisting a breech birth down on the Sawtooth Prairie, and fatigue had made Clover goose brained.

She knew she looked ragged even though her dark curls were bound into tight braids. Being a doctor's daughter was messy work, and Clover hated to have her hair yanked by deranged patients. She'd been tending to the sick in the foothills of the Centurion Mountains with her father for as long as she could remember. She helped him grind powders and hold patients down during surgery. She even stitched up the easy wounds herself, dipping the silk in brandy before making the tight, clean loops that kept a body together.

Now Clover shifted in her saddle, close to giggling or cursing. Or both. She watched her father, the model of propriety. Constantine Elkin had high cheekbones and a black beard that tapered to a handsome ink brush point. In recent years, Clover had seen the gray hair creep into his temples. His clothes were threadbare, but even now, after twenty-six hours of keeping a mother and baby alive in a sod house, his vest was still buttoned up—he was always a gentleman. He even chewed pine needles so his patients wouldn't smell the smoked trout he survived on.

They started up the red-clay slopes toward home. The forest thickened, and a squirrel squawked at them from the branches above. To Clover, there was nothing sillier than an angry squirrel, a fat governor of its own tree. She giggled, which only made the squirrel bark louder. Its tail waved like a battle flag. Clover wiggled her nose and showed her own teeth as she barked back, "Chuff, chuff!"

Clover's stomach grumbled. She hadn't had time to eat the raisin buns Widow Henshaw had made for her, and now they were as stale as oak galls. She pinched off a crust and cast it at the base of the tree, because even grumpy squirrels deserved something sweet now and then.

Her father shot her a look. He was suspicious. What would he do if he discovered the secret in her haversack? Nothing upset him as much as an oddity.

Clover noticed the bundle of gray fur swinging from her father's saddlebag and was suddenly as hungry as she was tired.

"Are you telling me that after two days of tending and a healthy baby against all odds, those settlers paid us with prairie rabbits?" Clover asked.

"You would prefer to be paid with snails? They're poor, *kroshka*," Constantine answered. "The poorest."

Clover usually liked it when he called her *kroshka*—it meant little bread crumb—but those rabbits galled her.

"Aren't we poor? Everyone pays us with turnips or jugs of sour cider. There's not even any fat on those rabbits. Look at your pants. I've mended them so many times the seat looks like a quilt."

Constantine sighed and shook his head.

"This is why the ties on my bonnet frayed and I switched to men's hats," Clover continued.

He looked back at her under a cocked eyebrow. "I thought you preferred dressing like a boy." There was a tender smile half-hidden under his mustache.

"I wear trousers so I can sit on a saddle properly, since I spend half my life on this horse. I wear men's gloves because they were made to get dirty and don't stretch or wear out." Clover knew she was beginning to sound like an angry squirrel herself, but after the cramped vigil in the damp birthing room it felt good to holler. "I'm not about to blister my backside sitting sidesaddle just because the world was made for men!"

"As you wish," he said.

It was just like her father to make her feel like she had chosen this life.

"A Prague-trained surgeon could have real paying customers if only we lived a little closer to New Manchester," she argued. "Or Brackenweed. Or any city. We could have fresh milk every day and new clothes. In New Manchester, we could buy turpentine instead of having to boil pine resin ourselves. That stuff never washes out! And you ask me why I don't wear dresses."

Her father was silent, allowing her outburst but refusing to participate. If Clover had wanted a response, she shouldn't have mentioned New Manchester. Nothing shut her father up as quickly as talk of the past. He had buried his history like a dead body.

Clover had been a toddler when they left New Manchester and didn't remember a thing about it. "Cities are swollen with woe," Constantine was fond of saying. Because of his Russian accent it sounded like *svollen vit voe*. The true name of that woe was Miniver Elkin. Clover knew only three things about her dead mother: that she had been a collector of oddities; that she was involved with a society of scholars who studied the singular objects; and that she had died in a tragic accident that her father would not explain.

Constantine's broken heart was the reason Clover had never walked the busy streets of New Manchester, never visited her mother's grave. Everyone said that Constantine Elkin was a generous doctor. But Clover knew how much he kept for himself. His high, learned forehead was a cabinet he had locked his secrets inside.

Now Clover had her own secret, something thrilling. Keeping an eye on the back of her father's head, she opened her haversack and reached in.

She gasped as it stung her finger. Biting cold! She opened the bag a little wider to let the light in.

It could have been an ordinary ice hook: an iron curve like an eagle's talon with a simple wooden handle, gray and splitting. Clover thought it was lovely, its flank dimpled where the smith's hammer had shaped it. If polished, it might even have fit among her father's surgical tools.

Just last week, while looking for mushrooms, she'd found the Ice Hook under the leaf mulch on the western side of the lake. It was the kind of tool used to carry blocks of ice in the fancy cities, where they could keep food cold for weeks in icehouses. Salamander Lake, where Clover lived, had smokehouses but no icehouse. No one she knew had any use for a tool like this, but then, this wasn't just an ice hook.

The minute she'd touched it, she'd known it was odd. The iron was ice-cold, even though the rocks around it had been warm from the afternoon sun. Clover hadn't had time to really examine it or wonder at her luck, because her father had hollered for her to saddle up for the ride down to the prairie. Now, three days later, the tool was still thrillingly chilled.

There was no denying it; the Ice Hook was an oddity, one of the fabled objects that her mother had collected and her father refused to discuss.

What he didn't know was that Clover had studied issues four, seven, and twenty-one of the *Journal of Anomalous Objects*, which their landlady, Widow Henshaw, kept hidden in her pantry under rags and bundles of lavender. While the old woman napped by the stove, Clover memorized the brittle pages.

She lay awake most nights enchanted by the entries. In Spain, there was a Fishing Net that pulled trout from the water fully cooked, with herbs and butter. In the southern coastal town of Juniper, there existed a Button that whistled a cheery melody whenever it rained. Clover had memorized the entry:

The Button has been proudly worn on the jacket of every mayor since the founding of the city. Juniper hosts a music festival in March, inviting composers to perform their variations on the Button melody. Should you attend, bring an umbrella and an appetite for the local delicacy, chowder pie . . .

But no matter how much she committed to memory, Clover was fixated on the missing pieces. The journals in the pantry were out of date, their lists incomplete. She ached to know what other wonders were hidden in the world. It didn't help that this strange disclaimer could be found on the first page of each issue:

Be it known that portions of this periodical contain intentional errors and outright fabrications. For reasons of safety, the locations of specific oddities have been omitted. Due to incidents of poaching, some collections can no longer be publicly displayed. Please report poachers and criminal traffickers to your local sheriff.

It was intended to frustrate thieves, but it frustrated Clover too, casting a dreamlike uncertainty over the entire subject. Every entry in the journal was as intriguing as it was unbelievable: a Mirror that led to another world, a talking Rooster that had risen to the rank of army colonel, an Umbrella that trapped lightning . . . Clover could never be sure which oddities were real, actually out there in the world, and which were decoys imagined by the Society of Anomalogists. Before she found the Ice Hook, Clover had worried that oddities were just another fantasy adults indulged in, like wishing wells, shooting stars, and Father Christmas.

But now she knew better. Now she had *touched* the truth.

She let her horse fall back a bit to give herself some privacy and pulled the Ice Hook out of her bag. She lifted it to the sunlight to see the white fuzz gathering on the steel near the handle, the moisture in the air turning to frost. It was as if winter itself had been forged into the tool. She touched it lightly with her tongue. It stuck fast, frozen instantly to the metal. She pulled it off with a whimper.

A wonder, a marvel! Though she had no idea what to do with it, just holding the Ice Hook made Clover breathless. Her hand trembled, like the first time she'd used her father's scalpel to remove a wart.

Something as stubbornly strange as the Ice Hook didn't belong hidden away in sleepy Salamander Lake. Clover knew it was the key to a wider world. Why shouldn't she become a collector like her mother, or maybe even an adventurer like the famous Aaron Agate, searching the wilds for priceless items to write about in the journal? And because she was also her father's daughter, Clover might discover medical uses for oddities. Now that she knew oddities were as real as the boots on her feet, she felt that anything was possible: a cure for the pox, for scarlet fever, for any of the pests that gnawed on human bones. Her father would have to smile on that.

But knowing he could turn around at any moment, she hid the Ice Hook beneath the raisin buns, closed the bag, and promised herself not to look again until she was alone.

They were close to home now. They turned onto a narrow trail near the cliffs that overlooked the lake. They pulled their horses to a stop, and together the two Elkins watched the boats on the water. The lake was a glistening emerald in the late-morning light. As always, Clover tried to make out the salamander shape in the edges of the water. But to her the lake looked more like the hand of a lady who had fainted.

The village itself was just a squat row of cottages on the bank, pine needles gathering on the roofs like coonskin caps. It had been settled years ago by simple folk fleeing the Louisiana War. Whites, Italians, Blacks, and one grumpy Russian doctor, they all ate the same smoked trout, drank the same river water.

Clover's father sat very still as the horses twitched flies away. Finally, he said, "You have something in your bag."

He wasn't angry yet, but he was close. Clover held her breath, watching the muscles of his jaw twitch. There was no escape: he knew.

She pulled the Ice Hook out and held it toward her father. He wouldn't touch it, though. In fact, he seemed afraid to look at it.

"I suppose it is odd?"

"It's always cold," Clover whispered. "Freezing cold. No matter what."

"I don't care what it does!" His eyebrows knitted together. "You know how I feel about oddities."

He shifted in his saddle, as if he couldn't bear to sit so close to the Ice Hook, and glared at Clover. "Put such interests behind you. They are corrupt. They are *dangerous.*"

"Horses are dangerous before we tame them." Clover had rehearsed this argument in her mind. Her voice trembled, but she kept speaking. "Every tool in your bag could be dangerous in the wrong hands. This Ice Hook is simply cold . . ."

"Then why do you hide it like a crown of jewels? Trouble breeds trouble. You may think you've found something special, but there will always be another little secret to protect, and before you know it, you'll be obsessed. You'll sell everything for a button that whistles when it rains or something equally ridiculous. A person may think she is collecting oddities, but in fact the oddities are collecting her."

He brushed the front of his vest off and looked as if he might ride away. But after a moment he said, "It's perverse, isn't it? For it to be cold when nature wants it otherwise?"

"It could make ice," Clover suggested. "Ice can stop pain. You could use it to help—"

"You see? It's already worked its way into your mind," he said. "Made itself indispensable."

Clover was alarmed to see tears welling in her father's eyes.

"There is always an excuse to keep them," Constantine said. "But I have seen what they do, Clover. They took your mother from us." He paused. "This is how she died."

Clover gripped the pommel of her saddle to stay steady. Maybe he would tell her now. "Did she have . . . many?" She faltered, seeing the pain in his face.

"Shelves of them: a Quill that wrote in different languages, a Mirror that swallowed people whole, an Ember that burned and *burned* and refused to be extinguished! She thought they could be . . . useful." He shook his head. "They devoured her."

Clover knew some of these treasures from the journals, and before she could think better of it she blurted, "The Mirror doesn't swallow people. Brave explorers have entered—"

"Never to return!"

It was more than he'd ever admitted before. The Ember! The Quill! Clover had *dreamed* about their magic. Had Miniver really touched them, seen their astonishing effects with her own eyes? Had she looked into that Mirror, a door to a twin world? But there was one question Clover needed answered more than any other.

"How?" Her voice wavered. She'd never been this close to knowing. "How did oddities kill Mother?"

Constantine's hat cast a shadow over his face, and Clover felt his silence returning.

"Where, at least, is she buried?" she pushed. "Haven't I the right to know where my own mother rests?"

Clover expected him to snap at her, but when he finally spoke, it was in a weary whisper. "This simple world is good enough for us. A pitcher that holds water. A needle that pulls thread. These are good enough. Do not become a collector of oddities, Clover Elkin."

Clover scratched the frost off the Ice Hook with her thumbnail. Just last year she would have cried at this disappointment, but she kept her eyes on the oddity. She'd learned to take deep breaths to keep the tears from welling up.

"Promise me," he said.

Clover bit her cheek until it bled. "I promise," she said.

"What do you promise?"

Now the tears came. "I promise not to collect oddities."

Clover made one last effort. "But this one. It's unique—*wondrous* . . . !" Her words failed her.

"How do you intend to get rid of it?"

He was giving her no room to argue, no choice at all. She'd found, at last, something of her own, a door to her mother's world, to answers, and her father was shutting it. Locking it. He had to control everything, even her dreams.

She opened her mouth, but outrage choked her.

Clover gripped the Ice Hook, its shameless chill stinging her palm. She raised it over her head like a weapon and threw it as hard as she could. It flashed briefly and dropped into the lake.

"Are you satisfied?" she muttered through clenched teeth. "It's gone forever! And I'll never find another."

"I pray you don't," Constantine said gently.

He reached out and patted her arm, but she pulled away and swallowed a sob. Her father waited as Clover composed herself. He was as patient as a statue—and just as heartless.

A cloud blotted the sun, and the lake turned a deep olive.

"You'll be hungry, no doubt," Constantine said, heeling his horse toward their cabin.

Clover hesitated, watching the ripples where her treasure had disappeared, her hopes sinking with it. She wiped her eyes and followed her father.

"We have earned a proper meal," he said. "You can't survive on raisin buns alone. Tomorrow we'll ride out and see how that new baby is faring." The horses picked up their pace, eager for their oats and bedding. "What will we give to fortify the mother's blood?" he asked.

"Tincture of vervain," Clover muttered, pulling her hat down so he wouldn't see her tears.

"You'll make a good doctor yet," he said.

· · · · · · · · · · ·

The forest air cooled Clover's burning cheeks. Even before she heard the mill wheel, she could smell the particular perfume of home: cut pine, smoked fish, and Widow Henshaw's yeasty doughs.

It was almost noon when they clopped onto the bridge. The mill wheel turned gaily in the high waters of the river that fed the lake—the ceaseless *plish-plash* that had been Clover's lullaby for as long as she could remember. She saw a thin stream of smoke coming from the chimney of their cabin. This meant Widow Henshaw had kept their rooms warm. For all her yearning for adventure, Clover was glad to see home. Soon she would be pulling off her boots and curling under a quilt for a long nap.

The river was a rapid hiss under the bridge. Clover was trying not to think about the Ice Hook stuck in the mud at the bottom of the lake, when her father pulled his horse to a sudden stop.

On the far side of the bridge, a band of strangers sat waiting on their horses, blocking the path.

It was dark under the pines, but Clover could see they were hard men dressed like trappers, with beaver-fur coats and fringed boots.

"I have a rash that itches terrible!" one of them shouted. He was the only one without a beard. "You have a remedy for that, good doctor?"

Clover wondered if she was dreaming when she saw rabbit ears coming out of his hat. But when he scratched his neck, Clover saw that the ears had been sewn there.

Another trapper, big as a bear, laughed. "An' my urine smells like oysters!"

"Oh, shut up, Bolete," the rabbit-eared man said. "The doctor ain't interested in your urine."

Constantine whispered to Clover, "Dismount."

"Why—?"

"*Dismount!*"

Clover obeyed, putting her feet on the bridge and patting her nervous horse on the neck.

Constantine swung himself down and unstrapped his medical bag. Clover pulled her own haversack over her shoulder, her heart pounding.

"Don't you have a salve or ointment or some such?" The rabbit-eared man took a pipe from his mouth and used it to scratch the back of his neck. "No cure but the grave, I reckon. Eh, Dr. Elkin?"

Constantine pressed his medical bag into Clover's hands. He kept pushing until her back was against the low rail of the bridge.

"Father, who are those men?"

"I only kept one oddity," Constantine whispered, his whiskers against her cheek. "Only one."

"What are you saying?" Clover was trembling. She'd never seen her father this way.

"It is . . . *neobkhodimyy*," he said.

It was one of the few Russian words that Clover knew. It meant "necessary." Her father used it only for things that really mattered. A heart was *neobkhodimyy*. An eye, a hand, even a kidney were not.

He pressed the bag against her until she was hugging it. "It holds hope. You must keep it safe. The Society will protect you."

Clover gasped, but he kept talking, his voice gritty with urgency. "Go to Aaron Agate in New Manchester. Look for the canary among doves."

The man named Bolete interrupted. "Don't be rude! Come greet us proper."

The rabbit-eared man said, "That *is* Miniver's girl there, ain't it? String me up if I didn't think you all was dead."

"Take a deep breath," Constantine whispered.

"Father, I'm sorry," Clover blurted. "I'll never touch another oddity—"

Constantine gripped her shoulders hard, stopping her words.

"You won't let them catch you," he said. "You'll hide. You will find the Society and you won't come back here looking for me, ever." He kissed her forehead, then ducked low and grabbed Clover's boots.

Before she knew it, Clover was lifted, toppling over the railing. She turned once in the air and heard the men shouting as she fell.

The water punched the breath out of her. Clover rolled in a roaring darkness. It was everything she could do to hold on to the bags. She twisted in the current, her shoulder knocking hard against a rock.

When she found the surface, she gasped and tried to keep her head up as the river shoved her toward the lake. The eddies spun her around, and she saw the bandits seize her father. They struggled. A gunshot cracked the air and an arterial arc of blood leaped from her father's chest.

From the churning water, she watched her father fall lifeless.

Clover choked on her scream and felt herself going numb. She saw herself from above, as a doll twisting in the pitiless river.

The paddle of the waterwheel chopped down, bruising her arm and bringing Clover back to her body. She looked up to see the next paddle dropping like a hammer. She dove deep to avoid being clobbered. When she emerged, sputtering, on the other side, she could no longer see the bridge.

Suddenly, the rabbit-eared man appeared on the bank just a few yards away. He held a smoldering match in his hand. Not even a hummingbird could have darted around the mill that quickly. He had somehow snapped from one place to the other in an instant.

With a snarl, he dropped the blackened match and dashed into the water to grab at Clover. Terror blurred her vision as the current pulled her just out of his reach.

He tried to wade after her, holding his pistol and a box of matches over his head. He was up to his belt and hollered to the others, "Hurry, boys, I can't swim! She's floatin' away!"

The river raked her over a rocky shoal, and then Clover found herself in the wide lake. The rush of the current continued to push her far from shore, until she could no longer see the murderous men on the riverbank. With the bags weighing her down, she struggled to keep her head above the water. The boats were on the other side of the lake, chasing the schools of lunkhead fish, too far away to hear her screams.

YOUR OWN BATTLES

T he northern bank was so muddy that Clover scrambled on her hands and knees to keep from losing her boots in the sludge, dragging her bags behind her. From this side of the lake, the village looked like a handful of chestnuts scattered on shore. When she could finally stand, Clover found herself stumbling over something slick and uneven.

The shore of the lake was covered with stranded fish.

Heaps of them lay dead and dying, their mouths open in dumb surprise. Striped bass and bluegills shimmered in the afternoon light. So many crowded the shore that Clover kicked them aside as she made her way up the bank. Thousands of eyes stared unblinking at the sky. Pickerels and perch, even a deep-water catfish the size of her leg. Their heads pointed away from the water, as if they'd all gotten the mad notion to up and walk away from their home.

A steam of panic rose, cooking Clover from the inside. She could not draw the attention of those monsters on the other side of the lake. With her braid between her teeth to muffle her wails, she ran into the forest.

In just a minute, Father will appear behind that crooked oak yonder, Clover thought, sobbing. *He'll be waxing his mustache and he'll explain.*

She crashed through huckleberry and bracken fern. Her shoulder ached where it had hit the stone. She hoped it was only a contusion and not a fracture. The bags had doubled their weight by soaking up water, and they tugged with every step.

. . . it holds hope.

How could he have kept an oddity? It must have been in the medical bag all this time. That was why he'd pushed it into her hands. But Clover couldn't look for it now. She kept moving.

He'll be just behind that tree, she assured herself.

But Constantine was not waiting behind any of the trees she passed. He was not sitting in the lee of the fallen birch or sipping water from the moss-cushioned spring.

Clover followed a deer trail, little more than stitches of dust woven into the mulch, hoping it would lead her to a path she knew. The mud dried and fell from her boots in flakes.

She considered cleaning her boots to make them presentable— a ridiculous notion. Her medical training told her that delirium was setting in. A violent shock could make a person daft. The best treatment was to wrap the patient in a warm blanket near a fire and administer brandy. Such a patient should never be left alone.

The sound of a galloping horse made her stop.

Help was near! She pushed through a bramble toward an open dirt trail and was about to call out when she saw one of the bandits charging toward her.

Clover dropped into the bushes, praying she hadn't been seen. As the rider thundered past, she froze. Terror gripped her throat as she heard the hooves rumble to a stop. The murderer was coming back.

The tangles of the winceberry bush were too thick to run through. The thorns left beads of blood on her arms, but Clover pressed deeper into the thicket.

The bandit pulled the horse to a stop just three feet from Clover, scanning the foliage for movement. He was the big one, called Bolete, breathing as heavily as his horse. Clover was close enough to see the man's nostrils flaring, close enough to see, through the trembling leaves, the skulls of rodents that he'd knotted into his greasy beard.

The murderer whistled a lonesome trill, as if summoning a wayward hound. "Girly?" he called. "Is that you?"

For thirty seconds, a minute, Clover didn't breathe. Despite the fire in her lungs, she held stone-still. A minute stretched toward two. Her heart slammed itself into her ribs, desperate for air.

The horse stamped, impatient, but the bandit didn't move. He was listening, watching. "Olly olly oxen free!" he called.

Purple spots crowded into Clover's vision. In a few seconds, she knew she would pass out. If she did, Bolete would hear her collapse into the branches and it would be over.

Clover closed her eyes and turned inward, looking for silent strength. Instead of silence, she heard the grinding of a millstone.

· · · · · · · · · · ·

When Clover was nine years old, she and her father had been called to the bedside of a miller who had lost a duel. The bullet had missed the liver but not the kidney.

"Find the source of the bleeding," Constantine lectured as he worked. The surgery lasted almost ten hours, and the blood and screaming washed over Clover, but the thump and groan of the grain mill in the next room rattled her. There the miller's wife was turning barley into flour because she could not afford to stop working. The relentless growl of that mill, like bone against bone, whispered something to Clover about life and death and hunger that she wished she hadn't heard.

And after all of her effort, tying the miller's hands to the bed-posts, pouring brandy into him until he couldn't speak, preparing the poultices, holding the lamp and the scalpel, boiling rags, and after all of Constantine's immaculate focus, his steady implements searching for the bullet without nicking the arteries, peering into that lurid cavern hour upon hour while the mill shook the walls, after all of that, the miller up and died. He'd waited until the bullet was out at last, dropped like a cherry pit onto the plate Clover held. He'd waited until the last suture was knotted, and the poultice was applied, and the bandage tied snug, then he'd heaved an impatient sigh and died.

Clover hated him for it. And she hated the wife who had worked all night long. She hated that cold grindstone, even hated the powdery sacks of flour. She knew it wasn't right, but she couldn't help it. She packed up their supplies in a hurry while Constantine whispered to the new widow, refusing payment as he always did when things didn't go well.

On the way home, Clover felt the shudder of the mill in her ribs, turning into something icy. She spent three days in bed with a bad fever, nightmares of grinding teeth.

Find the source of the bleeding.

When she woke, she saw that her father had gone off again to attend to some distant suffering, leaving their neighbor and landlord, Widow Henshaw, to wipe her brow.

The widow, fond of poems and boiled nettles, was so old that her face looked like a bowl of steamed prunes. She had been born into slavery but purchased and freed by northern abolitionists as a girl. She'd lived in New Manchester most of her life, working as a midwife, until her sons died in the Louisiana War. After that, grief drove Mrs. Henshaw and her husband to the quiet village by the lake, where they took solace in the filtered light and frog song.

Mr. Henshaw cleared trees and built half the houses in the village. When he fell from a rooftop, the properties passed to his widow. Folks generally paid their rent in salted fish, dried mushrooms, and firewood.

"What hurts?" Widow Henshaw asked. The pewter locket around her neck had tinted the skin there midnight blue.

"That miller's wife," Clover said. "She wouldn't stop working, even to hold his dying hand. I asked Father, and he just said, 'See to the body before you.'"

Widow Henshaw dipped the cloth in lemon balm tea and pressed it to Clover's hot cheeks.

"Your father heals the broken bone, the rattling lungs. Those are the battles he can win," Widow Henshaw said. "He doesn't have medicine for poverty, for war, for the broken heart."

Hearing this, Clover felt ashamed for judging that miller woman. She felt small in the shadow of her father, who gave his best even to the hopeless cases. Then Clover heard herself say something she'd been afraid to even think. "What if I'm not strong enough?"

The widow didn't answer right away. She never hurried; she endured. "You'll have your own battles to win," Widow Henshaw finally said. "And lose." She lifted a spoonful of duck soup to Clover's lips. "Now eat."

· · · · · · · · · · ·

Clover could hold it no longer—air burst from her and she gasped, filling her lungs as she opened her eyes. The memory of the widow's bedside tenderness had given her a few more seconds. Just enough. The bandit was gone.

Clover drew ragged breaths as she freed herself from the briar. "You are hunted, Clover Elkin," she whispered to herself. "No trails. No roads. No more stupid mistakes."

She pushed through the forest, making a confused course that even a fox would have trouble tracking.

When the ground began to slope upward, Clover knew she'd reached the edge of the little valley she'd called home. Before her loomed the breathless expanse of the Centurion Mountains, stretching north through the state of Farrington. Sometimes called "the shrouded mountains" because of the veils of fog that furled through its valleys, the range formed a natural barrier between the French plains and the American cities of the East Coast. The Centurions were largely unmapped, untamed, dense with bears and crumbling cliffs and worse. She'd never been this deep in the woods alone.

A robin in the leaves startled her into motion again. She tied her haversack to the medical bag so she could wear both over her shoulders like a yoke and pushed deeper into the woodland, where, even at midday, crickets trilled in the shadows.

She realized that a good tracker might be able to follow the flakes of mud from her boots, so she scrubbed them hard on a rotten log and then wiped them clean with a wad of fern, staining them green.

Staying off trail made it impossible to get her bearings. "When unsure of your position," Clover reminded herself, "the best course of action is to stay put. Build a fire." Clover did the opposite. She stamped through a little creek, zigzagged up into dells she was sure no one had walked before.

Clover got herself good and lost.

It was late afternoon when she found a lightning-struck oak whose hollow trunk created a den with a carpet of leaves and lichen. At last, she set the bags down.

She sat, surrounded by a shield of gray wood. Everything hurt: her legs, her shoulder, the blisters on her heels, the chafing where the bags had hung from her neck, but none of that mattered. There was nowhere to hide from the awful fact.

"Father is dead."

She choked on her tears until she felt like a wrung-out rag and the shadows leaned toward dusk.

"I'm sorry. I'm sorry . . ." She chewed her braid until it was soaked with spit.

She tried to make sense of his last words. Why would he have kept an oddity? Why would he send her to Aaron Agate if he despised collectors? Agate had been an explorer in his younger days, charting the Melapoma River in a bearskin canoe. He'd edited the journals Clover had secretly read. She'd studied the portrait of Mr. Agate in a beaver-skin hat and had longed to shake his hand someday. If she had known this was how her wish would be granted, she would have burned those journals herself.

"So sorry . . ."

The answers were in the medical bag. Clover snapped open the brass latch. The odors were comforting: the mink oil her father applied to keep the leather supple, camphor and turpentine, mercury salts. The implements, blurred by tears, swam before her as if still under water. She grabbed the first thing her fingers grazed: a bundle of mustard plasters. The medicated gauze was usually placed on the chest to pull infection out of the lungs.

Clover gasped. The gauze was heavier than it ought to be. Her hand began tingling, then burning . . .

Then she realized her mistake and threw it back into the bag, feeling foolish. The plasters weren't odd, they were just soggy. The lake water was activating the mustard powder, irritating her skin. They were useless now, ruined.

Clover tried again, reaching in and retrieving the silver-plated pincers. Could they be the oddity her father meant? They'd pulled splinters, chips of bone, and bullets from hundreds of patients. With trembling hands, Clover gripped her thumbnail with the pincers and gave it a painful tug. She tugged the hem of her shirt, and then her hair. Nothing. She placed them back in the bag, just so.

Clover shook her head, baffled. Constantine was a man who would sterilize tools with vinegar if hot water wasn't available, who would happily survive on dry oats and manzanita berries for days at a time. For him, few things were truly necessary. He used the word *neobkhodimyy* only for things he couldn't do without: clean hands, patience . . .

"What is it?" The tears came again. Clover tried to remember if her father had ever given her another hint, any clue, any—

A scream echoed through the trees.

It wasn't a human voice, exactly. And it wasn't the lovesick wail of a fox, or the glassy screech of an owl. It shook the air again, urgent and pained. People said a witch used to walk these woods, a shifting shadow, like something seen through a broken window. Widow Henshaw called her the Seamstress and said she spoke with two voices, wore a necklace of teeth she'd stolen from sleeping kids, and smelled like the dead animals she carried in her basket.

"The witch isn't real," Clover told herself. "Just a story to scare children . . ."

But oddities were real. And that scream was real.

When she heard it a second time, Clover lifted the bags and headed for a rocky outcropping. Before a flank of boulders, like a theater erected for no one, Clover witnessed a lonely battle.

A feral dog had caught a rooster and was shaking it savagely between its teeth. The dog was a hunting breed, but it had been a long time since it had seen its owner, and lean ribs showed under its brindle coat. The rooster's feathers were brilliant and glistened even as the animals struggled. It was the expensive kind of fowl that won prizes in farmers' almanacs.

The bird was hopelessly outmatched, and it let out the tortured howls that had brought Clover running. The violence of the dog's attack broke the rooster's wing. The bird let out another shriek and twisted frantically.

Clover looked for a long stick to separate them, but suddenly it was the dog that was yowling. The rooster, having turned over the broken wing, had planted one long spur deep into the meat of the dog's nose. It clawed at the dog's eyes with the other foot.

The dog immediately opened its mouth, releasing the bird, but the rooster held on, dragged along as the dog tried to retreat.

When they finally parted, the dog ran yelping into the trees. The rooster paced in a wounded circle, its wrenched wing dragging in the dust behind.

Looking at that broken bird, confused and bleeding, felt like looking into a mirror. Clover was still crying, but she set down her bags and wiped her cheeks with her palms. Pity softened her ragged voice as she said, "Come here, you poor thing."

The rooster jumped and turned to fight her, the hackles of its neck and chest bristling. It tried to flap its wings, but the broken one only shuddered on the ground. Then it wobbled and fainted into a heap of black and turquoise feathers.

Clover sat on a log and held the rooster between her knees, its good wing pinned tightly, keeping the brutal spurs pointed away from her. The head dangled loose over her thigh, but the bird was still breathing.

The smart thing would have been to put the bird out of its misery and roast it over a fire. Clover didn't know when she would see another meal. She pulled her knife out of her haversack but couldn't bring herself to slit the rooster's throat. There had been too much blood already. It seemed the wing was broken in only one place. If Clover helped, this bird might live.

It was foolish to doctor a bird. But just moments ago, Clover had felt so lost, so utterly helpless, that she was glad to find something she knew how to do. All of the sticks she could see nearby were either too gnarled or too gummed with sap to be of any use. Clover fished around in the medical bag and found the chestnut tongue depressor. She had whittled it herself. It wasn't the oddity she was looking for, but it fit the wing well enough.

"This will hurt," Clover said, pulling on the joints to set the bone.

The rooster woke with a wild squawk. It didn't struggle, though, as she went about applying the splint. Its plumage made a tight wrap difficult until Clover found that if she pushed the secondary feathers down, she could provide more support for the bandage. She could tell by the way its claws clenched that the bird was in considerable pain, but it held bravely still, cocking its head to peer at her with brick-colored eyes.

"That is competent work," the Rooster said. "For a field dressing, at least."

CHAPTER 3

BREAD PUDDING

Clover *almost threw the bird to the ground. "Oh dear," she said.* It was only her years of training that kept her still in this moment of shock. "Are you talking?"

"I am wounded. But I take solace in the fact that I am in the care of a medic. You are a medic, I hope?"

"I . . . am."

"Good, then. Kindly keep to your task."

Clover blinked at the Rooster. There was no reason not to finish the splint. Maybe she was losing her mind, but she knew better than to panic during a medical procedure. She could almost hear her father behind her, saying, *See to the body in front of you.*

Holding the splint in place while binding it took a long time; Clover was learning the angles of bird anatomy as she went. She made a final loop of gauze and began to tie the bandage.

"A good medic is invaluable. I thank you for your service," the Rooster said. It spoke rapidly. This was something Clover had seen in other wounded patients. "Are you part of the State Watch?

We are in dire need of trained field nurses, and I'll personally arrange to have you promoted—"

"You're stunned," Clover said quietly. The Rooster's tail feathers, long and curled like the strips of wood from a carpenter's lathe, were getting tangled in the gauze. "Sit still and let me finish."

"Stunned? It would take more than a hooligan ambush to stun a decorated officer of the Federal Army! "Perturbed" is the word. "Inconvenienced," perhaps, but hardly "stunned"! I don't want to intimidate you, but you're speaking to none other than Colonel—"

"Colonel Hannibal Furlong," Clover interrupted. "Of course you are."

The *Journal of Anomalous Objects* listed Hannibal Furlong as a rare "living oddity," but the idea of a talking rooster commanding an army was too peculiar even for Clover. She'd always suspected his entry was a fabrication, or at least an exaggeration. The "Cockerel Colonel" was one of the tall tales passed around by old veterans. He was a legendary hero of the Louisiana War, famous for defending Fort Kimball through a four-day siege by the French. Then, during the notorious "Furlong Retreat," he had ordered his men to sit backward on their horses so they could fire on their pursuers.

"If you know who I am, then there's no excuse for a saucy tongue," Hannibal said. "Don't tie it too tightly."

"Just calm down," Clover said, more to herself than to Hannibal. It was like meeting the sandman or Jack Frost. But this rooster was no folktale; his mustard-colored feet clenched as Clover tightened the bandage. Clover felt the world spinning under her and tried to take deep breaths. "I'm almost done."

"Who tells their commanding officer to 'calm down'? A tongue-wag is bad for morale—"

"Colonel?"

"What is it?"

"I apologize for my insubordination." Clover saluted, hoping to calm the Rooster.

"Finally you show some sense," Hannibal said. "Apology accepted."

"Will you stop flapping and let me finish the splint?"

Hannibal lay still, studying her as she completed her work. Clover folded the splinted wing gently back against his body, made one last adjustment to the wrapping, and set the bird on his feet.

He pecked and prodded at the bandage, shrugging a few times before saying, "Well done! Despite the fact that you saluted with the wrong hand, you're a fine medic. Now tell me, before we get any further, have you seen anything suspicious in these woods?"

"Suspicious?"

"Louisianan hideouts? Evidence of passing Frenchmen? Spies?"

"But the war is over," Clover said, remembering her father's lessons. "We signed a treaty. Napoléon Bonaparte kept his territory and we kept ours."

"And what did we profit?" Hannibal wagged one pinion feather like a schoolteacher. "Just what did that flimsy paper treaty afford us?"

"Peace!" Clover answered, remembering her father's lectures. "We have eleven states and peace with the French and with the Indians too. That's a good deal. That's plenty."

"You are too young to know what we lost," Hannibal said. "What a great nation we nearly were." Then he chuckled kindly.

"But I should know better than to argue history with a child. I was there. You were not." Hannibal gave his feathers a good shake and scanned the timberline with suspicion. "What is your name, medic?"

"Clover Elkin."

"Elkin, is it?" Hannibal's stare was unnerving. Suddenly he hopped up and crowed, making Clover flinch.

"Clover Elkin, fortune has thrown us together. Victory is on our side! We'll rest here for a spell before proceeding together," Hannibal announced.

Was the Rooster overly glad to meet her or was Clover losing her wits? She began to giggle, unable to contain the dizzy bubbles that welled up inside her.

"Do you have a joke?" Hannibal asked. "I have never objected to a tasteful joke."

"I have just met one of the only living oddities, the famous Hannibal Furlong!" Clover said. "It's not funny. I'm sorry . . . I've had a shock." The giggles turned to tears. Clover wiped her eyes with a gritty sleeve. She felt as though she were still tumbling down the river, carried blindly on a swift and unkind course.

She recalled the heaps of fish that had lined the shore of the lake and gasped at a sudden understanding: the fish had been driven out of the water by the frigid power of the Ice Hook.

"What have I done?" Guilt frosted her skin. "I wanted to see New Manchester, wanted to carry an oddity, wanted to be like *her*. He warned me," Clover said. "How many times did he warn me they would bring trouble?"

"What are you talking about?" Hannibal asked.

"Trouble came. I killed the lake. I killed Father—"

"Just what is this about?"

"I have to put it right. Somehow I have to . . ."

Clover reached into the bag, desperate to find her father's oddity. Hannibal watched her with a judge's silence as she pulled a tourniquet out of its leather pouch, the brass screw green with age. Clover quieted her breath to focus on the task, trying to put her feelings aside. She tightened the tourniquet above her elbow until her pulse disappeared. Then released the buckle and shook her hand as the blood returned. The tourniquet worked just as it always had. It kept people from bleeding to death during amputations . . . but it was not odd.

There were glass vials of peppercorn-size pills in the bag: quinine, mandrake, poppy, ginseng, and digitalis. Clover removed the corks and crushed one of each kind between her nails, giving them a sniff. The odors were sharp and familiar. Nothing remarkable.

Hannibal's attention had turned to the wood lice in the mossy crags, but as he pecked, he cast concerned glances at Clover. She peered through the little tin funnel, blew air through the catheter tubes. With every item she dismissed she got closer to her father's secret.

Three surgical needles, she knew them well. She'd been suturing since she was eleven. If there was anything odd about them, she would have noticed.

The Ice Hook had been overflowing with power; she'd felt it immediately. Whatever oddity her father had carried was holding its power close, hiding until it was needed.

Clover realized that she was afraid of finding it. For Constantine to harbor an oddity, it had to be desperately important. Suddenly "necessary" sounded like a threat.

Hannibal preened his injured wing. "The bandage will keep," he announced. "I need no more of your doctoring now, so if this frenzy is—"

"It's not for you," Clover said. The fading light came through the trees at a lonesome angle. "Oh dear." Clover set the bag down. "We're going spend the night out here."

"We all miss the comforts of home," Hannibal said kindly. "But don't fear, I've already spotted a good site to pitch camp. Now, if you've completed . . . whatever that was, fall in behind me."

She could imagine how a voice like his could command troops, and she had no better plan. Clover didn't want to be alone, so she gathered her bags and followed the bird to a shallow overhang in the side of the mountain.

From this height they could see the last embers of the sunset fading behind the dog-toothed peaks. In the valley below, the fog was thick as quilt batting. All her life, Clover had walked through that mist, but now she was perched high enough to see its unfurled beauty, a silver scarf muffling the indigo shadows.

"We cannot make a fire, of course," Hannibal said.

"Someone might see us," Clover said, thinking of the bandits.

"Now you're thinking like a proper soldier. These rocks have been warming in the sun. If we stay close to them, we won't freeze."

"It's just as well," Clover said, setting herself down in the hollow. "I'm skittish around fires anyway."

"Are you?"

"Worse than skittish. I'd rather see a pack of wolves than a fire burning free."

"Is that so?" Hannibal was surprised. "I mean to say, what a thing to fear when there are vermin and voyageurs lurking about. Never you mind, though. We've got good vantage here, and I'll keep the first watch."

"Well, I didn't choose to fear it." Clover turned her back on Hannibal and opened her haversack.

Hannibal cleared his throat and said, "I myself am not overly fond of snakes."

"No one is fond of snakes," Clover said. She found Widow Henshaw's raisin buns flattened into a wet mush. She scooped the mess out with her tin cup and looked at it in the gloom.

"I have . . . Let's call it bread pudding," Clover said. "Would you like some?"

He hopped onto her knee to peer into the tin cup. "Hunger trumps formality, I suppose."

They took turns picking the mush from the cup, Clover scooping with her finger, Hannibal dipping his whole head in and emerging with smeared cheeks. When the food was gone, darkness came quickly, like a blanket thrown over the earth.

Hannibal hunkered into a pile of leaves and asked, "Clover Elkin, what exactly is your mission?"

"All I know is that I'm supposed to find Aaron Agate in New Manchester."

"Well, there you go," Hannibal said, cleaning his beak on a stone as if sharpening a knife. "I myself am headed to New Manchester to deliver my report to Senator Auburn. You'll be safe with me."

Hannibal spoke so confidently that Clover wanted to believe him. But he reminded her of the old fishermen of Salamander Lake who traded war stories while they mended nets. Those stories changed a little with every telling, threaded through and knotted with feats of bravery and other fantasies. Even though Hannibal was a legendary hero of the Louisiana War, it was hard to take him too seriously. Anyway, he'd already tucked his head under his good wing and was fast asleep.

"I thought you were taking the first watch." Clover sighed. She lay down, clutching her father's bag to her chest, feeling the items shifting as she breathed.

Darkness soaked into the world like ink on silk. Coyotes cackled in the valley below. Bats stirred the air. Clover sat up at every rustle, peering into the depths. The unblinking moon stared with her, its cataract light casting uncertain shadows.

When she could hardly keep her eyes open, she saw her father looking down at her, his ghostly features cleaved with worry.

"How will you ever forgive me?" Clover begged. She saw now the bullet hole perfectly centered in his chest—a bloodless cavity, small enough for a caterpillar to have chewed, but it still looked as if it could swallow Clover whole. "You warned me they were trouble. I was too stubborn to listen. I know I brought this on us somehow."

"Trouble breeds trouble," he said, placing his hand over the wound as if to hide a stain.

"The trouble isn't over, is it? Please tell me how to set things right."

"Sweet child, I taught you to find the source of the bleeding and to mend it. I taught you to proceed with focus until the task was complete. A doctor must be composed even in the bloody tumult."

"I will find a way to avenge you."

"Vengeance is a coward's game," he said, sitting next to his daughter. His body was only moonlit mist, but his voice had warmth and weight. "I didn't raise a wolf," he said. "I raised a physician."

"But how do I—?"

"I told you. Protect the oddity. Take it to the Society."

"I will. Father, I am trying. But which one is the oddity? I can't tell."

"It is necessary," Constantine answered. "It holds hope."

CHAPTER 4

A POWERFUL MEDICINE

Hannibal crowed at the rising sun as if it were the enemy he was looking for. Clover was awake already. She had arranged her father's tools on a flat rock. "Bleeding cups, sulfur molasses . . ." she muttered. "Tincture of belladonna . . ."

These tools were supposed to be her life's work, the mending of bodies, one stitch at a time, and yet now they were the letters of an unknown language.

"What have I missed?" she wondered aloud. "Hannibal, do you see an oddity here?"

Hannibal scanned the assorted tools with an eager eye. "Is it something that can be used in the war effort?" He pecked at a bottle of bitter walnut syrup.

"Don't touch that," Clover said, shooing him away. "He said it held hope," Clover reasoned. "What better hope is there than health? A cure of some kind." But Clover couldn't remember her father using anything special to treat the sick. Grateful patients sometimes praised his "miracles," but he never hid his methods, and Clover had been taught that medicine was built of hard work and hard study. "And it is necessary."

Clover held the tincture of walnut to the light, peering through its dark ink. She shook the empty bag, and a single dime fell out, the only evidence that her father had ever been paid with actual money.

"Nothing here was listed in the journal. But Widow Henshaw had only three issues, and those were printed before I was born. There could be discoveries, entire collections I don't know about."

A heart was necessary. A brain. Water to drink . . .

Her mind was straying. She'd chewed on the word so long that "necessary" was unraveling into nonsense, the sounds blurring like smoke.

"If you've finished your inventory, fall in line," Hannibal ordered, strutting down the mountainside. "It's a long way to New Manchester."

It occurred to Clover, as she repacked her bags, that she didn't need to find the oddity herself. After all, Aaron Agate was an expert, famous for his lectures and essays. He would know the necessary oddity on sight. He would tell Clover why Constantine had hidden it. He would explain why this had happened. The hummingbird of hope lit on the thinnest branch inside her as she followed the Rooster.

· . · . · . · . · . ·

The smell of baking bread carried from the whitewashed buildings of Rose Rock *as Clover and Hannibal looked down at the wide dirt* road *through the little town. The mounds of drying hay in the* fields *looked like the pills of felt Clover used to shave from Con-* stantine's *woolen coat so he wouldn't look so unkempt.*

Hannibal flapped his good wing impatiently. "This road leads to the Regent's Highway, which will take us straight to New Manchester."

Clover turned and looked back into the shrouded mountains, her legs aching from the steep slopes. Her home lay on the other side now. She hoped Widow Henshaw had buried her father in his good suit.

"I had planned to rejoin my comrades here, but I see no sign of my men," Hannibal said. "How much money do you have toward hiring a coach?"

"None," Clover answered. "Just a dime."

"We'll have to sell those tools," Hannibal declared.

"I'd see you in a soup pot before I sell these tools," Clover said.

"Don't forget you're talking to a decorated colonel!"

"I'd see you in a soup pot, *sir*."

Hannibal glared but didn't argue. "In that case, we'll have to commandeer a mount."

"We're not stealing a horse." Clover started down the hill.

"Stealing wouldn't cross my mind!" Hannibal said, marching beside her. "We'll return the animal in good fetter, and with a generous fee, once we've made it to New Manchester. We don't have time to amble up the highway like a couple of shiftless farmhands."

"If you take a horse from these people, they'll tar us," Clover said. "We'll have to figure something else out."

They scrabbled down a gravel slope toward the road. An old goat grazed near the ruins of a toppled windmill. Once her father had pointed them out, Clover had begun seeing these ruins everywhere, the silent scars of the war. A poster had been recently pasted to the remaining brick foundation.

AUBURN FOR PRESIDENT!

It featured a portrait of the senator with his chin held hero-ically high. Underneath, in scarlet print, it read:

FOR A FEARLESS FUTURE, VOTE AUBURN!

"The senator is a man of great vision who sees both the dan-ger and the potential of our times," Hannibal mused. "The pride of Farrington. A gentleman who is not satisfied with the ashes of a lost war."

Clover decided not to tell him that her father used to call Auburn a "war-hungry slug who has sold arms to both sides." With her feet on the cobble road that led to the town square, she felt suddenly vulnerable back among people. She'd seen the horrors of scurvy and starvation, stabbings and typhus, but nothing had prepared her for those bandits on the bridge. They'd come from darker waters, a tide of trouble deep enough to swallow everything.

Passing a livery, Clover blinked at the smudged ink of another sign tacked to the wall:

$$ REWARD FOR RUNAWAY SLAVES! $$

The state of Farrington had outlawed slavery along with five other northern states, but federal law still made it illegal to help a fugitive slave. Clover looked away, feeling queasy. She needed to get to New Manchester quickly. She needed the safety her father had promised.

To her relief, no one looked twice at the weary girl coming

up the road with her rooster. They were more interested in the commotion in the center square, where a traveling performer was striking a gong.

A small crowd had gathered around a paneled wagon whose flaking yellow paint made it look like a cracked egg. The performer, a girl about Clover's age, struck the gong again and sang over the tone: *"Come witness a miracle, wondrous to see!"*

Her stout figure was festooned with sashes. Brass bells sewn to the hem of her rainbow quilted skirt tinkled as she strode across the stage.

"Marvels and miracles for the smallest of fees!"

Someone in the crowd shouted, "Get on with it!"

The performer reached up to free a latch on the wagon. The doors popped open, releasing a striped awning that unfurled over the plank stage. The shelves inside were lined with bottles of an unsettling purple hue. One nook was occupied by an ominous jar covered by an oilcloth. The girl smacked a tambourine and shouted, "What have you gathered to witness, I hear you asking!"

She shook out a banner and hung it proudly next to the bottles. Its faded letters read:

MYSTIC SECRETS AND RARE HERBS
A MIRACLE IN EVERY BOTTLE!
BLEAKERMAN'S CURE-ALL TONIC!

Clover had never seen a medicine show, but she was fairly sure this one was going badly. The singer started into another song, but one of the horses tied to the wagon had a case of diarrhea and interrupted the song with splashes that were hard to ignore.

Mutters of disappointment rippled through the crowd, and some turned to walk away. The girl stomped a heeled boot and shouted, "Yes! Go home to your lumbago, consumption, and constipation. Go home to your restless nights and toothaches and infernal boils."

This made the people pause, and the girl pointed at a man in the crowd, demanding, "You there! Guess my age! How old am I?" She turned her round face sideways, as if posing for a portrait.

"I'll guess you're sixteen at most," said the man.

The girl set her hands on her hips and said, "Ladies and gentlemen, my name is Nessa Applewhite Branagan, and I am forty-two years old."

There were howls of laughter, and someone yelled, "Hogwash! If you're forty-two, I'm a plate of pickled eggs!"

"Bleakerman's has kept me young!" Nessa insisted over the laughter. "This tonic will thrash a rash and beat the butter out of a headache!" She grabbed one of the bottles from the wagon and shook it. "This is as sure a medicine as you'll ever find!"

"It don't look like any medicine I've ever seen!" A bald man pointed at the storm-colored liquid. "It looks like something I'd poison a rat with!"

"Sir, I would advise you not to waste even a single drop of Bleakerman's on a rat," Nessa replied, "unless you want the healthiest, fattest rat in town. A rat with sparkling eyes and the glossiest hair doing gymnastics in your kitchen, sir!"

Someone yelled, "If it works so well, why not give it to your horse?"

Nessa was losing the crowd. Frustrated, she stormed across the stage and leaned her freckled face close to Clover. Clover found herself looking into eyes as green as Bramley apples. She noted the girl's sunburned neck and scabbed knuckles, signs of a rugged life.

"Do me a favor, sister," Nessa whispered.

"I can't," Clover said.

"You can't shake a tambourine?" Nessa cocked an eyebrow.

"Even a donkey can shake a tambourine if you tie it right," Clover said.

"Well, there you go!" Nessa shoved the tambourine into Clover's hands and began stomping out a rhythm. She sang:

It'll knock the bunions off,
Sure to cure a shotgun's cough—Bleakerman's!
Removes rheumatism with ease,
Sworn enemy of ticks and fleas—Bleakerman's!

The lyrics were nonsense, but Nessa's voice was deep and glorious, as if a small cathedral hid behind her double chin. Clover stared. No one in Salamander Lake sang like this.

When Nessa saw that Clover wasn't playing, she gave her an exasperated look. A thought occurred to Clover as she began to shake the tambourine. "This may be our ride," she whispered to Hannibal.

"A sham medicine show?" Hannibal snorted.

"A *traveling* medicine show," Clover corrected him. "She could take us a good way toward New Manchester."

Nessa was still singing, *"It'll put silk in your hair and steal away your every care—Bleakerman's!"*

An old women in the crowd shouted, "Does the tonic work or don't it?"

"Ma'am, you are rushing me," Nessa said.

"I aim to rush you! Who has time for dancing in the middle of the day?"

Nessa crossed her arms and scowled at the crowd. "You want to see the tonic work its wonders?"

"Yes!" the crowd shouted as one.

Without any further ceremony, Nessa yanked the cloth away from the large glass jar. Inside, an enormous snake rose from its coil, disturbed by the sudden light. It tested the glass with a gray tongue.

Everyone gasped.

"Well, there it is, if you're in such a rush," Nessa said. "This is the monster you think it is. See the oak-leaf pattern of its scales"— she rapped the glass, and the snake reared up, its tail vibrating furiously—"and a rattle like a sleigh bell. They say that when the angels hear that sound they open heaven's gates because some poor soul is getting ready to put this world behind them. This is a Sweetwater rattlesnake, the deadliest serpent on earth! God rolled this beast together from the dregs of the pot he boiled the devil in."

The crowd had backed away from the stage, but all watched closely as Nessa drew a lazy figure eight on the glass with her finger. The snake's angular head followed.

"No one survives a kiss from the Sweetwater viper," Nessa said. "In fact, no one has walked more than three steps after such a bite. But don't you worry. It can't hurt you through the glass."

Hannibal shuddered at the sight of the serpent. "Clover, let's be done with this!"

"Wait," she whispered, clutching the tambourine to her chest.

People groaned as Nessa lifted the lid off the jar. The snake reared, its rattle amplified by the glass, shrill as a cicada summer.

"The only way to get hurt," Nessa said, dangling her hand over the exposed snake, "is to do something foolish."

Nessa shoved her hand deep into the jar, and someone in the crowd screamed.

The serpent struck immediately, and struck again. Nessa was bitten twice before she yanked her hand out and clapped the lid back on the jar. She fell to her knees immediately, holding her bitten hand lamely against her belly and looking very ill. She fumbled with a bottle of tonic.

"Heavens," she moaned. "I am too weak . . . to get the cork out. Someone please . . ."

The woman who had been heckling her rushed forward and pulled the cork out of the bottle, but too late. Nessa had collapsed on the stage. She thrashed about horrifically for a moment and finally lay still. There were more screams as others rushed to help. They managed to get some of the tonic into her mouth. It splashed on her blouse, staining the collar a deep purple. The crowd pressed forward, riveted by the spectacle. Someone cried, "Send for the doctor!"

Others muttered, "Well, she asked for it."

"The girl is dead!"

"She sang like an angel, but the poor fool had porridge for brains."

Clover, clutching her father's bag, was trying to push through to help, when suddenly one of Nessa's legs shot up, startling everyone. Nessa sat up as if struck by lightning. Clover gasped along with the rest of the crowd.

Nessa rose and spun, her skirt a vivid pinwheel, and clicked her heels together, whooping and singing, *"I am alive! Thanks to Bleakerman's, I—Am—Alive!"*

Clover couldn't help but smile at Nessa's theatrics. The girl could certainly put on a show.

Clover stepped clear as the crowd pressed forward to slap their coins into Nessa's hands. One man was so eager for the tonic that he grabbed a bottle right from the shelf before paying. Nessa snatched it away and threatened to crack it over his head. "There's enough for everyone, mister!" she said.

Some took swigs of the tonic right in the square, their faces wrenched into masks of disgust. Nessa winked at them. "A powerful taste for a powerful medicine!"

Clover and Hannibal watched the hubbub from the shade of a mulberry tree. When the crowd began to disperse, Nessa rolled the awning and gathered the stage boards with practiced efficiency. She disappeared behind the wagon and emerged having traded her color and bells for a threadbare hemp traveling dress.

"We can still commandeer a horse," Hannibal whispered as Clover stood to return the tambourine.

"No free samples," Nessa said, adjusting her pantaloons with an unladylike grimace.

"Oh, I don't want any of that . . ." Clover couldn't bring herself to call the mysterious fluid a tonic.

"The snake's not for sale," Nessa said.

"I don't want the snake. I need a ride north. I don't have any money, but I am helpful and will not be a nuisance."

"Can you speak Italian?"

"Well, no," Clover said, blinking in surprise. "Only a little medical Latin."

Nessa wrinkled her nose as she climbed up onto the driver's seat. "That's not the same thing."

Clover turned toward Hannibal with an apologetic look.

"Well? Ain't you coming?" Nessa shouted. Then in a hoarse whisper she said, "Best to leave before they ask for refunds."

CHAPTER 5

FIRST WE CHEW . . .

"There is some trick to it," Hannibal huffed as Clover picked him up. "No one survives a Sweetwater bite."

"Of course there is a trick to it," Clover whispered, lifting him up onto the roof of the show wagon. "But we could be waiting for days before we find another ride."

And just like that, the three of them were rattling out of Rose Rock together on the wagon. Nessa put her dust-caked feet up on the dashboard, wriggling her plump toes with satisfaction. "Help yourself," she said. "There's wind enough for everyone."

"No, thank you."

"My name is Nessa Applewhite Branagan," the girl announced. "My favorite food is rhubarb jam on salt pork. But I *will* take leek soup, and winceberry pie when I can get it. A witch stole my tooth when I was eight years old. Look here, see?" She pulled her cheek back to show Clover the wet gap in her molars. "And I am the only authentic vendor of Bleakerman's Cure-All Tonic in this whole Unified States. Well?"

"Well what?"

"Aren't you going to introduce yourself?"

"I'm Clover Elkin. And this is Colonel Hannibal Furlong."

"Salutations." Hannibal saluted with his good wing.

Nessa yelped and stared bug-eyed at the Rooster. She fumbled the reins so much that Clover had to take over the driving for a while.

Hannibal peered into the seams of the wagon, saying, "Look here. We're grateful for the ride, but are you certain that snake can't escape? They can insinuate themselves through all manner of crevices."

Nessa only shook her head, stunned to be in the presence of the historic talking Rooster.

"What exactly is in that tonic of yours?" Hannibal asked.

Nessa swallowed hard and said, "Well, sir, Bleakerman's consists of a secret recipe of Indian herbs and miracle roots . . ."

"Aha! You're a charlatan." Hannibal laughed. "A mountebank if ever I saw one. A chiseler and a cheat."

"Just hold on, now!" Nessa blinked vigorously, as if through a cloud of gnats. "They pay for the tonic, they get the tonic. That's an honest business."

"The chief ingredient is probably horse urine." Hannibal winked at Clover.

Nessa flinched and glanced around, though they were far from town. "It is not!"

Clover couldn't help pushing. "What is it, then?"

"A secret is a secret," Nessa said, looking miserable. She took the reins from Clover. "Uncle used to say, 'Nothing works better than a secret ingredient.'"

"A steaming heap of taradiddle!" Hannibal chuckled as he sat and tucked his head under his wing. Soon he was snoring loudly from his perch on the top of the wagon.

Clover realized that the old bird must be exhausted. After all, he had fought in a war before Clover was born.

Nessa was clearly upset by his accusation. With one hand holding the reins, she tugged a comb through her thick hair until it shone like amber. Her earlobes, furred with nearly invisible down, reminded Clover of piglets.

"You sing beautifully," Clover offered.

"That's a fact." Nessa nodded, happy to be in agreement. "What I really want"—Nessa leaned toward Clover in confidence—"is to sing in the opera. But you have to speak Italian to stand on that spangled stage. And fate put plain old English on my tongue, so . . ." She shrugged. "You take what you get. Me and Uncle used to sell peanuts on the steps of the opera house in New Manchester. Oh, the rhapsody that rolled through those marbled columns! Uncle translated their woeful stories so I could follow, and they sang like their hearts were near to popping!"

Clover watched Nessa reveling in the memory. She made a mockery of medicine, she aired her feet in public, but her feelings rose right to the surface of her face, like trout feeding. It was hard not to like the girl.

"Look there!" Nessa half stood and pointed to a fallen tree that seemed, at first glance, to be enameled with molten rubies: a massive swarm of ladybugs. "Good thing we're here or that would go unseen, which would be a crime for certain." Nessa nodded with the satisfaction of a job well done. With no sound other than Hannibal muttering occasionally in his sleep, the girls craned their necks, watching until the marvelous swarm disappeared behind them.

They rode for a while in companionable silence. Perhaps it was the beauty of those jewel-toned bugs, the grass-scented breeze, or simply the knowledge that she was on the way to New Manchester, but for a moment Clover forgot her worries. Up ahead they saw a covered bridge over the Nominam River. It was guarded by two soldiers who put down their playing cards as the wagon approached.

One wore no coat. The other had removed a boot to whittle at his calluses.

Nessa cooed reassuringly to the horses as the wagon slowed to a stop. "There are checkpoints on most every highway now," she whispered to Clover. "Searching everyone for . . ." Nessa turned to the soldiers. "Just what exactly are you looking for?"

"French influence!" the limping soldier said, hopping on one foot to get his boot back on. The coatless soldier fumbled with the latches on the wagon-side cabinets.

Clover asked, "What gives you the right to search travelers?"

"Auburn's law, kid," the coatless soldier said, peering through a murky bottle of tonic.

"I've never heard of it."

"Don't make no difference to the law. Do you have any hazardous, uncommon, or seditious materials on you?"

"He means oddities," Nessa explained.

"You're confiscating oddities?" Clover gaped at the soldiers.

"We're monitoring the traffic of hazardous effects and suspicious persons during a period of national danger, is what we're doing. If you're a law-fearing American, you've got nothing to worry about. Just hand your bags over."

"And if I refuse?" Clover asked.

The sore-footed soldier swung his gun from his shoulder, saying, "Everyone knows we've got the French spying around, spreading their notions and burning our border settlements. Why would you refuse unless you were in with them? It's not my habit to point a gun at a lass, but unless you turn your pockets out, I may forget my manners, miss."

"Well, you'll find nothing on this wagon but the same tonics I rode into town with," Nessa said. "As well as a Sweetwater rattlesnake."

The soldier yelped and slammed the doors shut.

The sound woke Hannibal, who jumped to his feet, shouting, "Hold your fire!"

The soldiers' eyes bugged, and the sore-footed soldier dropped his rifle in surprise.

"Didn't know it was you, sir!" The soldiers scrambled to attention, pulling their suspenders up. Their hands trembled as they held their salutes.

"Your uniforms are a disgrace. Where is your coat?"

"Lost down the river when I was washing it, sir!"

"Miserable." Hannibal shook his head. "Who is your commanding officer? If I find you disgracing this uniform again, I'll have you both stationed in a fever swamp for the rest of your days."

"Sorry, sir!"

"Now, let us pass; we're in a hurry. Go on ahead, charlatan."

Nessa chuckled as she started the wagon rolling again. "Doesn't hurt to have a war hero along for the ride, does it?"

They were halfway across the bridge when one of the soldiers called to them, "Is it true we're headed to war, sir?"

"We are headed to victory, soldier!" Hannibal barked.

Clover turned to watch the guards disappear behind them.

"They may call it security, but it looks a lot like highway robbery," Clover said.

"The coming war will not be won with rifles and grenades," Hannibal said. "Have you heard of the bulletproof Thimble? During the battle of Serenade, when the Indians were still allied with Louisiana, my officers saw with their own eyes a Sehanna warrior wearing that Thimble. He strode through rifle fire like it was a gentle rain, the bullets bursting against his shaved scalp without leaving so much as a bruise."

"If his head was shaved, he was probably Okikwa, not Sehanna," Clover said, remembering her father's descriptions of the tribes that belonged to the Confederation.

"He fought under the Sehanna flag, regardless." Hannibal sighed. "The point is that we lost an entire platoon trying to capture that oddity. What has become of it? Does Bonaparte have it? These are the questions upon which our future rests. We cannot afford to leave such powers in the hands of hobbyists. How can we hope to mount a defense against Bonaparte if we as a nation have not gathered our own strengths? The checkpoints"—Hannibal tucked his head under his wing and trailed off—"keep our assets from slipping through . . . fingers . . ."

When the tired old bird began to snore, Clover whispered, "What if he's right? What if there's a war coming?"

Nessa held up a finger and did her best impression of Hannibal. "Take heed, children! Who do you suppose has been sneaking into our pens to steal our cracked corn?" Nessa's chin doubled as she deepened her voice, "Why, Napoléon Bonaparte!"

Clover tried to stifle a chuckle, but Nessa's puckered lips, a terrible impression of Hannibal's beak, were too funny. Her clowning was contagious, and Clover found herself trying the imitation herself: "And, morning after morning, who has taken the eggs from our very nests?" Clover's voice cracked as she matched Hannibal's tone. "Why, Bonaparte!"

Both the girls broke out in laughter, but Clover clapped a hand over her mouth. Her eyes watered with shame. How had she been tricked into laughing?

Nessa leaned out to snatch a sprig of roadside fennel as it passed and chewed until her teeth were green. "You can tell me," she whispered to Clover. "Was it vermin?"

"What?"

"You have the look of a kettle about to boil. And your boots are stained, like you've been running through weeds." Nessa arched her eyebrows knowingly. "Anyone can see you've had a fright."

Clover touched her father's bag to be sure it was safe. A fright? Everything had shattered all at once, and Clover knew the breaking wasn't over. She felt that the shards of her life were still turning in the air, looking for a place to land. She shook her head. "It wasn't vermin."

"Oh," Nessa seemed disappointed. Then her eyes widened and she whispered, "It wasn't the witch, was it?"

"What witch?"

"We've only got but one witch around here," Nessa said. "I'm talking about the Seamstress. The one that stitches pelts and carcasses together and revivifies them into vermin. The witch that comes in the night to rip teeth from the mouths of sleeping children."

"I'm not interested in ghost stories," Clover said.

"I saw the hag with my own eyes!" Nessa pulled her cheek back to show Clover the gap in her molars again. "I was sleeping by the creek because it was a hot summer night. It was the smell that woke me, like burning hair. When I opened my eyes, the witch was leaning over me, her eyes glimmering like broken glass and her face sewn together like a tinkerman's purse. I wanted to scream, to wake Uncle in the wagon . . ." Nessa paused here, and Clover held her breath. "But the Seamstress had already yanked my mouth open. I thought she was going to rip me in half. She leaned down close, that stench wrapping around me. She looked into me like . . . well, the same way you look into that bag of yours. I just knew she was going to suck out my soul, or eat my tongue. And then she said something I'll never understand."

Clover's breath quickened. "What did she say?"

"'Croak, croak.'"

"Like a frog?"

Nessa shrugged. "I've never been able to make no sense of it. Naturally, she didn't find a frog in my throat. So she made a disappointed hiss and grabbed one of my teeth and just"—Nessa snapped her fingers, making Clover wince—"yanked it out of my skull. Then she was gone."

"Was it a loose tooth?"

"Not until she tore it out."

"What did you do?"

"I did what any child would do," Nessa said. "I peed. You can be too scared to scream, but you're never too scared to wet yourself."

Clover shuddered. She believed Nessa's story and wished she

hadn't heard it. "My only interest is in finding Aaron Agate," Clover said, trying to focus on the road ahead. "In New Manchester."

She imagined catching the famed adventurer after a lecture, marching right up to the podium to whisper her predicament into his ear. Mr. Agate would appraise her with a wise eye, seeing the truth in her weary face and stained clothes. He would tell his assistants to postpone his scheduled meetings and sit Clover down in his library. After offering her tea and almond cookies, the learned man would pull on his maple-colored beard, take a deep breath, and patiently explain everything.

"Oh, you won't find him." Nessa shook her head, the fennel wagging. "The celebrated professor has up and disappeared."

"Disappeared?"

"They say he still lives somewhere in New Manchester, but no one knows exactly where."

"The canary among doves," Clover said, remembering her father's words.

Nessa squinted at her. "That sounds like a riddle. What does it mean?"

"I don't know, but I will find out." Just saying it gave Clover a feeling of confidence.

It felt good to set her heavy bags down and be carried along for once. This road would take her to New Manchester; all Clover had to do was stay on the wagon. Nessa was nosy and loud, but she handled the wagon confidently, giving the horses encouraging clicks and whistles. Her father would have called Nessa a "huckster," but at least Clover was moving north at a good pace with someone who knew the road well.

She rarely met anyone her own age. Salamander Lake was

populated by people who'd fled the war, old people. The children she met on doctor's visits were either too sick or too frightened to talk. Clover had never thought she needed friends, but now, sitting next to Nessa, she found she wanted one.

"Is it safe?" Clover asked. "Traveling this road alone?"

Nessa shrugged. "If anyone gets too pushy, I tell them I work for a parcel of nasty characters. People leave me well enough alone."

"You're in league with criminals?" Clover asked.

"I am not *in league*," Nessa scoffed. "I'm working off an honest debt. They get a cut of my profits, that's all. Like a tax. Anyway, it keeps me from getting robbed, so I can't complain, at least about that."

"If you don't like this business, why do you do it?" Clover asked.

"I just told you: I have debts. Selling medicine is my sole occupation."

"Tumbling around like a clown does not qualify you to dispense medicine," Clover said.

"Didn't you see me recover from the deadliest venom known to man?"

"I saw you thrash about that stage like a rabid muskrat. That's what I saw."

"That was the powerful effects of a potent poison!" Nessa said.

"Oh, just stop it!" Clover crossed her arms. "I've seen folks bit by rattlers and by scorpions too, and none of them hopped about as foolishly as you did."

"Just what do you know about medicine?" Nessa demanded.

"I am the daughter of a Prague-trained surgeon."

"Oh." That took the steam out of Nessa for a moment. "He didn't see my show, did he?"

"No," Clover said, trying to keep her voice even. "He did not."

"Well, then," Nessa said, "he missed a miracle and an opportunity. Every man of medicine would benefit from Bleakerman's, unless . . ." Nessa seemed to see something in Clover's face. "He died, didn't he? I mean to say, it's none of my business, I guess."

"It is none of your business," Clover said, her eyes brimming.

"I can see that." Nessa combed her hair and scowled at the road ahead. For a few miles the only sounds were the huffing of the horses and the buzz of flies drawn to the smell of the tonic.

Then Nessa leaned forward, squinting. "I do believe we're getting close!" she said.

"Close to the city already?"

"Close to pie." Nessa winked. "It's just beyond these trees. That should put a smile on your face."

"I would not object to a well-made pie," Hannibal mumbled sleepily.

"Prepare yourselves for the only winceberry pastry in the entire Unified States with the Branagan seal of approval," Nessa announced in her full-throated stage voice.

"Do we have to stop?" Clover asked.

"The Regent's Highway is sometimes cobbled," Nessa said, "sometimes just a muddy rut, but it is the only road that threads all eleven states, and I have traveled every inch of it selling Bleakerman's and I have eaten every manner of roadside grub, from fur trapper's gristle to the jellied aspics of the citified gentry. When pie is on the menu, I take it as my solemn duty to investigate. So you see, there is no judge better suited to determine which pie is the best. And I, Nessa Applewhite Branagan, declare that the winceberry pie we are, right this minute, approaching is practically perfect. I refuse to pass it by."

"I am in a hurry." Clover said. "To get to the city."

"And you're welcome to go on ahead on your own two legs," Nessa said, slowing the horses with gentle tugs of the reins. "When I come along again, you can hop back on and ride. Or you can take two minutes to enjoy the best pie of your life. You're going to thank me."

They stopped near the gate of a ranch. Across a sloping meadow of sorrel and chickweed was a farmhouse surrounded by the evidence of a full life. Stoic sheep nibbled the grass between the washtub and the laundry line. A young man straddled the peak of the house, his mouth bristling with tacks. He was replacing the gray roof shingles with new caramel-colored shakes, his hammer smacking out a neat rhythm. Three children came wheeling around the side of a corncrib, flapping their arms like crows.

"I don't see a sign," Clover said.

"We're not here to eat a sign." Nessa pulled on her boots and leaped from the wagon, humming.

Seeing the strangers at the gate, the children fell into a giggling heap and hollered, "Customers!"

Clover had been to homesteads like this before. It was refreshing to arrive without someone screaming for the doctor. Usually children ran in fear when Clover appeared—but here she wouldn't have to hold anyone down for the needle or a bitter pill. Now the children were taking turns crawling under the woolly-eyed sheep, who tolerated their shenanigans with cud-chewing patience.

A farmer wiped his hands on a rag and shouted from the door of the house, "Eggs, pie, wool, or cheese?"

"Just the pie and thank you please!" Nessa shouted back. "Three of your finest!"

Soon the farmer was crossing the yard, carrying bundles wrapped in newsprint. Clover noted that the man's left arm was stiff and held close to his ribs. He passed the pies over the fence, handsome pastries, each the size of a sparrow's nest, with a lace of blackened berry juice at the edges. Nessa unwrapped hers, cradling her hands to catch every crumb.

"Could that be Hannibal Furlong?" the farmer wanted to know.

Nessa's cheeks were too full to answer, but Hannibal hopped off the wagon and saluted. "At your service."

"I was a rifleman in the Eighth Regiment, sir. I fought at Chalmer's Gorge."

"A braver regiment has never worn boots," Hannibal said kindly. "That push broke Bonaparte's hold on the southern front. But what a price we paid. We lost too many that day."

"My own two brothers fell beside me," the farmer said. "One on each side." He touched his arm. "I was hit too, but for some reason I didn't go down." He glanced over his shoulder at the young man on the roof. "Is it true there's trouble coming?"

"Hoo!" Nessa gasped for breath, syrup running down her chin. Half her pie was already gone. "M'golly, but that's as good as I remember."

Hannibal said, "We're doing everything we can to ensure that the next engagement will be decisive."

Nessa rolled her pie over and kissed its flaking crust. "Who's the sweetest? Yes, you are!"

The children gathered around their father to stare at the talking Rooster. Nessa shoved the last edge of crust into her mouth, making faces for the children, who squealed in delight as they tried to hide behind their father. "You're living in paradise," she told them. "Pie cannot cure every ill, but it will try its best."

The young man on the roof took a break from hammering and played a bouncy tune on a jaw harp. Even the sheep looked up to see where the warbler twang was coming from. Clover didn't want to think what would happen to this peaceful homestead if war broke out.

"Go on, now." The farmer shooed the children back toward the corncrib, where they took up smacking one another with turnip greens. He tugged on his beard, looking for the right words. "What will you do about"—he cleared his throat and whispered—"the blue devil?"

"This time will be different, soldier," Hannibal promised.

The farmer didn't ask any more questions, and when Nessa tried to pay, he shook his head. "I can't take money from friends of Hannibal Furlong."

Hannibal stretched his neck and saluted with pride, but Clover could not tell if it was admiration or fear that made the farmer stare at Hannibal that way.

"Begging your pardon, there's wood to chop," the farmer said, and he turned to herd his children back to the house.

On the wagon again, Nessa asked, "Just what is the blue devil?"

Hannibal waited until the ranch was well behind them before answering. "That's what our boys called the *accablant,* Bonaparte's endless army. We still don't know what oddity created them."

Clover remembered her father's descriptions of the injured

soldiers during the war. Constantine had refused to fight, so he'd been conscripted as a field surgeon, one of three doctors in a medical tent, trying to keep boys alive. He spoke of the tent only once, because Clover had demanded to know, and the details still made her shudder: the blackened bone saw sterilized over a lantern flame, the waxed cotton he stuffed his ears with to block out the screams.

Once, when US forces reclaimed the Grendel Valley, Constantine saw French soldiers on his table. "We treated twenty, maybe thirty of the *accablant* infantry. Prisoners of war," Constantine told her. "It is true what they say: they were all the same man."

"Like twins?" Clover asked.

"No twins were ever so similar," Constantine said. "Every *accablant* had birthmarks, scars, palm creases in the same place. They were all the same man . . . repeated. But they suffered, each of them."

Now Nessa wanted to know: "How do you fight an endless army?"

"How indeed?" Hannibal said. "You've pie on your face, child."

· · · · · · · · · · ·

Nearing the Shepherd's Crick forest, they passed a woodsman with a stack of logs on his teetering wagon. "Avoid those woods, children!" he hollered. "There's a vermin lurking there!"

"What kind of vermin?" Nessa asked.

"The cursed kind!" The woodsman rolled toward Rose Rock as quickly as his mule would pull him. "What other kind is there?"

"But which one is it?" Nessa shouted at the man's back. "The Vulture? The Badger?"

The woodsman only hurried on, eager to get to the safety of the town.

"There are more of them every year . . ." Nessa rummaged through a storage box under the seat. "Sundry scraps cobbled together into infernal beasts. They spy on the living world and whisper to that old witch in the mountains."

"A plague," Hannibal agreed. "Killing livestock, stealing oddities."

Nessa pulled a long hunting knife from beneath the seat. She pointed her chin bravely toward the trees. "Uncle used to say, 'If you can't face the day . . .'" But she trailed off. "On the bright side, I might get to cut a vermin today."

"Can't we go around the forest?" Clover asked.

"Do you want to add a week to our journey?"

Clover didn't.

"Then this is the road for us," Nessa said, clenching her teeth. "Don't worry—they don't usually kill people."

Clover's pulse quickened as the wagon approached the towering alders. Visiting hunters told stories, but no one in Salamander Lake had ever seen a vermin. The village was hidden away in a pocket valley like an acorn under autumn leaves. No tax collector had ever found the village, and vermin hadn't either. But those bandits had. Would they be followed by vermin? Suddenly Clover felt that she'd lived her whole life protected by a veil of her father's silences. Now even that was gone.

The trees leaned together so thickly that the road seemed for a moment like an underground cavern. Nessa jabbered nervously as they were enveloped by shadows. "My uncle could cut hair and pull teeth at the same time. But people really came for his songs. Some people let him pull teeth that weren't even rotten, just to hear his voice."

Pale vines crept in loose spirals up the trunks of the passing trees. Tiny moon-colored flowers that Clover had never seen before bloomed between the ferns. They wavered in the darkness like the lingering glow left on the eye by a candle. It was so dark under the trees that an owl screeched nearby, cutting through the mesmerizing thrum of frogs and crickets.

"For my ninth birthday," Nessa prattled on, "Uncle traded all his bottles of tonic for a single balcony ticket. It was the last performance of *Orpheus* at Lucher Hall, and I had a bag of roasted peanuts on my lap, but I didn't eat a single one—didn't want nothing to interrupt the glory on that stage. I didn't hardly blink, just sat there with tears on my cheeks. If you don't cry at *Orpheus*, then you don't have a heart. That's a fact. Tragic beauty! It was Italian, but the story was clear: a love greater than death, and the arias, oh!" She sang a melody, and wound it back on itself into a haunting echo that stopped even the frogs and sent a shiver down Clover's neck.

"Hush, now!" Hannibal commanded. "We could be in for an ambush here." He paced the roof of the wagon behind them, his claws tapping out a military tempo. "Perhaps we ought to find another route after all. This place smells like old blood."

"Too late for that," Nessa said. "Road's too narrow to turn the horses—"

She was cut short by the sound of something skittering in the branches above. The travelers fell silent as they craned their necks, hoping that it was just some woodland fowl moving through the thicket.

The road narrowed, and twice Clover took the reins as Nessa leaped down to push the wagon around a tight corner. At last they saw daylight glowing like a hearth ahead, and the horses picked up their pace.

They were nearly out of the woods when they spotted the vermin perched like a gargoyle on a sunlit branch.

Clover froze, her hand clamped over her mouth to keep from screaming.

It moved like a squirrel, and parts of it were. But even from a distance it was clear that this creature was unnatural. Someone had stitched its stiff carcass together with pieces of an old saddle. It was, just as Nessa had said, an effigy made of this and that: the ribs showed through gaps in its skin, the belly had been stuffed with knots of rope and bits of punky wood. It hopped down the branch and turned its eyeless skull to watch them.

Clover's scalp tingled with revulsion.

Then, with a sudden leap, it landed on a branch that hung directly over the wagon.

"Law and lye!" Nessa cursed.

"Don't stop," Clover shouted. Her heart was stuck in her throat, but she was determined to get to New Manchester.

The horses groaned and shook their spooked heads as Nessa gave the reins a snap. Clover got a good look at the vermin as they passed under it. A knot of sky-blue thread had been sewn into the hide of its neck.

The Squirrel returned her stare, cocking its morbid gaze right at Clover. It clung to the branch with feet made of rusted baling wire.

"Steady on," Hannibal intoned. "Steady!"

Then, just as they were nearly out of danger, the creature bounded down and landed on the back of the wagon.

Hannibal leaped at it, spurs first, shouting, "Away, fiend!" His injured wing failed to carry him, and he tumbled off the wagon with a squawk. He righted himself on the ground and raced ahead, but the vermin was entirely focused on Clover. Its wire feet *scritched* against the roof of the wagon while the assorted components of its body ground together in a harsh whisper. It came quickly, the whispers growing louder, clotting into words:

"First we chew . . . Then we swallow . . ."

"Off my wagon!" Nessa shouted. She turned and stabbed the creature, pinning its pelt to the wood. It squirmed with bloodless violence and yanked itself free. The knife clattered to the floorboards as the vermin seized Nessa's forearm with tooth and claw. Nessa bellowed like a bull. The wagon veered, threatening to crash into the trees, but Nessa managed to hold the reins as the Squirrel dug in.

Swallowing her terror, Clover grabbed the beast with both

hands and ripped it from Nessa's arm. As it writhed, she felt uncanny organs grinding under the matted fur. Clover smashed it hard against the dashboard and flung it far into the trees, where it tumbled into darkness.

Nessa threw her knife after the abomination, bellowing, "Off my wagon!" Scrambling for more ammunition, she threw first one boot, then the other. "Off!" But the vermin had disappeared in the underbrush. She cracked the reins, making the horses bolt. The wagon burst out of the forest with such speed that the travelers nearly careened into a ditch, the wheels shuddering beneath them.

Hannibal leaped up as they shot past, and Clover caught him.

Nessa's rage was veering toward a wild-eyed triumph. "We gave it a good thrashing, didn't we?" she wheezed.

"You gave it your best shot," Hannibal said, "along with your shoes. Chins up, it was a brave effort. I would like to say we came away victorious, but judging by that wound on your arm, we'll have to be content with a stalemate."

Clover had been eyeing it too, a grimy gash, doomed to infection. She opened her father's bag, looking for the jar of cleansing powder, but the cork had failed in the lake. The medicine was a useless slime.

She looked back at the dark woods. "Stop the wagon."

"Why?"

"I said stop!"

Clover leaped down and ran back toward a cluster of oaks. She forced herself to approach the tree line, knowing that the vermin could be waiting in the shadows. She heard a whisper, so faint she thought she might be imagining it. "First we chew . . ." Then she spotted what she needed: a mop of gray fibers hanging from a dead branch. She grabbed a handful of the lichen before sprinting back to the wagon.

As they rode on, Clover crushed the brittle lichen in her fist. "This is tree beard," she said, adding a few drops of water from Nessa's canteen. She spread the paste on Nessa's wound before wrapping it with the last of her father's gauze. "To keep the rot away."

"Is it bad?" Nessa winced as Clover pulled the bandage taut.

"It will heal before you know it," Clover said, remembering her father's knack for putting patients at ease. "You were in the middle of telling us about the *Orpheus* play."

"Not a play. An *opera*." Nessa brightened, glad for the distraction. "Orpheus loses his beloved when the devil sends a snake to bite her. She's truly dead and sitting in hell, but Orpheus loves her so much, he follows her there and sings such songs that even hell itself can't bear the heartbreak."

"It does sound like something lovely," Clover said.

Nessa gave Clover a crooked smile. "Best birthday gift a girl ever received."

Hannibal watched the procedure. "Never fear, young charlatan. Nurse Elkin knows her craft."

After that scare, it felt good to do something useful. Making the assured knots that would keep the poultice secure, Clover felt a deeper appreciation of her father's dedication. With beasts lurking in the shadows, simply mending a wound felt like a priceless skill. But splinting wings and bandaging arms couldn't bring her father back. Some things remained broken.

"How does the Seamstress make those creatures?" Clover asked.

"She's a witch." Nessa sniffed. "She does what she pleases."

CHAPTER 6

THE FATE THAT FELL

With the sun heavy as a fall pear in the west, the travelers rattled to a stop at a roadside well near an abandoned farmstead. Nessa watered the horses, and Clover walked around the sloping meadow until she found a private spot to pee. She couldn't shake the image of the vermin savaging Nessa's arm. But the beast had been headed for Clover before Nessa intervened. Why?

The fright had left her shaky, and her stomach grumbled for real food. The pie had been delicious, but she'd eaten nothing else since the soggy raisin buns. Her body ached for something substantial. On her way back to the wagon, she found a cluster of edible mushrooms. She was brushing the mulch off the top of a speckled cap when Nessa hollered, "You're not eating that, are you?" Nessa was setting a string of small traps in the high grass.

"It's saltcap," Clover said uncertainly. "It might taste like snot, but food is food."

"But those are blue alders," Nessa said, pointing to the tree behind Clover. "Don't you have those where you come from?"

Clover noted the slender leaves rustling in the overripe light. Half a dozen ruby-crested flycatchers spiraled the trunk, looking for spiders. Their heads flashed like precious stones against the ash-colored bark. In fact, Clover had never seen this tree anywhere around Salamander Lake.

"When saltcap grows under a blue alder, they'll make you puke till your toes curl," Nessa said.

Clover dropped the mushroom and wiped her hands on her shirt. "Oh."

"On the other hand, we might find some ramps." Nessa wandered away with her eyes focused on the ground.

Clover had seen people who'd eaten the wrong mushrooms. Her father could rarely help them. The world was full of hidden poisons, secret threats.

Pulling her father's bag from the wagon, she peered inside.

She searched the bag with revived hope. The vial of clove oil shone in the light. It was the most expensive thing in her father's bag. Clover let a priceless drop fall on her tongue, numbing it with the nearly unbearable perfume. But that was what oil of clove was expected to do.

Clover dumped the tools out in the grass, suddenly struck with the idea that the *bag itself* might be odd.

She put her head inside, hoping to see fox fire, or to hear her father's ghost again, or . . . Nothing but musty darkness. She yanked the bag down hard over her head and screamed into the leather, "Show me!"

When she pulled her head out, Hannibal was watching her warily from a rotten stump where he was digging up grubs.

Clover crumpled the bag in her fists, ready to smash it onto the ground. But something inside the supple leather resisted, unyielding, like a kneecap under the skin. Clover ran her fingers along the inner seam and found a hidden pocket. Then, as if it wanted to be held—something heavy fell into her open hand.

Clover withdrew a pocket watch she had never seen before. It was open-faced, silver, with a chain and a winding dial at the top. The longer she stared at it, the more fascinated she became. Was this the necessary oddity, the hope her father had entrusted her with?

The inscription on the back, almost erased by time, read *Celeritate functa*. Clover's medical Latin told her this could mean "Act quickly" or maybe "Be on time."

Behind the cracked crystal stood stately roman numerals. The manufacturer's name was faded, but even with the silver tarnished storm-cloud blue, the object was breathtaking.

The silver warmed in her hand until it felt like a part of her, an organ of unknown function. And, as with the Ice Hook, Clover felt she was closer to her mother just for touching the thing.

She had an idea what the Watch might do. If a Wineglass could hold an ocean of wine, if an Ice Hook could hold winter's chilled heart in its mute steel, then might a Watch whisper to time itself?

There had been no mention of it in the journals. But Clover had seen only a fraction of those publications, and anyway, such a powerful tool would have to be kept secret, even from experts: ". . . *the locations of specific oddities have been omitted.*"

She examined the Watch in the fading light.

There were two fine dials side by side. One would wind the

clock, giving it life. The other would turn the hands, setting the time. Clover was terrified to touch either. What good could come from meddling with time? But what if she could go back and stop those bandits on the bridge? Clover could save her father. Was that what he wanted her to do? For that matter, she might fix every mistake, keep the Ice Hook out of the lake, put it back where she'd found it and good riddance.

Of course the Watch "held hope," as her father said. If it was possible to manipulate time, one could hope for anything. The hands hadn't moved. They were stuck at eight o'clock and twenty-two minutes—a tight-lipped frown on the moon-pale face.

If it truly had the power to change the path of history, her father would have used it on the bridge. This thought was followed by a shock: perhaps he *had* used it. Had Constantine, knowing murder awaited, repeated that terrible moment until he figured out a way to save Clover? She imagined him, bleeding on the bridge, twisting the dial of the Pocket Watch with his last effort. How many times had he lived through the horror before he found an escape for her?

Clover finally knew what she was protecting. "As soon as I learn how to use it," she swore, "I will put everything back in order."

Nessa returned with a fistful of ramps in one hand and a mop of miner's lettuce in the other. Her pockets bulged with chestnuts. From the wagon, she produced hunks of bread and cheese and a small skillet. They set up camp in the lee of the creaking barn. As the first stars appeared, a cloud of bats tumbled out of the loft and bled into the sky.

Nessa kindled a campfire, and Clover examined Hannibal's

injured wing, retying the splint and giving him a beak full of tree beard for good measure. They ate Nessa's greens raw as the chestnuts and wild onions roasted in the skillet. The nuts were a little green too, but cooking softened their bitterness. They took turns cracking them with the silver-plated surgical pincers. Clover ate the chestnuts as quickly as they were shelled, but Nessa took the time to press each into a nugget of cheese and wrap it with a whip of roasted onion.

"See that?" Nessa spread her hands as if she'd won an argument. "It's like Uncle used to say, 'a feast in the humblest meal.'"

Hannibal, who'd been pecking his cheese to bite-size crumbs, shook his comb out of his eyes. "This uncle of yours had a philosopher's tongue."

Nessa nodded proudly. "Capricious Branagan was a genuine genius. He could shave a chin smooth as a china pitcher. He had a story for every star and a song for every crossroads!" She began to hum a sweet aria between bites, a sound so lovely that Clover and Hannibal stopped eating to listen.

Clover was far from home in the company of some very peculiar characters. The hunger and shock of the past days had frayed her thoughts. But she had found the Pocket Watch at last, and something about this singing girl made her smile. "We're grateful, Nessa," Clover said. "For the ride and for the food. For the music too."

Nessa flexed her bandaged arm. "Uncle was killed by a vermin," she said suddenly.

"Oh, Nessa!" Clover gasped.

"It was a filthy little Sparrow made of a bent tin cup. It lit on the horses and spooked them. The wagon rolled into a ravine.

Uncle cracked his head and never woke up. I've been selling Bleak-erman's on my own ever since."

For a moment, there was a river of grief in her eyes, a reflec-tion of Clover's own drowning heart. Clover was about to give Nessa a hug when something snapped in the grass nearby. They all jumped to their feet, but it was only a mouse caught in Nessa's trap.

Clover followed Nessa to the side of the wagon to feed the Sweetwater rattlesnake. Hannibal stayed near the fire, grumbling, "That thing is a menace." Clover held the lantern while Nessa opened the wagon shutters. The snake was nearly as thick as Clo-ver's wrist, its ash-colored tongue darting irritably at its glass prison.

Nessa opened the lid carefully and dropped the wounded mouse in. A few seconds later, it was nothing but a bulge in the sinuous belly. "It looks to be a genuine Sweetwater viper," Clover said to Nessa.

"Of course she's genuine! She could kill a stampede of buf-falo before breakfast. She's a monster, but she's the only part of the medicine show that works anymore. Uncle could make the talk, songs, and jokes that swept the customers into a glorious swoon. But now this snake is the only thing that makes them pay."

"What's the trick?" Clover wanted to know. "How do you survive the bite? It's not the tonic."

Nessa hesitated, then turned the jar slightly. The snake writhed angrily at the disturbance. "Look from this angle," Nessa said. "What do you see?"

"It's all heaped up on one side . . ." Clover said.

"There's a glass partition right down the middle. If I slide my hand into the safe side, the snake strikes the glass. It only looks like I get bit. Now you know." Nessa shut the panel, closing the snake safely in the wagon. Her hand rested on the latch as if to keep everything from bursting forth. "I wasn't supposed to show that."

"It's a shame, what happened to your uncle," Clover said, wishing she had medicine for grieving hearts.

"It feels good to talk about these things."

"Secrets can be hard to carry," Clover said. "Especially for an openhearted person."

Nessa's eyes sparkled in the lantern light. "I am openhearted, aren't I?"

"I would say so," Clover said.

Nessa considered this for a moment. "Marsh wine!" she blurted, cracking into a guilty grin. "There, I said it. Bleakerman's Cure-All Tonic is marsh wine mixed with a little molasses to take the pucker out!"

"But I saw you drink it!" Clover gasped.

"It's not so bad," Nessa said, giggling. "I strain the chunky bits out. The trick is not to breathe through your nose."

Nessa was now laughing so hard she snorted, which made Clover laugh too. And soon they couldn't stop. Clover's heart was a tired tangle, and the laughter kept coming as they stumbled back to the light of the fire. Nessa brayed until she coughed. Clover found this hilarious. She was crying as she laughed, coming completely undone . . . but then, who was there to be tidy for? Hannibal's startled expression only tickled her more. Trying to stop laughing was like trying to get a cork back into one of Widow Henshaw's root beers. She let the laughter tumble out, opening her mouth wide to the sky and howling, startling the roosting pigeons out of the trees. The bewildered birds tumbled around them, like laughter made visible.

"So you've seen the Wine Marsh?" Clover asked, wiping her cheeks dry. "Seen it with your own eyes?"

"And smelled it!" Nessa said. "Law and lye, what a stench! A sea of wine turning to vinegar in the sun. Nothing lives there but flies and fiends."

Clover remembered her father's lectures about the catastrophe that made the marsh. "A Wineglass that is always full," he'd said. "It seems like a wonderful oddity, no? But someone left it overturned, and the wine pours out and out. Like a river, day and night, the wine gushes, knowing no decency, knowing no limits! A leak becomes a lake. Now the valley is flooded with it, and the marsh just grows year after year . . ."

"So the stories are true," Clover said.

"A vast sea of scum," Hannibal said. "They should call it the vinegar marsh. Many have tried to find that Wineglass. But the marsh has a way of turning a person around until they get lost and die of thirst. Even geese drop out of the sky above it, killed by the vapors."

"How can you sell that as medicine?" Clover asked.

Nessa was quiet for a long time.

"I am in debt to some unkind men. If I don't pay them . . ." She left the consequences unspoken. "Used to be, I worked for Uncle, and every day was stories and songs—and now I have to pay for the wagon repairs and the sick horses. This is the fate that fell to me. I don't have to apologize for it; I only have to survive it."

Her face flushed, her freckles seeming to multiply as emotion filled her.

"How much is your debt, child?" Hannibal asked gently.

"I don't rightly know." Nessa sniffed. "They fixed the wagon after the accident and told me they'd let me know when I was done paying them off."

"Why, you're getting robbed," Hannibal said.

"I know that." Nessa poked the fire with a stick, sending fire-fly cinders into the air.

"Why do you keep paying them?" Clover asked.

"Didn't I just say that they are unkind?"

"Mighty unkind, I guess," Clover said, trying to sound understanding.

"They're the meanest." With that, Nessa led the horses to a low-hanging oak to feed and tie them for the night. Then she unfurled a bedroll and sat sulking with her knees drawn to her chest.

Clover pulled a pear-yellow shawl from her haversack, one that Widow Henshaw had knitted years ago. It was still damp, but Clover drew it over her shoulders, knowing that wet wool was better than nothing. The smoke of the fire was between them. "Someday you'll put this behind you and sing opera instead," Clover said. "You could learn Italian."

"That voice of yours is one treasure that cannot be stolen," Hannibal said over his shoulder as he strutted away from the fire-light. "Until morning, brave soldiers!"

When Hannibal had roosted in the branches near the horses, Clover lay down, trying to ignore the dampness that crept through her shawl. Nessa lay with her back just a few feet from the embers, but Clover did not trust any fire enough to get that close.

· · · · · · · · · · ·

They were back on the road shortly after sunrise. The dew adorned the grass and the horses gave off the comforting smell of animal warmth. Nessa was in a foul mood, having woken with an ant in her ear, and Hannibal was pacing in restless circles on the roof of the wagon, so they rode in silence, which was fine with Clover, who liked a morning unsullied by talk.

Having examined everything else in her father's bag, Clover pulled out something she knew wasn't an oddity: a vial of dandelion seeds, no bigger than her little finger. She'd remembered it in the middle of the night but hadn't wanted to lose it in the darkness. Now she rolled it in the morning light, the fairy-fragile seeds shifting behind the thin glass, and the memory of her father's last patient washed over her.

· · · · · · · · · · · ·

"Clean towel!" Constantine called. "The baby will come soon."

The towels had not been clean for hours, but hot was almost as good as clean. Clover wrung the scalding water out of the rag before handing it to Constantine at the foot of the Washoes' cornhusk mattress.

The baby had gotten lost on its way into the world. Mrs. Washoe was so drained by her three days of labor that she opened her eyes only to moan and holler, as if trying to wake from a nightmare. Occasionally the horses outside added their huffs to her groans, but the only other sound was the muffled growl of the rain on the earthen walls.

Buffalo-shaped clouds shook sheets of water onto the grasslands. Puddles had already begun to seep up through the packed-clay floor. Clover didn't trust sod houses, slabs of earth leaning together like something a badger might hibernate in. The front door was only a stiff cowhide curtain, but Mrs. Washoe had decorated the walls with plaited grass wreaths and fragrant bundles of bee balm.

"And if the walls slip and bury us alive?" Clover muttered, but the men paid no attention; they were watching Mrs. Washoe fall asleep between contractions.

The Sawtooth Prairie was disputed territory, straddling the no-man's-land separating Louisiana from the eleven unified states. It was as lawless as it was shadeless; only locusts and cougars were really at home here. With no trees in sight, the rare houses were cut from the earth itself, and the cooking fires burned cow dung. Yet the free and arable soil still tempted some, like the Washoes, to try their luck farming the tattered edge of the Unified States. From a distance, their home looked as stubborn and exposed as a tick on a horse's back.

Mrs. Washoe whimpered. The baby had never turned the right way, which made things dangerous. Mr. Washoe was a stringy man with a sloppy beard like a used dish towel. Because there was no room to pace, he rocked on his heels, his loving eyes fixed on his laboring wife.

"The midwife never came?" Clover asked.

Mr. Washoe shook his head miserably.

"Because your wife is Louisianan," Constantine announced. "You know?"

"The pile of boiled snail shells in the yard tells your secret," Constantine said. "Do you season the escargot with wild mustard?"

Mr. Washoe nodded, stunned.

"*Ils ont meilleur goût de cette façon.*" Constantine patted Mrs.

Washoe's arm reassuringly. "They taste better that way. Twenty years since the war, and still people are poisoned by hate. Maybe this baby will be the one to show us how to live together, yes? Light!"

Clover turned the wick up until the flame danced in the glass and held it just over her father's shoulder.

She envied the little naps Mrs. Washoe was getting. She watched her father pull the woman's eyelid back and mutter, "Good, good."

Gute, gute.

Clover hardly noticed his accent, but she knew patients respected it. When their own remedies failed, they were glad to have the Old World medicines, and just the sight of his heavy leather bag with its steel implements and glass ampules was enough to make some of them feel better.

Mr. Washoe wrung his felt hat to a sorry wad, the portrait of desperation. Clover had seen men like that faint, and she'd also seen them lash out, breaking tables or bones with sudden violence. Neither mother nor baby was out of the woods, but it was this husband that worried Clover. She wished he *would* faint so they could drag him outside and be done with his panic.

"The baby's bungled because we slept in the moonlight," Mr. Washoe admitted suddenly. He stooped under the low ceiling, chewing his bottom lip. "It's my fault; I should have known better. A full moon and everything."

Clover waited for her father to set him straight. Constantine usually swatted superstitions down with the same ruthlessness he afforded horseflies. But, to her surprise, Constantine nodded and said, "In that case, we must have the dandelion seeds."

Clover straightened up, baffled. "The what?"

"Dan-de-lion," Constantine pronounced. "Don't tell me we have none?"

Before Clover could protest that they'd never carried such a remedy, Constantine grabbed an empty vial and shoved it into Mr. Washoe's hands. "Fill this with dandelion seeds. Go now."

And just like that, Mr. Washoe rushed out into the squelching prairie. Constantine examined Mrs. Washoe's belly again, placing the French stethoscope, like a little trumpet, above her navel until he could confirm the infant's heartbeat through the copper tube.

Clover waited until he was done and then whispered, "Dandelion seeds? It's a fool's errand to keep him out of our hair!"

"No," Constantine chided her. "The seeds are not for us. They are for him. Fear is its own agony and deserves treatment. When people are afraid, they need something to do."

Six contractions later, Mr. Washoe was back with a full vial, and Clover saw that the medicine had worked. Standing useless, Mr. Washoe had been as twitchy as a trapped rat, but now he was flushed and proud, his tortured hat back on his head where it belonged. The rain would have knocked every flower flat, and yet he had somehow found enough seeds to fill the glass.

"It's all I could get," he panted.

"It is enough." Constantine gave him a solemn nod and slipped the vial under Mrs. Washoe's pillow. "Good, good."

And then, as if the seeds really were magic, Mrs. Washoe woke with a new kind of wail, as if she were being torn in half. Clover held the lamp, and her father announced, "The child shows its arse at last! She is having a joke at us."

"But isn't that backward?" Mr. Washoe asked.

"It's far too late for forward," said Constantine, taking the lamp and surrendering his stool to Clover.

Clover had never caught a baby before, but she knew this test had been coming. She sat just in time for a slick leg to emerge. She tried to keep pressure in the right places, as she had seen her father do. The arse came out like an unripe peach, and the other leg, then the rest of the baby, all at once.

The baby mewled, alive and whole, a girl with a rumpled gray scowl already turning pink. Clover quickly wrapped her in a quilt that had been warming near the fire. When she tried to hand the bundle to Constantine, her father said, "It's not my baby! Put her on the mother's chest, first thing. Mother is the baby's best medicine."

He washed his hands with the last of the brandy, giving Clover a nod of approval before taking his seat on the stool to cut the cord and check for bad bleeding.

Clover helped Mrs. Washoe position the baby as it wailed. Welcome ruckus! Soon the baby was suckling to the sound of the parents' wet-eyed laughter. Everyone was alive and breathing. Clover saw then how Constantine had been taking care of them all in that sodden room. In all her life, he had never let Clover feel useless or afraid.

When the afterbirth came, Mrs. Washoe hardly noticed. She was weeping with a mix of exhaustion and love that Clover couldn't look away from. She'd seen it before with healthy births, and it made any woman, no matter how smeared, shine like the full moon. Had Miniver looked just this way when she first held Clover?

But Clover was exhausted too, and she spoke without

thinking: "Born butt first in the middle of a gulley washer. I hope you have a good name for her."

"We'll name her Dandelion," Mrs. Washoe said, giving Clover a knowing smile. She'd heard everything.

It was a brave thing they were doing, an American and a Louisianan making a family here in the unforgiving borderlands where the grass had been trampled red long ago. But, Clover thought, dandelions had a way of surviving.

"Keep baby clean, but warm is more important," Constantine told Mr. Washoe before taking up his medical bag and dropping the vial into it. "Mother needs to eat meat, but she drinks only boiled water. Teas and broth. Understood? Baby drinks only mother's milk."

The storm had wrung itself out, and Clover was glad to be saddling the horses in nothing more than a drizzle. Constantine emerged and began strapping the bags to the horses. The long bed-side vigil had bent his mustache, making him look like a clock dropped off the back of a wagon. But he was smiling.

"Your mother taught me that," he said. "The dandelions. She was helping during the cholera in New Manchester, a terrible time. We'd set up an emergency clinic in a church, and the pews were filled with families waiting, worried. Miniver saw their suffering, the suffering of the *healthy*. The whole churchyard was picked clean of dandelions that week!" Constantine chuckled, and the memory of that precious sound carried Clover into the present.

· · · · · · · · · · ·

Now, clutching the vial to her chest, Clover could almost hear it. She felt all of them together, Miniver, Constantine, and herself, held close for just a moment, seeds from the same flower. Then, like her father's laughter, the feeling faltered and was gone.

With the wagon rocking her, Clover tied the glass vial to a leather cord and hung it around her neck, making a necklace of her family. It was not an oddity, but it was powerful, proof of the goodness she had come from.

Clover filled her lungs with morning air and wanted music. "Do you have a song for us, Nessa?"

Nessa thought for a moment and then leaped into an anthem: *"What bright lights will lead us through the night, and what hope yet glimmers on the water?"* Nessa's throat trembled as she forged the silver notes. *"Press on, press on. Hope glimmers on the water!"*

"Do you know what water that is, children?" Hannibal interrupted. "That song recounts the battle of Herrod's Lake, during which I led a fleet of canoes under cover of night against the French fort in—"

"It's a war song?" Nessa looked disappointed.

"It is a patriotic commemoration of a key victory against Louisiana."

"It takes two to make a war," Nessa said.

"Another of your uncle's sayings?" Hannibal asked. "And just what was he doing during the Louisiana War?"

"My grandparents owned an inn on the Melapoma River," Nessa answered proudly. "Twenty clean rooms and hot food for the folks trading on the river. Music every night. But when the war came, neither side wanted the other to use the docks, so the inn was shelled from east and west, shot all to splinters. My grandparents were buried in rubble, and Uncle hid in a pickle barrel in a ditch for three days, listening to the muskets crackle. Then he ran barefoot all the way to New Manchester."

"Your uncle could have picked up a rifle and joined his country against Bonaparte." Hannibal's talons clicked on the top of the wagon as he paced in a tight circle. "Or, better yet, secured those docks for our boats."

Nessa shrugged. "Uncle had a short leg, and anyway, he said his time in the barrel put him off pickles and guns for the rest of his life."

"Pickles and guns?" Hannibal was offended.

"When Uncle got to New Manchester," Nessa said, "the opera hall was boarded up, but musicians were still practicing on the marble steps, playing free for anyone who cared to listen. Uncle said that the musicians were the brave ones."

"Musicians do not advance the front lines!" The hackles on Hannibal's neck frilled in exasperation.

"All I know is that both sides shot at the inn while my uncle waved a white kerchief out the attic window, begging them to stop. If not for that, my grandparents might be alive. Uncle might not have started selling Bleakerman's and he might be alive. I could be baking bread and singing for the guests and sleeping on a down bed every night, instead of riding this wagon over the bony ribs of the world."

The argument was interrupted when they turned a corner and had to pull the horses up abruptly. The highway was choked with travelers waiting for their turn at a borderland security checkpoint. Dozens of brusque soldiers had detained merchants on their way into the city, and some looked like they'd been sitting in the sun for hours. They watched as the soldiers cut open sacks of buckwheat and cornmeal in a field littered with possessions. Clover was relieved that the guards recognized Hannibal right away and waved Nessa's wagon through.

They rode in a tense silence, Nessa combing her hair and Hannibal pecking sullenly at a spider hiding between the boards of the wagon.

And then, before Clover had readied herself for the sight, the wagon crested a hill and New Manchester appeared like a bee-hive broken open, the bustling city spread across the earth. Clover gasped and held that breath. New Manchester was bigger than she had dreamed it could be.

Nessa stopped singing and reined the horses to the shoulder of the highway so the riders could admire the view. The city Clover had dreamed of visiting now stretched before her, arches and spires, aqueducts and cathedrals, the modern capital of Farrington. It was strange to think that she'd been born here. Some part of her belonged in New Manchester, Clover the city girl. She let her breath out at last, feeling chap-lipped and light-headed.

Hannibal hopped to the ground, saying, "It would not do for a colonel to be seen riding into the city on a charlatan's wagon. Now, if you'll follow me, Clover, I'll introduce you to Senator Auburn."

"That is not why I've come to New Manchester," Clover said, her giddy feeling dissolving.

"I assure you, he will be eager to meet you. This is the sort of introduction that changes the course of a person's life, isn't it? Just have tea with the man. Tell him of your experiences on the border. He'll be keen to hear it."

"Why would someone like Senator Auburn want to talk with me?"

Hannibal paused, then cleared his throat. "The good senator trusts my judgment, and when I meet a promising individual, like yourself—"

Clover shook her head. "But I must find Mr. Agate. I made a promise."

Hannibal considered her in silence. "A word of advice: learn your strengths before others do. I hope that, when you've finished your errand, our paths will cross again. To find me, ask any soldier. Now I must make my report. I wish you the very best, Nurse Elkin."

"What about me?" Nessa said. "Am I not a promising individual?"

"You are certainly individual." Hannibal chuckled. "Farewell, charlatan."

"Please!" Clover said, but she wasn't sure what she was pleading for. Did she really expect Hannibal to escort her every step? "I don't like to see you go, Colonel Furlong." Clover saluted, trying to be brave as she saw the Rooster turn to go. "Thank you for your help."

"It's fighters like you who will secure our victory in the end," Hannibal said, strutting away from the road. "Even if you're still saluting with the wrong hand."

Clover watched the Rooster until he had had disappeared into the roadside shrubs, and felt her chin tremble. She couldn't help feeling abandoned.

"You'll really miss the old bird?"

"Of course I will." Clover sniffed and sat up straight. "He gave me courage."

She turned her attention to the enormity of New Manchester,

a city that could swallow her as easily as the lake swallowed minnows. The Melapoma River ran through it like a jade-colored eel.

Nessa pulled the wagon to a stop at the city gates and waited as Clover gathered her bags and jumped to the ground.

"I should like to give you a memento to remember me by," Nessa said, fishing through a leather purse. She examined something small and glinting before handing it to Clover.

"A gold tooth?" Clover laughed.

"It's the only gold I have." Nessa shrugged. "Uncle pulled teeth. Do you want a bottle of tonic instead?"

"No, this will do just fine," Clover said, pocketing the strange gift. "But aren't you taking the wagon into the city?"

"I don't care to go in, myself."

"Oh, you mean you *can't* enter New Manchester," Clover said. "They won't let you."

"Not everyone likes the tonic." Nessa smiled. "I do my business with folks outside the walls."

"They found out what was in the tonic, didn't they?" Clover chuckled. "Kicked you out and said 'Never come back.'"

"Just be careful in there, sister," Nessa said, and gave the reins a quick slap. The wagon started down a side road shaded by willows and clouds of gnats.

"Did they tar and feather you?" Clover shouted.

Nessa didn't look back.

Clover watched, sorry to see Nessa go too, then set her bags down with the gates of New Manchester looming before her. She was about to enter the biggest, most modern city in the state, maybe in the world. She had hoped to do so with friends. The wall was too high to see over, but she could hear the bombination of city life just inside the gates.

And somewhere in that restless bustle was Aaron Agate, the man who had real answers. She touched the Watch in her pocket to check that it was still there, then grabbed her bags and walked toward the gates. She looked behind her once, but the yellow wagon was gone. Statues of falcons bearing shields stared down at her from the high walls. She straightened her hat and entered New Manchester.

CHAPTER 7

SUSANNA WILL NOT BE PLAYED WITH

New Manchester welcomed Clover by sweeping her into the carnival eddies of its busiest streets. Craning her neck to take in the ten-story marvels of granite and brick around her, Clover was elbowed down the avenues as much by noises and smells as by crowds and coaches.

She had only just covered her mouth against the insulting stench of a soap manufactory when that smell was replaced by the intoxicating steam rolling off a confectioner's cart, where the molten lacquer of caramel was being ladled onto roasted peanuts.

Modern lamps hung from posts on every corner of the main street, maintained by lithe men in red caps who carried ladders on their shoulders and clambered about like monkeys, trimming wicks and refilling the oil. Clover had expected modern marvels, but the inspiring audacity of lighting an entire city every night left her a little breathless.

Some blocks sparkled with finery. Even the sign above a cobbler's shop had been illuminated with gold leaf. Clover leaned against the tide to get a better look at a public drinking fountain inlaid with a mosaic of fish and octopuses. She dipped the ladle and drank. The water was surprisingly cold, tasted of iron, and bubbled forth end-lessly, like a mountain creek captured in a bowl. Clover wasn't sure if she was jealous or angry with these people who had lived here so long they passed such marvels without so much as a glance.

Clover didn't see the wagon that clipped her shoulder and spun her around. She was shoved and bumped down the avenue like a leaf on the wind, all the while saying, "Pardon! Excuse me!" The general etiquette on the streets of New Manchester had all the order and decorum of a slow-moving avalanche. Everything was jumbled together. Musicians on one corner played a giddy jig while, just a dozen yards away, another group was playing a funeral dirge. Gentlemen in swallowtail coats escorted women over wooden planks above dozing beggars.

Clover pressed her back against a brick wall to make way for a nanny clutching sheet music to her chest and scowling as if temper alone could cut a path through the crowd. Behind this jowled chap-erone was a flock of young women Clover's age, a tittering bustle of bonnets and silk. Hiked skirts revealed boot buttons ascending like the notes of a scale. They were students, no doubt, headed to music lessons, curls bobbing, cheeks scrubbed rose pink. As they passed, their lilac cologne swept over Clover like a breeze from paradise.

What would it feel like to be wrapped as carefully as a gift? It was rude to stare, but Clover let her head swivel after them until they were a vanishing bouquet in the distance. Did they feel as unsullied as they looked, parasols twirling like halos?

Clover looked down at her own muddy pants, her freckled forearms, her calloused palms, the moss-stained boots that had carried her all the way from the lake. It was too late, of course, far too late for a different life. The stains that mattered could not be scrubbed away. And, of course, Clover would never trade what she knew of the spine's viola curves or the heart's rhythm for any amount of chamber music frippery.

But, perhaps, if her mother had lived, Clover might have endured, might even have enjoyed, a corset's embrace. If things had been different, there might have been an untarnished blossom named Clover carried breathless and carefree in the wake of her chaperone.

In an open square, a gleaming pillar rose toward the sky, a monument to the treaty that had ended the Louisiana War twenty years ago. Marble doves spiraled up the monument, frozen in flight. It surprised Clover that something so fine could have come from war. She pressed her palm against the cold stone. Had Miniver touched this monument? As Clover moved through New Manchester, she couldn't help but wonder: had her mother walked on these cobbles, looked at this stained-glass window, heard this blacksmith's staccato rhythm?

But Clover had more pressing business. "Can you help me find Aaron Agate?" Clover asked shopkeepers and fruit vendors. "Where does Mr. Agate live?" she asked passing ladies and cart drivers. She asked a lamplighter. But the answer was invariably no. A sheriff blew beer foam out of his mustache to grumble, "Don't go looking for trouble, little miss."

Clover was so overcome by the feverish pulse of the city that she'd almost forgotten her father's directions.

"The canary among doves . . ."

She began studying the birds on the rooftops. Gargoyles

mocked her from above, their stone tongues black with soot. Someone with a sense of humor had put a real scarf around one of their necks. When Clover asked people about a canary, she got even less help. City folk were too busy to bother with a lost bird.

Walking with her eyes on the sky, Clover wandered into a different part of the city. Here the houses leaned together like boats thrown ashore by a storm. Clover stepped around beggars whose faces bloomed with sores. Many of the people she passed were dark-skinned. New Manchester was known as a haven for Black people, emancipated, born free, or fugitive. Clover had supposed everyone in the big city lived side by side, as they did in Salamander Lake. But this neighborhood might as well have been a different city altogether.

The manure sweepers carted their loads only as far as this street before heaping them into great flyblown dunes. Older Black men, too frail for more rigorous labor, sat around the mounds with buckets, mixing manure with clay to make fuel to stave off the night's chill. They teased and laughed, passing the time, but Clover saw that some of their legs were warped by beriberi, a disease whose simple cure was food.

Clover had sutured black skin. The needle knew no difference. Her father had treated slaves, freemen, and Indians, anyone who needed it. He'd taught Clover that all bodies were cured with the same medicine. Clover had expected this capital of the free state of Farrington to reflect that simple truth. Instead, New Manchester was cracked like a plate.

A flower girl sang out as Clover passed, "Pretty flowers for the lady!" Her hair was plaited against her scalp, the oiled braids tight as cords of licorice. She'd taken great care to look proper. Born somewhere in these stepped-on streets, the girl was more "tidy" than Clover had ever been.

Widow Henshaw had told Clover that when slave catchers couldn't find their fugitives, they sometimes kidnapped free people instead, selling them to the plantations whether they had papers or not. Clover had only just encountered men capable of something like that, but this girl had lived her whole life under such a threat. Yet she stood as fearless as a ship's figurehead, calling out, "Flowers! Flowers for the pretty lady!"

Clover did not feel like a pretty lady, so she shook her head and pushed on.

Her father's bag felt heavier with every passing moment, the weight of its mystery making her parched. More than water, more than food, more than sleep, Clover needed Aaron Agate to lift her burden.

Her search for the canary drew her eye to the handmade beauty that brightened the slums: jewel-colored shawls pressing babies tightly to their mothers' backs, doorways painted with geometric patterns. The smell of fried okra made Clover's mouth water. But she also recognized the smell of cholera and diphtheria. And below it all, so deep that it might have been coming from her own trembling bones, Clover heard the grinding of that terrible mill.

This was another secret her father had kept. "Cities are swollen with woe." He'd told her that much. But how could she have guessed that all of the woe had been pushed to one side of the city?

Clover felt queasy. She needed to find Aaron Agate. She half ran through the dust, then stopped. She'd seen something: a patch of yellow. Had it been the canary? She retraced her steps but found herself looking only at a dried yellow rose in a basket. "A flower for the pretty miss?" the girl said, her forehead shining like a brass bowl.

"Have you seen any canaries in this city?" Clover asked.

The girl couldn't have been much more than eight, but the wariness in her eyes looked older. She held the flowers up, a mass of muted colors. "Five cents for a single, seven for a nosegay."

Clover dug in her father's bag for the last dime and handed it over. "I'll take a nosegay."

The girl gave Clover a dried rose nested in lavender and pointed downtown. "The canary lives on the glue maker's roof. You won't catch it, though," she said, shaking her head ruefully. "It's too quick."

Clover hurried down the avenue.

Even without the sign painted over the door, Clover would have recognized the glue maker's shop from the abominable smell of boiled horse. She stuck her nose deeply into the brittle flowers as she stood before the building, craning her neck to see the roof.

It was there.

Surrounded by doves hunkering and cooing in their drowsy manner sat a canary. The city's soot had tarnished its once-bright plumage to a muddy brass. Still, it was a welcome shard of color in the smoke-woven air.

Clover watched as it dropped from the roof, lit into the street to snatch at some crumb, then darted away. She raced after it, clutching her bags, trying to keep her eye on the bird as it dipped behind a wagon, through a miasma of chimney smoke, and into the limbs of an ancient oak. She'd lost it.

Clover was so frustrated that she screamed through her teeth and dashed the dried flowers against her thigh. Only the horses tied to their posts looked at her. City folk had no trouble ignoring her.

Clover went back to the glue maker's to find that the bird had returned to the shade of the chimney. She followed it twice more, and both times, the bird came back. It seemed tethered, invisibly, to this particular rooftop.

Clover walked around the building. It was a brick-walled factory with several open doors, each one revealing another glimpse of the huge kettles. The workers moved in a shimmer of swampy heat. But there was no sign of a famous oddity expert.

On her second pass, Clover pushed through the hanging branches of a parched willow and found herself in the twilight of a hidden alley. It was quiet here, and at the bottom of three stairs, as if waiting for her, was a heavy basement door.

Clover knocked. She noticed that the canary had perched on the willow above, watching her. From behind the door, a man shouted, "Password!"

"How am I supposed to know that?"

The canary flew away. She knocked again. Pressing her ear to the wood, she heard a low ruckus coming from inside. "Hello?" She kicked the door and tried to peer through the gap between the door and the jamb. The sound of hammering and heavy scraping came from inside, but she could see nothing. She slumped, pressing her forehead against the wood. "My name is Clover! I have to find Aaron Agate," she hollered.

The voice behind the door said, "Clover who, exactly?"

"Clover Elkin," she said. "From Salamander Lake."

The canary appeared again, darting so close to her face that the wind from its wings parted the flies. The man inside cleared his throat. "Clover Constantinovna Elkin?"

"You know my name?"

After an uncertain moment, the voice delivered a string of strange words: "Travels footless. Hungers gutless. Bites toothless."

Clover swallowed. It was the same riddle Widow Henshaw had tested her with since she was a little girl. Even in deep winter, the widow had made Clover stand in the cold doorway until she'd recited the ritual words.

Now Clover answered by habit, "Soot's sire, fire. Latch and key, admit me."

Just "fire" would not do. Widow Henshaw had insisted that Clover say the whole thing before letting her into the kitchen for a bowl of chowder or a piece of oven-warmed molasses bread. And, remarkably, it worked here too. Clover heard the latches opening.

The bolts took a few seconds to free, but finally the door swung open.

The old man was a mess. He had no fewer than three pairs of spectacles on his head, one hanging low on his nose, one he stared through, and another pulling his rat's-nest hair away from his forehead.

"I'm looking for Mr. Aaron Agate," Clover said.

"You have found him." The man bowed, and the loosest of his spectacles clattered to the floor.

She had expected the strapping hero she had seen illustrated in the journals, a full-chested explorer in a beaver hat, overlooking a river with a bear cub heeled eagerly beside him. This man looked like a librarian who had recently lost a fight. He wore what used to be a fine suit, but the vest buttons were in the wrong holes. The only evidence of a lifetime spent squinting against the sun were the deep wrinkles radiating from the corners of his eyes.

"Is it really you?" Clover asked.

Mr. Agate fished around on his head for a hat. Finding none, he lifted a pair of spectacles instead and made a little bow. "Aaron Thomas Agate, at your service," he said.

Clover grabbed his hand and shook it as though she were trying to pump water. She trembled with relief. Before she knew what she was doing, she had wrapped him in a fierce hug, smelling wool and chicory coffee.

When she let go, Mr. Agate studied her face closely. "I am honored to meet you," he said. "As much for your pedigree as for your intrinsic nature."

"My what?" she asked.

"But you've come at a bad time. A terrible time, I'm afraid. Forgive me, but I must keep at it, distinguished company or no. Don't linger in the doorway."

Clover entered a long cellar that had been expanded and reinforced with brick. The smell of the glue had penetrated the walls. The floor was cluttered with wooden crates and bulky objects half-draped under dust cloths. High windows let in the afternoon glow, shafts of dusty air that fell on the disorder of the room.

She'd never seen such a sundry collection: candelabra, wooden idols, antique lanterns, horn spoons, and precarious piles of books. A writing desk in one corner seemed about to collapse under the weight of leaning towers of paper. In another corner, a sleeping roll sagged next to the stove, a night basin, and a pile of unwashed dishes with its own population of flies. It seemed that the great explorer now traveled no farther than to empty his night pot.

"I would welcome a hand; do you mind?" He gestured to the

piles of disorganized rubbish. "I've already moved this collection three times."

Mr. Agate was pulling books from the shelves and tossing them into piles. Some of the crates were already nailed shut, some only half-packed with bundles of straw padding. Clover saw a hobbyhorse in one, a crystal vase in another. China plates and teacups sat half-buried in barrels of oats, the best way to protect them for a long wagon ride.

"I must disperse the oddities. Between the poachers and the vermin, no collection is safe these days."

"Poachers?"

"They steal oddities and sell them to the highest bidder. It used to be the height of fashion to have an invisible Hairbrush in your salon or an Ice Hook that makes its own ice. But now that Senator Auburn is buying every oddity the poachers can get their hands on, no collection is safe."

"What does Auburn want them for?"

"He has never stopped looking for a solution to Bonaparte's advantage," Mr. Agate said. "During the war, the Unified States had the material advantage: munitions, steel, provisions, cotton. We should have won easily. But Louisiana overwhelmed us with sheer numbers. Of course, I have a purely scientific interest in just what sort of oddity could duplicate a person, turning a single French soldier into thousands. But Senator Auburn's interest is more . . . personal. The treaty of New Manchester is like a dagger in his heart."

"How can Auburn defeat an endless army?" Clover asked.

"I hope we never find out. Imagine the horror. The Heron burned the entire Hawthorn Forest in a single day. The Wineglass turned Sojourner Valley into a muddy waste. Oddities used as weapons are a threat to our survival. But Auburn will do anything to get himself elected president. He's trying to follow Bonaparte's example. If he gets his way, we won't have an election. We'll have a coronation."

Judging from the dark circles under his eyes, it was clear that Aaron Thomas Agate hadn't slept in days. "Collections must be scattered, for everyone's safety. We are entering a dark age."

Clover saw a teacup dangling above his back pocket—in putting on his belt that morning, he must have managed to loop it through the handle and either hadn't noticed yet or hadn't taken the time to remove it. Clover wondered if the old explorer's sanity might have been left somewhere on the muggy banks of the Melapoma River. Or maybe the basement air and locked windows had given him a touch of cabin fever. Or maybe this was what her father had warned her about, an example of what oddities would do to a mind.

Still, Clover's mouth went dry and her heart fluttered like a fish on the line. She was close to answers. "My father told me to seek the protection of the Society—before he died."

"Died? Constantine?" Mr. Agate covered his heart. "Then, my dear, consider yourself under our protection, such as it is. But . . . there aren't as many of us as there once were. Our membership is in decline. Keeping even a single oddity is dangerous now." He continued packing.

Clover gazed around the cluttered room. "Are these all oddities?"

Mr. Agate only grunted, moving a pile of books from one end of the room to the other. "You'll want to admire the press, no doubt." He pointed to a printing press with a great brass screw and lever. "We used to publish the journal on this old mule. Now, where did I put that spoon?"

Clover saw a broadsheet set in the printing tray. The lead letters were backward and ink had thickened to syrup in the crevices. At the bottom of the frame was the Society's crest: an egg in a nest. There was not a bird within the egg, as one would expect, but a rabbit, sleeping peacefully.

Clover spoke the Latin inscription under the crest, *"Custodia Insolitum."*

"It means 'protection of the unusual,'" Mr. Agate said. "We bickered over that for some time, but I still say it's a solid motto."

Clover picked up a journal from a pile on the floor. The issue, though years old, was still more recent than any Clover had seen in Widow Henshaw's collection, its pages bright and clean.

The introductory essay, "On the Purpose of Oddities," was written by none other than Miniver Elkin. Clover's breath caught in her chest as she read:

> . . . a simple prism, which breaks light itself, was once considered a mere curiosity. Then Newton used it to launch a rational revolution. If we see oddities as baubles, as trinkets for the entertainment of parlor guests, we will have squandered our greatest potential. Every oddity is an opportunity . . .

"May I take this?" Clover asked, her voice clotted with emotion.

"Why not? We printed it before the poachers began using the journals as shopping lists. That was a golden era, when our collections were displayed in libraries and town halls. Even the black market has collapsed. There is only one buyer now, and the poachers sell everything to him. I thought if I hid well enough, I might be able to keep this collection together. One light to carry us through the night. But it's just too dangerous."

"So the Society . . . ?"

"We're waiting out the storm. Our membership has"—Mr. Agate coughed—"dwindled."

Then Clover remembered why she was really here. She opened her father's bag and presented the Watch on her open palm. "At first I didn't know what it was," she said, "but I think I'm certain now. Mr. Agate, this is the Pocket Watch."

"What pocket watch?"

"Don't you know it?" Clover said. "It is *necessary*." She studied his face but saw only puzzlement, jowls in need of a shave, a nose veined like the petal of a wilting rose.

"Whose collection did it come from?" Mr. Agate asked. "Why haven't I heard of it?"

"Haven't you?" Clover's heart sank. She fell to her knees to dig through her father's bag, feeling hope drain from the room. "Or maybe it isn't the watch. It could be something else . . ." Her voice faltered.

"My dear, I haven't time for games. Are you carrying an oddity or not?"

"I am! It is in the bag. If it's not the watch . . ." She pushed the bag to his feet. "One of these things is odd," she declared. "Important."

"Odd how?" Mr. Agate asked, crouching over the bag.

"Hope," Clover said. "My father said it was necessary."

Mr. Agate licked his lips. "Which is it?" He fished out the lump of medicated beeswax Constantine had used to rub on arthritic joints. "Has it been catalogued?" He pulled the scalpel from its leather sheath.

"I don't know." Clover bit her lip. "Portions of this periodical contain intentional errors and outright fabrications." It had been so easy to invent the Pocket Watch, a desperate fantasy.

"My dear, I don't have time to fish through a sack of junk."

"It's not junk! These are medical tools. They belonged to my father, and he told me to bring them here."

"But I don't recognize any of these," Mr. Agate answered. "If an oddity held hope, such a thing would be sorely useful right now."

"Do you mean to say you have never heard of such an oddity?"

Could her father's secret be so powerful, Clover wondered, so crucial, that it had been hidden even from the Society scholars?

Mr. Agate gave her a weary look. "Don't fret. Today we flee to deeper obscurity. But someday, someone will resist the senator. Someone will be brave enough to hunt down those poachers and make them pay. Someday, someone will give us reason to hope . . . but today . . ." He trailed off and began packing again.

Tears welled in Clover's eyes. "Mr. Agate, I have come so far to find you. My father's last wish was that I place this oddity into your care."

"Maybe it's been noted in one of the foreign lists . . ." He disappeared, muttering, behind a bookshelf.

As she waited, Clover took a closer look at the objects around her. She touched the fur of a dried tarantula, tapped on an empty saltshaker, pulled the lever of the printing press to watch the tremendous screw turn.

In the middle of the room was a marble stand with a scuffed cigar box sitting on it like a piece of art. Curious what kind of tobacco deserved a pedestal, Clover picked up the box and opened it.

She had only a second to see what was inside: a rag doll of the simple type that settlers called a "Prairie-Sue." It was made of a rough hemp cloth, the color and size of an old sock. It had a yarn smile fading from plum to pale pink. Its button eyes stared in different directions with a sleepy, faraway look.

But the dreamy smile turned into a scowl as the Doll reached out and closed the lid with a snap, pinching Clover's thumb. Clover yelped and dropped the box. It opened mid-fall, and the rag doll tumbled out, rolling twice before pulling itself to its feet. Then it stood, hardly a foot tall, and frowned furiously about the room.

"Oh no!" Mr. Agate yelled, dropping a stack of books. "Oh heavens, no!"

Clover took a few steps back, but there was nowhere to run. Her thumb was throbbing, but more distressing was the fact that the doll had picked up a crowbar.

It flung the tool with such force that the crowbar stuck in the brick wall with a *thunk*, narrowly missing Clover's head. Clover screamed and scrambled to find shelter behind the press as the Doll searched for another weapon.

Mr. Agate crouched on the floor, holding the cigar box open toward the Doll. His hands were trembling, but he sang a child's lullaby as sweetly as he could: "*Susanna, don't be sore; the rain will stop by morning. Susanna, don't you cry; the clouds are only snoring.*"

The Doll had lifted the corner of a crate between the nubs of its stuffed hands. The crate rose as if it weighed no more than a bread roll. Clover had seen draft horses tear the earth with their hooves, she'd seen oxen pull chestnut stumps out of the ground, but she had never seen strength like this.

Mr. Agate kept singing, with sweat streaming down his face. He shook the box a little to draw the Doll's attention. "*Susanna, don't you fuss; the morning bird is singing.*"

Begrudgingly, the little Doll slammed the crate down and ambled back to the cigar box. She climbed in and gave Clover one last sour look before Mr. Agate closed the lid.

He placed the box gingerly on the stand, then, thinking better of it, set a heavy book on top to keep it shut.

He looked at Clover over his spectacles and said, "Susanna will not be played with."

ITEM NUMBER W17

Despite the scare, Clover let out a thrilled laugh. She was standing amid a genuine *collection*. She chewed on the end of her braid, panting with panic and awe.

"Do be careful," Mr. Agate said. "Anomalies can be quite dangerous, as you must already know. But there are boxes to pack! I have eighteen confirmed oddities here, the largest collection in the world, plus thirty-two unconfirmed, and it all has to go."

"Unconfirmed?"

"Suppose a man wears a particular glove and wins at cards. He wonders, 'Did the glove make me win? It must be an oddity!' But usually it isn't. This, for example," he said, twirling a green Umbrella over his head, "is said to have survived eight lightning strikes. If it's true, I'd be happy to include it in the books as a genuine oddity, but it's not an easy thing to test, and I don't want to be the one to do it. So for now it remains unconfirmed. The Birdcage, on the other hand . . ." He pulled a simple brass birdcage from a high hook and handed it to Clover. "Put your head inside."

Clover did and almost dropped to her knees with vertigo, for suddenly she was perched high above the street, looking down onto the bustle of people and carriages. Then, with stomach-lurching speed, she was flying with the gray birds around her. The noise of the street below was muffled by the soft applause of dove wings. She gasped and withdrew her head, blinking at Mr. Agate.

"I was flying!"

"The Canary was flying."

"But I saw—"

"What the Canary saw. When you're obliged to spend your days cowering in a basement, as I am, the Canary offers a much-needed perspective. We'll pack the Birdcage last." He gestured at the medical kit. "And we'll sort through that when we've safely moved."

As Clover repacked her father's bag, she blinked at the wonderland around her. The iron stove, the washbasin, the whisk broom—any of them might have strange and beguiling power.

"A collection like this must have taken decades to assemble. Where do they all come from?"

"Where indeed?" Mr. Agate was nailing a crate shut and spoke between hammer blows. "There are different schools of thought—" *Blam!* "Some say oddities are artifacts of an earlier draft of creation—" *Blam-blam!* "Detritus from a flawed universe, you might say. Some say they're merely random eventualities. In a field of clover, for example, there is bound to be one with four leaves, isn't there? Likewise, if you have enough"—he looked at the hammer—"hammers, there is bound to be one that is a little different."

"Is that hammer different?"

"No. This is just a hammer. But this—" He lifted a blue-glazed

Teapot from its box and gazed at it lovingly before removing the cork from its spout. "In the end we don't care where this Teapot came from. We are only concerned with its nature. Would you like some?" He scanned the littered room and, failing to find the teacup that dangled from his own belt, shrugged, and poured an amber stream right onto the brick floor.

"Chamomile," Clover whispered with reverence. "It is always chamomile." She knew the Teapot from the journals, but she'd never thought she would smell its perfume.

She stepped back and watched the dark puddle grow. A moment later, when a normal teapot would have emptied, the tea was still rushing out and showed no signs of stopping.

"Nice and hot," Mr. Agate said.

The redolent steam warmed Clover's cheeks, and she was overcome with the significance of the objects around her. She saw how easily this work could have coaxed Mr. Agate away from his explorations and turned him into a nearsighted archivist. The enthralling aroma insisted that this was the most important teapot in the world, the only teapot that mattered. And yet, after all, this was just wet tea, wasn't it? Was even an ocean of chamomile really important? Was it, as her father would have said, *neobkhodimyy*? What was the necessary oddity? What could overshadow even these heavenly artifacts? Clover had made it all this way and still had no answer.

"I could stand here and pour tea enough to drown us." Mr. Agate seemed as mesmerized as Clover was.

"You won't, though," Clover suggested, turning her attention to the eccentric scholar.

"I could fill this room, and this pot would still give and give!"

Mr. Agate was in a reverie, his eyes shining as he watched the tea flowing. "That's how . . . *generous* it is."

The tea surged and filled the cracks between the bricks, pushing out toward the walls and filling the air with moist fragrance.

"I should not like to drown today, Mr. Agate," Clover said sternly.

He blinked and finally pulled the pot upright, stopping the flow.

"The tea is perfectly safe to drink. But some don't like chamomile." Mr. Agate tapped the cork back into the spout and went back to packing, his feet now sloshing about in the liquid. "Philosophers say that the oddities slipped through the holes in our dreams and tumbled into this waking world. Of course, there was your mother's theory—that the oddities are puzzle pieces, or rungs of a ladder, so to speak, which, if arranged in the proper order, could lift us up from suffering, even from death! Rather unscientific, if you ask me. Newton, on the other hand, established that an object at rest tends to stay at rest—"

"Did you say my mother?"

The professor kicked a table hard. "You see, it takes a good deal of force to get it to move. But what if there was a table that tended not to rest? In Bangladesh, there is just such a table; it dances about the room, spinning its tablecloth—"

"But you said—"

"An oddity simply has a different tendency, a variation in the whims of nature. I am working on an addendum to Newton's principles, you see, a law of anomalous physics for—"

"Aaron Thomas Agate!" Clover shouted.

"What is it?"

"Did you know my mother?"

Mr. Agate looked up from his packing. Dust smeared his nose, and the pair of spectacles had slid down to hang in front of his mouth. "Of course! We all knew her well. Or as well as a correspondence allowed. She was a generous mentor. I still have her letters tucked away somewhere . . ."

"Mentor to . . . How . . . When . . . ?" Clover balled her fists, dumbfounded.

Mr. Agate placed a hand kindly on her shoulder. "Clover, your mother was not just a member; Miniver *founded* the Society. Miniver Elkin was the first one to write to other collectors, to classify oddities, to track them, and to lay rules for their proper use and care. Before Miniver, oddities were just rumors scattered in gossip, something a drunk cousin saw. Now there are verified collections like this one, and an international host of scholars dedicated to understanding them. She brought oddities out of the shadows into the light of modern scrutiny. She is the reason I started collecting. We all tried to keep pace with her, but she was, well, she was Miniver."

Mr. Agate looked embarrassed. "One would think your father would have told you these things," he said softly.

"He didn't tell me anything. Nothing at all."

Mr. Agate wrung his hands awkwardly. "Perhaps he was protecting you. We lost track of him almost immediately after the fire. He left his practice and fled to the edge of the world. Her death ruined him, I'm afraid."

Clover's knees shook, and she leaned against the printing press.

"Your mother . . ." Mr. Agate crouched beside Clover and put a gentle hand on her shoulder. "Well, she wanted to change the world. Some say her ambition ruined her, that she flew too close to the sun, so to speak. But those of us who knew her, we believed she could do it. She inspired us."

The strange man was telling the truth—Clover saw it in his eyes. The warmth she felt kindled inside her. Pride for being Miniver Elkin's daughter was an answer Clover hadn't known she needed.

"Now, I'm sorry," Mr. Agate stood and returned to his boxes. "We *must* pack as we talk. I'm told that poachers have been spotted here in New Manchester, just this last week, sniffing about. I don't know how much time we have."

"Father said oddities killed her."

"Well, yes," Mr. Agate said, rolling a tapestry and tying it with a scrap of twine. "In a manner of speaking. But a spoon is a shovel in a manner of speaking. A wolf is a running shark in a manner of speaking. A turtle—"

"Mr. Agate."

"What is it?"

"How did my mother die?"

The professor sat on a pile of books next to Clover and put his head between his hands. "The *fire*, of course. My dear girl, how is it that I know more about you than you know about yourself?"

Just then, someone hollered from outside: "Aaron Agate! I've come to hear a lecture from the learned man!"

Mr. Agate seized the Birdcage and thrust his head inside, only to groan and withdraw it just as quickly. Clover put her own head in and saw, from the rooftop, five rough horsemen with the fur-clad look of trappers. They wore slouch hats, long rifles, and

knives strapped to their thighs. Their unkempt beards made them look like brothers, except for one man, who was tall and beardless. He had rabbit ears on his hat where other men might put feathers.

Clover's legs went numb.

The rabbit-eared man knocked his pipe clean on his boot. Then he hollered again, "Agate! I know you're home!"

Clover pulled her head out of the cage with a desperate moan.

Mr. Agate stood still. He was very pale. "We're lost. It's Willit Rummage. They've found us."

"That's them," Clover whispered. Her pulse roared in her ears like a storm-swollen river. "It's the men who killed my father. Where are your guns?"

"A gun fight with these men is not something we would survive."

"Call for the sheriff. A big city like this must have a strong sheriff," said Clover.

"But someone must go and fetch the sheriff," Mr. Agate said. "And the sheriff isn't eager to get killed by poachers. These men don't fight fairly. Hush now, I'm thinking of a plan."

A moment passed, and Willit hollered again, "Have I caught you over the chamber pot? Do you need a minute?"

"Well?" Clover whispered. "Do you have a plan?"

Mr. Agate held up his finger. Then he said, "No."

Clover recognized another voice outside. The big man named Bolete said, "Maybe he prefers to be called 'professor.'"

"Do you reckon?" Willit asked. "*Professor* Agate! I get bored of peekaboo. I happen to be holding, in my hand, item number W Seventeen! I trust you remember it?"

Mr. Agate paced back and forth, muttering to himself, "Of course I remember it; I catalogued the thing."

"W Seventeen." Clover searched her memory. "The Pistol!"

Clover made a dash for the printing press and crouched behind it, gripping the end of her braid between her teeth.

A moment later a shot echoed in the alley. The bullet buzzed down the stovepipe like a hornet, through the grate, trailing hot ash, and punched a hole through Mr. Agate's right ear. The metal passing through the flesh made a wet snapping sound. Mr. Agate screamed and dropped to his knees, cupping a hand over the bloody wound.

"I only winged you this time!" Willit hollered. "The next one goes through your eye! I'm going to clean my pipe before I reload."

"I'm sorry, dear girl," Mr. Agate said as he stood and wadded a kerchief against his dripping ear. "We're cornered."

When Clover saw that he was going to open the door to let them in, she tried to hold him back, but Mr. Agate pushed her aside and freed the bolts. She turned in a terrified circle; there was no escape. She retreated to the back of the room as the gang sauntered in.

Bolete entered first. He was built like a walking pickle barrel. The others followed, cackling and tugging on their beards. Their leathery faces were mostly hidden by their low-slung hats and unruly whiskers, and they smelled like a pot of burned onions. Their hunting knives clattered against boxes as they shoved their way around the room. Clover counted five of them, a herd of brutes.

But it was Willit Rummage who terrified her most. Tall and narrow, he looked as if he'd been rolled through a laundry wringer.

His hands trembled as he took the pipe from his mouth, and he scratched himself constantly, tugging his tawny coat up to reach bare skin. The stubble clinging to his cheeks was the color of sawdust. He wore a crude necklace made from half a walnut shell. He sniffed at a painting on the wall and gingerly touched the same dried tarantula Clover had.

"You've even packed up the goods! How helpful," Willit said. As he spoke, he scratched under his arm, then under his chin. He was like a man scrubbing himself in the bath, plagued by some terrible itch. In some places his skin was worn to bruises and scabs. "Here are the terms," he continued. "We get your collection, and you get to live. Everyone wins."

Clover hardly heard the words; the icy river water was rising within her.

When Willit spotted her trembling behind the press, his face lit up. "No river to jump into this time?"

"Why?" she whispered, her tongue dry.

"Why what?"

"Why did you kill my father?"

"That was a heat-of-the-moment thing." Willit spat a wad of yellow mucus on the floor and scuffed at it with his boot. "Bolete don't enjoy killing folks, do you, Bolete?"

Bolete shrugged.

"We were following a lead on the Ice Hook when this sweet old woman told us her warts had been cured by 'the Russian doctor.' Well, who could that be but long-lost Constantine? I thought to myself, he might just have something better than the Ice Hook. I was going to ask nicely, but then your father went and got everybody agitated."

Willit held the Birdcage out the open door and whistled. The Canary flew obediently into the cage, and the poacher closed it with a satisfied grin. He handed the cage to Bolete. "All this time looking for you, Mr. Agate, and now I come to learn that I should have been looking for a songbird."

Clover wrenched the crowbar from the wall behind her and ran at him, screaming. She was going to smash his skull.

But she was caught up by Bolete before she reached Willit. The ursine fiend crushed her in his arms. Her legs kicked in the air, and the crowbar rang as it hit the ground. She kept struggling until the breath was pressed from her lungs and purple fireflies spun before her eyes.

Willit tapped her forehead with the bowl of his pipe. "That's the agitation we just talked about. Listen, kid, I can put a bullet through your nose and have it come out your belly button. Tell her, Professor."

"It's true," Mr. Agate moaned. "Don't test him."

"That's fine advice. This here is a wise man."

"Take what you will and leave us alone," Agate said.

"Yes . . ." Willit said, studying Clover, "and no." He lit his pipe and brought the smoldering bowl slowly under her chin. Clover held her head bravely still, trying not to flinch.

Just before it burned her, Bolete said, "Professor might have sent a signal. He's got his tricks, don't he? Best to get on before something surprises us."

Willit sighed. He removed his hat to scratch his sweaty hair. The rabbit ears were worn furless in places and swung pathetically from where they were stitched to the hatband. Looking deeply into her eyes and exhaling a plume of smoke, Willit said, "Load it up!"

Bolete threw Clover to the ground, and the poacher they called Digger stood on her braid. Clover was shaking, with her cheek pressed against the tea-damp floor. Death had found her and the entire journey had been for nothing. She'd never even seen her mother's grave. She had failed her father again, her best efforts unraveling into a new nightmare. The watch was just a broken timepiece. She'd squandered even the hope her father had offered with his last breath, leading these monsters right to Mr. Agate's collection. She watched the poachers carry the collection out. They were the worst kind of men. None of them had been anywhere near kindness or bathwater for a very long time. Their eyes looked like the holes a crow might peck in a heel of bread.

As his men carried crates and paper-wrapped packages out the door, Willit sauntered around, tapping at oddities with the end of his pipe. He took a moment to scrub his back against a wall, like a raccoon with mange. He picked up a long chain with a small iron box dangling from one end. "Is the Heron's Heart in here?" he asked.

Mr. Agate nodded miserably, the blood from his wound blackening his shirt.

Willit jumped up and clopped his heels together. He whooped and smacked his hat on his thigh as he danced a manic jig to music no one else heard. "I knew I'd find your little hidey-hole. Better than a gold mine, because there ain't no digging. If even half of these are genuine, I'm going to be rich." He pulled Mr. Agate toward him by his bloody ear and kissed him on the mouth.

"We'll be crapping money!" Bolete hollered as he hefted a crate. "Money just tumblin' out our backsides!"

Willit whistled as he wiped Mr. Agate's blood from his fingers and began to sprinkle more tobacco into the bowl of his pipe.

Clover reached for the crowbar, which lay just feet away, but Willit winked at her and touched the pistol in its holster. "Is this loaded? That's the question you need to ask yourself." His pipe waggled at her. He picked and scratched at himself like a monkey. Clover thought it might be the worst case of bedbugs she had ever seen. Or it could have been chiggers or a half-dozen diseases that she had helped her father cure. Whatever it was, she wanted Willit to die of it.

When the room was empty except for books, Willit shook Mr. Agate's hand and said, "You collect them; I sell them to the buyer. I can pay you a small finder's fee in the future if you like. Don't you go trying to disappear, Aaron. I'll sniff you out."

Then Bolete came back in and lifted Clover off her feet, kicking and screaming, into the alley. Outside, a delivery wagon was heaped with the stolen crates. A wooden cage sat on the back of the wagon, open and waiting.

Clover fought hard, but Bolete squeezed the air out of her again, and soon she found herself crammed inside the cage. She was forced to crouch with her thighs against her chest because the cage was too small to kneel in, let alone stand.

Bolete slammed the lid shut and bent down to whisper, "You ever see a hog eat a duck? Feet first, face first, it don't matter. Feathers and all. Crunch crunch. It ain't polite, but it's how things go. Life is like that; sometimes you're the hog, and sometimes you're the duck. I guess you know which one you are today. It ain't your fault and nothing you can do, so don't worry too much."

Frightened faces peered down at her from the windows in the buildings above. The people did nothing but watch. Terror was turning her lungs into a burlap sack, but Clover managed to wail, "Send for the sheriff!"

"Oh, don't bother," Willit said, leaping onto his saddle and scratching at his chest. "He's probably a busy man."

Among the stacked crates, Clover spotted Hannibal imprisoned in his own little wicker cage. They'd gotten him too! His bandage was gone and his wounded wing sagged. He nodded bravely and whispered, "Salutations, Nurse Elkin. I am glad to see you again, but wish it were under better circumstances."

Bolete threw her haversack and her father's bag onto the heap and then covered her cage with a blanket, shutting out the light.

PART II

CHAPTER 9

LIAR

The slats might as well have been the ribs of a wolf that had swallowed Clover whole. She screamed herself hoarse as the wagon shuddered down the cobblestone streets. But her cries were thin notes against the city's orchestra of vendors, musicians, beggars' bells, and workshops. Bolete and the other poachers bellowed drinking songs to drown her out completely. Soon the wagon rumbled out the city gates, and the clamor of New Manchester fell away behind them.

"Father, I'm sorry." Clover shook the slats and growled in the desperate darkness. Worse than the humiliation, worse than the fear, was the guilt of having failed her father. The oddity he had told her to protect, that last hope, now belonged to the poachers. The monsters had won.

"Hannibal?" Clover whispered. "What happened?"

"I had just sent my correspondence on to Senator Auburn's caravan when I learned that poachers were roaming the city," Hannibal said. "I rushed to find you, but just as I was getting

close, these cowards ambushed me in an unfair fight."

Bolete interrupted, "That's what you get for sticking your beak where it don't belong. Willit don't like his plans meddled with."

"Willit knows better than to cross Senator Auburn," Hannibal declared. "You'll all face a firing squad when this comes to light."

"Well, best not tell the senator, then! Maybe we'll give you to the witch. On occasion, Willit has been known to make a generous donation to that hag. Or maybe we'll just do a simple roast with gizzard-and-rosemary gravy—"

"How dare you—"

But Bolete burst into a drunken song, drowning Hannibal out.

To market, to market to buy a fat pig!

Home again, home again, jiggety-jig!

The Rooster was as helpless as Clover was, trapped in his own cage. And the Society that was supposed to protect her was nothing but an addled old man. Agate had given her a few scraps of information about her mother, but there were more questions than ever, and Clover couldn't help but think that if she'd known enough, if she'd been given the whole story, she might have avoided this fate.

The wagon jolted off the regular cobbles of the main highway into the softer ruts of a dirt road.

Clover found that if she pinched the blanket over her cage between her fingers, she could tug it down half an inch at a time, widening a crack of light. She saw sheets of algae glittering in a roadside ditch. The leaves of apple orchards trembled, and starlings tumbled through the air like a school of minnows. She tugged the blanket until she could see the untarnished sky, like an enamel pot clapped over the earth.

The world was stubbornly beautiful to the last, ignoring her entirely.

She stopped crying as anger lit her nerves. What if a wolf *had* swallowed her? Wouldn't she kick and claw and do her best to kill that wolf with indigestion?

"Clover Elkin," she said, "will not die without a fight." She pulled the blanket off and let it drop behind them. Squinting against the light, she saw two of the poachers sitting in the driver's seat: Bolete and Digger, a man whose knobby head bobbed on the end of a long neck like a pelican's. The others must have ridden ahead.

Hannibal gave her a sly nod and whispered, "Don't fret, Nurse Elkin. We'll find our way to victory."

When the blanket had disappeared in the distance, Clover wiped the snot from her upper lip and spoke. "Mr. Bolete, was it your bullet that killed my father?"

Bolete turned and blinked at her. He was chewing a wad of tobacco thoughtfully, and he peered around the wagon, looking for the blanket.

"Willit don't like to waste bullets on easy pickings," Bolete finally answered. "So he leaves the sure shots to me." He leaned over to spit in the road, giving Clover a good view of a chapped neck between his greasy strands of hair.

Bolete wore a necklace made of half a walnut strung on a leather cord, just as Willit did. Clover had never wanted anything as badly as she wanted to seize that cord and choke him with it. But all she could do was tremble in her cage like malaria itself, her vision blurred by white blooms of shame and rage. She heard herself say, "You're rabid. You should be put down. Every one of you."

"Who will put us down? You?" Bolete chuckled, picking pinches of tobacco out of the skulls he had woven into his beard. "I don't see that coming to pass—do you, Digger?" The long-necked man only cleared his throat, as if that were an answer. "For one thing," Bolete continued, "you're in a cage, little miss. And anyway, you'd have to come at us with better than a crowbar."

The wagon slowed as they approached a crossroads. Clover's heart leaped when she saw the unmistakable yellow wagon parked on the side of the road, with the bright lettering on the side announcing *BLEAKERMAN'S CURE-ALL!*

"Nessa!" Clover screamed. "Help me!"

"Shut your hole!" Bolete snapped.

Digger leaned back and whipped at her with the riding crop. A few of the lashes came through the slats to sting her, but Clover kept screaming.

Willit and the other poachers were waiting in the shade of an oak tree. Clover twisted and leaned. "Nessa, it's me!"

Then Clover saw Nessa standing among them. She was looking at Clover with such bewilderment that the poachers burst out laughing.

"Help you?" Willit crowed. "Why, Nessa just sold you."

Nessa took a few steps toward the wagon, her face red as a hammered thumb. "Why is Clover in a cage?" she blurted. "You said you only wanted the goods! You said you'd leave her alone!"

Willit smacked Nessa's ear. "She *is* the goods."

"You're with *them?*" Clover stared at Nessa, the truth sinking in.

"Don't take it hard," Willit said, climbing onto his horse. "Nessa comes by it naturally. Her uncle was the best swindler I ever met! He spun golden lies and picked a pocket with every song."

"Shut your mouth!" Nessa raged, her fists balling at her sides. She looked like a bull about to charge. "You do not talk about Uncle!"

"Pick up the pace, boys," Willit said, ignoring her. "And someone throw a jacket over that cage." He half stood in his stirrups to scratch his calf, then heeled his horse into a gallop.

Digger clicked his tongue and whipped the horses pulling the wagon.

"You liar! You . . . *pox*!" Clover cursed as the wagon lurched past Nessa. She felt her heart, just moments ago ripening with hope, withering to a rotten apple.

"Hold up!" Nessa shouted at the poachers. "Wait!"

She made a dash toward Clover and leaped up to catch hold of the wagon. Bracing herself against the cage with one hand, Nessa started tugging on the latch, saying, "They said they only wanted the oddities—"

CRACK!

Nessa went rigid as the sleeve of her shirt shredded. The cloth fell away, exposing a spiral of welted skin. A brand circled her upper arm, blisters rising even as Clover watched. Stunned, Nessa landed on her butt in the road.

Willit held up his smoking Pistol. "Last warning, Nessa!" He had fired without looking, and still the bullet had cut a sinister path through the fabric of Nessa's sleeve, leaving her arm intact.

Nessa got to her feet and stood in the billowing dust, her tears cutting bright lines down her cheeks.

Clover found the gold tooth in her pocket and threw it into the dirt.

"You killed me, charlatan!" she spat.

Bolete and Digger exchanged some tense words, and then the long-necked man removed his duster and draped it over Clover's cage. It smelled like cheese and only covered two sides of her view.

"Nice and comfy?" Bolete asked.

Clover didn't answer.

Willit had gone ahead again, but Clover heard the other

poachers lingering on the trail—probably scouting for trouble. Peering out from under the coat, she saw crows sitting in the trees like bottles of Bleakerman's tonic. She felt the pockets of Digger's long coat but found only smears of lard and crumbs of coal.

"Where are you taking me?" Clover asked, swallowing her fear.

"Most of our hauls go to Senator Auburn these days," Bolete said. "He's got a hunger for every oddity he can lay his hands on."

"What happens then?"

"What do you think happens?" Bolete said. "We sell you with the rest of the mess and come away rich as bear fat."

"But what would Senator Auburn want with me?" Clover asked, her voice quavering.

"He'll burn you, I expect."

Clover shuddered. "Burn me?"

"What else are you good for?"

At this, Clover's mouth went dry and her vision narrowed. She pushed the desperate words out. "I am a doctor's apprentice. Tell Willit that if he sets me and Hannibal free I can cure him of that rash."

"It ain't a rash," Bolete said. "It's a curse. He's been smote by the witch, and she gives him no rest, even though he's tried an' tried to get on her good side."

They were passing a derelict hunting shack when Bolete cussed, pulling the wagon to a shuddering stop. "Aw, bung worms! It's Smalt!"

The coat had slipped down enough for Clover to see Willit standing by the road, talking with a tall dandy dressed in a blue satin suit that could have come from a prince's closet. Even in

New Manchester, Clover hadn't seen anyone wearing such a lavish costume, though she had seen illustrations of styles like this from before the Louisiana War. Lace frothed at the ends of his sleeves, and his cravat was so thick it looked like it was strangling him. The preposterous curls of Smalt's wig were held in place with periwinkle ribbons. The wig sat high on his head, slightly off center, and the faint breeze blew clouds of white powder off it like snow from a mountaintop.

Behind him stood a hound the size of a pony, its cheeks like steaks dripping with gravy.

CHAPTER 10

THEY ALWAYS LOOK

Smalt leaned toward Willit like a rotten tree. Clover remembered the word "Smalt" mentioned briefly in a journal paragraph about dangerous oddities, but she had imagined Smalt to be a bottomless pit or a poisonous cloud hovering in a desert somewhere. Now she saw that Smalt was a man.

"You see?" Willit said, pointing at the wagon. "It's nothing but a load of junk. We have nothing you want. Begone, devil."

Smalt spoke with a curdled voice. "You forget your manners. Shall Smalt tell your cohort why you wear the ears?"

Willit said, "There's no reason for threats. I'm in a hurry, is all."

"But you hurry east, when your esteemed buyer is northwest, in Brackenweed, where I myself am headed. You must be running side errands. For whom?"

Willit looked over his shoulder before saying, "The one who makes the dead birds sing."

"Oh, her." Smalt dismissed this with a flick of his wrist. "Smalt already knows about your sordid history with the Seamstress. Stop stalling and give me my due!"

"What more do you want? You've already milked us dry!"

Smalt wrinkled his nose. The huge dog took its cue and lunged, backing Willit against a tree. With the hound's paws pinning his shoulders, Willit's hand went to his Pistol, and Bolete raised a rifle. But Smalt didn't flinch. He adjusted his wig and said, "Consider carefully, ragpickers. Recall that Smalt's messengers are posted in every city. If something happens to me, they will deliver the envelopes exposing you."

Smalt's slick voice made Clover's skin crawl. His accent was high society, but every syllable came up wet, like a frog trying to escape a butter churn. "Even your Pistol cannot reach my messengers," he continued. "Shoot me only if you wish the newspapers to print your every secret. Your deepest, most ruinous—but what is this?"

He pointed to Hannibal. "Is that who I think it is? The senator will have your hide—"

Willit said, "The senator don't need to know."

"You know I'm happy to keep a secret." Smalt spotted Clover half-hidden under the coat. "Are you trading in urchins now?"

"She's nothing," Willit said. "A mountain girl with a bounty on her head."

While the growling hound kept Willit pinned to the tree, Smalt strolled to the wagon. This wasn't the kind of rescue Clover wanted.

Smalt tugged the coat off the cage, and the two examined each other. Smalt's suit and wig looked antique, but it was impossible to guess his age, for his face was caked with a cosmetic so thick it cracked and crumbled at the corners of his mouth. His false teeth seemed too large, and he spoke around them like a horse considering the bit. He held an enormous top hat of blue silk.

"Has she got secrets?" Smalt asked, his teeth clicking wetly behind his lips.

He snapped his fingers, and the dog let Willit go.

"No," Willit said. "Just a prairie surgeon's daughter."

"But a bounty means there's surely something in there. Smalt will find out."

"Ten dollars and I get to listen," Willit said, edging warily around the hound.

Smalt's chin lifted with disdain. "Out of the question!" He teetered a bit in his heeled boots and steadied himself with his silver-headed cane. "A secret shared is no secret at all. In exchange for not telling the senator that you've abducted his prized chicken, Smalt will give this mountain girl a little squeeze. It won't take long. You and your idiots take a stroll. Find some weeds to water. We'll be done here before you can shake it dry."

Bolete and Digger climbed down from their seats as Hannibal squawked, "This mistreatment is an affront to the dignity of a decorated officer—"

Smalt sniffed once and gestured for the dog, which placed its paws up on the wagon on either side of Hannibal's cage, growling. "Take that with you!" Smalt said. "My Hat doesn't work on beasts."

Bolete hoisted Hannibal, cage and all, off the wagon. Then the poachers sauntered down the trail, leaving Clover alone with Smalt.

His suit bunched at the joints as if his limbs were held together with twine. Despite its obvious expense, his sky-blue coat seemed too small one moment, then clownishly large the next. Between the heavy face-cake, the towering wig, and the gloves, not an inch of his skin was visible. By the way his clothes warped and buckled, it was clear he was the frailest of men, doused in a geranium perfume that gave Clover an instant headache. But of all the unsettling things about Smalt, the worst was the way he looked at Clover, as if she were a pudding he intended to eat.

"Salutations." He smiled, and his lips puckered around the teeth to keep them from slipping out. He opened the lid of the cage, and Clover pulled herself up with a grunt. She would have leaped out, but her legs were bloodless from the cramped quarters, so she just stood in the cage. This close, Smalt's perfume stung her eyes.

"Don't you touch me," she said, trying to sound brave while she waited for feeling to return to her feet.

Smalt laughed as he turned his Hat in his hands. "Touch? Creature, you are filthy! No, Smalt shan't touch you."

With his cane, he rapped the crown of his Hat like a drum. He ran his gloved finger around the velvet rim, which was spattered by purple stains, as if someone had spilled wine on it. Then he presented the Hat before her, like a server offering a meal.

"Whatever you do," he said, "don't look inside."

Before she could think better of it, Clover looked into the empty Hat, and the darkness inside seized her. She could not look away, no matter how hard she tried. Waves of nausea churned her gut.

Smalt grinned. "They always look."

Clover tried to wrench her face away, but her eyes were pinned to the bottom of the Hat. She couldn't even blink.

"For a doctor's daughter, this shouldn't be unfamiliar," Smalt said. "Think of it as a purging."

A sickly gasp escaped Clover's lips as the cramps got worse. She was going to vomit.

"Come on, then," Smalt said. "Out with it."

Then Clover was retching, but instead of bile, tendrils of moist indigo dripped from her mouth and nose. The inky mist coagulated into twitching forms as it pattered into the Hat, forming letters and words, scurrying ants dancing out a horrid calligraphy. Clover heard a whisper:

I stole molasses from Widow Henshaw's pantry.

Smalt tsked. "Smalt isn't wasting time on molasses. Come now, pest, reach deep."

I threw the Ice Hook in the lake.

"Who cares what trash you threw in a lake? Do you have a secret or not?"

Father died because I wanted to be like Mother.

The words fluttered like drowning moths into the Hat. Clover almost fainted with the shame of the confession, but Smalt pursed his lips reproachfully.

"I have a feeling you can do better."

He flicked the rim of the Hat, and Clover doubled over as the secret she was trying to keep clawed up her throat. She swallowed hard, her guts turning inside out. She almost passed out trying to keep the secret down.

"This must be a good one!" Smalt said, shaking the Hat a little, as if he were begging for alms. "Go on, don't be stingy."

Clover groaned as a surge of sour fluid filled her throat, writhing into a grub. It whispered as it slowly emerged:

I carry . . . the necessary oddity . . . something so secret not even Agate knew about it . . .

Clover's eyes bulged, bloodshot. She clenched her jaw shut, nearly fainting with the effort, but the bitter larva slipped through her teeth and plopped into the Hat.

. . . in the medical bag.

"Much better," Smalt purred. "What does this oddity do?"

Clover shook her head. She didn't know.

"Necessary, is it? Could it be the oddity that a particular senator has been searching for? The key to beating Bonaparte? No matter; I'll ask him myself." The ghoul pulled his Hat away, and Clover could finally blink. She clutched the top of the cage to keep from falling over. Smalt brushed the last wisps of sticky vapor into his hat before placing it over his wig and giving it a jaunty tap to keep it in place.

He grinned at her and said, "Don't you feel lighter now? Unburdened? Cleansed?"

"Please." She coughed. "You mustn't take it."

"Of course Smalt will take the bag. How could I not, after you've told me what's in it?"

Smalt pushed Clover back into the cage with a single finger, making a disgusted face, and locked it. "I don't normally trade in oddities. Secrets are my particular passion, but if it is as special as you say . . ." He peered about the wagon until his eyes fell on the medical bag, and he snatched it with a spidery arm.

"Certain entities are paying top dollar for such things these days." He snapped for his dog and untied his horse. "Senator Auburn is, as we speak, traveling the state gathering his support. Democracy is not a lucrative business, but war is, and the senator puts on a grand party."

"Please," Clover begged. "I promised to protect it."

Smalt was already in his saddle. Over his shoulder, he said, "Well, you tried your feeble best. Don't punish yourself. A juicy secret like that, who could keep it to herself?"

Before Smalt could ride away, Willit and the other poachers emerged from the trees with their pistols drawn, blocking his exit. The dog growled, but the poachers stood their ground.

"What's in the bag?" Willit asked.

"That's between Smalt and the girl. You know how secrets work."

Willit scratched and twitched, following an itch down his neck and into his shirt. He scratched so hard, Clover could see welts rising on his skin. "I said you could take a secret. I didn't agree to the bag."

"You lied. She's more than a mountain girl. And Auburn would be unhappy to know you're dealing with the Seamstress on the side. So I will keep your secret and this bag," Smalt said. "Now, have your apes step aside; I have a distance to cover."

Willit stared at Clover and then at Smalt again. "If you want the bag so bad," he said, "it must be something good in there."

"Are you proposing an exchange?" Smalt cocked an eyebrow.

"You only got one thing that I want."

"Very well," Smalt sighed. He removed his Hat and held it toward Willit, who flinched away from it.

Clover watched that Hat with disgusted fascination, careful not to let her sight fall inside the rim. The body of the Hat buckled and swelled, churning with an ocean of secrets. How many people had been its victim? What truths were trapped inside that awful oddity?

"Go on, then," Smalt said with a treacly smile. "Fish it out."

"Just reach in?" Willit was nervous.

"Hurry up. I have appointments to meet."

Turning his head away, Willit reached a shaking hand into the Hat and felt around. Clover heard distant voices, screams, even a lullaby coming from the hat, as if a rabble of ghosts were trapped in the velvet lining. One woman's voice was so familiar that Clover's breath caught in her throat. She stared at the Hat, straining to hear the words. But they were too faint and faded back into the river-hiss of whispers before she could understand them. Wincing, Willit finally pulled out a dark and dripping cockroach. Its legs scrambled in the air, and Clover heard bits of Willit's secret hissing from its steaming carapace:

. . . give me my due . . . used the Pistol . . . Seamstress's curse . . .

"Hold on tightly, now," Smalt warned. "Once released, a secret may cling to the underside of a shoe or scamper under a pillow. It might spread it wings and fly for miles. When it finds a warm, unsuspecting ear, it will crawl inside to lay its eggs . . ."

Willit clutched it as it squirmed. "What do I do now?"

"Put it back where it came from," Smalt said.

"Put it back?"

"Isn't that what you want? To keep the truth all to yourself?"

Willit shoved the secret into his mouth. It fought, choking him, and he was forced to chew it. Clover nearly retched again, watching bits of the secret falling out, only to be caught and put back in Willit's mouth. Finally Willit had swallowed the whole mess.

"There, now," said Smalt. "Your little secret belongs to no one but you."

"But what's to keep you from telling it anyway?" Willit blurted, looking very ill.

"Without proof in the Hat, such stories are nothing but wind. Smalt does not trade in rumors. Anyway, your secret wasn't worth much. Pitiful as it was, no one would have paid for it but you. I only kept it as leverage."

Willit sat on the ground with his head between his knees, trying not to vomit. He waved his Pistol, and the other poachers stepped aside. Smalt pulled the Hat firmly onto his wig, mounted his horse, and started off down the trail, heading northwest with the hound loping behind.

As he passed her cage, Smalt gave Clover a wink and touched the rim of his Hat, a gentleman's gesture warped into a threat. Faint threads of indigo unfurled from the Hat behind him, as if the secrets wanted out. Clover could almost make out words in the soft hiss of whispers trailing behind him as he hurried away, *mischief . . . malevolence . . . Miniver . . .*

Clover pressed her forehead against the slats. Had it said Miniver? "Stop him!" Clover said, clutching the slats. "Bring him back!"

"Let it go," Willit sighed, setting Hannibal's cage back on the wagon. "Smalt has done it to all of us. Everyone wants to kill him, but no one is brave enough to try."

Hannibal continued his protests, ". . . you'll face the fires of justice . . ."

Willit ignored him and put his face close to Clover's cage. "All my life I've been looking for just a piece of the luck that others got," he said. "But what becomes of a man who tries to crawl out of the scorched beans and squalor of life? He gets cursed by a witch. At night I can't sleep for the itching. All the sweaty day I can't get no rest from the itching."

"Have you tried a bath?" Clover said.

"This ain't no joke!" Willit shouted. "I am telling you how the world works. I am telling you about the misery of man."

"The misery of a murderer is nothing I care about," Clover said.

"Well, you are going to fix it for me." Willit mounted his horse. "Auburn may want you, but there's another who wants you more. You're the belle of the ball, and everyone wants a dance."

Before Clover could ask what he meant, Bolete climbed into the driver's seat of the wagon beside Digger and gave the reins a flip. The wagon creaked as they followed Willit, the road sloping toward a shady vesper-pine forest. The blanket of pine needles crackled under the wheels.

Only a few minutes later, Willit slowed, his horse munching at a thatch of grass as he loaded the Pistol. "I'll say this much, though," he muttered, scratching his ear with the butt of the gun. "I do not appreciate being drooled upon." He pointed the appalling weapon at the sky and hesitated, an uncertain scowl on his face. Then he fired. Everyone had been waiting for it, but the blast made them all flinch. "That is one thing I do not appreciate," he said, holstering the Pistol.

"Who is that for?" Bolete demanded. "Not Smalt?"

"It's for that consarn dog."

"Well, a dog is only as good as its owner," Bolete said. "It can hardly help how it was raised."

"Don't start weeping into your silk kerchief, Bolete. I only hobbled the sloppy cur."

Clover imagined the bullet darting into the sky before cutting a sharp curve toward Smalt's unsuspecting hound.

"Smalt won't take kindly to you taking bites out of his dog," Bolete said.

"Maybe next time Smalt will steer clear of me and mine." Willit heeled his horse and darted ahead.

Bolete nodded approvingly and elbowed Digger. "That right there is why he's boss. Willit's always thinking of the future. He's got a mind for the grand scheme of things."

When they caught up with Willit again, the poacher was staring hard at deep shadows cast by a boulder.

"What now, boss?" Bolete said, pulling the wagon to a stop.

Something moved in the shadows, then hissed. The horses snorted and wagged their heads.

"What is it?" Digger asked.

"Can't you smell it?" Bolete whispered. "If it smells dead but don't act dead, it can only be one thing: vermin."

"Who's there?" Willit shouted.

The voice that came from the shadows was parched as pebbles in a skillet. "Why have you summoned my mistress?"

The vermin lowered its head into the light, scratching at the ground with a broad paw. It had once been a badger. The patches of fur that weren't clotted with blood were thickly striped. Its lips had dried into a permanent snarl, revealing savage upper fangs and a lower jaw made from a bent saw. Its rib cage had been replaced by a dented teakettle.

Seeing it, the horses hitched to the wagon reared onto their hind legs, wheezing. Bolete and Digger tried to keep them calm with cooing and clicks of the tongue, but the horses backed into the wagon, shoving it onto a rocky slope. The heavy load lurched and leaned. Crates shifted around Clover, kept in place only by straining leather straps and a slim margin of gravity.

"I don't want to talk to you," Willit told the vermin. "I want to talk to the Seamstress. She knows me."

"She knows you for a thief," the hideous thing hissed.

"I ain't denying that," Willit said, scratching the back of his neck. "But I have what she wants. Tell her to come get it. If she removes the curse, she can have it."

"Mistress wants nothing from you."

The horses squealed, tugging their bits bloody and knocking their heads together. The vermin paced hungrily toward them, seeming to enjoy their terror. The dirt beneath was muddy with urine, and the horses leaned hard against their harnesses. The wagon lurched and then tilted as they pushed it farther into the roadside boulders. As it leaned, Clover pushed her weight against the slats of her cage, trying to tip it.

"I have the frog," Willit said. "I have Clover Elkin."

"Impossible," said the vermin.

"See for yourself," Willit answered.

The Badger crept toward the back of the wagon and rose on its hind legs to look at Clover with empty eye sockets. She could see its frightful design clearly. The beast had been forged in a fit of rage. Its back legs were fastened to the spine with hammered forks, and the sticky hide was secured around the internal clutter with fencing wire.

Bolete struggled to keep the horses from toppling the wagon.

"Want I should shoot it?" Digger asked.

"No!" Willit shouted.

The vermin cocked its brutal head and asked Clover, "Are you she?"

Clover was trembling as much as the horses, her palms sweaty against the slats of the cage, but she forced herself to speak bravely. "I am Clover Elkin."

"Hush, girl!" Hannibal hissed. "If the Seamstress did that to a badger, what will she do to you?"

Willit said, "You see? From her own mouth the girl admits it. Go and tell the Seamstress. Smalt came this close to taking her. He has all the pieces, but Auburn is the one who has put the puzzle together, and it's only a matter of time. Don't you see? The Seamstress will want to get the frog from me. She won't like Auburn's terms."

"If you are lying, the Seamstress will grind your teeth and hang your pelt to dry—"

"Enough! I know the witch's wrath! Get gone and tell her what I have."

The Badger sniffed the air, as if memorizing Clover's odor, then turned and shuffled toward the shadows. The grinding sound of bone on metal disappeared into the forest.

"I thought we were selling the girl to the senator," Digger moaned. "I don't want nothing to do with no Seamstress."

Bolete turned on Digger. "Then jump on down and walk home, you tender kitten! You bar rag! Don't nobody want nothing to do with a witch, but if Willit says we got to, we got to!"

Digger struggled with the horses' tangled lines, muttering, "This won't come to nothing good."

CHAPTER 11

GIVE A LITTLE RUN

T he horses strained *against their lines, eager to get away from the* place. As they picked up speed, Clover felt she was tumbling slowly into her own grave. She didn't know which was worse, being burned for no reason by the senator or having her skin hung to dry by the Seamstress.

Her knuckles white against the slats of her cage, she searched desperately for a way out. Then she saw the cigar box pressed between two crates that had shifted. Now it was held in place only by a slim leather strap.

"Hannibal," she whispered, "can you reach that?"

Hannibal squeezed his head through the gaps in the wicker and stretched his neck toward the cigar box, the sliver of his tongue quivering with effort. Finally, he managed to get the end of the strap in his beak, but he couldn't budge the tether.

"That's enough of that!" Bolete drew his knife and turned around to reach back into her cage. He slid the long blade between the slats until it rested against Clover's throat. She froze, feeling her own pulse beating against the steel.

"I ain't supposed to kill you," Bolete whispered. "But I will shuck your ears from your skull like oysters. I will cut a pocket in you big enough to hide a pickled egg if you two don't stop whispering."

Hannibal gave one final tug, and the cigar box slipped under the strap and tumbled down. It bounced once on the boards before dropping to the road below. They heard it crunch under a wheel.

"Infernal confoundery!" Bolete hollered. "I am going to beat you till you talk backward! Digger, stop the—"

But before Digger could pull the reins, the wagon came to a violent stop on its own. Something powerful had seized a back wheel. The horses squealed at the sudden strain.

Clover knew that Susanna, the Doll, was out of her box and had a hold on the wagon. It pitched like a ship at sea, then tilted up at an extreme angle. Agate's collection slipped and tumbled in an avalanche of crates.

Bolete fell forward into the reins, and his knife took a bite out of Clover's ear before he vanished. The crates crashed and scattered as the wagon began to rock. Hannibal crowed, and Digger leaped into the nearby bushes for safety. Clover hung on to the slats of the cage as the forest swung upside-down, until finally the wagon landed on top of her. The cage shattered, and Clover found her cheek pressed against pine mulch.

She kicked at the splintered wood and pulled herself out from under the heap, slats scraping her shins as she emerged. Without the cage shielding her, she would have been crushed.

The forest swam. She was faintly aware of the chaos around

her as she scrambled toward the trees. One of the horses lay pinned under the wagon, kicking its front legs and gasping for air. Somewhere nearby, Bolete was hollering obscenities.

As Clover crawled away from the wreck, she spotted Hannibal's cage in the dust. She tugged the bottom out to find him alive and wild-eyed. He rolled upright and jumped swiftly toward the forest ahead of her, shouting, "That's it, Nurse Elkin! Run!"

Clover tried, but her feet were numb, and she pitched onto her belly. In the distance she heard Willit shouting, "What is happening back there?"

Meanwhile, the overturned wagon shuddered as if a bear were waking from hibernation beneath the planks. The poachers were all shooting at it, and pine needles rained down around them. Then, even louder than the gunshots, there was a wail of wrenched steel as little Susanna broke the axle from the wagon bed.

Clover got to her feet again and was making a wobbly dash toward the cover of the trees when a wagon wheel flew past her head, ricocheting off the trunk in front of her. She ducked just in time to escape decapitation.

Peering over her shoulder, Clover caught a glimpse of the Doll; the yarn mouth buckled in rage as Susanna pulled the heavy beam of the bed free, picking the wagon apart piece by piece.

The poachers had taken shelter behind trees and boulders. They leaned out only far enough to aim their rifles at the rattling wagon.

Willit was shouting, "Never shoot at oddities! That's our fortune, you idiots!"

"But she's tearing it all to hell!" Bolete screamed.

"You're hitting everything but the Doll. Here, let me do it."

Willit drew his infamous Pistol, the gun that could not miss, and shot Susanna through the belly.

From behind a tree, Clover watched Susanna stop short and place a hand on the hole, where cotton wadding poked out. Digger approached with a sword drawn, ready to finish her.

Susanna charged. When Digger turned to run, she caught his boot and tripped him. Seizing him by the belt, she swung him like a sack of oats. He screamed as he sailed into the canopy above.

Rifles crackled. Some of the bullets sizzled past Clover and smacked into the trees around her. She hunkered behind a boulder, panting and covering her head with her hands. She could see wretched Digger twenty feet above. He hung from one trouser leg in the branches, his twisted sword having fallen from his hand.

Beneath the thunder of gunfire, Clover heard a voice calling her name. Hannibal was in the trees somewhere nearby, like a seraph guiding her to safety. She rose to her feet and tried to follow his directions.

"Stay low, brave girl!" Hannibal shouted. "Run. Now duck!"

Clover went low as a jagged piece of the wagon cut through the air above her.

"Up now and run! Left. Go left!" Hannibal shouted. "There is a rifle near the horses. No, leave it be; someone else got it."

She followed his instructions blindly, tripping sometimes over fallen branches.

"Take cover there!"

Clover dove to the ground behind a log. She could see the area around the wagon cloaked in the blue haze of gun smoke. Susanna continued to hurl debris into the trees.

Willit shouted, "Where's the girl? Find Clover!"

But the poachers were still firing at the wagon.

Something moved past the log Clover had hidden behind. The Badger vermin lifted its mummified head over the wood and croaked, "Don't go wandering off, frog."

Clover screamed and leaped up, sprinting madly as Hannibal warned, "Not yet! They'll see you!"

But Clover needed to leave that savage grin far behind. She was relieved to spot Hannibal ahead, hopping from branch to branch.

"Look out!" Hannibal shouted. "He's upon you!"

One of the poachers caught Clover by the hair and yanked her off her feet. He dragged her back toward the road, hollering, "I've got her! I've got the—"

A crate slammed into the poacher with the force of a cannon-ball, plastering him against a tree.

In her tantrum, Susanna was throwing everything she could get her tiny hands on. She'd pulled the wagon apart like an over-cooked turkey and was now scattering debris throughout the forest. Clover covered her ears as she ran again. A bullet tore a branch off a tree nearby, and she veered blindly in another direction.

As the forest blurred past, she saw the Badger leap on a poacher that had gotten in its way. The man went down screaming.

Then Willit appeared in front of her, sudden as a sneeze. He was holding a Match that had just gone out, and he was twitch-ing with rage. Clover remembered how he had appeared on the riverbank, the Matches giving him the power to jump from place to place.

"I have burned too many of these chasing after you, kid," he said. "And now you've gone and ruined a whole haul of oddities."

He dropped the blackened Match and pulled the Pistol from his belt. With his other hand he reached for his purse of bullets.

"You go on and run," he said, scratching his neck with the barrel of the gun. "Now that I've got a bead on you, I am going to take my time putting a bullet through your leg. Don't worry; I'll only take the kneecap off—won't hit nothing vital."

But Clover didn't run. Through a torrent of terror, she waited until Willit held the bullets in his hand.

"Go on, now. Give a little run," Willit said. "It feels like a waste if you just stand there."

Still Clover held her ground, trembling, trying not to imagine what a bullet through the knee would feel like. Willit opened the back of the Pistol to load it.

Then, just as he tugged the mouth of the purse open, Clover lunged past him, snatching it as she went. She kept running as fast as her aching legs would carry her, clutching the bullets to her chest.

Willit filled the air with curses, making a mad dash after her. But Clover was faster, and after a few quick turns, she'd lost him in the trees.

Another crate came sailing through the air in an arc. It exploded just feet away, releasing a heap of debris: twisted ladles, splayed books, candleholders. A small iron box popped open, and a red-hot coal tumbled out. Immediately, the pine needles beneath it began to smolder. The smoke gathered in a disturbing cloud above the oddity.

Clover stared, transfixed, as the Ember blackened the ground. She watched as smoke rose, watched as white tendrils twined together in the air like spun wool.

The vapors bundled into a ghostly, long-legged shape. Sparks illuminated the smoke from inside like lightning in a thundercloud, and Clover saw long, dark bones knitting together in the maelstrom.

Hannibal hollered, "That's not something you want to linger over, is it? Don't you know the Heron when you see it?"

His voice freed Clover from her shock, and she dashed away. When she looked back, the plume had grown darker. A long neck with a dagger-like head emerged. The braided smoke took the shape of a large fisher bird.

Light crackled at the tip of its beak, and in a flash, a bright-blue flame rolled down the neck, igniting the smoke as it went until a fiery Heron lit the forest with an eerie glow. It was no bigger than a marsh egret, but, even yards away, Clover felt the heat on her face as the Heron stretched its luminous neck over the Ember. It snatched up the glowing coal and gobbled it down. The faint shadow of the Ember spun in the Heron's belly. The only solid thing in the beast, it became a smoldering heart, barely visible behind the glowing feathers. Then the Heron cocked its hungry head toward Clover.

Clover knew this oddity had killed hundreds during the Louisiana War. The journal said it had burned an entire forest to ash. Of all the dangers around her, it would be fire that killed her after all. Her nightmares were finding her one by one.

Clover ran from her greatest fear. With a predator's instinct, the Heron ran after her, branding the ground behind it with seared tracks. Clover tried to duck behind trees, but the Heron was always close, lowering its head and making leaping strides.

She couldn't outrun it. Clover had no choice but to turn and make a stand. She grabbed a sturdy stick and pivoted to fight. She took a strong swing, screaming as she aimed for the shadow of the Ember in the furnace of its belly. She missed and swung again, but this time the Heron snatched at the branch. The wood turned to ash where the white-hot beak cut through it, and Clover's weapon fell to pieces.

A poacher emerged from the trees behind the Heron, lifting his rifle. The Heron turned on him and pounced, its inferno wings enveloping his torso.

His screams didn't last long. Clover made a mad, sinuous path between the trunks. Finally she collapsed, panting, under an ancient crab apple tree festooned with mistletoe and thick hanging lichen. Clover hunkered in the den under the branches, her heart a furious drum.

The Heron stalked through the trees nearby, casting a light on the forest like a harvest moon. The air around it wobbled with heat as the bird paced, peering between trees and nudging the damp heaps of leaves. Fire itself was hunting Clover.

She remembered nothing from the journal about how to stop it. When it finished with her, it would burn the entire countryside, then the world.

"You were right about oddities, Father," Clover whispered. "I'm so sorry. You were right."

The Badger's voice replied, "If you run again, I'll rip the tendons from your ankles."

Clover screamed, pressing herself against the trunk of the tree, as the Badger crept under the canopy.

But just when the Badger was close enough to bite, the shadows shifted. The Badger hissed as the Heron snatched it up. Clover watched through the branches as the Badger squirmed in the bird's blazing beak. The hide went first, then the bones turned to ash. Bits of scalding metal fell around the Heron's feet. Just like that, the vermin was gone.

Now the Heron was peering into the branches where Clover was gasping. It had already grown larger. It spotted her with comet eyes.

Clover ran as the Heron strode right through the crab apple tree, flaming branches tumbling aside.

As she ran, Clover pulled her bandanna over her mouth. The air was choked with smoke. Over her shoulder, she saw the Heron lower its frame into a full run, closing the distance with a few strides. It was now as tall as she was.

Clover stumbled downhill toward what she hoped was a river. But the creek held only shallow puddles. She followed it into an algae-slick gorge, the Heron trailing closely. Clover dashed toward a leaning log, hoping to find safety on the other side of the natural bridge.

Before she made it over the log, the Heron leaped across the gorge, cutting her off. It was huge now, as if the sun itself had fallen to the earth. It opened its beak with a piercing howl and flapped its wings, sending a baking wind that buckled the bark of the surrounding trees. Clover fell backward, rolling off the log and landing hard on the rocks below.

"Help!" Clover screamed. "Someone, please!"

With the Heron peering over her, Clover felt like a minnow, doomed in the muddy shallows. The air scalded her lungs. She rolled toward a boulder, scrambling for shelter, but the Heron's blazing claws slammed into the mud beside her, blocking her escape with a blast of steam. There was nowhere to go. Clover knew this was her last living moment.

The Heron plunged its searing beak into Clover's heart.

CHAPTER 12

DOCTORING A SOCK

lover tried to scream but was paralyzed with pain.

The Heron stabbed her twice more, its head like a blacksmith's hammer striking sparks in a forge. But, despite the agony, Clover's heart refused to stop.

There was no blood, no smell of burned skin. The Heron cocked its head, perplexed, and tried to pierce her again, but its beak merely vanished into Clover's chest. It flapped its wings furiously, letting out another long, haunted howl.

Somehow, Clover was alive.

Just as the Heron was about to make another attack, Willit appeared, a smoldering Match held between his teeth.

The iron box that the Ember had come from dangled on the end of the chain he was twirling. Before the Heron could turn on him, he swung the chain hard and knocked the Ember right out of the bird's chest.

The blazing bird sputtered like a poorly made candle, then disappeared into a tower of white smoke. The Heron was gone.

The Ember hit the ground and immediately started smoldering, building toward another incarnation of the Heron, but Willit scooped it into the box before it could kindle. He latched the box, shaking his singed fingers, and looped the chain into his belt. Clover tried to get to her knees as he pulled out a long knife.

"That's another wasted Match, kid. I don't need bullets to take off your kneecap, but it will hurt more this way."

"What do you want with me?" Clover wheezed. She was too rubbery with shock to run.

"It ain't me who wants you."

Just as Willit grabbed her ankle, Hannibal slammed into the side of his head, a flurry of spurs and feathers.

Willit wailed, smacking at Hannibal, who clung to his hair like a fury. Willit made a blind stab at Hannibal but missed, cutting a red line above his own eyebrow. He cursed as blood spilled into his eyes. The chain and iron box fell from his belt as he stumbled toward his horse, Hannibal still leaping viciously at his back. A bugle sounded just as Willit spurred his horse away, frantically wiping blood from his face with the sleeve of his shirt.

"Hurrah!" Hannibal cried. The Rooster was winded but clearly thrilled by the events of the day. "A hard-earned victory!" he crowed.

"But how?" Clover touched the places where the Heron had hit her, feeling for cauterized gashes. But her skin was whole; she could feel no damage at all. Her shirt was singed, but there was not a single mark on her skin.

"Pure gallantry!" Hannibal shouted.

"I should be incinerated," Clover gasped. "Like that Badger, like those men."

"But you have lived"—Hannibal laughed—"to fight another day! You see, you are more than a match, indeed you are the answer to the Heron problem. You've proved your value as a key asset—"

"Shh!" Clover said, hunkering into the gulley. They weren't far from the road and might be heard. Clover's terrified flight had brought her in a broad circle back toward the site of the smashed wagon. She buttoned her jacket over her ruined shirt and grabbed the chain Willit had dropped. The box containing the Ember was the size of an apple, groaning and pinging like a kettle without water.

Clover and Hannibal crept up a small embankment, pulling the Ember box behind them, and peered through a hedge of winceberry bushes at the wreckage on the road.

The wagon was obliterated. The trees nearby had been stripped of their bark by the force of Susanna's tantrum, and some had been completed toppled, muddy roots clutching at the air. But it was very still now. The poachers were nowhere to be seen.

Clover whispered, "Keep watch," and stepped toward the road.

"Are you mad?" Hannibal whispered.

"We have to get the oddities." Clover said. "We can't let the poachers have them."

The smoke from the brushfires clouded the road. Clover found her haversack half-hidden under a crate. She moved carefully toward the wreck of the wagon.

Hannibal tugged at the hem of her pants, saying, "Those poachers are only temporarily discouraged. They'll come back—"

"Hush! There she is." Clover pointed to Susanna, who was clambering over the splintered planks of the wagon. The Doll picked up a rifle, bent the barrel like a length of licorice, then slammed it into the ground, shattering the stock. Susanna dropped the gun and tottered in a dazed circle, looking for something else to destroy. She seemed, finally, to be losing steam. She had not escaped unscathed. One of her arms hung by a few stitches, and wads of wool were visible in the holes in her belly. One button eye hung loose, giving the impression that she was weeping. Her fury seemed to have ebbed, and now, she was sifting through the debris, looking for something specific.

"She wants the cigar box," Clover said.

When Susanna saw Clover, the Doll squared her shoulders for a fight. She picked up a length of timber and looked ready to beat Clover to a paste.

Clover began to sing, "*Susanna, don't be sore; the rain will stop by morning.*"

The Doll took two furious steps toward her, but Clover crouched as she had seen Mr. Agate do, holding out her hands and singing, "*Susanna, don't you cry; the clouds are only snoring.*"

"You'll be torn to pieces!" Hannibal whispered.

But Clover kept singing. "*Susanna, don't you fuss; the morning bird is singing.*"

The Doll stopped short. She dropped the splintered beam, looking suddenly like a baby in need of a nap. Clover held the side pocket of her haversack open. Susanna took a tentative step toward the bag, peering inside. This was no cigar box.

"*Susanna, don't you fret; the daffodils are blooming.*"

The sound of a bugle again, closer now, and horses on the road startled them. Susanna gave Clover one more mistrusting glance, then climbed into her sack. Clover fastened the leather ties and leaped behind the bushes with Hannibal. She ducked just as Willit, Bolete, and two remaining poachers came galloping past. They spurred their horses around the wreckage and beat a hasty pace up the road.

"But our haul!" Bolete wailed.

"We'll return for it," Willit shouted, "when I get more bullets."

The poachers disappeared into the forest.

Only a few breaths later, their pursuers, half a dozen armed men, arrived with a flurry of hoofbeats. They were led by none other than Aaron Agate. A few of them raced after Willit and Bolete while Mr. Agate pulled his horse to a stop and took in the catastrophic scene. He was wearing his old explorer's clothes, a bearskin cap and tasseled leather jacket. He held a rifle comfortably under his arm, but he was no longer the young adventurer from the journal.

Here was a shadow of what the Society had been, the brave league riding to protect the unusual.

Mr. Agate dismounted with a grunt. "What happened here?"

"Susanna happened," Clover said, emerging from the bushes.

"Oh, Clover, you're alive!" Mr. Agate embraced her before sorting through the wreckage. He found the cigar box, split and damp with horse urine, but Susanna wasn't in it. He shook the box, looking terrified. "But where is she?"

Clover felt a little kick as Susanna made herself comfortable in the bag. Suddenly, Clover didn't trust Mr. Agate. She knew he meant well, but then, Clover's father had meant well when he told her to throw the Ice Hook in the lake. She slung the bag over her shoulder and lied, "Gone, I guess."

"Gone where?"

"Into the forest, I suppose." Clover knew she should give

Susanna back to Mr. Agate, but the forlorn way the Doll searched for her cigar box made Clover feel protective of her. The Doll was no safer with Mr. Agate than she was with the poachers.

"God help us all," Mr. Agate wheezed.

Hannibal had wandered off to talk with a man wearing a deputy badge on his hat.

"At least the Heron is contained," Clover said. "Something as dangerous as that . . ." She handed Mr. Agate the chain with the iron box attached. "That thing is a monster."

"But you are . . . unhurt?" he asked, looking at her singed clothes.

"I can't explain it."

Mr. Agate shook his head as he gazed at her. "When you've been in the company of oddities as long as I have, you stop hunting for explanations and learn to live with wonder. Now, marvelous child, the poachers will be back as soon as they see how small our party is." A chill wind sent oak leaves spinning into his hair as he watched his comrades picking through the ruin. "We really must hurry."

Clover touched the base of her neck where the Heron had tried to incinerate her heart. The skin there was still warm but unblistered. "How did I survive? Was it something my mother did?"

"Miniver's notebooks burned along with everything else," Mr. Agate said. "We cannot know what her final experiments were. What the fire didn't consume, the witch picked over like a crow in the midden, just as we are now . . ." He trailed off, crouching to examine a crystal inkwell briefly before shoving it into his pocket. "The last of the great collections, dashed in the dust!" He swept his arm across the wreckage as if it were Clover's fault. "Tragic loss!"

"But why did the poachers . . . What am I . . . ?" Clover's words stopped coming.

Mr. Agate wasn't listening anyway. He let out a moan and fell to his knees, cradling the cracked Teapot in his hands. He was trying to fit the grinding shards back together, dribbles of steaming tea pattering through his fingers. Clover suddenly pitied the old collector, weeping for tea. All of the intoxicating marvels seemed a heap of useless trinkets to her now. Clover had a glimpse of the madness her father had warned her about. She pressed her gritty palms against her eyes, her head swimming. Nothing made sense. And yet her father's last words had been very clear. In the fever of her confusion, Clover clung to them. They were all she had left.

"I promised I would guard the bag," she announced. Saying it aloud felt good. "Smalt has it. I'm going after him."

Mr. Agate shook his head. "Smalt is extremely dangerous, a scorpion in a suit. No, you and the Rooster must stay with us. We'll keep you safe."

"Safe? You let the poachers carry me away like a Christmas cake!" Clover said.

"It was that or a bullet through the eye." Mr. Agate said. "We've caught up with you now, haven't we? I didn't see anything in that bag worth risking your life for." When he looked at her, Clover saw tears in his eyes. The poor man was sitting in the ruin of his life's work.

"Father wouldn't lie to me," Clover said.

"Even if there is an unknown oddity in that bag, it is gone now," Mr. Agate said slowly, the kindness in his voice strained, as if explaining to an exasperating toddler. "The malice of that Hat has hollowed Smalt out. There can be no happy ending where that wraith is concerned. I am sorry, but that's the truth of it. We can, however, still salvage some of this. Oh, treasures strewn about like so much garbage!"

"I swore I would protect it," she said softly, grateful for something to hold on to. "A promise is a promise, Mr. Agate."

Mr. Agate and the other men began to throw objects into burlap sacks: a tin pipe flattened to a dull blade, a brass knocker still attached to the oak slab cut from a door. With every piece, Mr. Agate emitted a pained gasp.

"We should go right away if we're to catch Smalt," Hannibal said.

Hope caught in Clover's throat. "You mean you'll come with me to Brackenweed?"

"Most certainly, brave girl. Escorting you is a privilege, and since I must make my reports in any case . . ."

It felt fitting, in a strange way, to be setting off once again to the music of Hannibal's proud prattle.

"Clover, don't wander off," Mr. Agate pleaded, but Clover ran through the woods with Hannibal beside her.

· · · · · · · · · · ·

Night felt like an ocean that Clover was creeping at the bottom of. When they could no longer see the road, they made camp in the shelter of a crumbling roadside altar. It had been abandoned long ago, and it was impossible to say what saint or ancestor people had been praying to there.

Clover fished blindly in her haversack until she found her oil lamp. She hesitated before lighting it. After the Heron, Clover didn't want to start even the smallest fire. But she was not ready to sleep in complete darkness. Constantine had given her the lamp on her twelfth birthday and said, "A doctor does not squint in the smoke of tallow candles. Whale oil is expensive, but it burns bright and clean."

At least it used to. Now the wick, dampened by lake water, sputtered. In the quavering light, Clover spotted piles of scat and upturned earth that suggested wild pigs used this place more often than people did.

As Hannibal investigated the shadows, Clover watched the tongue of flame lapping the air. On an impulse, she passed the end of her braid quickly over the lantern.

Her hair didn't burn. She held it directly over the fire, waiting for it to curl and smoke. After a minute, the end of her braid was glowing, each strand red-hot, but still it didn't burn. She put her little finger in the flame—and gasped. It hurt, but she forced herself to hold it there for five full seconds, then twenty seconds, then pulled it out to look. No charring, no blisters, no inflammation of any kind.

"But why?" she whispered, feeling her sanity shudder. Of all the things she had seen since beginning this terrible journey, this deviance of her own flesh was the most terrifying.

"Something is wrong with me," Clover said to herself. "Those poachers knew it. Why didn't I?"

"The perimeter is safe!" Hannibal strutted into the light, making her jump. "Now, before we discuss that battle and our noble future together, what victuals shall we fortify ourselves with?"

"There is no more bread pudding," Clover said, grateful for the interruption. She set the lamp at a safer distance and focused on simpler things. As she removed the handkerchief from around her neck, moths fretted above the lamp, and Hannibal hopped up, picking them out of the air. It was how a rooster ought to behave, but it struck Clover as ridiculous. Still, she wished she could eat moths.

Clover folded the edge of the cotton over the blade of her pocket knife and cut until she had two small squares of cloth. She pulled a sturdy thread from the scorched part of her shirt. Then she found the needle she carried in a little leather sheath, perfect for mending during long bedside vigils.

"What is that you're doing?" Hannibal wanted to know.

"I'm going to operate on Susanna, if she'll let me."

"On the Doll? You are courting disaster!"

"She was shot helping us escape," Clover said. "Didn't you see those holes in her belly?"

"She wasn't helping us escape. She was turning the forest into kindling."

"Who wants to walk around with a hole in their gut?" Clover asked.

Taking deep breaths for courage, she unfastened the brass clasp of her haversack's side pocket.

"Your ear is still bleeding from that poacher's knife," Hannibal warned, hurrying behind a stone to watch from a safe vantage. "You may be fireproof, but you're not indestructible!"

"Come on, you little thing. Let me see you," Clover cooed.

The Doll pouted in the cozy corner of the bag, her doughy arms crossed over her wounds.

Clover gave the bag a shake and began to sing: "*Susanna, don't be sore; the rain will stop by morning.*"

Susanna finally climbed out of the pocket, eyeing Clover warily. She held one hand over the yellowing wool of the wounds.

"Normally I'd give you some willow bark tea, but I guess we can skip that," Clover said, patting her knee. "Can you set yourself here?" Clover knew to keep talking, because it gave a patient something to focus on instead of the needle. "I'd clean the needle with brandy, but I don't think you're in danger of blood poisoning, are you?"

Clover used her finger to gently nudge Susanna across her thigh. "Don't watch. Just look at the lamp and think of good things."

Clover held her breath as she made the first stitch. The cotton swatch was frayed at the edges, but Clover made tight loops. Susanna lay still, her button eyes shining in the flickering light.

Clover noted the blue thread used for Susanna's original seams. Much of the Doll's fabric was dingy and worn soft as a horse's nose, but the blue thread was bright as spun candy.

Clover made quick work of the rest of the patch, then she turned Susanna over and made an identical patch on the other side where the bullets had gone through. She mended the tear in Susanna's arm and then retied the loose button of her eye. Throughout it all, the Doll hardly twitched, a perfect patient.

"There you go," Clover said, setting Susanna on the ground. "Like doctoring a sock. Easier than real suturing, at least. And it looks better too."

Susanna patted her newly mended belly and turned in a circle, trying to see her own back. The patch was a bright square on a dun body, and Clover thought if anything could make the Doll smile it was this. But Susanna just climbed back into the bag and pulled it closed behind her.

"You're welcome," Clover said.

"At least she didn't crush you with a rock," Hannibal said, emerging from his hiding spot. "Your courage almost makes up for your recklessness, Nurse Elkin. Lock her up, then, and we'll make good use of her in the war effort."

"Why do you suppose she is so ornery?" Clover asked, ignoring his last comment.

"Why does the wind blow? That Doll is a bundle of rage. You'd be safer with a rattlesnake in your pocket."

"In my experience, folks are angry for a reason," Clover said. "She has a temper, but she's not so bad."

"She is a hurricane! There is only one use for something like that."

"All my life I tried to be quiet, helpful, tidy," Clover said. "Where has it gotten me? Susanna is none of those things. I like her. Anyway, she's with us now, and we'll just have to be careful."

"Best to lob her from a distance, with a catapult, perhaps, into a fortified stronghold." Hannibal paced and chopped the air with his wing. "Imagine the effect on enemy morale! We'll consult with the senator when we catch up with him in Brackenweed—"

"Susanna is not a weapon." Clover insisted, trying to remain calm.

"What is she, then?"

"Well, I don't know exactly. What are you?" Clover asked.

"I am a colonel of the Federal Army and field commander of the State Watch. I am a decorated hero of the battles of—"

"And what am I, if I can't be burned?" Clover asked, remembering the scorching pain.

"You, my dear, are a born fighter. The bravery you've shown already cannot be faked. I've seen seasoned soldiers crack under less. With a little training, I am certain you'll be one of our most powerful assets—"

Despite the storm in her heart, Clover's voice didn't waver. "I won't let you throw Susanna at some imagined enemy! After we find Smalt, we'll find a home for Susanna. If not with Agate, maybe another Society member . . ."

"Have you considered," Hannibal said gently, "that Smalt may not have what you're looking for?"

"Of course he does. He stole my secrets, the oddity inside my father's bag . . ." Now her voice quavered. "I promised to protect it."

"But surely you've figured out that there is no oddity in that bag," Hannibal said.

Clover held her breath, not wanting to hear what he was going to say next.

"How many young women have a miraculous immunity to

fire? You are a singular specimen, Clover Elkin. *You* are the oddity. Your father obviously knew what a stubborn girl you are. If he told you to keep yourself safe, you would get killed trying to avenge him. But if he told you to keep that bag safe—well, you'd stay alive in order to do it. And so you have."

"He wouldn't lie to me," Clover said through clenched teeth.

"He didn't lie. He said he kept one oddity, the only one necessary to him: you."

Even as he said it, Clover knew she'd been avoiding this truth. Mr. Agate had been more interested in her than the medical bag. Hadn't Bolete threatened to burn her? And the Heron's attack could not have been survived by anything other than . . . But hearing the plain truth spoken aloud made her knees go soft. There was nothing in the bag but tools and an old watch someone had hidden long ago.

"But Father abhorred oddities," Clover whispered. "When he looked at me, what did he see?" Her fingers tingled, and she felt like she might faint. Then a terrible wish entered her head: *Would that he had died without knowing what I am.* Clover dropped her head into her hands. She regretted the thought. All of this horribleness was corroding her heart.

"For reasons of safety, the locations of specific oddities have been omitted," Clover whispered to herself. "That's why we never visited the cities. He was hiding me in Salamander Lake."

"A fireproof girl!" Hannibal marveled. "Nothing more than a rumor until I stumbled upon you while searching for Louisianan interlopers! Do you see how fate is in our favor? Your father was right, young Elkin. You do indeed carry hope. It wasn't fire you feared, my girl, but your own strength! You must let me introduce you personally to the senator. He trusts me."

"Why do you work for him?"

"He is the chair of the Wartime Powers Committee and the Borderlands Security Committee. He is the man with the vision and daring to protect our nation—"

"But what would he want with me?"

"I cannot discuss sensitive strategies in the open field. But, if you let me, I will answer all of your questions once we're safely reunited with the senator."

"I want no part of it."

"We all must play a part. I can help you choose what part you play."

"Hannibal," Clover begged, "we're still recovering from the first war. How many will die this time? I don't want to fight."

"Of course you don't. No good-hearted person wants war. But, twenty years ago, Bonaparte stole victory with an oddity that created an endless army. In the past six months, the senator's investigations have proven that the French are massing troops at the borders again. We have no choice but to defend our nation. Do you intend to go home and wait for the enemy to arrive at your front door?

"And when war is declared, we still don't know which side the Sehanna Confederation will fight for. Their ambassadors promise neutrality, but we believe Bonaparte already has the loyalty of the Ormanliot chief, and this could drive a wedge between them and the other tribes. So you see, we could be facing enemies to the north as well, and the stakes are nothing less than survival. We would be fools not to use our own oddities in the fight. We must utilize every weapon at our disposal to tip the scales in our favor. That includes the Doll and the Heron—"

"No—"

"Of course, there are risks. There is really only one person who can safely wield the Heron. Consider it. Together you will be unstoppable. You were born for this duty. I will no longer call you Nurse Elkin. You will be, henceforth, Lieutenant Elkin, First Rank. It is a high honor I am offering, but I have seen your bravery. You might just win this war for us. I will make certain that the senator understands your value."

"But the poachers work for Auburn too!"

Hannibal's hackles rose as he barked, "The poachers work for themselves! The senator cannot be blamed for the duplicity of notorious bandits!" He regained his composure, letting his feathers settle before continuing, "It is true that, on occasion, the senator sees fit to relieve those poachers of dangerous items they've acquired. Would you prefer he leave oddities in their hands?"

"No . . . but . . . I . . ." This was not an argument Clover felt she could ever win. She looked at the Rooster, the livid ridge of his comb glistening in the lamplight. She forced herself to stand. "I am not a weapon."

"Of course not. You're a soldier. A strategic agent—"

"No." Clover clenched her fists, blinking tears away.

Hannibal sighed, his comb deflated. "I cannot make this decision for you, of course. But the question remains." Hannibal's unblinking gaze seemed to pierce Clover's skin. "What will Clover Elkin do? I myself am a born tactician, a commander of brave men with thousands depending on me. I am a defender of the Unified States. That is my proud purpose. What is yours?"

Clover picked up her bag but immediately dropped it again.

"I . . . don't know." She turned in a circle, but the forest offered nothing more than shadows and the dizzying chorus of crickets. She sat again, utterly lost. "Am I even human?"

Hannibal clucked dismissively. "An overrated trait. The celebrated Incitatus Germanicus, Caesar's most trusted magistrate, was a horse."

"But how did this happen?" Clover asked, choked by the things she didn't know. "Did Mother . . . meddle with me somehow? Why did the poachers call me 'frog'?"

"Everyone knows that combining oddities is dangerous and unpredictable."

"So I was a mistake? A disaster . . . misbegotten. " Her chin trembled.

Hannibal stood defiantly at her feet and beamed up at Clover. "A few sniffles are understandable after surviving a shameless kidnapping and a direct assault from a hell-wrought fiend. But this is no tender milkmaid I see before me, weeping over a ripped seam. No, indeed. Clover Elkin is nothing less than a warrior of the first degree. With a little training, I make this pledge to you: that Heron will be your cringing pet."

Clover shook her head. "I have to find Smalt. I made a promise . . ." She trailed off, staring at the searing ring of soot on the edge of the lantern's glass.

"Let's stop pretending it's the bag you're after." Hannibal shook his head sadly. "Your father is gone. Aaron Agate is addled and naive. You think Smalt is the only one left who can tell you what you want to know about your family."

"Willit said Smalt took secrets from everyone, so perhaps my mother . . ." Clover bit her lip, then blurted out. "I think I heard her voice coming from the Hat. Smalt must know something that can lead me—"

"You can't afford his secrets! You won't get a thing from that wraith! You must learn to abide the mystery of your existence."

"It's not a mystery, it's a curse! Oddities and Willit and the witch, they're all tangled up with my family somehow. Father tried to hide from it, and it came *hunting us*. If I don't know where I come from, how can I know where I am supposed to go, what I'm supposed to be? If Smalt knows anything about my mother, I have to find him." Clover sat, feeling exhausted.

Hannibal touched her back with a gentle wing and said, "I myself do not know what egg I came from. And I too wondered if heaven had made a cruel joke: a man's upright spirit crushed into the frame of a farmyard beast. But while others were scratching in the dirt, I taught myself to read discarded tracts. A library, its window left ajar for summer ventilation, was my university. Before my pinions were grown, I had read every military history on the shelves and begun a correspondence with Auburn himself. And when war provided the opportunity to prove my tactical merits, I leaped at my chance to defend our glorious nation.

"Let go of eggs and mothers! The past is a shackle. March toward that which is greater than yourself, the integrity of a nation." Hannibal considered her quietly, a glint of compassion in his eyes. "I can offer you a generous enlistment bonus," he said. "Maybe it hasn't occurred to you that a ranking officer is entitled to lifelong benefits, which include not only the privileges of status and—"

"You haven't heard a word I've said. I don't want your money! I don't want your war! If you're so eager to hand me over to Auburn, why not let the guards at the checkpoint take me?" Clover said.

Hannibal bristled. "I am doing everything in my power to protect you, to guide you along a safe path." Then he softened, his neck feathers settling into a brass-colored collar. "But clearly all I'm doing is upsetting you. I'll let you consider in peace." Hannibal started to turn away.

"Wait, you aren't leaving, are you?"

"You need time to clear your head and heart. Unfortunately, that is not time I have." Hannibal stood and shook the dust from his plumage. "My report is expected and, given the events of the last few days, rather consequential. So ruminate in these woods like a hermit or pester Smalt if you must, but hear this: if you don't choose your fate, it will be chosen for you."

"Don't go!"

Hannibal said over his shoulder, "Fear not. We'll meet again soon. I'm sure of it. I'll try to give you the time you need to reach a sensible decision."

Hannibal sauntered into the shifting shadows and was gone.

Clover lay down by the fire and worried. She worried about the poachers, who could be creeping up on her in this unfathomable darkness. She worried that Hannibal was right and she would never know what she was or how she had come to be.

She touched the dandelion seeds in the vial on her necklace and thought about Mrs. Washoe's face, lit with love as she held her newborn. Had Miniver held her that way? She wished her father's ghost would appear. He would say something calm and infuriating. He would tell her to blow out the lamp because she was wasting oil.

Instead, she heard a strange voice, like a cricket song, coming from her bag.

"Mean old bird," Susanna said.

BITS AND SCRAPS

lover peered into the bag. "You can talk!"

"Talk is junk," Susanna said.

"I have so many questions," Clover said, pulling the Doll gently from the haversack. In the dim light she could see that the mouth was not sewn shut. It was a tiny buttonhole, and the voice that emerged was raspy, like that of a toddler recovering from a bad cough.

"Junk questions." Susanna crossed her arms irritably.

"I haven't asked them yet."

"Junk!"

Clover found herself admiring the grumpy Doll again. "Let me ask you this," she said. "Do you wish I had let Mr. Agate take you back?"

"Stinky old cigar box."

"You don't mind sleeping in my bag? I mean—do you miss your home?"

"Need no home."

"Where do you come from?"

"Old Missus Seamstress."

"The Seamstress made you?" Clover was shocked. "But she makes vermin. You're not scraps of skin and wire."

"I am many stitches strong," Susanna said, arms proudly akimbo to show off her little body.

"I don't understand," Clover said. "You are nothing like those nasty beasts."

"I am first best," Susanna said. "Before junk. Old Missus makes me to carry bags and wood and rocks. To clear the tumbledowns. To dig deeper tumbledowns. To make the mountain home. Then Old Seamstress wants more."

"More Dolls?"

"She wants tooth bringers and junk whisperers. She tries to steal my stitches so she can make junk."

Clover remembered the blue Thread she'd seen in the neck of the vermin Squirrel and understood the connection. "She tried to pull you apart to make vermin?"

"So I leave mountain home. Need no home. Stinky old hole."

"That's terrible," Clover said. "But how did she make the vermin without your Thread?"

"Bits and scraps. Junk whisperers just one stitch. Not strong. I am many stitches strong. Want to see?"

"I have seen your strength."

"I am not afraid."

"I believe you, Susanna. I think I understand now."

Susanna climbed back into the haversack.

Clover blew out the lamp. She couldn't claim to be fearless. But with Susanna nearby, she found the courage to sleep.

· . · . · . · . · . · . ·

The wind brought the stench of Brackenweed's famous leather works long before Clover saw its chimneys. What had begun as a rustic market for fur trappers had grown into a bustling economy of furriers, milliners, and merchants, the second-biggest city in the state. It was rumored that the only reason Brackenweed wasn't chosen as state capital was a general objection to the caustic odors of the tanneries.

The road toward the city brought Clover past a paddock full of plucked geese, who waggled their necks and honked, but Clover had no crusts of bread to throw for them. A butter-colored brightness spilled out of a barn's open doors and lit the morning mist like the entrance to paradise. Fiddle and piano trills mingled with the hoots and boots stamping on wood. A sound like a mule braying was actually a man laughing. As Clover passed, she asked a red-faced farmer just emerging from the shindig, "It's mighty early for a dance, isn't it?"

"Wasn't early when we started last night!" He laughed as he climbed up to the seat of a wagon and slipped a piece of ham to the dog that had been patiently guarding the load of potatoes in the back.

"What are you celebrating?"

"'Hain't you heard? The senator's coming to Brackenweed! He's gonna be president!"

If the senator hadn't arrived yet, then Smalt was still waiting for his meeting, which meant Clover had a chance to find him first. As she entered the main square, Clover was impressed by the number of sage wreaths and pots of smoldering cedar placed about the main square, a respectable effort at masking the tannery odors.

The merchants were doing a brisk business. The town was bustling, and everywhere people were haggling over furs and saddles, boots, belts, and gloves. Anything that could be made from an animal's skin was for sale here. Clover saw a man wearing a bearskin jacket with the claws still attached at the cuff.

A brass band clattered down a narrow alley where people had gathered around a roasted goat. But not every conversation was joyous. Here and there, Clover heard whispers about another settlement burned on the Sawtooth Prairie. Some said that the French had done it, some said it was Indians. Everyone agreed that the senator would have answers.

Clover peered into the darker corners of the city, eyeing the shops, alleys, and even the jailhouse, all built of the same jaundiced bricks, as if the city had risen whole from the tannery-poisoned mud. She felt Smalt waiting nearby like a scorpion under a log. She was not looking forward to confronting him, but having a strength like Susanna in her bag gave her courage.

Clover paused at a copper-green statue of a soldier clutching a rifle in the main square, a tribute to those lost in the Louisiana War. She felt the invisible web of history tightening around her. Her family, Senator Auburn, even Emperor Bonaparte were all bound together. When one tugged, the other felt it. Some of the connections were clear: the uncertain boundary between Louisiana and the US had led to the war, to this mute monument, and to Senator Auburn's insatiable need for power. Auburn's craving for oddity weapons had led the poachers to hunt her father down. But some connections were still invisible. What did the Seamstress want with her? How exactly had her mother died? And why was Clover odd?

If Hannibal was right and this new war was upon them, Clover couldn't survive such a future stumbling blindly. Every step she'd taken since the Ice Hook had resulted in calamity.

"If I am to make the right choices," Clover whispered to the solemn statue, "I must *know*."

Clover had to untangle her own history, see the threads that—

"Bleakerman's!"

The voice turned Clover's head. She followed it and spotted Nessa Branagan across the square, smacking her tambourine against her hip.

"A strong taste for a strong medicine!"

Nessa had set up in a sunny corner of the square, trying to draw a crowd. There were half a dozen tonic bottles arranged on the ground before her. She wasn't wearing the rainbow skirt, but she'd woven a hurried crown of daisies while waiting for customers. There was no sign of the wagon and, instead of a stage, she was standing on a horse trough.

"Liar!" Clover shouted, stomping toward the girl who had betrayed her. "Cutthroat!"

When she saw Clover, Nessa jumped off the trough and opened her arms for a hug. "You escaped!"

Clover ducked the hug and shoved Nessa into a trough. "Fiend!"

Green water slopped onto the cobbles. Nessa looked pitiful. She was barefoot, one meaty arm still bandaged and the other bare and scarred where Willit's bullet had burned her. Her skirt spread like mud in the water around her. She made no move to pull herself out.

But Clover could not afford pity. "Those poachers killed my father, and you helped them find me!" she raged.

"I didn't know all that. Willit promised to leave you be." A blush spread across Nessa's cheeks like a tonic stain.

Clover wanted to believe Nessa. She was angry at herself for thinking she'd made a friend, for enjoying those sweet songs. Tears threatened to quench Clover's anger, so she shouted at people passing by. "Don't you drink any of this poison! She will sell you to bandits the first chance she gets!" She was surprised to see a smile creeping onto Nessa's face, as if the horse water were a soothing bath. "What are you smiling at?"

"You're alive!" Nessa said, almost laughing. She removed the ring of daisies from her hair and offered it to Clover. "We're free!"

Clover smacked the flowers to the ground, but she felt a glimmer of Nessa's stubborn gratitude breaking through her rage. "What do you mean 'free'?"

"I thought it was my fate to work for Willit Rummage. I owed him. But when I saw you in that cage, I felt like I was in there with you. I said to myself, 'Nessa Branagan, spit on fate. Fear don't play no part in it. You have to help Clover.'"

"I almost died escaping that cage," Clover said. "With no help from you."

"I didn't know how I was going to beat Willit's Pistol and Matches. But Clover, I swear I was trying to find you."

"Why didn't you?"

"Smalt stole my wagon to carry his dog." Nessa spread her hands helplessly. "He said the hound was slowing him down. A thorn in his paw or something. I offered to take his horse for a swap, but he said, 'Smalt doesn't swap,' and just took everything. I know better than to pick a fight with Smalt. But I didn't give up. I've been trying to sell enough tonic to buy a horse to keep looking for you."

Smalt's name startled Clover back to her senses. "Is he here?"

"Who?"

"Smalt!"

"He stays at the Golden Cannon—why?"

Clover ran, leaving Nessa behind.

The Bleakerman's wagon was parked in front of the Golden Cannon Inn. The smell of beer, urine pots, and roasted peanuts wafted from the door of the tavern.

A hulking barkeep gave Clover a hostile stare as she pushed her way in. His bald head was tattooed with dark script she couldn't make out, and he wiped the sweat from his neck with a dirty rag.

The high-beamed drinking hall was thick with chatter and pipe smoke. Raucous revelers crowded around small tables, arguing about the rumors of burning settlements.

When her eyes adjusted to the gloom, Clover noted an ancient cannon mounted in one corner, another monument to the Louisiana War. By some local custom it had been covered with gold foil. One red-faced patron sat atop the cannon, delivering a lecture to no one in particular, occasionally patting the cannon as if it were a favorite donkey. "And who will lead us to a proper victory against the scoundrels at our borders? Why, Pres'dent Auburn, who else?"

Every few minutes a newspaper boy entered to announce, "No sign of the senator yet!" The barkeep rewarded the messenger with pinches of the greasy ham that hung on a string over the fire.

But for all the noise and commotion, one part of the hall was strangely still. A stairway led to an open mezzanine with three tables and plenty of empty chairs. There, a single figure sat hunched over a carafe of cloudy liquid, like a spider in the rafters.

Clover took a deep breath to gather her courage. Then she shouted, "Smalt!" and started toward the stairs.

The barkeep grabbed her arm. "Best not to meddle with that one, little thing." His grip was strong, but his voice was gentle.

"I have business with that man," Clover said.

"That ain't a man," the barkeep whispered. "That is Smalt.

He never eats. He only drinks vinegar. Nothing good ever came from messing with Smalt. You just leave him be."

"I have business."

The barkeep gave her a pitying look. "Whatever he took from you, you must let it go." He turned back to his work.

Clover's mouth had gone dry. She couldn't lie to herself anymore. She wasn't here to recover what Smalt had taken from her. She was here for what he had taken from someone else, anyone who knew about her family. Did it matter where such secrets came from? Her history belonged to her. Clover shook her arm free and marched up the stairs.

"Don't look in the Hat," she whispered to herself. "Do not look."

Clover felt her father's ghost behind her, pushing her up the stairs. With every step, the hall grew quieter. By the time she could see Smalt's boots, the crowd below was watching her. Smalt, though, took no notice. He peered into the dusty shadows and slurped his vinegar through his loose teeth. His wig sat crooked on his head, its edges crusted with old makeup.

In the silence, she heard a hiss coming from the diabolical Hat on the table. It bubbled and whispered as if the secrets were simmering inside it. Clover spotted her father's bag under the table; the slobbering hound was using it as a pillow. A rag had been tied hurriedly around the beast's front paw; Willit's bullet had found its mark.

Smalt still believed the bag contained a powerful oddity. Clover had carried it like a bomb about to detonate, but the only power it held was her father's memory. In the past few days, Clover had been battered by infernal forces. But what power did she herself contain? She'd told Hannibal that she was no weapon. But every oddity was dangerous—there was no denying that now.

She had no idea how she was going to get what she wanted, but she forced herself to take the last step. Smalt regarded her with disgust. Clover started to speak, but a brittle sound made her stop. A *rattle*. Near the mezzanine railing, almost invisible in the shadows, Nessa's Sweetwater viper lay coiled in its jar. Smalt had taken a new pet.

UNDER EVERY FLOWER

The hound growled in its sleep, a dollop of drool sliding down the medical bag. Clover didn't have a plan for this moment. Now that she had found Smalt, she had no idea what to do next.

"Mr. Smalt," she said, "I have come——"

"*Mister* Smalt?" He sucked the liquid from his teeth and turned to Clover. "Why not call me 'Your Excellency'? 'Your Majesty'? 'Vaunted, Inestimable Potentate'? If you must use a title, pest, put some effort into it."

"I have come for my father's bag." Clover's voice shook. "For the oddity inside and for the secrets you took from me."

Smalt leaned out of the shadows. His sunken eyes were like caves carved in the sallow plaster of his face. "I liked you better wearing a cage."

"Or"—Clover lowered her voice—"you can keep them in exchange for what you know about Miniver Elkin."

Fear and shame painted Clover's cheeks. She was lying about the bag, about her secrets, and at the same time she was confessing her deepest desire. She was trying to strike a deal with a devil.

Smalt cocked his head, intrigued, his ear like the wormhole in a rotten apple. He swished a mouthful of vinegar and spat it, cloudy, back into his glass. "No," Smalt finally sighed. "Smalt will keep the trinkets. I have a buyer in mind. Senator Auburn will do almost anything for an oddity these days. It can't hurt to have the future president in my debt. "

He scratched under his wig with a long gloved finger. "But the wait is ever so dreary. They say he's been just around the corner for days now."

"You must give me one or the other," Clover said.

"I must? Is the pest telling Smalt what he must and must not do?"

Snickers came from the hall below, where the crowd was waiting on every word like a theater audience.

"Just tell me how she died or—"

"Oh dear, this is getting dull." Smalt snapped his fingers, and the barkeep stomped up the stairs to grab Clover by the collar. As the patrons hooted and cheered, the man dragged Clover halfway down the stairs.

Clover shouted over her shoulder, "I challenge you, Mr. Smalt!"

The hall went quiet again, and the barkeep stopped.

"Challenge Smalt to what, exactly?" Smalt asked.

"I can find a secret as well as you can," Clover said. "And I don't need a raggedy old Hat to do it."

"The poor girl is cracked!" someone in the crowd shouted.

"Let her try," someone else said.

Smalt said, "All right, pest, show me your little trick."

"If I can do it, you must tell me what I want to know and give my father's bag back."

Smalt cackled, a dry sound like acorns rolling down a shake roof. "The pest wants to play my game?" Smalt leaned over the railing and pointed to a hairy man in crowd. "That man there. Milo Talbot—"

"I beg you," the man named Milo quavered. "Please—"

"You see, pest? Milo is already begging. Milo's secret isn't worth much money, but he would do just about anything to keep Smalt from telling his sister, wouldn't you, Milo? Do you think Milo would eat his shirt? Let's see if he would."

Milo was very still.

Smalt said, "Well? Get to it."

Suddenly Milo pulled off his shirt and tore it into shreds, wadding them up and stuffing them into his mouth. He poured beer into his mouth, trying to wash the wads of cotton down his throat.

"Stop it!" Clover shouted.

"Put some heart into it, man." Smalt lifted his glass to the effort.

Milo ate faster, gagging and choking. He had a sleeve halfway down his throat when he turned blue and fell over. The others nearby managed to pull the shirt out and pounded his back until he was breathing again.

Smalt grinned at Clover. "Can you make a man eat his own shirt?"

Clover was speechless.

"Secrets run deeper than blood," Smalt purred. "Secrets are power. Go home, pest, before you get hurt."

"I am not cruel," Clover said. "But I can find secrets all the same. Do you accept my challenge?"

"Let her try!" someone said again.

"Fine." Smalt flicked his wrist. "Find me something juicy."

"If I can do it," she insisted, "you'll give me what I want?"

"Yes, yes. Shall we draw up a contract before a judge? Get on with it."

Clover took slow steps through the crowd, scanning the drunken faces. Poor Milo sobbed quietly in a corner. Clover tried to calm herself and see these people with a doctor's eye. Most of them lived and worked here in Brackenweed. She focused on the smallest details: the calluses on their index fingers from leather-working tools, the soot behind their ears from stoking fires, the rashes on their forearms from caustic tanning liquids.

One man was different, though. The scars were on his knuckles. He had a cauliflower ear and a nose like a flattened fig.

"This man spent his youth as a pugilist," Clover announced.

"That ain't no secret," the man replied. "I was the toughest fighter in the state!"

The crowd muttered with disappointment. Clover had to do better. She noticed that one man's breath smelled like wet feathers.

"This man," she announced, "went to bed with a headache last night and woke up with joints so stiff he had to waddle like a duck until he warmed up."

"It's true," the man said. "How do you know that?"

Only those with rubella smelled that way, but Clover didn't say so. She moved on, looking for more secrets.

"And this man," she said, smelling the squashed-pear scent of sugar sickness, "has tingling toes and wishes, right at this moment, that there was a piss pot nearby."

"Are you a witch?" the man asked.

Several people clapped and cheered. Clover looked up, but Smalt only rolled his eyes. "Petty ailments?" he said. "These are not real secrets."

The crowd was still murmuring. Everyone hated Smalt, and they were excited about this strange girl brave enough to challenge him.

"Do it again!" someone shouted, and the crowd quieted as Clover climbed onto a table to get a better look. This was her only chance to salvage something of her family: some truth about her mother or at least the memento of her father's tools. If she failed she would have nothing left.

She peered into the faces of the inn patrons, listened to their breathing, noted how they shifted and scratched in anticipation. It was no good to find things that they would tell just anyone. She had to uncover things that they wanted to keep hidden.

She saw the worn shoe of a clubfoot, the broken mustache of a cleft lip. She saw the yellow skin of a failing liver and the squint of the nearsighted. She saw bodies shaped by misery and accident that went on as best they could, no different than the patients in Rose Rock or the Sawtooth Prairie. Clover saw a room full of stories. The chisels of life had whittled these bodies into their current shapes. The quills of hope and chance had left their faint calligraphy, if only she could read it.

In the expectant hush, the Sweetwater rattlesnake twitched its tail once, striking the jar like a glass bell. The sound sent a chill down Clover's spine. Finally, Clover pointed to three men, one after the other, and made her pronouncements.

The first had the sagging lip and hand tremor of an old soldier who had been poisoned by bad rations. "This man celebrated the end of the Louisiana War from a sickbed." The second wore a thin silver bracelet with a pigeon-shaped bangle that Clover's father had told her about. "This man married an Okikwa woman." At last she pointed to a man whose head sat atop his stiff neck in a way she had seen only once before.

"And this man . . ." She paused. She was not sure, but this was her only chance. "Was a criminal. Hanged from a gallows. A long time ago . . . but the rope did not kill him."

"She's true, Smalt!" the first two men shouted.

All eyes went to the last man, who stared so coldly at her that she realized she was right. She also realized she had said too much. In her eagerness to win, she had done the same thing Smalt did, dug too greedily into another's life, exposed something that should have stayed buried.

"I'm wrong about him," she shouted, trying to undo what she had done. "I made a mista—"

"No!" the hanged man said. "It is no mistake. If someone must tell my secret, let it be this strange girl. She can do what you do, Smalt. Without the Hat. She has won the bet!"

"She has done nothing special," Smalt grumbled.

"She won!" the crowd shouted. "Give her what she's due!" The hall filled with cheers in Clover's favor.

Smalt rose to his feet, leaning his long blue frame over the banister, and roared, "Rabble! Do you dare?"

The room went quiet. A mist of vinegar and spittle rained down as Smalt hollered. "*Why* was Jonah hanged? Isn't that the real secret? Why did those villagers drag him to the hanging tree? Does the girl know? Do any of you? *Smalt knows.* Why does the baker's wife wash her hands in the middle of the night? What poison began the Louisiana War? Why does Willit Rummage wear the rabbit ears? In what warren are the vermin wrought? Only Smalt knows. In the blooming field there is a body buried under every flower. Who knows their names? Smalt!"

He turned to Clover and said, "The ocean of secrets crashes against your little world, wanting in. Do you want the flood? I owe you nothing. Shut your mouth and go."

The crowd clucked and hissed, but there were no more shouts. The barkeep shook his head. It was no use; Clover had failed. But she could not just walk away. She made her way back up the stairs, her knees trembling.

"I don't know about all that horribleness," she said. "But I know a bully, Mr. Smalt. A deal is a deal. You owe me more than just the bag you stole. I will have what's mine."

"No, pest," Smalt said, pushing the viper's jar to the staircase with the tip of his boot. "You won't." The jar wobbled precariously on the edge of the topmost stair.

Then it fell, tumbling over the first two stairs and bouncing high. Time seemed to slow as everyone watched the pale serpent floating in its glass bubble.

Clover recoiled and stumbled down the stairs. Panic shook the tavern as the jar shattered on the floorboards. The Sweetwater rattlesnake writhed like boiling porridge near the bottom stair. Clover was knocked down by the flood of patrons rushing for the door. She lifted her head to see the viper tightened into a coil just a few feet away, its arrowhead face pointed right at her.

Screams filled the hall, but the only sound Clover heard was that furious rattle, blurring in the air. With her eyes locked on the snake, Clover slowly lifted herself to her feet. She took a cautious step backward, but her foot rolled off a beer mug, and she fell hard on her back. To her horror, the snake came right for her, its rattle rising in pitch like the sound of fear itself.

The viper struck.

It happened so quickly that Clover hardly felt it. She turned her head to watch the snake disappear into a dark corner of the suddenly empty tavern.

Then Nessa came rushing toward her, her skirt still dripping with horse water. She must have been watching with the rest of them. Clover was so glad to see Nessa's round face that she almost kissed her. Instead she struggled to pull her own pant leg over her boot.

"Am I bit? Nessa, I think I'm bit."

Exposing her calf, Clover saw the twin fang marks on her shin. They looked too small to matter, but the skin around them was already turning a sooty green.

Nessa gasped. "No . . . oh no, Clover!"

"Quickly! My father's bag!" But Clover was already too dizzy to operate on herself. "Go for a doctor, Nessa. I need a doctor to draw the poison!"

Nessa ran out the door, screaming, "Doctor!"

"Hurry . . ." Clover whispered, finding her head on the floor again.

High above her, Clover saw Smalt's face peering down with a gargoyle grin. "How are you feeling?" he asked.

Clover remembered the tourniquet inside the medical bag, a spark of hope. She got to her knees and shuffled toward the stairs, but it felt like the sky itself had clubbed her on the head, and she dropped. A taste like maple syrup filled her mouth.

Clover remembered Susanna. She fumbled with the leather strap, but her fingers were too numb to open her bag.

Her legs felt wooden except for the place where the snake had bitten her. There, she felt every hair follicle, every pore. She even felt the burning wad of venom the viper had left under her skin. It seemed to be unwinding and making its way deeper into her leg. As her limbs stiffened, she felt the poison's milky tendrils reaching out, threading up into her veins.

"Hurry . . ." she tried to say, but her tongue was as useless as a cotton rag, and her ears were ringing as if the rattle were now inside her. It might be minutes before Nessa brought a doctor. Clover didn't have minutes. She had seconds.

Her clothes were soaked with sweat, but she couldn't feel them. All sensations had faded except for the venom creeping deeper. It seemed to be growing as it found the larger veins. When it had writhed its way to the small of her back, Clover felt that the venom had become a viper itself. She felt it bite one of her kidneys.

Smalt whistled down at her from his perch high above. "Be a good sport and tell Smalt how it feels."

It was too late.

Clover closed her eyes, not wanting Smalt's face to be her last sight. She tried to think of good things, of her father, of the sound of oars on the lake. But the venom was still moving, forking its tongue at her liver and crowding her lungs. Now the viper was coiling around her heart. Her heartbeat accelerated, thrumming like a rabbit caught in its burrow, before slowing.

It beat feebly twice more.

Father, forgive me.

Once more.

Mother . . .

Clover's heart stopped.

When the snake moved up the wide arteries of her neck and coiled into the warm cave of her skull, Clover's eyes popped open, but she saw nothing. Clover Elkin was dead.

CHAPTER 15

THE RISKS
SHE TOOK

T here were *pinpricks of color in the darkness. Clover's mind was going cold.* As she sank into the shadow of oblivion, she saw flickers of long-buried memories. A dead rabbit. The smell of sulfur. The sounds of breaking glass and Willit's voice. These were her earliest sensations, coming to her in a dream as she perished. They were clues to the mystery of her past, too faint and too late.

· · · · · · · · · ·

Clover woke on a horsehair mattress in a humid canvas tent. A stack of books sat atop a bundle of clothes nearby. The tent was smaller than she'd expected heaven to be, but it smelled pleasantly of lavender and duck soup.

Clover made out the blurry outline of an old woman knitting at the foot of the bed. Her neck was wrapped thickly in the same green scarf that her woody hands were knitting, one slow stitch at a time.

"Am I dead?" Clover asked, rubbing her eyes.

"You were," the crone said, her voice like the crackle of autumn-blown leaves. "Now, take a sip of this broth."

Clover rolled onto her back with a moan and leaned against the folded quilt at the head of the bed, feeling woozy. Near her head was a bowl of hot soup, an aroma so familiar it was its own memory. There was a salted duck foot floating among dark strips of collards. Her mouth watered, but she was too shaky to eat.

"Do I know you?" Clover asked.

"You had better!"

"Widow Henshaw?" Clover cried, her vision clearing enough to recognize her neighbor from Salamander Lake. "You're here? How did you save me?"

The widow pulled her pewter locket from the tangled scarf around her neck and opened it. The interior was dusted with a sky-blue Powder.

"I gave you the last of the Powder. I'd been saving it for an emergency. I guess you're that emergency.

"A lifetime ago, the Society entrusted me with item Forty-one, the Pestle," the widow said. "If you grind teeth in the Pestle—and it is not easy to grind teeth—it produces a blue Powder that can cure almost any ailment."

"The Society? That's why you had those journals. You left them for me to find, didn't you?"

"I promised your father I wouldn't tell you about oddities. But what you read yourself . . ." She shrugged mischievously. "You'd learn the truth eventually."

"Father . . ."

"The Powder wouldn't have worked on him. He was too far gone. There are some injuries that even the Powder can't . . ." The widow paused, seeing Clover's agony. "We took care of everything, lamb. He's resting now."

"What are you doing here in Brackenweed?"

"I came here after the ice," the widow said. "I can't afford to rent a room, but this tent is home enough for now."

"What ice?"

The widow fished a large wooden spoon out of her apron and cupped it behind her ear. It was something Clover had seen hundreds of times, and it still made her smile. The widow was nearly deaf, so Clover leaned close and spoke loudly into the spoon. "I said, 'What ice?'"

"After your father was murdered," the widow whispered, "and you disappeared, a frost bloomed across the water, like the lake itself was mourning. Froze solid as glass in a single night. A wrenching and popping like you never heard! Great slabs and splinters pushed up like knives, and that ice is still creeping right up the river."

"Oh no . . ." Clover whispered. She couldn't bring herself to say aloud what she knew about the ice, but she felt that the old widow knew more than she was saying.

"We were half-frozen ourselves," the widow continued. "Some went to relatives or to the Sawtooth to wait it out. I went to New Manchester to find Agate. But I gather he left the city in some commotion. No one can find the man. They say poachers rousted him. So I came here to find help."

"From Auburn?"

"Heavens, no. My boys fought for Auburn during the Louisiana War, and they died for nothing, because all the promise of freedom and equality disappeared as soon as the smoke cleared. No, I've come to find some old friends. Ruth Yamada. Ephram Carter. They've gone underground like the rest, but I'm going to sniff them out."

Clover recognized the names from the journal. "You're join-ing the Society again."

"It's going to take something powerful to stop that ice. Don't you fret, lamb; we'll see things sorted out."

"But is it safe for you here, in a big city, I mean?"

"No one promised us 'safe.'" Widow Henshaw blew her nose into a kerchief and resumed her knitting. "My freedom papers were lost in a flood before you were born. But I'm too old for slavers to come snatching me up."

Clover closed her eyes as the tent spun around her. Widow Henshaw was putting a brave face on a desperate situation. What could possibly pull the Ice Hook from the bottom of a frozen lake? It was as hopeless as trying to find the Wineglass under the Wine Marsh. And now the kindest woman Clover had ever known had left her home because of Clover's recklessness, her stupidity, her heedless—

Seeing Clover's tears, the widow poked her with the spoon. "No need for all that. At least you're alive! Drink up, lamb."

The woman jutted her chin at the bowl, and Clover took a sip. A sheen of oil shimmered on the surface of the broth. Clover found herself slurping up mouthful after mouthful. She chewed some of the greens and wiped her chin with her sleeve.

The widow gave her a toothless grin. "When you can't chew, you get good at making soup."

It soaked into Clover's bones, giving her strength. "Do you still have the Pestle?"

"Haven't seen it for years. When I was a midwife, the Pestle saved many lives before I loaned it to Miniver for her experiments."

"You knew her?"

"I knew her work. The Pestle was a miracle, but it was infernal to use. It took thirty human teeth to make the smallest pinch of Powder. But when Miniver saw one person cured, she wanted to cure ten, a hundred. She wanted to . . . *expand* its power, combine it with other oddities to cure more than the one body's affliction."

"More than one body?"

"I mean the afflictions of poverty, slavery, war." The widow shook her head sadly. "It sounds outrageous now, but your mother had a way of making wonderful things seem possible."

"Did Willit Rummage kill her?"

For a moment, Widow Henshaw seemed not to have heard the question. Her gums worked idly, her lips bunching and stretching. Just as Clover was about to ask again, the old woman set her knitting down.

"Your father wanted to tell you when you were ready, but he can't now, can he? You're not a child anymore. You've just died and come back, which is more than I've done. So I'll give you the hard truth. Your mother isn't dead."

Clover opened her mouth but couldn't speak; a hundred questions seized in her throat.

The widow whispered, "She's a witch."

"How can . . . What are you—?"

"I won't tell you a thing if you keep squirming like that," Widow Henshaw said, taking Clover's bowl away before it spilled. "She wasn't just a collector, your mother. She was always tinkering. What would happen if you poured an ocean of tea over the Ember? She produced a lot of steam, that's a fact. What would happen if you ground emeralds in the Pestle instead of teeth? Well, she ruined some perfectly good emeralds. Maybe with more time, Miniver could have changed the world, saved us from ourselves, but something went wrong, and there was a terrible accident."

"The fire . . ."

"It was quick and mean. Half the city came to help, but there wasn't much could be done. The Heron . . ."

Clover flinched.

"So you know about the Heron? Don't worry—there was a thunderstorm that night, and the Heron was doused by simple rain. Without that bit of luck, the whole city would have burned. But that wasn't the only thing lurking in the fire that ate up your house. Everyone had a different story to tell about what they witnessed in those flames: bursts of music, a sour green smoke—but most everyone saw a smoldering figure hunting through the inferno, burning alive, eyes glinting like lightning. Some said it was a demon Miniver had summoned. Some said it was a jealous witch come to destroy your mother before she became too powerful. Later, after the vermin, they named this witch the Seamstress. Most think she killed your mother. Hush now and listen.

"Your father was on his way to a country call, halfway out of the city when he saw the sky lit up and came back in a hurry. Folks tried to hold him, but he ran into that furnace three times, trying to find you. His head was wrapped with a wool blanket, and still the beard burned right off his face. And finally, when the roof came down, Constantine collapsed in the gutter, half-dead himself, and that's when you came crawling through the cinders like a lizard from the kindling. He said you were sooty and hot as a kettle, but you were whole.

"And as he was wrapping you up, and using his tears to clean your face because he could hardly believe it was really you, he looked and he saw that witch up close. She was roasting alive, her hair like a torch, as she dug through the timbers, looking for you. No one got as close as your father—no one saw her as clear as he did. And what he saw scared him so bad that he left the city right then and never returned. Left his practice, his friends, everything, to hide you in a tiny village in a distant valley. Far from trouble."

Clover's mouth was parched, her heart struggling under a smoking ruin. "Was it really—?"

"He never said. Not exactly. You know how hard it was to get Constantine to tell something he didn't want to. But I can guess, and maybe you can too."

"Mother? She's the Seamstress?" It was a truth that fit into the deepest holes in Clover's heart. "But why did he leave her? Why didn't he—"

"She'd become something terrible. They say the Seamstress screams with two voices, that she's pieced together like a broken plate. A wraith. A haunt. And I think . . . Well, I am only guessing—"

"*Please.*"

"I think Constantine was angry. To see what Miniver had done. To see the risks she took with you."

Clover gripped the widow's arm tightly. "But how did I survive? Why am I odd?"

The widow eased Clover back down, saying, "Whatever happened that night, it changed you, and it changed your mother so much that Constantine never looked back. And here is what I want you to hear: it's better to say Miniver died. Can you see that?

What came out of that fire after you, maybe it had once been your mother, but it isn't now. You both walked away from those flames— but you're the only one who really survived."

"What changed us?"

"No one knows."

"*She* knows!"

The widow tsked. "Go and ask her, then. Even if you knew where to find her. Even if you could make your way through the wilderness, past the vermin, to her secret den in the mountains, do you think she'll sit for tea and cookies? The witch who steals teeth from children is not Miniver Elkin. Not anymore."

Clover wanted to scream. She was closer than ever to understanding what had happened to her family, the spark of trouble that had set her whole world alight. And it was still unreachable. She felt dizzy.

"Why didn't you tell me?"

"I promised your father. He wanted to give you a quiet life. A safe life."

Clover shook her head. "Safe . . ."

The widow shrugged. "We tried." The old woman wrapped her arms around Clover and held her for a long time. Clover wanted to stay there forever, soup warming her, protected in the widow's embrace. She recalled the last person who'd tried to hug her.

"Where is Nessa?"

"Who?"

"Wasn't it Nessa who . . . How did I get here?" Clover asked.

The widow pointed a crooked finger at Clover's bag. "Your friend pulled you."

Susanna peered over the edge of the doctor's bag, smiling to see Clover alive.

"When I heard people saying that a mountain girl had insulted Smalt, well, I had to see for myself. You were pale as milk in the moonlight by the time I got there, with Susanna dragging you out the door."

"You know Susanna?"

"Agate introduced us, long ago. She threw a chair at me then. But she remembers a friend, don't you, Doll?"

Clover tried to eat another bite of soup, but she choked and started crying again. "Father should have told me. These secrets feel like a web," Clover cried. "I'm caught, and every strand I cut gets me more tangled!"

"Your father wanted an orderly world, predictable and safe. And I want a cow that spits nickels." The widow chuckled.

"But I have to know what happened. How else can I set things right, mend this mess I've made?" Clover started to sit up, but the gentle weight of the widow's hand on her chest was all it took to keep her pinned to the mattress.

Mrs. Henshaw clucked. "This mess is older than you."

"Those bandits came to Salamander Lake because of me," Clover said, the words like bile on her tongue. "I know it. You know it too."

"Oh, child." Mrs. Henshaw's words finally failed her, so she just patted Clover's head. Clover let herself crumple into the widow's arms.

"You have a healer's heart," Mrs. Henshaw whispered. "You want to fix things. You're an Elkin."

It felt good to let the tears roll down her cheeks, each sob making Clover a little lighter until she felt something like clarity. "I *will* find her."

"People have looked. Those who hunt for the witch don't return. No one knows where she is."

"Smalt knows." Clover shuddered, remembering his crackling face, the glass jar tumbling through the air. "He said it himself: 'where the vermin are wrought.'"

"But you tried that."

"I'll try again." Clover pushed herself up, determined, and scanned the room for her boots. She saw a wool blanket atop a pile of straw and worried for the old woman, trying to stay warm far from home.

"It isn't going to be as easy as that," the widow said.

"What do you mean? Aren't I cured?" Clover pulled the blanket away and saw the wound on her leg. The skin around the snakebite had swollen purple, like a mouth of a boxer who's lost a fight. It was tender to the touch, but Clover could see that it was not infected. Still, the sight of it made her wish her father were alive to treat it.

"The healing power of the Powder is strong," said the widow, "but the venom of a Sweetwater rattlesnake is too. It is still in your veins. The Powder couldn't pull it out of you, so it managed something like a truce, I suppose. You are alive, but your blood and the venom are mingled for good."

"Mingled?"

"Just one more ingredient in your soup. No one has to know. But here's the tricky part," the widow said. "Look here."

Widow Henshaw pulled the blanket off the heap of straw to reveal the Sweetwater viper coiled like a noose. Clover covered her mouth to stifle a scream.

"It followed you here, and it's been waiting all this time."

"Waiting for what?"

"For you to die, I suppose."

"Can't we push it out with a broom or something?"

"I tried that," the widow said. "But every time I got it out the door, you took a turn for the worse."

"Susanna, will you dispose of this beast for us?" Clover asked.

Susanna jumped out of the bag, eager to help.

The widow climbed onto the mattress with Clover, gathering

the trailing loops of her scarf, then Clover nodded at Susanna.

Susanna grabbed the serpent by the tail. The snake hissed like frying bacon and, in a flurry, struck Susanna three times with savage bites. But the Doll just marched toward the door, dragging the writhing snake behind her. With no blood to poison, the fang marks were nothing more than a few more stitches in Susanna's quilted body.

As the snake disappeared out the door, Clover felt suddenly dizzy and breathless. "Oh dear," she whispered. "What is happening?"

"You see?" said the widow. "Susanna, you'd best let it go."

As soon as Susanna released its tail, the serpent darted back toward the bed. Clover had nearly fainted against the widow's shoulder. She couldn't lift her head until the viper was coiled again in the straw nest, its tongue unsheathed to taste the air.

"I felt it," Clover whispered, recovering. "I felt Susanna pulling *me* by the tail. And the farther I got away from myself, the worse I felt."

"You and the rattlesnake are knotted together now," the widow declared, holding up her knitting needles. "Knitted! Your fates are joined. It is the best the medicine could manage. It looks like you have another traveling companion, dear."

CHAPTER 16

NEVER LIKED CORSETS

Clover limped toward the Golden Cannon Inn. The Sweetwater viper hung in a heavy coil around her neck, the weight of danger itself. Yet Clover was not dead.

"Thanks for nothing, Nessa," Clover muttered as she weaved through town. "I've got your memento close to my heart."

She had tried to get the serpent into her haversack, but Susanna had crumpled Clover's tin mug into a gray wad in protest. Anyway, Sweetwater seemed to want to be as close as possible, and as terrifying as it was, Clover felt the same way. When the snake was even five feet away, the bite wound throbbed and a flu-like vertigo threatened to topple her. But if the snake was actually touching her, she felt perfectly healthy. In fact, she felt even stronger, braver than she had before she'd been bitten.

Clover knew she couldn't walk around holding the world's deadliest viper in her hands, so after some fumbling negotiations, Sweetwater found comfort draped around Clover's collarbone, mostly hidden under her coat.

Clover passed a crowd of people on the corner, pointing at the Golden Cannon and talking about Smalt.

Murdered her on a whim. I saw it!

As Clover staggered past, one of the bystanders spotted her.

Isn't that her?

Impossible.

But it is!

Clover ignored them. Her leg was still throbbing, and walking took all her focus.

She's going back!

A crowd had gathered, following her and filling the air with awed whispers.

But she was bitten! I saw it myself!

When the Sweetwater viper poked its head out of her collar, the crowd gasped. Clover reached to push the snake's head back under her shirt, but the serpent retreated before she touched it. Clover paused.

She willed the snake to rattle. A piercing hiss rose from her coat.

The crowd behind her scattered.

So this was how tangled they were. Clover imagined the snake wrapping around her waist. The snake obeyed, dry scales hugging her rib cage. "I never liked corsets," Clover muttered. "Now I've got a poisonous one."

Braced by the creature that had killed her, Clover looked toward the inn where Smalt waited. Her courage was as unsteady as her knees, and her heart felt like a fish gasping on the shore, but there was no other way to find her mother.

"If Smalt won't tell me," she muttered to the snake, "maybe he'll tell you."

She paused at the door of the Golden Cannon, leaning on

the jamb to gather her wits before stepping into the darkened hall. The barkeep was cleaning up broken chairs and spilled food. He pointed at her. "You, out!"

"Who is it?" Smalt asked, still in the rafters. He leaned over the railing and clapped his gloved hands. "Pest?" He tittered. "Didn't I watch you die?"

The crowd had regrouped in the doorway, larger than before. Dozens gathered to watch the strange girl confront Smalt a second time. They followed her inside, and their muttering echoed off the rafters. *She's a witch. She has the snake. I saw her familiar dragging her dead body.*

Clover hobbled toward the stairway. Her leg ached, but Sweetwater tightened around her, giving her courage. Susanna shifted in the haversack. Clover felt the intimidating heft of her companions.

"I'm here for the secrets you owe me, Mr. Smalt. I will not leave without them."

"No one can lie to the Hat," Smalt said. "So why do I feel lied to? What exactly is your game, pest?"

"You're a bully," Clover said, reaching the middle stair. Smalt's dog woke up growling. When it saw Clover, it stood, lifting the table and knocking over the vinegar glass.

"Enough!" Smalt said, and the hound lunged at Clover.

It leaped from the top stair, its yellow fangs bared as it barreled toward her. Its wounded paw seemed only to have made it angrier. Clover ducked its bite, but the dog's chest hit her hard, and together they fell over the railing onto a table below. The dog rolled to the floor, scrambling for footing in the spilled beer and broken glass. The crowd backed away from the fearsome animal.

Clover got to her feet just as the hound put its front paws

on the table. As the table wobbled beneath her, Clover jumped as high as she could, catching hold of the iron ring of lanterns above. There she hung, like the ham over the fire, with the hound growling and snapping at her feet.

The swaying lanterns spilled oil down her arm as she scrambled with the other to reach the buckle on the haversack. Susanna tumbled out and landed at the feet of the hound. The dog bent to snatch the Doll up, but it might as well have tried to attack a ship's anchor. Susanna grabbed it by the ear and slammed its massive head onto the ground. Before it could get back up, Susanna had gotten a grip on the scruff of its neck.

Susanna threw the hound. It shattered a window and disappeared, yelping as it went.

"Barkeep!" Smalt yelled. "Put this urchin out!"

The barkeep pulled an old musket from beneath the bar and came toward Clover, saying, "C'mon now, girl. This has gone too far."

At that moment Clover screamed with excruciating pain. At first she thought the barkeep had shot her. Then she saw the flames. The lantern oil had caught fire, and her right arm was blazing. Clover dropped to the table, squirming in agony.

Time seemed to slow as her mind raced. Memories of blistered and scarred patients flashed in her mind. She tried to remember that she was different, but the pain was real, like shards of glass raking down her arm. As she scrambled for something to put the flames out, she saw Smalt at the top of the stairs, trying to escape.

Every tendon and muscle screamed, but Clover forced herself to ignore the pain. As the flames crept to her neck, she climbed over the banister, blocking Smalt's exit. She marched up the stairs, backing Smalt into a corner of the mezzanine, leaving a trail of fire as she went.

Down below, Susanna smashed tables with the barkeep's gun.

As the flames reached their crescendo, the pain was a banshee in her skull. But she kept her eyes locked on Smalt. In the corner of her vision, she saw wisps of her hair glowing red-hot.

Smalt was cowering against a wall, eyes wide. "What are you?" he asked.

The question stopped Clover at the top of the stairs. The Sweetwater viper cramped against her in agony, but, wedded to Clover, it did not burn.

Just as the unbearable incandescence threatened to devour her mind, she heard her own molten voice saying, "My name is Clover Constantinovna Elkin, and I am angry with you, Mr. Smalt." The flames roiling around her were matched by a rage within that felt very old, like unseen magma rising into the light. "You take what is not yours. You manipulate. You bully . . ."

Finally the oil exhausted itself, and the flames began to sputter and die. The cool air on her bare arm was the sweetest sensation she had ever felt. She snatched the Hat straight from Smalt's hands and held it behind her back for a moment as if she were about to do a magic trick.

"We all have our secrets, Mr. Smalt. But you have more than your share. Kindly tell me what you know about my mother," she said, holding the Hat toward Smalt.

Smalt shook his head, powder falling like snow from his wig.

"I forgot to say, 'Don't look inside the hat.'"

"Do you think that would work on me?" Smalt snapped. But a strange sound came from the Hat, a sharp jingle like the sound of a crystal bell. Startled, Smalt looked inside and gasped.

As the power of the Hat seized Smalt, the Sweetwater viper

crawled out of the Hat where it had hidden and, still steaming, encircled Clover's waist.

Smalt let out a haunting moan. His eyes bugged, and his knees buckled. Clover placed the Hat on the floor and stepped away as Smalt writhed in his ridiculous clothes.

Then, all at once, a great gush of sticky secrets burst out of Smalt and poured into the Hat. It kept coming, a deluge of wet whispers and distant screams. Clover had only hoped to use the serpent to get an advantage, to convince Smalt to tell her what she wanted to know. But now the Hat was in control. After a few seconds, Smalt's clothes began to bunch on his thinning frame. His false teeth clattered to the floor, and his wig slipped off, revealing a pale, dimpled skull.

"Why am I odd?" Clover shouted, not knowing if she was asking the Hat or Smalt. "What can counter the Ice Hook? Where can I find the Seamstress?"

But if the answers were in the clotted river of sludge, Clover could not grasp them. Years of hoarded secrets rushed into the Hat until Smalt was lifted off his feet by the force of it. He floated in midair like a marionette caught up by an angry child. Smalt was so steeped in secrets that every dram of his blood and tissue was being squeezed up and out of him. Even his ears leaked streams of indigo fluid.

Clover covered her mouth, gagging, but she forced herself to keep her eyes open, watching for any hint of her mother's secrets in the acrid outpour.

Smalt's shoes fell from his withering stockings, and his gloves went slack as the Hat consumed him. Not everything made it into the whirlpool of the Hat. Some secrets floated in the air like smoke;

some pooled in puddles on the floor. They spread into the cracks of the walls and nattered out the windows on wasp wings. Those with spider legs scattered quickly; the slugs smacked wetly against the walls. The room filled with haunted voices.

The torrent slopped over the Hat's brim, and Clover flinched as the voices of the ghosts howled past her. She covered her ears against the deafening wails. For several desperate seconds, the floor was flooded, and Clover scrambled to keep her footing in the riotous filth. Then she was on her feet again.

Smalt was gone. He'd been completely wrung out. With mist still swirling in an eddy above the rim of the hat, nothing was left but his clothes, his false teeth, and his crusty wig.

It was over. The hall was a creaking ruin. The smashed window let in a shaft of ragged light, the staircase was charred, and everyone had fled. Clover wasn't sure how much of the deluge the Hat had swallowed, but she knew plenty had escaped out into the city.

She slumped to the floor, touching the arm that had, moments ago, blazed oven hot. She touched her neck, her hair, her side. The pain was fading to a dull throb. She was unharmed, but if Smalt had said anything about her mother, she hadn't heard.

"I missed it," she whispered. "I'll never know."

Susanna pulled herself over the top step and nuzzled Clover's leg like a tired puppy. Clover hummed a few bars of Susanna's song, and the Doll crawled back into the haversack.

The Hat bubbled and burped, a cauldron of putrid stew. Clover was careful not to look inside. The purple mist hissed over the brim. Clover knew it would be madness to reach in searching for her mother's secrets. This was an unclean object, sloppy and contaminating. After corrupting Smalt's heart, saturating his flesh until he was no longer human, this Hat had gobbled him up as a dog swallows a sausage.

Clover knew she was looking at evil itself.

She watched as the Hat digested Smalt. Shameful memories, the wretched thoughts that victims had hoped to take to the grave, now stained the room, shimmering images and rank odors. Just when it looked as if the Hat had absorbed the mess and gone quiet, one last dollop burped over the brim, buzzing into the air like a horsefly. Clover tried to catch it, but it darted out the door, whispering about a sunken ship.

At last the Hat went still and began to look again like any old hat, dropped by a drunkard. Was Clover's secret history still inside? Clover kicked it over. It seemed empty, but she knew better than to reach in. Still, she couldn't leave it here to seize some poor victim. She considered burning it in the cooking fire, but she feared it might release more haunted voices to rain onto the city.

Already people outside were calling for the sheriff. "Witchcraft and mayhem!" they shouted.

Clover reached into her father's bag and found the cool weight of the tools: the rolled leathers of scalpels and lancets, the rows of glass vials. Everything in its place. Then she hefted her haversack onto one shoulder, her father's bag onto the other. The Hat wouldn't fit in either. She knew she had no other choice.

With a shudder, Clover put the Hat on her head and carefully descended the groaning stairway. Outside, the commotion grew, as if the panic she had just survived had spread. The Hat occasionally slipped over her eyes as she went. Clover didn't know that an oyster-colored secret lingered just inside the rim, where she dared not look. This secret, heavier than the others, carrying, as it did, the secrets of an entire nation, had barely escaped the Hat's gravity. It clung to the velvet lining with fierce mandibles. It had waited decades for the unsuspecting warmth of a host.

When Clover reached the last step, this secret uncurled its centipede loops and scuttled down into her hair. Clover gasped and knocked the hat off her head, but the secret was already surging into her right ear. And just like that, Clover knew how the Louisiana War really began.

• . • . • . • . • . • . •

The French ambassadors still smelled of the mildew and tar of their ship cabins. Ambassador Durand was tall and horse chinned, dignified despite the white splotch a seagull had left on his vest. Ambassador Bertolette was short and still wore his woolen traveling mantle, which he used to wipe his dripping nose. In need of baths, sleep, and a good meal, the men were out of place in the marble chamber whose echoes were muffled by draped tapestries. They held their teacups with both hands to warm them.

Gerald Lee Auburn, secretary to the president, lounged on a silk couch across from his guests, opening pecans with a silver nutcracker.

"First France gives the territories to Spain," he was saying, "and now Spanish nobles have traded New Orleans for plum titles. Grease-fingered royals are using the continent as a bargaining chip. Everyone is profiting from our furs, our tobacco, our silver. Everyone but us."

Durand reached into his purse and withdrew a letter bearing the crimson seal of Napoléon Bonaparte. "Happily, these frustrations will soon be behind you, Secretary Auburn." He handed the letter to Auburn. "This is to be delivered to your President Cooper without delay. It relays the final terms for the purchase of New Orleans, including"—the ambassador grinned generously before delivering the good news—"the entirety of the Louisiana territories. The West will finally be yours."

Auburn leaned over the dwindling pecans, poking around for a promising nut. It was not the reaction the ambassador had expected.

Bertolette cleared his throat. "Did you hear? Your Congress can buy your beloved West! You will double the size of your nation in a single day. Ride a carriage from the Atlantic to Spanish California and never leave the Unified States!"

Auburn was not impressed. "I was born into a family so poor that we celebrated Christmas by whitewashing the grave posts behind our house." Auburn paused to pick a bit of pecan out of his teeth. "My seven siblings planted in the earth like so much corn. Later, my father and older brother died in a factory explosion. But I survived the fevers and the hunger and the debtors' houses, and now I own that munitions factory and five more."

"You have every reason to be proud," Bertolette said, touching his lips as if they'd gone numb. "You're a specimen of American enterprise."

"This humble estate"—Auburn's gesture encompassed the chandelier and the marble statue of Aphrodite in the corner—"was earned by selling a better rifle. A dependable firearm."

"Commendable, sir, but what does this have to do with—"

"I was not born into wealth," Auburn said. "I wrenched it

from an unyielding world. The industrious man sees a need and fills it. But the wealthy man creates the need. I'll say it outright: your emperor is desperate."

Durant coughed and turned red. "We will not sit idle while you dishonor—"

Pop! The burst pecan made the ambassadors jump.

"Napoléon Bonaparte needs money to fund his European wars and he needs it now," Secretary Auburn continued. "He can't wait for the tobacco to grow, so to speak. His plan to build a palace in Hispaniola was frustrated by the slave revolt there. So he wants to sell his New World colonies to keep his throne in France. The British control his seas. He is not in a position to negotiate."

Bertolette held his stomach. "Something disagrees with me."

"Listen, friends." Auburn laughed. "Why don't you explain to me how you French settled Louisiana so quickly?"

"Our negotiations with the Indians—"

"I am not talking about trading beads with the mud-eaters." Auburn set his nutcracker down with a clatter. "I am talking about the settlers themselves. So many! While our industrious pioneers are squatting in sod hovels, your people build three-story villas with European oak. Now, tell me: whence the timber? Whence the settlers? You control no ports." Auburn leaned intently toward the ambassadors. "And there are no caravans from the north. So how does he manage it?"

"Who?"

"Bonaparte! How does he populate the interior of our continent?"

Durand cleared his throat, but his voice was raspy. "Our trade secrets are—"

"It's not a trade secret," Auburn hissed. "It's an oddity! Your soldiers, your settlers, look identical. I believe they are somehow pulled from a single mold, duplicated in the manner of a plaster bust. I believe that you have multiplied your timber and spices in the same manner. Tell me I am wrong."

The ambassadors exchanged anxious glances. Bertolette stood and gathered his cape around him. "From now on we will communicate with President Cooper directly—" Then his legs collapsed under him. The ambassador lay in a heap on the floor.

Auburn made no move to help. Durand was struggling to stand but only trembled in his chair.

The ambassadors looked vainly to the door for help, both of them knowing they'd been poisoned. "*Traîtrise!* You would start a war," Durand groaned, "for an oddity?"

"The world has watched your squat emperor storm through every country he laid his covetous eyes on," Auburn said. "His victories aren't natural. How could we ever feel secure against invasion unless we knew his secret? And what good would owning the territories do us if the French continue to multiply? You would merely reclaim Louisiana in a matter of years anyway. Gentlemen, I am a patriot who wants nothing but the safety of my country. Anyway, I own the rifle factories. A little shooting is good for business."

"You cannot murder two ambassadors of New France and hope to—"

"Oh, not two," Auburn interrupted. "One of you will live." Auburn produced a tiny vial of sky-blue Powder. "I have the antidote here, extremely expensive stuff. One of you will come to your senses and tell me all about Bonaparte's oddity. The other will die—in just a few minutes, it seems. Now, which will it be?"

Clover blinked the vision away. She found herself leaning against the gilded cannon, trembling with a rage so intense her teeth chattered. The secret that had crawled into her mind swept away the lies she'd been told since she was a child. Napoléon Bonaparte hadn't started the Louisiana War. It had been Auburn. In retaliation for the missing ambassadors, the French had seized shipments on the Melapoma. Congress ordered troops to reclaim them, and the New World tumbled into anarchy—pushed from a great height by Auburn, who made a fortune selling arms before being elected senator.

But Auburn's plan for conquering the Louisiana Territories by force did not go well. When the US Army marched west, they found fortified French forts and ranks of soldiers, well armed and decently fed. The Louisiana War lasted four years, killing thousands and bankrupting the nation.

It was a truth too big for one exhausted girl, and for several moments she wobbled on her knees, trying to digest it. Then she steeled herself. She had to be sure there was not another secret waiting to pounce. With her eyes tightly closed, she forced a hand into Smalt's Hat, running her fingers blindly over its damp nap. She found no more pests lurking near the rim, but she could feel an eager surge from deeper within, like carp jostling for a scrap of bread. Suddenly her hand was enveloped in warmth, as if the faint whispers inside were the steam of a hot bath. Clover yanked her hand out with a yelp and waited. Her hand was clean. The Hat was still. She turned it over and smacked the top. Nothing else slipped out. The Hat was hardly empty, but it was finally holding its secrets.

Did it still hold the one that Clover wanted more than

anything? Not wanted. *Needed.* She closed her eyes and whispered, "Where is Miniver Elkin?"

The hat lurched and mewled like a sack of kittens. A hiss of whispers, too muffled to understand, sent a mist of spittle onto the brim. The Hat wanted to tell her as badly as she wanted to know. Having asked the question, all Clover would have to do was reach in and retrieve it. But this oddity had devoured Smalt's soul long before it devoured the shell of his body.

"It would be safer to crawl into a loaded cannon than to use this Hat," Clover told herself. With the wrecked inn creaking around her, she pressed her palms to her face, wishing there were another way. Someone else must know where the witch was hiding.

"Mean old dog," Susanna muttered from inside the haversack.

Clover gasped. Of course. She opened the flap and squinted in at the Doll. "Susanna! You must remember where the Seamstress lives!"

PART III

CHAPTER 17

WARMONGER

C lover rushed out of the ruined inn and into the bright chaos of Brackenweed. The roof of the tannery was smoking. Mill oxen had broken free and were roaming the streets, bellowing. People hurried around the square, hollering, "Smalt is dead! We're free!" Others cried, "Smalt is dead! We're doomed!" The newspaper boy ran out of the printing office, his hands and face covered with ink. Above it all, stray secrets could be seen dipping and darting like bats in a fog.

Gunshots and screaming echoed in the distance. Whether blown in a wet wind or carried by his couriers upon news of his death, Smalt's secrets were spreading quickly. Everywhere Clover looked, people argued:

You stole my goat!

You poisoned my well!

Scoundrel! Liar! Thief!

The city of Brackenweed was coming undone.

A banker ran down the street, his silk coat stuffed with

money, dollar bills trailing in his wake like autumn leaves. The sheriff's deputy sat on a mule backward, both of them braying. A group of laughing children ran after airborne secrets, trying to catch them in a burlap sack. Clover heard snippets of the secrets dancing on the wind:

The dairyman adds plaster to his cheese.

The priest gambles with donations.

The mayor's father was a voyageur.

Clover watched a secret scuttle quickly up a carriage driver's sleeve. The man hollered and smacked at it, but the secret slipped into his ear, quick as a word. The driver went very still, then turned and marched into the butcher shop. Seconds later, the skinned head of a pig flew through the doorway and landed in the street, looking surprised.

What secret had provoked this? Why was a high-class lady digging through the bedding of a horse stall? Clover didn't want to know.

Clutching her possessions, she hurried through the square, hoping no one would recognize the Hat. She knew she made a strange sight, her clothes singed, the bulk of a viper moving under her shirt, the oversize blue Hat bobbling atop her head. But the city was too frenzied to pay her any mind.

It was into this riot that Senator Auburn finally arrived. First his military escort was spotted at the doors of the courthouse, regal in their brass buttons and blue coats. Auburn soon appeared on the balcony above, bracketed by rifle-bearing bodyguards. He was not a tall man, but his striped suit was spotless, with a starched collar and a coat that tapered to his girdled waist.

"Liar," Clover muttered. "Murderer."

The agitated crowd surged toward the balcony. The Brackenweed brass band struck up a welcoming march, but they were buffeted by the crowd, their song mangled as the horns were bullied in different directions.

A thunderous roar split the air and the crowd went still. Auburn had ordered the cannon blast, an empty shot that shocked the mob into silence.

Now his voice carried easily over the square: "You are right to be afraid! The French curs are massing on our borders to attack. Their ranks swell with a single goal: to push us into the sea! They attacked us once without warning. This time we will not be taken by surprise."

The senator tugged at his tie until it dangled loose and swayed with his frenetic energy. He scowled and shook his fist. He was working a charismatic spell not to quiet the fears of the people but to focus them.

"The wolves are at the door. The time has come to stand and fight."

Lies. Not one of these people knew what Clover knew, a truth that overturned history. Time had silvered Auburn's hair, but this was the same man Clover had just watched poison the ambassadors. His arrogance and greed had broken the nation. And now he was doing it again, bent on ruling the entire continent, no matter how many died. He was insatiable.

"Trust not the vile gossip spreading like a contagion," Senator Auburn shouted. "Trust only your own ears, which hear the distant gunshots. Trust your nose, which smells the smoke of the approaching conflagration! Trust your eyes, which see the skulking stranger, the voyageur among us."

The crowd bristled with suspicious glares, frightened eyes sweeping for someone to accuse. Some fell on Clover, the strange girl who had destroyed the inn, who had survived the snake's poison.

It was time for Clover to go. As she pushed her way out of the square, the senator's voice echoed, "Rise to the defense of your country! Rise against French tyranny!"

The crowd chanted with him. The senator was guiding Brackenweed's frightened cries into a chorus. "Rise against tyranny!"

Clover shouldered her way through the shouting crowd. She knew, finally, where she had to go. Susanna had told her that the witch's lair was deep in the abandoned silver mine at Harper's Ridge. Clutching her belongings, Clover headed for the main road out of the city. But just as she slipped through the throng and into an open alley, the barkeep from the Golden Cannon cut her off. He was wild-eyed, still clutching the soiled bar rag.

"Destroyed my inn!" he snarled, grabbing Clover by the shoulders. He looked ready to strangle her but pulled up short when the barrel of a rifle caught him under the chin. The brute let go and backed away as a squad of uniformed soldiers surrounded them both.

"I was just talking to her," the barkeep said, rubbing his beard.

"You're finished talking now, friend."

Clover knew the voice. The soldiers parted for Hannibal Furlong, sitting atop a white horse. He rode comfortably on a custom-made saddle, grasping the slender reins with one claw.

The barkeep fled into the crowd, and Hannibal winked at Clover. "I should know by now that the place to find you is in a tangle of trouble."

"Oh, Hannibal! I have to talk to you," Clover said. "It's important."

"Indeed. Come with me," he said.

Hannibal's squad guided Clover down the narrow alley, all but empty now that most of the city had converged on the square. Silent and obedient, the soldiers around Clover were nothing like the bumbling guards she'd seen at the checkpoints. All this time Clover could hardly imagine Hannibal actually commanding soldiers, but these intimidating men were clearly his own elite guard. They wore cockerel insignia on their shoulders and kept a tight formation as they hurried through Brackenweed's streets.

They passed a courtyard where a straw-haired boy was milking a goat. The goat stamped and tugged its halter, alarmed, no doubt, by the chaotic sounds echoing over the rooftops: shouts, occasional gunshots, the brass band trying again to finish a song. But the boy cooed and shushed the goat, filling his bucket one hissing tug at a time. Clover wanted to trade places with the boy, to carry the bucket inside and sip some of the sweet froth off the top. The comfort of simple chores seemed so far away. Clover's head was still spinning, a chill blew through the burned holes in her clothes, and the viper was still hot as a fever around her ribs.

She looked at Hannibal, so regal atop his horse. She knew Hannibal wouldn't like the truth about Auburn's evil history, but he deserved to know.

"Hannibal, I must speak with you—" But Clover's words caught in her throat when she saw where she was being taken.

A splendid caravan was parked in the middle of a high-walled terrace. The vehicle was beetle black, trimmed with gold ornamentation, and twice as long as Nessa's wagon.

One of the soldiers opened the caravan door and bowed deeply, waiting for Clover and Hannibal to enter. Stepping in, Clover gaped at the extravagant chamber: walls and couches upholstered in scarlet velvet, the ceiling elaborated with mother-of-pearl palmettes. A custom-forged stove sat opposite a writing desk strewn with loose piles of correspondence. The caravan smelled of brandy and calfskin.

"The senator will be with us shortly," Hannibal announced as the door snapped shut behind them. "And, I assure you, everything will be sorted out." He hopped onto a seat and stretched his wings. "Rest yourself, my dear girl. Today you fought a monster most were afraid to face, and you came away victorious."

"Listen, Hannibal; Smalt wasn't the only monster. Look around. Is this how a servant of the people travels?"

"You cannot blame the senator for wanting a bit of comfort on the long road."

"Auburn started the first war for his own profit," Clover whispered, not knowing how much could be heard through the caravan walls.

"A shameful rumor."

"I'm telling you. I *saw* it. It came from Smalt's Hat—"

But the sound of the soldiers outside clicking their arms to attention shut Clover's mouth. Then, before Clover was ready, Senator Auburn himself ducked into the caravan, pulling off his wrinkled necktie. This close, close enough for Clover to see a spot of stubble under his chin that the barber had missed, Senator Auburn was shorter than he had appeared on his balcony, though he was still flushed pink from his theatrics. The tufts of his eyebrows swept up toward his hairline.

"Hannibal tells me you're difficult to find," the senator said as he dropped into a seat opposite Clover. The caravan felt suddenly much too small. "But I am terribly happy to meet you at last. I hear such promising things."

Leaning to push a small kettle onto the stove, he said, "I'll have some tea ready shortly."

"I know better than to take tea from you, Mr. Auburn," Clover blurted, remembering the faces of those poisoned ambassadors.

It was a dangerous thing to say, but Clover couldn't take it back. For a moment, Senator Auburn blinked at Clover, saying nothing.

"Please understand," Hannibal intervened. "Her nerves are in tatters. She has survived ordeals, several, and she . . . says things."

"The air today is literally filled with lies," Senator Auburn said. His rabble-rousing had left him hoarse. He squeezed a dropper full of laudanum into a glass of lavender water and gargled it before continuing. "And who can we thank for that? You've kicked over Pandora's box. Quite the mess. But even this may be to our advantage, wouldn't you say, Hannibal? I thought it would take another year of campaigning before we had total support for the war, but now old wounds are opening. Smalt's gossip will only spread panic from city to city, and frightened people deserve security. Clover, you have helped our cause already."

"That's as I've been trying to tell you," Hannibal said. "Nurse Elkin is a force of consequence, and we must position her accordingly. I have seen her bravery, her determination. When she sets her heart to it, she is practically unstoppable."

Hannibal talked about Clover as if she weren't there. She tried to take deep breaths, but the red-upholstered walls seemed to press in like the gut of a beast digesting her. She considered kicking the door open to leap out, but those soldiers were waiting just outside.

"You see how Hannibal has taken a liking to you," the senator told her. "We can't blame him. You're clearly a remarkable child, so remarkable, it seems, that he's been keeping your exact whereabouts from me."

"Sir, I assure you—"

Auburn flicked his hand at Hannibal dismissively and leaned close to Clover, bringing a waft of ambergris perfume and tobacco. "The witch wants you, poor child." Senator Auburn sat back and crossed his arms as if to ponder a riddle. "Now, why in the world would that be?"

Clover shook her head.

"I don't know either. Who knows what goes on in the mind of a mountain hag? But it puts us in a difficult position because we sorely need something from the witch. I am showing you my every card, Clover, so you know you can trust me." He licked the pad of his thumb and ran it along his eyebrows, grooming them the way another man might wax his mustache. "You are going to help us acquire a crucial element only she possesses."

"You'd have to know where to find her," Clover said.

"But I do. I paid Smalt for that secret years ago. Very expensive. Knowing where she hides isn't enough, though. Here's the dilemma: the witch has what I need, and it seems you're the only way to get it."

"But, to lure the witch out of her lair, we would have to leave Clover unprotected at the mine," Hannibal objected. "Senator, I respectfully remind you that bait is frequently eaten."

"Am I to be bait?" Clover asked, staring shocked at the Rooster she had thought was her friend.

Hannibal ignored her and continued, "As you know, sir, vermin are unpredictable and savage. That mountain is crawling with them. Even with the best planning, we could not both capture the witch and protect Clover. It's an unacceptable risk."

"You've just told the girl our plan," Auburn said sourly.

"She deserves to know what is to become of her. Clover is more valuable than any of the oddities we've acquired at highway checkpoints. It would be folly to lose her to vermin."

"Age has made a hen of you," Auburn said, but he turned to Clover, his eyebrows raised. "The honorable Colonel Furlong here, whose counsel I've trusted for decades, insists that you're more valuable on the battlefield. 'Unstoppable,' he says."

"After what just happened in that inn," Hannibal pleaded with Clover, "you can't deny being a fighter. First the Heron, then Smalt. Some of my men saw it with their own eyes."

"Well?" Senator Auburn asked. "Are you the secret weapon Hannibal says you are?"

Clover understood, at last, that Hannibal had been arguing for her fate like a lawyer at trial. He was afraid for her and now Clover was afraid too. She was caught up in something much larger than herself, falling in a capsizing wagon, and Hannibal was trying to guide her to safety. The wise thing would be to follow his voice as she had before, to accept the arrangement he offered.

The kettle began to tick and hiss, but no one moved to take it from the stove. Hannibal and Auburn waited for her answer.

The idea of helping Auburn made her stomach clench. The groans of those ambassadors echoed in her mind. What would the world have been like if he hadn't poisoned them, if the first war hadn't happened? How could Clover hope to resist this murderer on his way to the presidency, this manipulator of mobs and nations? She could not risk taking part in his deadly schemes.

"I'll never fight for you, Senator," Clover heard herself say. "You're a liar and a warmonger and worse . . ." She clenched her teeth as words failed her. She didn't know what to do, but she knew what she couldn't. "I'm sorry, Hannibal," she whispered.

Auburn wrinkled his nose as if he'd smelled something rotten and reached for a silver cigar box. "She'd rather be eaten alive by vermin," he said. "She's practically feral. I can see why you're fond of this brazen girl, Hannibal, but she has made her own decision." He lit a cigar and sat back, puffing thoughtfully. "On the other hand, if she is as valuable as you say—"

"She is, sir," Hannibal said hopefully. "I assure you."

Clover flushed with rage and humiliation, listening to them haggle over her like a piece of market beef.

"Then we must lock this Clover away immediately and send the witch something tempting," Senator Auburn said. "One of Clover's fingers should do. Wouldn't that be enough to convince the Seamstress to come to us?"

Hannibal closed his eyes and shook his head wearily. "You can't mean it."

The senator chuckled, "Does the hero of a hundred battles blanch now at the loss of a single finger?" But his smile became savage as he pointed at Hannibal with the smoldering cigar. "You have frittered away precious time while the French sharpen their bayonets! The Seamstress cannot fall into Bonaparte's hands, and if this misguided mountain girl is what you say she is, she must remain in our control."

"I understand," Hannibal said.

"Leave the witch alone," Clover said, her voice quavering. "Leave us alone, you miserable man."

Auburn turned to Clover, his voice icy. "Your sacrifice will not be in vain. The Seamstress is the key to our victory. Without her, we will be overrun by the endless army." He looked again at Hannibal. "I will have that witch. Are we quite clear, Colonel?"

Hannibal held very still, looking for a moment like a stuffed trophy. Then he said, "Yes, sir. Leave it to me."

"Hannibal you can't—" Clover started.

"Shut up, Clover!" Hannibal barked with such authority that Clover was stunned into silence.

Senator Auburn drew on his cigar contentedly. "It would

be an unfortunate end to your glorious career if a hill-born brat clouded your duty to your country."

"Nothing of the sort, Senator."

As Hannibal and Clover stood to leave, Auburn delivered a final warning. "Though, if you are ready to retire, I'm sure we can find a barnyard worthy of the fabled Hannibal Furlong: clean straw and a bevy of hens, plenty of cracked corn, and a farmer willing to postpone the butcher block for a few years. After all, you've served us so faithfully."

Hannibal received this insulting threat with a stiff nod. "I will secure the asset."

As Hannibal and Clover stood to leave, Auburn delivered a final warning. "This girl," he said through a cloud of smoke, "and everything she carries are now your responsibility."

· · · · · · · · · · ·

"Don't you see it's madness?" Clover pleaded.

In a meadow outside the city, a camp of fifty soldiers scrambled like a kicked anthill, saddling horses and rolling up tents. Clover and Hannibal watched from a low hill as bugle calls and the glint of armaments lit the air.

"We could have purchased Louisiana, all of it, with no bloodshed," she said. "Bonaparte wanted to sell it to us. The war could have been avoided!"

"The time for political theory is long past," Hannibal said soberly. "We have no choice but to face the challenge of the present. There is still time for us to secure our advantage. The Seamstress has hoarded her oddities in the abandoned silver mine at Harper's Ridge. Now that her location may be on the wind with the rest of Smalt's secrets, we must make our move before Bonaparte does. It will take my platoon eighteen minutes to break camp. In that time, you must decide: will you be escorted to a training camp or to a dungeon? I would rather have you as a comrade than a prisoner."

Clover shook her head. "I think Auburn knows what Bonaparte's oddity is, the one that makes the endless army," she said. "He wants it for himself. Auburn doesn't just want to be president. He wants to be emperor!"

"Would you rather be ruled by Bonaparte?"

Nothing Clover could say would penetrate his plumage. She looked at the soldiers pulling up stakes, smelled the scorched stews dumped over cook fires, heard the clicks and whistles of tenders luring mules into their yokes.

Most were young men, not much older than she was, proud in federal coats with brass buttons, their chins high and brave. Could it be that there really were fighters like this just beyond the border, waiting to attack, the Louisiana army, with their blue coats and yellow sashes, all of them proud and young and ready to die?

"All this time I've trusted you," Clover said. "But you were planning to hand me over to that madman so he could sacrifice me to the Seamstress."

"Isn't it clear by now that I've risked everything to protect you, to find a better role for you? We all must play our part!" Then he softened. "We do not get to choose the body or world we are born into, only what we do with them. You have greatness in you. If half these men had your mettle, I'd have Bonaparte rowing back to France in a pickle barrel. The war is coming. You can help us win. You can help me."

"I didn't meet you by chance, did I?"

Hannibal sighed wearily. "During our search for useful oddi-ties, we became aware of a rumor, whispered among the older Society members. A fireside yarn that Dr. Constantine Elkin had pulled a baby out of the inferno before riding off into the night, whispers that a Russian doctor was still tending to the sick in the mountain villages, that there was a girl with him. Auburn tasked me with dispelling that rumor. I expected to find old fishermen and spiders and more tall tales." He looked kindly at her. "Instead I found you."

Soldiers were beginning to gather in a loose group at the edge of the meadow, making last-minute adjustments to their bags and harnesses, a small army to take on a single old woman.

Clover spotted five of Hannibal's elite squad guarding a wagon covered with a canvas. A breeze lifted the sheet just enough for Clover to recognize the Society logo stamped on one of the crates beneath. Nearby, a soldier held a heavy chain attached to a smoldering iron box just big enough to hold the Ember.

"The Heron!" Clover said. "That belongs to Mr. Agate!"

"Temporarily commandeered for the just cause of defense," Hannibal explained.

"You're no better than a poacher!"

"Quite an accusation from someone wearing the Hat."

Clover snatched the Hat off her head in embarrassment. She had already forgotten it was there. "I'm going to give it to Mr. Agate," she said.

"Don't bother." Hannibal sniffed. "It is my responsibility to oversee all our tactical assets. That includes your own collection. I'd say you have five minutes left to make your decision."

"Tell me this: what weapon does the Seamstress have that Auburn wants so badly? What could possibly defeat Bonaparte's endless army?"

Hannibal shook his head. "It's enough to say that the witch is key to our strategy."

"No," Clover growled. "No more riddles. No more secrets. If you're asking me to play a part, I deserve to know."

Hannibal sighed and stretching his neck uncomfortably. "The senator wants the technique, the . . . *method* used to create vermin."

"But the French won't be intimidated by tin-bellied skunks and dead-eyed crows."

"Indeed. Not skunks and crows," Hannibal said, refusing to look her in the eye.

"You don't mean soldiers?" The horror of it hit Clover all at once. "Auburn wants to turn *people* into vermin?"

"To pick soldiers up when they fall," Hannibal said quietly. "To make the brave sacrifice of our boys mean more. Once dead they will not suffer, you see. Will not feel pain . . ."

"Look at them!" Clover pointed to the young men in the knee-high grass. "Those boys trust you. You plan to sew them together with whatever limbs you find on the field, stuff them like scarecrows, and send them back out to be shot again and again. They will keep marching, won't they, even if a cannonball whistles through them?"

"We hope it won't be necessary. War demands distasteful decisions."

"It's a nightmare! The infinite army against the unkillable army. Hannibal, a war like that would never end." Clover's voice quavered. "We can't let it happen."

Hannibal regarded her with tired eyes. "The senator did not invent vermin. If we don't obtain this advantage, the French will. Better for us to have the method than Bonaparte."

"And after she's told you the secret," Clover asked, "what will become of the Seamstress?"

"We'll take her into comfortable custody, to ensure that her powers can't be used by the enemy."

"And when she refuses?"

Hannibal shook his head.

"You'll kill her." Now Clover was crying.

"Weigh your next steps very carefully, Nurse Elkin. Would you really sacrifice your future to protect a witch?"

"She's my mother!" Clover said between clenched teeth.

Hannibal stared at Clover with shock. So he hadn't known. It didn't matter.

Clover wiped her cheeks. The decision had made itself. "I will not help you create an army of the undead. I will reach the Seamstress before you," she said. Remembering the Society motto, she added: "Custodia Insolitum."

The platoon was now lined up in five clean rows, facing the shrouded mountains, as still as wooden soldiers.

Hannibal sighed. "It breaks my heart, but I will have to arrest you to keep you from meddling. A few days in a cell, I hope, will clear your head." He nodded, signaling to the guards who had been watching from a distance. Immediately, three soldiers came forward on horseback to seize her.

"I don't intend to be arrested," Clover said, summoning her courage.

Sweetwater emerged from the neckline of her shirt, rose up

tall on her shoulder, and swayed there with cold-blooded focus. The soldiers' horses reared and snorted.

"Anyone who touches me will feel Sweetwater's kiss. She's got plenty of venom for each of you. And Hannibal, you know I carry another friend in my bag."

Hannibal waved his men back with a flick of his wing. He regarded Clover with a jewel-bright eye. "We will reach the silver mines before you, of course. You don't even have a horse."

At his signal, the lieutenant blew a whistle. The entire platoon started off toward the blue-stained mountains, their footfalls making a drum of the earth.

Before following them, Hannibal said softly, "You are choosing the wrong side, Nurse Elkin. If I don't bring you in, Senator Auburn will send someone else. But you know the mountains. You can disappear. As your friend, I beg you, do not interfere with our mission."

"I saved your life." Clover placed the Hat back on her head.

"And I saved yours. Please don't make me remove you from the field."

"The world won't survive the kind of war you're making," Clover said. "Despite everything, I know you have a good heart, Hannibal. Consider it."

NO MORE TREES
TO CLIMB

Clover kept the snowy peaks of the Centurion Mountains on her left as she trudged northwest.

To bring the entire platoon to the mine at Harper's Ridge, Hannibal would have to take Abbot's Highway, the only real road to the peak. It was wide and safe for heavy wagons, but it threaded through the foothills, switching back so often that frustrated travelers called it "the snarl." Clover couldn't hope to travel the same highway and beat them. She'd have to cut through the wilderness, a direct route, but one with no roads to aid her.

She glanced back at the mustard-colored chimneys of Brackenweed, wishing she had time to see Widow Henshaw again. Her heart ached to think of the old woman camping alone in the strange city.

"I'll set this right," Clover whispered, knowing in her gut that there was no solution for the ice on the lake. Then she turned her attention back to the race against Hannibal.

The borderlands were teeming with bandits, and Clover's

route would also take her through Sehanna Indian territory. What would they make of a mountain girl cutting through their land? There was more than one kind of Indian in that area, and not all were tolerant of strangers. The Ormanliot were known as friendly traders, bringing their canoes right up to shore loaded with pelts, wampum, and bottles of maple syrup, but the Quamit were said to shoot from the trees without so much as a "hello." Her father had described the Sehanna themselves, the tribe the Sehanna Confederation was named for, as fiercely loyal to their friends and "rather unkind" to their enemies. Clover's best bet was to move quickly and hope she wasn't noticed.

Clover found that crumpling the Hat did not squeeze secrets out, so she shoved it into her father's bag. She wanted to leave the thing under some rotting log, but she had a fear that oddities *wanted* to be found. She couldn't let some new villain pick it up. The world didn't need another Smalt. When the wind stilled, she thought she could hear the Hat's sinister whispers.

Sweetwater's grip around her waist wasn't the same as having a friend to talk to, so Clover pulled Susanna out of her pocket and set the Doll on her shoulder. Susanna braced herself by holding on to Clover's braid, seeming satisfied to be riding high. She peered at the mountain peaks with button eyes.

"Mean old Missus."

"Yes. We're going to the Seamstress. No one else can tell me who I am, *what* I am. I have to go. If Hannibal reaches that mine first, he'll kill her. I can't let that happen."

"Mean old bird."

"He's right in some things," Clover said. "If I am not a soldier, what am I? Blood sister to a snake, keeper of a cursed Hat and a foul-tempered Doll. I mean . . . you can't deny that you are foul tempered."

Susanna didn't seem offended.

"We're sisters, you and I," Clover continued. "Both of us made by Miniver." She thought about the tools in her father's bag. "What is a scalpel? Only a blade. And a blade can be used to kill or to cure. And you, Susanna, you are practically a hurricane, but you've saved my life. Oddities are like that. Full of harm or help, depending on their use. Auburn wants to chop me up as bait. Hannibal wants me to be a weapon. But maybe, if I know where I came from, I can find a better purpose."

Winter's breath rolled down the mountain. Clover pulled her shawl tightly over her shoulders. She was small in the shadow of the peaks, but she felt a strong sense of direction for the first time since her ordeal began. It had felt good to argue with Hannibal, to speak the truth, even if he refused to hear it.

"I almost have the whole picture now," Clover said. "There are only a few questions left, but I know where to find the answers."

"You're not scared," Susanna offered helpfully.

"Oh, Susanna, I'm terrified. I don't know if we'll make it to that mine, or what will happen when we get there. Even if I get through Sehanna territory and the Wine Marsh, we're liable to see more vermin. Sweetwater has to come with me or we'll both get sick, but you have a choice. I know you tried to put the Seamstress behind you."

Susanna crossed her arms, pouting.

"There is no shame in it," Clover said. "I am afraid of fire, even though it can't kill me. It still hurts, and I am still scared."

Clover didn't tell Susanna that, right now, she was more

afraid of the Seamstress than she was of anything. Compared with the shadowy creator of vermin, even Smalt seemed like a feeble old man. Something horrible had transformed Miniver Elkin. If the founder of the Society hadn't been able to defend herself from it, it must have been terrible indeed. Clover needed to find her mother, but she might never be ready to see the monster she'd become.

"You need me," Susanna said.

"You have saved my hide already," Clover agreed. "But I won't have any hard feelings if you want to part ways now. You could just tell me how to get there."

"Not scared," Susanna said, and she gripped Clover's braid tighter as the slope became steeper. The hunting trail they were following narrowed as they approached the border of the state of Farrington, and then it disappeared completely. Clover was leaving the Unified States and everything she knew behind as she pressed on into the no-man's-land between the US, Louisiana, and the Sehanna Confederation. Her breath made fleeting clouds that she broke through as she trudged ahead, step by step. She longed for Nessa's rumbling wagon.

They crested a ridge, and Clover watched sunset rain raking the Sawtooth Prairie in the southwest. Somewhere beyond those grasslands were the French. It was said that they were building tracks for steam locomotives right through the continent toward the Spanish coast, but Clover saw only the felted beige of the prairies.

Before all of this, Clover had longed to see the world. Now, from this vantage, she saw more than ever before. In the northwest was the appalling purple stain of the Wine Marsh, a bruise left from the last war surrounded by bone-colored crags. Beyond that, the dense forests and rivers of the Sehanna Confederation stretched all the way to the northern horizon. Four northern tribes, the Okikwa, Quamit, Ormanliot, and Sehanna, had banded together under the leadership of Yellow Mouse to fight alongside Louisiana in the early days of the war. In the second year of the war, they withdrew their support for Bonaparte, consolidating their territory east of the Inland Seas as a sovereign nation and defending their own borders. Most fur coats and beaver-skin hats in the world had come from this river-rich land, and Constantine had told her that the Sehanna used their wealth to provide for the Indian refugees who had fled north, escaping US and French aggression.

To the south lay her own hill-furrowed country and the quilted farmland of western Farrington. Clover imagined all eleven states of the union along the coast. It was an unimaginable expanse, yet Auburn and Hannibal wanted more.

Clover hurried down the next slope into a dark valley, letting the mountains rise around her. When darkness fell, she kicked the ground clear under the low-hanging arms of a roadside willow and lay down for the night.

She realized she was no longer afraid of bandits riding up in the dark. The world's deadliest viper, the unstoppable Doll, and the fireproof girl. Clover had started this journey alone, but she'd forged alliances with uncanny comrades.

Owls swept the stars and the wind shook the vines, and somewhere near dreaming, Clover felt her father sitting on a branch near her. He cleared his throat politely, smelling of pine and smoked fish.

"I'm sorry you have to haunt me," Clover said softly. "I wish you could rest."

"Don't tell me you believe in ghosts!" Constantine chuckled, that rarest of sounds.

"I know you're only an echo," Clover said. "Sorrow casting shadows on a troubled memory. But . . . a ghost is a ghost."

Constantine looked at the stars between the branches, keeping his judgment silent, a skill practiced in life, perfected in death.

"Why didn't you tell me what I was?" Shivering made Clover's voice brittle.

"I wanted a life for you. A safe life."

"I could have done something on that bridge. I could have helped you," Clover said. "I let them kill you."

Constantine sighed, a dismissive sound inseparable from the hush of the willow leaves.

"Well, I'm not powerless now," Clover said. "If the world is set on war, I have to do what I can to push it in the other direction."

"A doctor's role is to serve the body before her."

"Thousands will die! Every oddity they get their hands on will make this war worse. Those are the bodies I see before me."

Clover felt her father's gaze on her, diagnosing even in the dark.

"What is necessary? What is hope?" Clover said. "I won't sit by while warmongers turn this continent into a graveyard. You taught me to find the source of the bleeding, to mend it if I could."

"It's an impressive argument, but don't forget that I know my willful Clover. I know when you're hiding something," Constantine said. "What is the real reason you are marching toward the witch's den?"

"I have to know," Clover admitted. "I'm strangled by the questions you refused to answer. What did she do to me? Why do the vermin call me frog?"

Clover waited for her father's answer, but he'd retreated into his perfect silence.

"Why wasn't she content"—Clover turned her face to the sky and let her father disappear into a restless wind—"to be my mother?"

. . . .

In the hollow-bellied morning, Clover descended toward what looked like a lake of tarnished copper, a grassy plain bordered by a dense forest, the southern Sehanna border.

"We must cross straight through to get to the mountain pass yonder," Clover told Susanna, who peered from the safety of her haversack pocket. "It looks harmless enough."

But Clover didn't speak any Indian languages, and she could almost feel the scouts watching from the forest. Aside from a few scattered cottonwood trees, there was nowhere to hide on the prairie. Like the mule deer that had left clear trails, Clover would be visible for miles. She'd feel less exposed picking her way through the forest, but entering those woods would be asking for a confrontation with Sehanna patrols.

"If we cut across the grass, they'll probably let us pass, and we should reach the Wine Marsh by evening."

Of course the Wine Marsh was notorious for killing those stupid enough to venture into it. But Clover put that out of her mind and skittered down the last slopes above the grassland. Speed was her only strategy.

The grass came up to her elbows, thick as a bear's hide, but it was dry and didn't slow her march. The spent heads crackled, having scattered their grain weeks ago.

Sweetwater was happy to have her belly on dry ground.

She darted ahead, exploring the hidden veins that rodents had dug through the undergrowth. Clover wished she could also crawl beneath the surface of things, unnoticed. Instead she was leaving a wake of trampled grass behind her.

She was far from any kind of shelter when she heard a sound that made her stop, a scraping, dry and out of place. Clover held her breath, listening hard. It was the unsettling rasp of grinding bones, but Clover couldn't tell where it was coming from.

"Susanna, do you hear that?"

"Junk," Susanna whispered.

A shadow darted over them, and Clover spun around just in time to see a Vulture swooping toward her. Its head was made from a claw hammer, and it hit her just as hard. Clover was knocked off her feet and rolled in the grass. She got up, head throbbing, and saw that she was surrounded.

The Vulture circled above while three other vermin emerged from the grass: a Hare, the Squirrel, and a tattered old Hound. They were refuse masquerading as life: broken milk jugs and candlesticks, threadbare rugs and dented pie pans, all sewn tightly into the hides of long-dead animals.

"Is this it?" the Hare rasped.

The Hound circled with its nose to the ground. "Yes, yes, yes."

The Vulture swung close, and Clover tried to keep an eye on it. Her head was aching from the blow. The next one might kill her. Responding to Clover's fear, Sweetwater coiled tightly around her shin.

If her venom had no effect on Susanna, it would be useless on scarecrows like these. Clover opened Susanna's pocket.

"Susanna? I could really use you right about now."

But Susanna didn't leap out ready for a fight. In fact, the Doll had curled up inside, trembling.

"Don't tell me you're afraid of vermin?"

"Junk! Nasty junk!" Susanna wailed, and tucked her head under her arms.

"We're in trouble," Clover said just as the Vulture plunged. The hammer missed her, but the pitchfork claws caught her shoulder and nearly lifted her off her feet, dragging her through the grass before dropping her on the ground again.

The Hound snatched Clover's pant leg and tugged, snarling. The Hare grabbed at her braid with its teeth, and Clover found herself pulled between the vermin, taut as a clothesline.

Sweetwater struck out at the Hound. Her fangs pierced the dry hide easily but not the scrap tin underneath. Clover's own teeth ached, an echo of the snake's pain, then the Squirrel leaped to her chest. Clover swatted at it, but the vermin dodged easily.

"This is it," the Squirrel said. "This is what Mistress wants."

"This is no frog," the Hare grumbled through Clover's braid.

"Smells like frog," said the Hound. "Yes, yes."

"Does Mistress want the frog dead?" the Hare asked.

"We were dead when she found us," answered the Squirrel.

"She will be heavy."

"Tear her into pieces, then," the Squirrel offered. "Let the sun dry her out. The Seamstress can patch her together."

"Yes, yes," the Hound whispered.

The Squirrel opened its mouth, and Clover saw that its teeth were tin snips. She scrambled, trying to keep the monster away from her throat. When it clamped down on her arm, Clover wailed.

An arrow cut through the Squirrel's neck. Another arrow

pinned the Hare to the ground. Clover got to her feet just as a rifle shot smashed through the Hound's washbasin chest. It yelped and made a splayed dash into the grass.

Clover turned and spotted her saviors, a small band of Sehanna runner-scouts, bristling with weapons. The Indians were not happy to see her.

The Vulture dove toward the closest of them, a scowling young woman with a long lance in her hands. She speared the vermin out of the air and tore its wings off with one swift motion.

Holding the writhing Vulture at arm's length with a look of disgust, the woman pulled a blue thread out of the feathery mess. The bird fell apart, scattering into pieces that did not move again.

One of the runners pursued the Hound into the meadow, but the other three surrounded Clover with their rifles pointed at her chest.

The young woman who had killed the Vulture wore a breast shield made of porcupine quills and the silver arm cuffs of an honored warrior. Her braids were decorated with beads that looked to be carved from antlers. She nodded, and one of the other fighters snatched up Clover's bags and began to fish through their contents.

The young woman asked, *"Qui es-tu?"*

Clover shook her head. "My name is Clover Elkin, but I don't speak French. I am requesting passage to the Wine Marsh. Who are you?"

She stared at Clover for a moment before saying, "Margaret."

"I thank you for your help, Margaret. I am in a terrible hurry."

"Are you alone?"

"In a manner of speaking," Clover answered.

Just then, Sweetwater emerged from Clover's shirt. One of

the scouts dropped the haversack with a gasp as Susanna crawled out and peered around. Seeing the vermin destroyed, the Doll started bravely toward the Indians, her little frame bunching for a fight.

"Susanna, wait!" Clover said.

But Susanna had grabbed the blade of one of the lances and yanked it out of its owner's grasp.

"*Susanna, don't be sore!*" Clover sang, and Susanna turned back grumpily.

"Ain't afraid," Susanna muttered.

"I know you're not. But this isn't a fight," Clover assured her. She picked Susanna up and put her on her shoulder. In one last fit of frustration, the Doll broke the head off the lance and threw the splintered remains at the ground.

The warriors' eyes were wide, and they cocked their rifles, waiting for a cue to shoot.

Margaret said, "You're a witch."

"I am not a witch. But I am in a hurry."

"Why do the vermin want you?" Margaret asked.

"I don't know."

The one who had lost his lance to Susanna picked up the medical bag again, and Clover said, "Leave that alone. Those are my father's things."

"Is your father a doctor?" Margaret asked.

"My father was Constantine Elkin, and he was the best doctor in the territories," Clover said.

The runners exchanged glances.

"Come with us," Margaret said.

· · · · · · · · · ·

Hundreds of Indian fighters were camped in the oak forest north of the grasslands. Clover's father had told her that Sehanna Indians lived in multifamily straw-thatched houses, but this was a cluster of tents and open-air fires, an army on the move. Clover recognized some, the Okikwa with shorn hair and blue-stained hands, the Quamit with their red-wool caps and silver crescent necklaces, but judging by the variations in clothing and jewelry, there were several tribes represented here, and they were all prepared for battle. Even some children carried weapons, and not the bows and torches that Clover had seen in illustrations. These were modern rifles. Mules pulled cannons and crates of ammunition. In the distance, Clover saw a group in a mock skirmish, the raptor battle cries cutting the air. Clover felt sick to her stomach. If Senator Auburn wanted a war, he was going to get it.

At last they entered the central circle of tents, a little boy, nearly a toddler, charged the group and demanded something of Margaret. Margaret tried to wave him away, but the boy insisted. She finally relented, leaning down to scoop him up onto her shoulders. The boy tugged her braids, thrilled to be riding high, and Margaret tolerated it with a sigh.

At last they arrived at a sprawling tent attended by guards in scarlet mantles. The canvas walls had been embellished with deer running under blue storm clouds, their antlers branching like lightning. Margaret whistled and was allowed inside, ducking under a lintel of braided cedar with the little boy. Clover listened through the fabric, but the only words she understood were "Dr. Elkin."

Then the chief emerged. He was tall in a beaver-pelt robe, and as wrinkled as a cider apple. The guards looked at the ground in deference, and everyone nearby went silent. But it was his eyes that

told Clover without a doubt who this was; they were as white as boiled eggs. This was the legendary leader who had unified the four tribes of the Confederation. It was this man's strategic brilliance that had forced the US and Louisiana to include the Sehanna in the treaty at the end of the war. Yellow Mouse was now in his eighties, completely blind since birth. He cocked his head at Clover as if he could see her.

He spoke softly in Sehanna, with a voice as ragged as a crow's.

Margaret translated: "Are you really Dr. Elkin's daughter?"

"My name is Clover Elkin, and I am in a hurry, sir."

"In a hurry?" Margaret interrupted. "You're talking to Yellow Mouse himself and you're in a hurry?"

"I just said I was."

Yellow Mouse chuckled and muttered something, ducking into the tent and pulling his robe close with a shudder.

Margaret translated: "Then you must be his daughter." She held the tent door open until Clover entered.

The tent walls were thick with pelts and beaded sashes, and a cast-iron stove in the middle radiated a welcome warmth. Men and women sat in a corner around a low table, looking at maps and drinking sweet-smelling tea. Clover had interrupted a war meeting.

The toddler ran in giddy circles, splashing his hands in a bowl of water and drying them on Margaret's deerskin leggings before settling down on Yellow Mouse's lap.

"This is my great-grandson," Margaret translated for Yellow Mouse. "He's learning to wash his hands."

The boy tugged on the beads in the chief's braids and sang a little song, staring at Clover warily. Yellow Mouse hugged the boy close and smiled.

Clover said, "I know I am here without permission."

Margaret translated Yellow Mouse's response. "Who asks permission anymore? US soldiers come through dressed as French trappers. We've lost more than twenty men in skirmishes since spring."

"Well, that's Senator Auburn's doing," Clover answered. "He's trying to provoke you. This war is not real."

"They are shooting real bullets," Margaret interrupted. She prodded Clover's bags warily with the toe of her deerskin boot.

"But it's only a scheme to get him elected president," Clover explained. "It doesn't have to happen."

"What shall we do?" Margaret's earrings glinted in the lamplight. "Shall we lay down our weapons and let them raid through our crops and orchards?"

Yellow Mouse spoke next. "A long time ago," Margaret translated, "people came up to this world through a badger hole and were happy here. But there came a flood and then a famine and then the world caught fire. The wise ones took seeds and climbed up a tall tree, through a hole in the sky, into the world above. They are up there now, happy and fat. The rest of the people stayed behind while the tree burned. We are the children of those who stayed."

There was a silence, and then Margaret said, "He means we have no more trees to climb."

Clover felt like a leaf blown by a strong wind. How could she stop a war that the rest of the world insisted on?

"Did you come all this way to ask us not to fight in a war you started?" Margaret asked.

"No," Clover said. "I am headed to the abandoned mine at Harper's Ridge."

"To the witch's den," Yellow Mouse said in English. He rocked his great-grandson almost imperceptibly, as if feeling the gentle waves of a hidden ocean.

"You know about it?" Clover wondered if the Sehanna had spies in the US or if Smalt's secrets had flown here on their own. She decided it didn't matter.

"Auburn cannot create . . ." Yellow Mouse could not find the word he was looking for and continued in Sehanna with Margaret translating, ". . . he cannot create *accablant* soldiers, so he wants the next best thing. But now that the witch's location is no longer a secret, Auburn isn't the only one interested. It is not safe to go there."

"I know that."

"Dr. Elkin rode across battle lines to bring medicine during the pox. He risked his life to tend to our sick," Yellow Mouse said.

"I know." It kindled a warmth in Clover's belly to meet someone who knew who her father really was.

"He was stubborn and reckless," Yellow Mouse went on. "His medicine didn't work. But once he set on a path, there was no turning him off it."

Margaret broke in, "Even if this girl is not a spy, she will still tell what she's seen here."

Yellow Mouse turned his cloud-colored eyes skyward. "What have you seen here?"

"I've seen armaments as good as any we have," Clover answered, "and lots of them. I've seen Yellow Mouse alive and making plans, and I've seen more than just the four Sehanna tribes here. It looks like some plains Indians are here too, ready to fight under your banner."

Yellow Mouse laughed. "Let her tell them that!"

The chief and Margaret argued briefly in their own tongue, then she grabbed her rifle and left. Yellow Mouse sat in silence for a minute, squeezing his great-grandson's feet.

"I'm telling you, there will be trouble at the mine," Yellow Mouse said.

"I know that."

"If you come here again, you will be shot from a distance," he said.

"Yes, sir," Clover replied.

• . • . • . • . • . • . •

At last, Clover had a horse. It was a strong breed with short legs and an oatmeal-colored coat. It wasn't terribly fast, but it didn't flag even though Clover pushed it hard past the stake walls of the camp and down a wooded trail, hoping she was moving in the right direction. As the sun set, Clover heeled the little horse into a faster gallop. She'd lost too much time already.

Yellow Mouse had given her a cake of smoked pigeon, pumpkin, and cranberries wrapped in a corn husk. Clover had gobbled it as soon as she rode out of the camp, licking the grease from the husk shamelessly. It reminded her so much of something she might have eaten at home, she almost felt happy. For once the heavy bags were off her shoulders and her belly was full.

She cut across a shallow stream and emerged from the trees just as the sun notched itself into the slot made by the mountains, and the light cut through in great shafts of pink glory. Soon the foothills rose up around her. She shot out of the grasslands and charged through a narrow passage cut by floodwaters at the beginning of time. The cliffs were painted dream colors by the setting sun. She heeled the horse again, ignoring the chafing from the unfamiliar saddle and ignoring too the Indian riders who followed her at a distance.

The Sehanna tribes weren't much for horses, preferring their hidden networks of running trails or a swift canoe, but some of the plains warriors who had joined their ranks at the camp were practically centaurs, and Yellow Mouse had arranged the loan. Clover didn't know enough about plains tribes to identify them, but the horsemen who followed her wore buffalo-fur mantles and sweeping leather tassels that danced behind them as they rode. Clover wondered what would happen if more plains tribes migrated north to join the Sehanna. Would the Confederation crack under the strain of so many different cultures? Or would it become stronger with every new member?

Her thoughts were interrupted by an unsettling odor. She smelled the Wine Marsh miles before she saw it.

The cliffs fell away, revealing an uneven terrain dotted with stunted trees. Clover heard the horse's hooves squishing and looked down to see rivulets of dark mud. The riders behind her whistled, and she pulled the horse to a stop. She patted its cheek gratefully, then dismounted to remove her bags.

The riders whistled again, and the horse returned to them. Then they took a trail up into the hills. Clover waved her thanks, but the riders did not wave back.

Susanna muttered to herself contentedly in the haversack, but Clover could feel that Sweetwater was hungry. She let the serpent slide down into the stunted shrubbery to find prey.

With her eyes closed, Clover could almost smell the rodent

that trembled somewhere nearby, sense the warmth coming from a little hole in the ground. She didn't want to see what came next. She opened her eyes and forced herself to focus on what was before her: the vast, turgid wasteland called the Wine Marsh. The smell coated her nostrils, as if she'd stuck her nose in a jar of pickled fish.

She felt the Indian riders watching her from the hills, even if she couldn't see them. If they knew a safe route through the marsh, they had not told her.

The sun was long gone by the time Sweetwater returned, belly thick with some swallowed rodent. Clover looped the snake around her neck like a scarf and walked through a stand of sickly-looking trees. She knew better than to attempt a crossing in the dark. She found a pile of dry leaves under a leaning tree and curled up under her shawl.

Clover tried to guess at Hannibal's progress. Parts of Abbot's Highway were snow covered year-round, and Clover prayed that Hannibal was half-buried in a blue drift. Her shortcut through the prairie at the Sehanna border had saved her miles. If she could cross the marsh, she'd be nearly there. The marsh gave off an unnatural warmth that kept winter's chill at bay. Her belly was full. Sweetwater's belly was full. She used the bags as a pillow and was asleep before the moon rose. Clover slept strangely well.

· . · . · . · . · . ·

In the morning, Clover picked her way between fetid upwellings to stand on the edge of the purple sea. Her heart sank. Swarms of flies roiled overhead, droning like a warped cello. The bone-gray trunks of dead hawthorns reached skyward like the arms of drowning men.

Unkind vapors bubbled up: hot wine and rotten eggs. A wandering haze drifted over the surface of the wine. Clover was already dizzy, and she was only on the edge of the disaster.

How many had become disoriented here, walking in circles until they collapsed? And if the vapors weren't enough, there was the sinking mud and the thirst.

The carcasses of migratory birds punctuated the inky muck, ducks and geese that had made the mistake of landing. Their brittle bones crunched as Clover worked her way around the edge, looking for some sign of safe passage.

A legendary oddity, the Wineglass had touched the lips of kings and queens before being lost in the Louisiana War. No one really knew who dropped it. Now it lay overturned somewhere under all the muck, pouring more and more wine into the mud. Wine enough for all the world to celebrate.

When the drifting haze encompassed her, Clover held her nose, but the smallest breath made her so dizzy she knelt to keep from falling face-first into the muck. She couldn't go around. The marsh was too wide and the edges were so steep she'd surely fall in. She was thirsty already, and wished she'd asked Yellow Mouse for water.

But she'd stalled long enough. Every moment she spent looking for a better course, Hannibal was moving toward the mine.

Clover removed her boots and took a tentative step, sinking up to her shins.

As she tried to pick her way through the shallow areas, she saw odds and ends in the wine: combs, lanterns, rifles—all cast off by desperate wanderers trying to lighten their loads.

When she looked up again, Clover was already lost. The

mountains had shifted around her. The dead trees she'd been using as landmarks all looked the same. The marsh branched into inlets and fingers, and even the sun was hidden behind the haze.

Clover pushed on, trying not to think about the bodies beneath her, the half-preserved corpses of fallen soldiers. Knee-deep in bubbling contagion, she tried to sing a song but couldn't remember any words. Step after step, she pushed deeper.

Sitting on a slick log to catch her breath, Clover felt her father's ghost catch up with her.

"What an unholy mess," Constantine declared.

His voice was patient and steady, and Clover longed to go back to the simpler time when all she had to do was follow his orders. She looked at him. His jaw was shaded with stubble, and his coat was fraying at the shoulder seam. Clover had the irrational impulse to mend it.

"Well, it's our mess," Clover said. "This marsh is still bleeding from the last war. There's no avoiding the past. "

"A good doctor—"

Clover interrupted him. "How could you ask me to be tidy when you knew what I was?"

"Trouble breeds trouble," Constantine said.

"I *am* the trouble. It's *in me*." Clover felt the anger welling up. "What happened the night mother died?"

Constantine calmly shooed flies away from his face, the same infuriating cipher.

"You promised to teach me everything you knew. You didn't even tell me what I am."

"I gave you the tools to become a respectable doctor, to live a simple—"

"Was I born this way?" Clover cut him off. "Am I one of her experiments? Was she . . . pleased with what she'd made?"

"It is enough that you are my daughter."

"Are you so afraid of me?"

Constantine looked hurt, but he didn't answer.

"I can't change what happened to you," Clover said. "But if I figure out what happened to *us*, I might be able to change what happens next, for everyone. If you have answers, real answers, speak. I've had my fill of lectures."

Constantine looked at Clover as if he didn't recognize her. Clover knew she was filthy, trudging through this toppled world. Tidy was far behind her. Maybe she wasn't his daughter any longer.

"I fear *for* you," Constantine said at last. It was the simplest truth he'd ever given her.

Clover looked at the fetid expanse of wine, feeling the ghost shimmering beside her, nearly vapor. "I have to do what you couldn't. I have to face Mother."

She left her father behind her and trudged on through the muck.

MASTERPIECE OF CRUELTY

lover's toes pickled as flies braided past her head. She was so thirsty she caught herself considering a drink from the thick liquid. Susanna's muffled grumbles mingled with the faint whispers of the Hat.

Most of the marsh was deep enough to swim in, but Clover knew her bags would pull her under, so she sloshed through the shallows. If the muck hadn't been filling her footprints, Clover would have had proof that she was going in circles.

She panicked when she saw the sun already setting. But it wasn't the sun. It was a bright yellow patch on the edge of the marsh. Clover rushed toward it, fell face-first in the muck, and pulled herself up. She wasn't hallucinating. It was a wagon, a yellow wagon.

Bleakerman's

In the distance, Nessa Branagan was filling her tonic bottles with marsh wine.

"Nessa!" Clover called, but the sour air had curdled her voice, and she sounded like a crow. The vapors made the shore swim. It was hard to know how far away salvation was.

Clover made a desperate dash across a slimy mat of algae and found herself chest deep in the filth. She tried to pull herself out, but with every move she sank deeper. The flies settled on her lips and neck, impatient for a feast.

Sweetwater spiraled up her arm to safety, then darted away, a pale current on the surface.

Clover sank fast, lifting her chin to keep the wine out of her mouth. Sweetwater had gone too far, and Clover didn't know if she was going to throw up or faint. Susanna climbed out of the bag and tried to pull Clover by her braids, but there was no solid ground to pull from. The Doll sank deeper with every tug.

Clover tried screaming, but a splash of rancid liquid slipped into her mouth, and she choked and spluttered.

The haversack tugged her down, so she let it slip off her shoulder and sink. But the medical bag floated, its thick leather holding air. She rolled over it and managed to pull her upper body out of the muck. With Susanna tugging and Clover kicking, inch by inch, they managed to thrash onto a shallow bar of sludge.

My father's bag saved me, Clover thought.

When she finally reached half-solid ground, Clover picked up Sweetwater and stumbled toward the wagon, covered in inky mud.

Nessa knelt on the bank, bottles clinking. "She was stubborn," Nessa muttered to herself. "I told her that snake was deadly . . ."

"Charlatan," Clover croaked.

When Nessa saw Clover, she turned pale. "Don't haunt me! I found a doctor as fast as I could!"

"I'm too stubborn to die in a drunkards' inn." Clover

coughed. Despite herself, she was glad to see Nessa. "Water?"

"No one survives a Sweetwater bite." Nessa trembled as she handed over her canteen.

"I did," Clover said, and poured clean water into her mouth.

A splash of water revealed the snake hanging in loose loops around Clover's neck.

Nessa screamed as she ran. "Vengeful spirit! Show mercy!" In her panic she ran straight for the spot where Clover had almost drowned.

Clover sent Sweetwater to cut her off. It was only the sight of the viper skating across the water that stopped Nessa from tumbling into the sinking mud.

"Now, come here," Clover commanded, slumping exhausted against the wagon wheel. "Ghost or not, you owe me an apology."

For a moment Nessa was too rattled to speak. She stood gawking at Clover and her companions. Susanna scrubbed her muddy back against a tree, shaking leaves down around them. Her cotton was stained indigo, probably for good.

Clover felt the serpent return, twirling up her leg to hang like heavy rope over her shoulder. "Sweetwater is mine now," Clover said. "Or I am hers. In any case, she's not going back to your jar."

Nessa blinked. "But how did you . . . ? I mean, where did you go? I found a doctor, but you'd vanished. No one would tell us where you went. Those people were afraid of you." Nessa squinted. "They think you're a witch."

"Not a ghost. Not a witch. I don't know what I am." Clover sighed.

"I had a terrible time trying to get my wagon out of Brackenweed. That city went mad. I've never seen anything like it."

"Do you know a passage through this marsh?" Clover asked.

"On foot? Impossible."

"Can't cross with horses," Clover said. "They would sink faster than we would."

"There is one way to get across." Nessa shook her head. "But you won't like it."

"Nessa Branagan, I didn't ask for a birthday cake. If you know a way across this marsh, you best tell it."

"I would do anything to help you, Clover. I feel so sorry for how things went."

"Then show me how to cross."

They climbed into the wagon and rode along the shore in silence, Nessa casting glances at Clover from time to time.

"Where are you going?" Nessa asked.

"To the Seamstress. I'm going to stop this war if I can."

"Why do you care so much?"

"It's a war!"

"But you seem to take it personally."

"This mess just keeps getting bigger," Clover said. "I thought Father had hidden his secret in the bag, but it was hidden in me." She looked at the marsh. "It's also hidden out here. In New Manchester, in Louisiana, in the old mine. It is all around us."

Nessa said, "You're looking to uncover business buried long ago. But some things are buried for a reason."

"And you just accept the stories your uncle told you," Clover countered. "Some of us need more than opera lyrics."

If Nessa was hurt, she hid it by combing her hair. "Uncle was a storyteller, it's true," she said finally. "He painted the world in brighter colors. He wanted people to smile. So I smile when I can.

That's how I remember him. When you talk about your father . . ." Nessa shook her head.

"What? Say it."

Nessa squinted at her.

"I loved him!" Clover said.

Nessa shrugged. Then, as they passed through a curtain of brittle willow branches, she opened her mouth again. "It's OK to be angry at him, you know. Even though he's your pa. Even though he died."

"You have no right," Clover said. "No right to say that."

"Getting yourself killed won't bring him back."

Clover caught her breath as if she'd been slapped.

"I know you want to set things right," Nessa continued. "But some things just stay broken and we have to go on living with it."

"You," Clover bit each word off. "Don't. Know. What I'm *living* with."

"We both lost—"

"Your uncle died in an accident," Clover shouted. "A spooked horse! The men who killed my father were there because of me. They were looking for *me*!"

"How is that your fault?"

"My father hated oddities. He *abhorred* them. What did he think of me? You can't understand."

But Nessa was right. Clover was angry. She was angry at Nessa, angry at those murderers, and yes, angry at her father, who could have warned her, could have told her so much, could have saved her all this trouble if only he'd explained things, if only . . .

She was close to tears, but she tried to play it off by wiping the grime from her forehead.

"Your father lied too," Nessa said gently. "He lied to keep you safe."

Clover waited for the anger to flare—waited for the words to scream at Nessa—but instead she felt melted inside, tired and sad.

Suddenly Nessa was holding Clover. Irrepressible, appalling Nessa had taken the reins in her teeth and draped her heavy arms around Clover's, squeezing her tightly.

And with the hum of flies around them, the stiff remnants of a dead bison stinking nearby, Clover returned the hug, because she needed it. She had needed it for a very long time. Nessa had a way of accepting things just as they were. Her arms created a shelter that Clover hid inside for three breaths, four . . .

"You've got your wagon back," Clover said.

Nessa took up the reins again and gave her a smile. "They said Smalt was dead, so I reclaimed what was mine to begin with."

They came at last to a narrow inlet hidden by stunted trees. There, hanging from a thick branch, was a large brass bell.

"Are you sure you must cross?" Nessa asked.

Clover just nodded. Nessa leaped down to ring the bell three times.

"Don't tell me there is a ferryman," Clover said.

"Not exactly."

They waited, watching the mists dance over the wine, until a shadow emerged. It was a pontoon with a little shack atop, a shabby home built to skim over the wastes. A man with a long pole guided the pontoon toward the shore. He scratched himself, and rabbit ears flopped from his hat. Even at a distance, Clover recognized Willit Rummage.

The poacher banked his pontoon on the shore and yelled up at them, "Is it payday again already? Who is that with you?"

"I said you wouldn't like it," Nessa whispered to Clover. "Willit knows the marsh better than anyone. What do you want me to tell him?"

But Clover was already jumping off the wagon.

"Wait," Nessa said. "He's dangerous."

"So am I," Clover answered, running straight for the pontoon.

"Is that Clover under all that mud?" Willit said, his eyes bugging. "Glory, I thought we'd lost her! Nessa, you have outdone yourself, girl! Shouldn't we tie her up, though?"

When she reached the wine's edge, Clover sent Sweetwater across the shallows straight onto the pontoon.

Willit danced in fear as Sweetwater coiled around his ankle, fangs exposed. "What the blazes?" he shouted, reaching for his Pistol.

"Can you pull a trigger faster than a viper can strike?" Clover called out.

Willit froze where he stood, and Clover tossed Susanna onto the pontoon behind him. Before he could see what was happening, Susanna yanked his feet out from under him. Then, with one swift snap, the Doll smacked him onto the planks like a dirty rug. The Pistol clattered out of his hand. Clover leaped onto the planks and snatched it up.

"That's enough, Susanna; don't kill him."

"A swell idea," Willit groaned. "Don't kill me." His nose was bloody.

Susanna grumbled but let him go.

Nessa stood gawking on the bank.

Clover yelled out, "If you want to help, come steer this pontoon."

After watering and setting her horses loose so they wouldn't drink marsh wine, Nessa guided the pontoon out onto the purple lake. Willit sat with his back against the wall of the shack, guarded by Sweetwater. Clover peered inside the shack. It was a lonesome kind of filthy, with piles of newspapers and empty liquor bottles. Beside a stained straw mattress was a collection of Society journals. She could imagine Willit reading the lists of oddities, sleepless with greed, and wondering, as she had, which were real.

"Didn't know I was receiving such dignified guests," Willit mumbled, cupping his tender nose. "Or I would have cleaned up."

"So when you aren't murdering innocent men, you live here alone?" Clover asked.

"No place safer! No lawman has so much as tried to find me here. Sometimes Bolete stays with me. He's a better cook than I am. I believe my nose is broken," he groused.

"You deserve worse. Where is Bolete now?" Clover asked.

"Gone to town for bacon and coffee, but he'll come looking for me."

Clover examined the Pistol.

"You don't want to mess with that, kid," Willit said.

"I don't want to do any of the things I've been forced to do since I met you," Clover said, putting the Pistol in her father's bag. "I don't want to be in this stinking marsh and I don't want to travel with a devil like you, but I have to."

"Travel with me? You mean you ain't going to kill me?" Willit asked.

"You're going to guide us across the marsh to the abandoned silver mine."

"Is that right?" Willit sat up straighter. "Well, that's what you'd call a partnership."

"It's not."

"It sounds like one to me. Do you mind if I light my pipe?" Willit produced a box of Matches and started to remove one, but Sweetwater hissed and exposed her fangs near his ear. A droplet of venom fell onto his shoulder. The wool there sizzled like frying oil.

"Sweetwater will bite before you can get that Match lit."

"Well, of course," Willit said. "You've seen that trick . . ."

Clover took the box and examined it. Only seven Matchsticks remained.

"What other oddities do you have?" she asked.

Willit shrugged. "I guess you've got them all. The tables have turned. You're a regular poacher now, ain't you?"

"Pull legs off?" Susanna asked.

"Not yet," Clover said. "I have questions. What kind of curse did the witch put on you, Willit?"

"Want to see it?" Willit asked.

"See the curse?"

"You got to lean close." Willit pulled his collar wide, as if the curse were on his neck.

Clover hesitated, then leaned in and peered at his grimy neck, welted and scabbed from his endless scratching.

"Do you see it?" Willit asked.

At first it looked like a grain of crushed pepper. But it jumped from his neck to his earlobe, then onto his arm.

"That's a flea," Clover said.

Willit scratched and smacked at it, but it was faster than he was, and everywhere it landed, it bit him.

"This Flea is the nastiest vermin the Seamstress ever stitched. It's her masterpiece of cruelty."

Suddenly the Flea leaped onto Clover's arm, and she gasped. Its body was made from an onion seed, its delicate legs from the smallest watch springs. Its mandibles were steel filings, and it was all held together with a single stitch of blue Thread. It was a miracle of rage and craftsmanship, a testament to the witch's hatred. The Flea leaped back onto Willit and crawled under his shirt as he scratched after it.

For a moment, Clover almost felt sorry for Willit. Then she said, "You deserve a hundred more."

They were far from shore now, rolling on a lake of wine, and the vapors hung thick around them. Occasionally, Willit grumbled directions to Nessa—"Go left when you see the bubbles foaming up, and keep left!"—and Nessa pushed the pole deep into the muck to steer the pontoon.

Clover glanced at the distant slopes, hoping Hannibal had not reached the mine. She turned to Willit, who looked as beaten and harmless as a churchyard tramp. "Why did you sew rabbit ears to your hat?"

"Oh, he'll never tell you that," Nessa said.

"I was once in love with a woman who kept a pet rabbit," Willit announced.

Nessa stared at the poacher, shocked. "Well, don't believe what he says, anyhow."

"Don't tell me you're a romantic," Clover said.

"Why not? A man has a heart, doesn't he?" Willit said

wistfully. "But when I confessed my feelings to my beloved, she threw me out a window. I keep these ears to remind myself that behind every tender smile there are teeth waiting to bite."

Clover shook her head, the vapors making her dizzy. She didn't want to hear any more, but there were answers here, if only she could find them. She kicked Willit in the knee. "Were you there the night of the fire? Why did the Seamstress set the curse on you?"

"That much is my personal history, and a secret besides," Willit said.

Clover nodded at Susanna, and the Doll grabbed him by the shin, preparing to break his leg.

Willit yelped and looked at Clover pleadingly. "I don't think you're the violent kind, kid!"

She wanted to throw Willit into the drowning mud, but he was right. She wasn't going to let Susanna rip him apart.

Still, she was tired of his games. She pulled out Smalt's terrible Hat and held it between them, her hands shaking with rage. "Are you really going to make me use this, Mr. Willit?"

"Isn't that what you come here to do? Why, you already look like a witch, covered with mud and carrying your little goblins." He tried to shake Susanna off his leg, but she held fast to his ankle.

"This is your last chance," Clover warned. "I don't want to use the Hat, but I will . . ."

Willit said, "I could tell you the truth as pure as the angels saw it, but you wouldn't believe a word that came out of my mouth. Because I am a liar. But no one can lie to the Hat." Willit laughed, tickled to see her squirm. "You've got all the power now. I'm just a cursed man, caught up in your story."

Clover knew Willit was trying to rattle her, to keep her off balance so he could get the upper hand. But the poacher also knew things she didn't, and Clover needed to find the threads of truth in his words. "My story?"

Willit smiled. "Of course it's your story. The Pistol, the Matches—well, I was just holding them for you, wasn't I? And now you've come to claim them."

"Don't listen to him," Nessa warned. "He can talk a bird into a cat's mouth."

"Oh, but Clover understands me, don't you, girl? Nessa was happy to take orders, but you are no one's fool. You know now how the game is played. You know that sometimes you have to take control—"

"Enough," Clover said.

"—so you can get things done."

"I said *enough*!"

Sweetwater rattled, and Willit raised his hands in surrender. Then he removed his hat and scratched furiously. "Whatever you say, little witch."

She gripped the Hat, trembling with indecision. *I can use the Hat just this once, then never again*, she thought. But Clover remembered the tortured man in the Golden Cannon Inn, trying to eat his shirt. The Hat would tempt her again and again. She remembered her father's words: "A person may think she is collecting oddities, but in fact the oddities are collecting her."

She stuffed the Hat back into the bag. "I am not Smalt."

Willit seemed disappointed. He blew a bloody wad into his handkerchief and continued scratching after the Flea.

The middle of the marsh was too deep for the pole, but the sun-warmed wine carried the pontoon on a dark current. They floated in silence for several minutes, and Clover tried not to panic; she was far from solid ground on a flimsy pontoon with a murderer.

Nessa guided the craft through a cluster of dead trees, pushing against the bleached trunks with strong arms. Her upper arm was scarred where Willit's bullet had branded her, a pale coil on the freckled skin. Clover wondered if she could really trust her.

Nessa pointed to a tassel of dust rising from the distant mountains. "There's riders on Abbot's Highway," she said. "A bunch of them."

"That's Hannibal's platoon," Clover said.

"Coming from Louisiana?"

Clover looked again, and it was true: the party was coming from the west. Louisiana. Smalt's secrets had flown quickly, and Hannibal wasn't the only one racing for the Seamstress.

"Can't you go faster?"

Nessa stuck the pole deep into the mud and managed to give the pontoon a little more speed.

At last, they saw the far side of the marsh, a steep cliff of ashy boulders that plunged right into the wine.

"So you work for Clover now?" Willit asked Nessa.

"I don't work for you no more," Nessa answered.

"You're quitting a solid business arrangement?"

"Wasn't ever solid for me," Nessa said. "You got all the money!"

"Don't be so quick to change teams, kid. We're headed into the lair of the beast, where we'll likely get skinned by the Seamstress, but not Clover here. She's got a special connection to the witch, don't you?"

"Stop it," Clover said.

"Something drawing you toward the vermin-makin' she-demon—"

"Shut your mouth!"

"What is he talking about?" Nessa's cheeks were flushed.

"Oh, hasn't she told you?" Willit spat blood. "I guess Clover and I share a secret, don't we? And that's a special bond, ain't it? We're practically family! It's the ones we're closest to, hurt us the most."

"Clover?" Nessa's eyes were wide.

Clover looked up at the cliffs. "After we cross the marsh, you can go back to your wagon. I'm headed for danger."

"Don't I know that? I've lost a tooth to this witch, remember? It's her pet that killed my uncle."

"When we get to shore you can take the pontoon back."

Nessa shook her head. "Every time I let you out of my sight, you get walloped."

"I don't know how this will end. I have to face it, but this isn't your problem."

"It is now," Nessa said, and amazingly, she was smiling. "Whatever business you've got, fate keeps crossing our paths. We're meant to stick together."

"The lovebirds twitter and prattle," Willit said.

The pontoon stopped abruptly on shallow shoals, and a silence came over them as they peered up at the walls of the unforgiving mountain. The mines were hidden in the cloud-covered peaks above them, and peering up the slopes made Clover dizzy.

Willit laughed. "This is your shortcut? I don't think even a goat could make its way up those slopes. You can't get to the mines from here."

Then Susanna piped up. "Follow me."

She led them up a winding path between piles of rubble and sheer rock faces. Clover considered leaving Willit on his pontoon but was afraid to turn her back on the man, figuring he'd sneak up and try to reclaim his Pistol. So she slung Sweetwater around his neck to keep him in line.

They followed Susanna on a trail that was so narrow they had to turn sideways to squeeze through shoulders of cold granite. The only things that survived here were crusts of lichen and blue-bearded lizards. Clover tried not to think about avalanches, but it was clear from the heaps of rockfall that the terrain was unstable, as if the mining had broken something deep inside the mountain.

Suddenly, the mountain was trembling. About a hundred yards away, a slope shifted, then came crashing down. It sounded as if the earth itself were growling as tons of rock dropped into the Wine Marsh, sending a wave of dark fluid rushing across the surface.

Through the dust and mist, they saw what had touched off the avalanche: the jittery movement of creatures scrambling over the rock, wounded but agile.

Willit shook his head. "Vermin. This mountain is infested with them. They're watching."

"Do you think they will come for us?" Nessa asked.

"They'll be on us like dogs on a sausage," Willit said.

Clover gripped her father's bag closer to her body, watching the shadows shifting on the hillside. Through clenched teeth she said, "Keep moving."

Susanna, who had been riding on Clover's shoulder, crawled into her pocket and pulled her head in. "Ain't afraid," she whispered.

"That's all right," Clover said. "You're being very brave."

Willit coughed. At last they emerged onto a plateau, where leaning pines shed their needles in the wind.

"We'll take a short rest," Clover announced, her legs wobbling from the climb.

They sat in a sullen circle, and Willit coughed again. Clover knew the sounds of illness, and this was malingering. Willit was up to something. The next time he did it, she watched closely and saw that he was whispering into his walnut shell necklace.

Sweetwater's rattle cut the air as Clover snatched the walnut off his chest.

"Is it an oddity?" Clover demanded. "Who are you talking to?"

Willit shrugged.

"Do you want Susanna to break your nose again?"

"No need for all that," Willit said. "I just remembered that I do have another little something in my pocket. I'll show it to you."

"Do it slowly," Clover ordered.

With dramatic care, Willit reached into his breast pocket and pulled out a single Match. "I always keep one handy for myself, just in case."

Before Clover could reach it, he struck the Match with his thumbnail and disappeared in a blink. Sweetwater fell to the ground with a thump that knocked the wind out of Clover.

Willit reappeared yards away, beside a gnarled pine.

Bolete, who had been hiding in the branches, tossed Willit a shotgun and leaped down to stand beside him. Clover remembered that Bolete had the other half of the Walnut. They'd been using it to arrange an ambush. In the brush behind them, Clover spotted the foam-flecked horse Bolete had spurred all the way up the mountain, lying panting on the ground.

The poachers started shooting immediately. Their bullets ricocheted off the cliff side, and Clover dove for cover in a spray of shattered rock.

"You should see your faces!" Willit laughed between shots.

Clover found herself crammed next to Nessa in a hollow no bigger than a closet. Sweetwater, bruised from her fall, came slithering in as the poachers reloaded.

Susanna leaped from Clover's pocket, climbed over a boulder, and charged madly toward Willit.

The Doll was only a few feet from him, her fists balled for wrecking, when he fired. The blast sent Susanna flying. She hit the wall behind Clover, smoldering and in tatters. The Doll lay still.

Clover screamed, "Susanna!"

"Use the Pistol!" Nessa yelled.

Clover pulled it out and cocked the hammer. She was thinking of a course for the bullet when she heard Bolete's voice coming through the Walnut shell in her pocket. "Just give up, girly," he said. "You forgot to take the bullets. Pistol isn't much good without 'em."

Then Willit's voice came through. "Now is a better time to choose teams, young Nessa."

Panicked, Clover looked and saw that it was true—the Pistol's chamber was empty. The bullets she had stolen earlier had sunk to the bottom of the Wine Marsh in her haversack. The oddity was useless.

Willit hollered, "Nessa, you like that mountain girl enough to die for her?"

Nessa put on a brave face and hollered back, "I have seen the error of my ways!"

There was a confused silence, and through the Walnut, they heard the poachers muttering, "Does that mean she's with us or against?"

"I'm with *her*!" Nessa shouted.

"Unwise," Willit hollered back. "I need the Elkin girl alive, but it don't bother me to shoot you dead."

Nessa moaned and knocked her forehead into the rock in terror.

"Come on now, little witch," Willit said. "Do more people have to die? Don't you have enough on your conscience?"

Clover trembled, clutching Nessa's hand and shouting, "I didn't kill anyone! You did!"

"I wasn't looking for your father," Willit said. "You know that now, don't you? He'd be alive today if only you'd played nice."

Clover shook her head, trying to keep his words from her ears. She searched desperately for something useful, but all she saw was rocky ruin.

"We'll give you the count of three to surrender before we come blastin'," Bolete said. "I'll wager that snake ain't immune to bullets."

"One," Willit shouted.

Susanna had managed to get to her feet but wobbled where she stood. The Doll looked as if she'd crawled through a meat grinder, one eyed and leaning, wool poking through ragged tears. Clover opened her father's bag, and Susanna crawled miserably inside.

"Two!" Bolete hollered.

"They're going to kill us." Nessa's eyes were wild with fear until she looked at Clover's face. Then her features softened, and she smiled. "This would make a tolerable opera. Tragic beauty!"

"The next one is 'three,'" Willit warned. "Here we come, children."

As the bandits approached, Clover remembered the Matches. She dug in her pocket for the box and managed to pull out a Match-stick just as Willit and Bolete came charging around the corner, their guns raised. Bolete's first shot blasted the cliff behind them, and Clover felt the sting of the dust hitting her face as she struck the Match on a rock, ready to disappear. But she did not disappear.

Everything stopped.

Willit and Bolete had frozen mid-run like statues. The air was frighteningly cold. Nothing moved—not Susanna, not Nessa. Bolete leaned on one foot at an impossible angle. Even the bits of shattered rock hung in the air as if trapped in ice. Only the Match continued to burn, the flame consuming the pine stick bit by bit.

Clover now understood how the oddity worked. The Matches didn't send the user anywhere; they simply gave her time to move. She let out a frightened laugh. It was what she thought the watch might have done. Time stopped, if only for a few moments. Time enough for hope.

But Clover didn't know where to go. The fire crept closer to her fingers; her opportunity was almost lost. She rushed toward the poachers and, having no other plan, grabbed hold of the shotgun barrels. The next shots would kill Nessa and Sweetwater if she didn't do something. She pulled down as hard as she could, but the guns didn't budge. They were as immobile as the rest of the world, fused in place like a badly healed joint.

The Match fell from her hand and sputtered on the ground, the last of its flame dying. Clover pulled with all her strength, and as the fire went out, reality rolled back into motion. The ends of the gun barrels dropped under her weight, and Willit's shotgun blew a hole in the dirt at her feet. With the Match gone out, the gun barrels were suddenly searing hot and lit Clover's palms with pain.

"Nessa!" Clover screamed as she wrestled with the poachers. Her palms felt like pancakes on a griddle, but she forced herself to hold on to the gun barrels. The rock dust was in her eyes, and she didn't see Bolete's fist coming. It landed in her ribs, knocking the wind out of her. She fell to her knees, gasping. Bolete yanked his gun back and aimed it at her head.

Then Bolete fell to her right and Willit collapsed to her left.

Willit was bleeding from the head but still breathing. Nessa stood over him, holding the rock she had brained him with.

Bolete was a heap. Sweetwater had bitten him twice. His arm twitched once. He was dead.

The mountainside was very quiet except for the groans coming from Willit Rummage, the murderer.

THE BULLET OR THE FANGS

C lover fished through Willit's pockets, looking for more secrets.

The poacher was in no state to resist. "I thought you weren't the violent kind," he moaned. Even in agony, he still scratched after the merciless Flea. Clover found the purse of bullets and stuffed it into her own pocket. The only other things she found were a lint-covered piece of dried cheese and the bloody handkerchief Willit had wiped his nose with. Clover felt strangely numb as she threw them both over the edge of the mountainside along with his belt and boots.

The words "violent kind" rattled in her head. Bolete's body was hard to look at. Clover's eyes swam with tears, but she couldn't be crying for that brute, could she? She was not herself. *But,* she thought, *what safety is there in being myself?*

Willit held his rabbit-ear hat in his lap and winced as he touched the injury on his head. Blood had crusted a few strands of remaining hair on the back of his pale scalp. Clover watched his eyes for signs of internal bleeding.

"The skull is not broken," she said. She opened the medical bag to find a bandage, falling back on old habits, and her hand touched the Hat.

Clover shoved the Hat on her head to get it out of the way.

It fit perfectly. Clover felt secrets stirring inside, like cobwebs swarming with hundreds of baby spiders. But she was beyond caring, her vision blurred, her palms throbbing, and the stench of gunpowder stinging in her nose. The whispering spiders trickled into her ears, and she learned about Willit's other crimes:

. . . Robbed a church . . . Bludgeoned a deputy with a horseshoe . . .

Clover set the bag down and turned to the poacher. All this time she'd been disgusted by the Hat, but after all, it was only trying to tell her the truth. She could not go back and save her parents, but she could keep this wolf from killing again. The truth was messy, but then, she'd never mastered "tidy."

. . . Kidnapped an actress . . . Burned a silo to raise the price of corn . . .

She pulled out the Pistol, loaded a bullet into the chamber, then aimed for the rabbit ears. She pulled the trigger and watched as the bullet obeyed, fur snowing onto the poacher's lap even as the shot's echo rattled off the hillsides. The fear on Willit's face was the best thing Clover had seen in a long time.

. . . Put a scorpion under the pillow . . . Robbed the mausoleum . . .

Were they all Willit's crimes or did these secrets belong to others as well? Clover decided it didn't really matter. "Drastic symptoms demand drastic measures," she said. "Shall I pass a bullet through the valves of your heart like a clot of blood? Or lodge one deep in your brain, one last stupid thought?"

"Clover, don't," Nessa whispered.

"Or I could take my time, start with the muscles of your right hand. I know how a body is built." Clover smiled. "So I know how to take it apart. If I removed the rotten parts of Willit Rummage, what would be left?"

. . . Fed a cow hemlock . . .

Clover saw now that the Hat was nothing to be afraid of. Smalt had been weak, vain, and greedy. But Clover wasn't going to profit from secrets; she was only going to do what needed to be done.

She opened the Pistol chamber and blew the smoke out of the barrel. Willit rolled and lurched to his feet. He limped a few steps before tumbling down a slope and landing with a yelp in a heap of stones ten feet below.

"You're not a killer," Nessa said.

"I killed Smalt," Clover said.

"That Hat killed him—several times over."

"Clover killed Bolete," Clover said. It felt good to speak in simple truths.

"The snake did that."

"And good riddance to them both."

Clover leaned to watch Willit scampering like a cockroach behind a lichen-crusted outcropping.

"You of all people know that you can't hide from the Pistol!" Clover shouted at him, and her laughter echoed with the cobbles that he stumbled over.

All the while, the Hat whispered like a chorus, faithfully guiding her toward this just act. She tasted something in the back of her throat, salty, sour, and enormously satisfying. It was the vinegar tang of brutal truths. Clover savored it as she sent

Sweetwater down the ravine at a leisurely pace.

"Which will find you first, Mr. Willit? The bullet or the fangs?"

Nessa grabbed Clover's shoulder. "You don't need to—"

"Now I know what felt so . . . *wrong*," Clover said, reveling in the clarity the Hat offered. "I wasn't *meant* to be a doctor. Father's tools never felt right in my hands. But this"—she examined the Pistol—"holds itself steady."

Just as Clover was reaching for a new bullet, Nessa snatched the purse from her and ran.

Clover shook her head. "I've played both sides of this game." She lit a Match, and Nessa froze, everything froze. Just as the universe stopped around her, a wave of nausea hit Clover like a punch to the gut; Sweetwater was too far away. Clover's vision blurred, but she clenched her teeth, blinking until she could see clearly again. The snake would return when it was finished, and Clover had her own work to do. She grimly hummed the tune of Nessa's opera, letting the Match burn her fingers as she walked to stand in front of the charlatan. When the flame surrendered to its thread of smoke, Nessa slammed into Clover and fell into the dirt.

"You've been a thorn in Clover's side, Ms. Branagan," Clover said, grabbing the bullets and loading the pistol. "You betrayed Clover. Sold Clover. Left Clover to die."

The Hat confirmed everything she said. While everyone else lied or hid the truth, the Hat offered solutions to every riddle, cast light into every shadow. Old debts were aching to be settled. "You worked for the poachers who robbed your uncle. You stole my heirloom silver," Clover said, listing Nessa's crimes, speaking out loud the truths the Hat whispered.

"What?" Nessa sputtered. "I never—"

"Poisoned my dog—you were jealous. Your hounds could never tree a fox as well as mine."

"What are you saying? This isn't you."

"Your gossip ruined my promotion. I would have been lieutenant of this ship," Clover said, seeing in Nessa everything that had soured the world.

"Clover, wake up." Nessa got to her feet. "You've got every right to kill Willit. But what you do right now will sit heavy on you for the rest of your days. *You'll* have to carry it, not him."

"I was carrying it," Clover said with wonder. "I thought it was all my fault somehow. But now I know better. Clover was not the problem, but Clover will be the solution."

"He deserves what's coming to him," Nessa pressed. "But you deserve better. He's got nothing left. You can leave him to his misery."

Clover pointed the Pistol toward the ravine. "Clover's first shot belongs to the poacher," she said. "You can have the second."

Nessa's punch landed on Clover's upper lip with a wet *plop*. Pain bloomed like a sunflower in Clover's skull. Tears rolled down her cheeks as blood slicked her teeth. The Hat fell in the dirt next to the dropped Pistol, but Clover was still standing. She lowered her head, baring crimson teeth, and lunged at Nessa. Nessa set her feet firmly and caught Clover's enraged rush, wrapping her in a fierce hug. Nessa held on as Clover twisted like a caught fish, her screams crumbling into whimpers. And then, all at once, the Hat's fevered clarity was gone. Fear, guilt, and confusion settled into Clover's gut again. With them came relief. She'd been pulled back from the cliff's edge.

Feeling Clover's body go slack, Nessa loosened her wrestler's grip just enough to examine her friend's face.

"Are you . . . *you?*"

Clover nodded, shame hot on her cheeks. Dizziness overwhelmed her and she sat on the ground, feeling very ill. They both looked at the Hat.

"I never thought I'd pity Smalt," Clover said shakily.

"You have to get rid of that thing."

"I will when I find a safe way to destroy it." Clover shoved the Hat into her bag, hearing the sour whispers protesting. "But it wasn't just the Hat."

"What do you mean?"

"I mean it fits me a little too well." She licked her swollen lip. "Thank you, Nessa."

"For the hug or the punch?"

They heard Willit scream in terror, and Clover gasped. "Sweetwater!" She felt the snake close to her prey, darting like an arrow toward the warm target, the cowering body. Clover closed her eyes and willed the snake away. It took all of her strength, like pulling a bull by the tail. Clover could feel the animal's fear. The poor beast was as miserable as Clover but didn't understand the reason. The snake surged closer to Willit, longing to lash out at the closest threat. But she finally felt Clover's call and relented. Soon enough Sweetwater returned, flowing over the gravel like molten bronze. Clover would not have Willit's death on her head today.

She hugged Nessa again, trembling. Clover sobbed once and buried her face in her friend's shoulder. Beneath the grime and marsh wine, Nessa smelled like wet hay.

"We both need a bath," Clover said.

"Ah . . . Clover?" Nessa whispered.

Clover pulled back and saw that Sweetwater had wrapped herself tightly around Nessa's neck, tucking her head cozily under her jaw.

"Oh, sorry," Clover said, coaxing the viper back onto her own person.

Nessa called into the ravine, "You just rot down there! Between the cold nights and the vermin, I guess you've got slim chances. We'll check in on you on our way back."

"You're going to the witch," Willit hollered. "You ain't coming back."

Clover and Nessa started toward the mines.

"It ain't right to leave an injured man alone on a mountaintop," Willit called after them. "Bootless!"

"Nothing about you is 'right,'" Nessa called back.

Clouds enveloped them as they crossed a plateau of grass and obsidian. Clover examined Susanna in the uncertain light. The Doll was in bad shape. The shots had shredded her belly, and she was loose, almost lifeless. Clover knew Susanna didn't feel pain, but there wasn't much holding the Doll together anymore. Soon she'd be nothing but a nest of wool and wine-stained cotton.

Clover set Susanna on her shoulder. Her voice cracked as she said, "I am sorry, Miss Susanna. As soon as we get off this mountain, I'll find good cotton and put you back together. Good as new."

"Not getting off this mountain," Susanna whispered.

"Why would she go and say something awful like that?" Nessa groaned.

"You did your part," Clover said to Nessa. "You can go home." For a long time there was no sound but the slip and crunch of their feet on the black, glassy gravel.

"You said I might write my own opera someday," Nessa said, looking straight ahead. "Well, in my opera, I'm going to keep knocking poachers in the head with rocks until you're home safe."

"Then it looks like you're going to meet the witch with us," Clover said.

They crossed a bleached field dotted with huge corroded mining pans holding green puddles. A massive stamp mill loomed nearby, the hammers that crushed the ore now mottled with rust. Even now the remnants of the copper and mercury used to extract the silver smelled like stale blood.

They heard a skitter of rocks and the hoarse whispers of vermin nearby. Susanna shuddered; her remaining eye wobbled. She pointed toward a clump of soot-colored bushes. "That way," she said. "To the bridge."

Beyond a copse of larch trees dripping mist from their bare branches, they discovered the abandoned mining town of Harper's Hope. Clouds moved like ghosts between the brick ruins. An echoing warehouse was surrounded by smaller structures: a bakery, a post office, a barracks, and more. The wooden roofs had rotted away years earlier, leaving them open to the sky.

Abbot's Highway, an ambitious road cobbled by stones brought up from the mine, was wide enough for the twelve-mule wagons that had once carried the precious silver down the mountain. The road cut away from the town in both directions, one toward the US, one toward Louisiana. But there was no sign of soldiers. It felt as though nothing living had passed this way in a long time.

Susanna pointed toward the edge of the town where the fog was thick. Brambles were woven between the fallen walls, and with every step, the click and scurry of hidden vermin got louder.

Susanna was too weak to climb down into the medical bag, so Clover tucked the Doll in. "Ain't scared," Susanna croaked.

The town ended abruptly at the edge of an enormous canyon. The chain-and-slat bridge had once been strong enough for carts of ore, but mist had rusted the links, and many of the planks were long gone. It hung like a toothless smile across what seemed to be a bottomless gorge. Here the wind whipped the clouds into a stampede whose whorls hid the distant reaches of the canyon.

On the other side of the bridge, a hole in the cliff wall looked like the entrance to the land of the dead.

"Missus waiting," Susanna said.

"What, in that hole? I don't think we should go in there." Nessa's voice wavered

"I'm not asking you to," Clover answered, testing the bridge with her foot.

"We could just go home," Nessa said.

"If I have any family left, it's in there. The Seamstress is my mother." It was a relief to say it aloud.

"Oh, Clover." Nessa groaned. "It's no wonder trouble follows you."

Clover put all her weight on the first plank she could reach. It creaked but held.

Then they heard the trumpet of approaching riders. The mountainside distorted the echoes, but Clover guessed they were only a few miles away. The clarion was followed by the crack of a gunshot rattling through the canyon.

Time was running out. Clover leaped to the next plank, grasping at the support chains.

"What if we moved to Italy?" Nessa called from the safety of solid ground behind her.

When she got no response, Nessa sighed and followed, grumbling.

They had made it halfway across the bridge when something monstrous rose from the mists below. At first Clover thought it was a giant spider. But it was a vermin as big as a bear. It scrambled up the opposite canyon wall on six legs, several hides bound together: bison, cougar, wolf. It leaped onto the bridge and roared like a steam engine rumbling to life. In its cavernous mouth, rows of teeth doubled where the pelts overlapped. The sharpened farm equipment that composed its skeleton shrieked and rattled.

With another roar it gave the bridge a violent shake, and Clover's feet slipped between the slats. Nessa caught her elbow, and Clover yelped, her feet dangling above the void. As Nessa pulled her up, Susanna clambered out of the bag and took a few shaky steps toward the beast.

"Susanna, wait!" Clover yelled.

"Ain't scared." The Doll's voice was very faint, but she picked up speed as she headed across the bridge, sometimes leaping over the gaps, sometimes teetering across the chains.

The sentinel vermin saw her coming and lunged to meet her, opening its nightmare maw.

They slammed into each other with a crash that sent the bridge swaying.

The beast bellowed, slashing at Susanna with steel claws. Susanna returned the blows, knocking bits of junk off the beast

with every punch. Clover and Nessa could do nothing but hang on as the battle swung the bridge.

Then the vermin swallowed Susanna whole. It closed its mouth like an oven and shook its mane of pelts. It lifted its patchwork head and filled the sky with an earsplitting victory howl.

"Susanna!" Clover screamed, rushing forward, but Nessa pulled her back.

The giant vermin shuddered, wagging its miserable head.

Then it burst open.

Susanna was wrenching it apart from the inside. Its limbs scrambled as she kicked and tore, tangled in the wreckage of its gutworks. The bridge shifted, and the beast's heavy machinery slid off the planks. As it went over, Susanna reached for a chain but missed her grip and went down with it.

Clover watched the speck of the Doll's body tumbling in the debris before disappearing into the depths below.

"No!" Clover wailed as Nessa held her. "Susanna, please!" The mists had swallowed them completely. "I need you!" Clover cried.

Nessa tugged her toward the mines. "We have to move! It isn't safe."

The trumpet cascaded off the cliff walls. It was answered by drums. The war-makers were converging.

Clover made one last precarious leap off the bridge onto solid rock. She knelt and peered into the gorge. The mists churned, but there was no sign of Susanna or the vermin.

"We can't just leave her."

"She's gone," Nessa said. "I'm sorry, Clover."

"But if she's alive . . ." Clover trailed off as she reached into the medical bag and removed the tourniquet from its leather pouch. She dropped the pouch over the edge, hoping it was big enough for Susanna. "She'll need something to rest in."

Clover stood on trembling legs. She turned toward the cave and forced herself to take a step, wiping tears from her cheeks with the palms of her hands.

The sun sent a thin wafer of light only a few feet into the tunnel. Beyond that, the darkness was thick. The mildew smells of the earth rose out of the old mine.

The whale oil lamp she found in the medical bag was battered and damp. It took the flint a long time to convince the wick, but it finally cast its beam into the rugged tunnel. Clover carried her father's light into the darkness.

CHAPTER 21

A KIND OF BRAVERY

The miners had carved the main tunnel at a steep descent, with side shafts branching off every fifty yards. Many of these intersections had collapsed, giving the mine a reputation as a widow-maker before it was abandoned altogether. Even the main tunnel had piles of rock that Clover and Nessa had to climb over.

The lamp revealed shimmering streaks in the walls, and they knew they were looking at veins of raw silver. There were still riches in the unstable walls, as if left there to tempt the foolish. And now the witch's vermin had given the entire mountainside a reputation for being haunted; it was no wonder the place was desolate.

The tunnel veered down, making a spiral into the mountain's belly. With every step, Clover's lungs tightened. The darkness felt thick enough to stain her bones. Perhaps her mind was finally cracking under the strain, for she felt that this hole in the earth was part of her, that she was being pulled into the unknowable gravity of her own soul.

"Don't think of avalanches . . . or witches . . . or vermin," Nessa whispered.

The smell of rotten meat overtook the mildew. Rasping voices in the darkness made them stop in their tracks. As if emboldened by the smell, the vermin began to whisper in the darkness.

"I told you. This is the frog."

"Careful, it has friends."

"The Seamstress will not like it to blunder in. Let's chew its ankles and drag it the rest of the way."

"Yes, yes."

Judging by the voices, there were at least half a dozen vermin, their shadows gathering to pounce.

"Tooth!" Nessa shouted, throwing a glint of white into the darkness.

The vermin scrambled after it.

"I saw it first!"

"Mine!"

"Where is it?"

Clover and Nessa hurried deeper into the mine.

"You carry teeth with you?" Clover whispered.

Nessa held up a small pouch. "They remind me of Uncle."

When they heard the vermin scuttling back toward them, Nessa threw another tooth deep into a side shaft, and the vermin disappeared again, chasing after the distant click. The girls pressed on, moving faster.

Nessa rambled nervously. "After Uncle died, I thought I'd never enjoy music again. I was angry at the birds for singing. But then one morning after a storm, I heard them. They were wet and tired as I was, but they sang like they were bringing the sun up note by note. And I saw that it was a kind of bravery. To keep singing."

"Sing now, Nessa," Clover begged.

So Nessa sang an aria she had heard on the steps of the opera house. Her voice, sweet as malt syrup, filled the cavern. Neither of them understood the words, but the echoes resonated like a chorus, giving them courage.

Then Clover's light was swallowed up by a tremendous cavern. She lifted the lamp, but the room was so big she couldn't see the ceiling. "These are the chambers that Susanna dug," Clover whispered. It was as big as a barn and filled with heaps of junk.

Clover took a closer look at the pile and saw a collection of butter churns and brooms, rolling pins, soup spoons. Hundreds of them, a hill of household implements. On the far wall was a doorway. They walked through it into another chamber. This one was filled with saddles and boots, bridles, and whips. The shadows shifted just beyond the light.

Nessa threw a tooth into the pile, and they watched in horror as vermin swarmed over it, a mass of fur and debris tumbling over the junk. There were dozens of the creatures nearby now.

The girls hurried into another chamber, which held silver spoons, candlesticks, forks, and knives. They ran through one chamber after another. One contained steel tools, plows, and wagon axles in rusting heaps. Another held a glittering pile of broken china, porcelain bowls, and bedpans.

"Are they all oddities?" Nessa asked as they dashed past washtubs and scrub brushes.

"Can't be."

The carrion smell grew to a nauseating intensity, and Clover knew what she would find in the next chamber. The storage room was piled high with dead animals. Most of them were dried and flat, but some still lay in the process of putrefaction.

Nessa retched.

"It's a vermin manufactory," Clover said.

They heard a familiar chant coming from deeper in the tunnel. They crept toward the voice, Clover's heart hammering in her chest.

First we chew, then we swallow.
First we lead, then we follow.
Grind it up, choke it down.
First we float, then we drown . . .

Behind them, the tunnel seethed with vermin, a hot wind of greedy whispers.

"Do you have any more teeth?" Clover asked.

Nessa lifted the bag to the light. Only a few remained. When the vermin surged toward them, she threw the bag into their writhing midst. The sound of the vermin fighting over the bag was like a storm in the trees.

A soft glow lit the rock ahead. Clover blew out her light and entered the room.

The tunnel opened onto a ledge above a room lit by dozens of lamps. The witch worked below.

From above, the Seamstress looked almost harmless, a beetle grubbing in its tunnel. She dropped a handful of teeth into the Pestle and ground them. Her figure shimmered and twitched, as if seen through restless water.

"Look!" Nessa whispered, pointing to the moving shadows

in the corners of the workroom. "Hundreds of vermin!"

"Hush!" Clover said, watching the witch's process.

As the Seamstress ground the teeth, they became the blue Powder that had saved Clover's life. But the work wasn't done. She roasted the Powder over a small stove until it sizzled.

"Now we burn," whispered the vermin in a haunting chorus, "now we churn."

When the Powder had melted into a dark liquid, the Seamstress poured it into a Churn. Clover began to understand what she was watching. There were more stages to the process, but at the other end of the table was a spindle, and beside that a small basket full of blue Thread. This was the process that gave the vermin life.

Clover couldn't take her eyes off the basket. "Enough Thread to make a hundred Susannas," she whispered.

The Churn turned the liquid into a thick paste, which the Seamstress kneaded wearing a pair of calfskin Gloves. Then, removing the Gloves, she flattened it into a sheet with a Rolling Pin. The Seamstress cut this into ribbons with Shears, and all the while the vermin whispered, "Now we clot, now we knot."

Clover was too overwhelmed to note the last steps of the process, but in the end, the Seamstress had another half-inch of blue Thread that she twined onto the bundle.

"What will you do with all that Thread?" Clover shouted down at the Seamstress.

"Quiet!" Nessa hissed as the witch peered up at them.

"What's this?" the Seamstress croaked. "Visitors? And no calling card? Nevertheless, bring them in. We don't keep guests waiting."

Like a sudden windstorm, the vermin swarmed over Clover and Nessa, lifting them up, pushing them forward.

"I already gave you all the teeth!" Nessa screamed at them.

Sweetwater lashed out, but the creatures, like Susanna, were immune to her poison.

The horde carried the girls down into the workshop, teeth and claws tugging, threatening to tear them apart. Clover and Nessa were pressed against the cavern wall, pinned by twitching abominations.

The Hound opened its maw and dropped several teeth at the feet of the Seamstress.

"They had a bag of them," the Hound muttered proudly.

Up close, Clover saw that the Seamstress was actually two women, impossibly sharing the same space. Glimpsed though kaleidoscopic shards of light, one was pale as a tallow candle, her hair matted into a thick bundle that hung over her shoulders like a beaver tail. The other was bald and covered with scars, her dried flesh stitched together with whips of leather, some patches replaced with animal hide. These splintered reflections of the witch, one bloodless, one wild-eyed as a hermit, stood on the same two feet, moved and spoke as one.

"What is all the Thread for?" Clover repeated, her eyes straining to focus on the shifting figure. "You have too many vermin already."

"Don't provoke the witch," Nessa pleaded. "Please, Clover . . ."

"But we are already provoked." The Seamstress crooked a finger, and the vermin dragged Clover toward the worktable. They pressed her face onto a heap of putrid fur. "How did you defeat my pet at the bridge? You must be quite strong, or clever, or quick . . ."

"There are people coming to steal all of that Thread," Clover said. "They want to create an army of undead soldiers."

"Is it true?" The Seamstress turned to the Hound, who nodded.

"Yes, mistress. Riders approach from east and west."

"Come to take our Thread? And the bridge is unguarded? But that won't do. We'll need a better pet, no? Yes. Something clever. Something quick," the Seamstress muttered to herself, her voice cracking in twain, sometimes only hoarse, sometimes the brittle whisper of dry bones. "A dead squirrel, a sunbaked raccoon. We've done our best with the sources at hand. But it is never enough." She caressed Clover's cheek with a gnarled finger, then picked up a knife and started sharpening it.

Clover tried to pull away, but the vermin held her against the table, their claws digging into her flesh. The Seamstress brought the blade close to Clover's neck.

"You don't need us," Clover gasped, choking back her fear. "Your vermin do everything you ask—"

The Seamstress hissed, "Not everything! They bring us teeth, pelts, oddities. But they can't find the one thing we want. Now we must do better. And here you are. Brave, aren't you, to have come this far? Clever and quick?" The witch's voice changed. "Must we kill her, the poor thing?"

The Seamstress was arguing with herself, her mind as shattered as her body. Which was the true Miniver?

Her mood swung like a flag in a storm, and suddenly the witch was smiling again. It was a toothless grin that told Clover exactly where she'd gotten her first Thread. "You'll only be dead for the time it takes us to put you back together!" she said to Clover. "We'll have to borrow your skin, and probably remove your skull as well. Quite the insult, I'm afraid, but strictly necessary. Look away, now. This will only hurt for a moment."

Sweetwater surged down Clover's arm, hissing and rattling her tail.

The witch flinched. "Kill it!"

"Don't touch her!" Clover screamed, but the vermin yanked Sweetwater away, dragging the writhing serpent to another skinning table.

Clover became instantly ill, feeling the blood draining from her face. Her feet went numb.

While the vermin stretched the snake out for slaughter, the Seamstress peered at Clover. "Oh, but look how she shivers! Do we have no mercy?" one voice begged. The corpse voice snapped a response, "We're giving her immortality! Don't fuss. There is work to do, and so much to work with. Bones, teeth, skin . . . a bounty!"

Clover struggled not to faint. "You gave me my bones, Mother," she said. "My skin and teeth too. Do you really want them back?"

"What did you call us?" The Seamstress stared. "Where are your manners?"

"I learned my manners from Constantine Elkin."

A stunned silence filled the chamber. Even the vermin holding Sweetwater stopped to watch.

"That," the Seamstress said, cocking her head as if hearing a distant, tiny thread of music, "is a name we know."

"You should. You married him."

The Seamstress froze, and the vermin, sensing a change, loosened their grip. Sweetwater wriggled free and darted back to Clover. As the snake wound up toward her shoulders, Clover felt her strength returning. She stood and shook the stunned vermin off.

"I'm here, Mother. It's Clover. Before vermin, before Susanna, you made me. I've come for answers."

"Impossible," the Seamstress whispered. "Our Clover is just a baby, barely walking."

"That was twelve years ago," Clover said. "I grew up."

"So long? Could it be?" Miniver searched Clover's face with milky eyes. "But Constantine died that night . . ."

"Father was shot by poachers just days ago."

"I thought we lost him in the fire . . ." Miniver faltered, her features collapsing in grief and confusion. Her face broke like a thrown plate, sorrow and anger merging in an inhuman mask. The Seamstress howled like a trapped beast. Her voice split into dissonance, and for a moment, Clover could hear both parts of her, one alive and bewildered, one dead and remembering every pain. Miniver wobbled and nearly collapsed. Clover caught her and was surprised how weightless the woman was—as if she were nothing but a bundle of chicken bones and yarn.

Touching her mother, Clover felt both the brittle leather of her stitched body and the soft sags of living skin, the cracks in reality grinding together like a poorly set bone. Pity flooded Clover's heart.

"Poor Constantine," Miniver whispered. "He hated a commotion . . . Is it really you? Seeing you is like water for our parched heart."

"We didn't die in that fire," Clover said. "We survived."

"We have made such a mess of things," Miniver whimpered. "A terrible mess."

"Will you tell me what happened?"

"How can we tell?" Miniver wavered. Then she pulled the calfskin Gloves off the worktable and put one on her left hand. She gave the other to Clover. "Here," she said. "See for yourself."

The Glove was tacky and had holes worn through the fingertips. If Clover had ever seen the Gloves mentioned in the journals, she could not remember what they did. Behind her, Nessa had taken an oil lamp from the table and was trying to shoo vermin into the shadows with it.

Clover took a deep breath, pulled on the Glove, and was no longer in the mine.

CHAPTER 22

GRANDER INTENTIONS

Clover found herself in a quiet room lit by the rose tones of a stained-glass window. The window contained the rabbit in the egg, the logo of the Society, backlit by the street lamps of New Manchester.

Miniver Elkin was young and lovely even in the dingy apron she wore over her blouse. She was kneeling near a brass cage. Clover saw it all as a dream, but she knew this was the past as it had happened.

On the tables behind Miniver was a bewilderment of items arranged like a chemist's workshop. A Quill tied to a swinging Pendulum drew an erratic scrawl on the paper below. A Horseshoe was lashed to a Music Box with leather straps. In a steel pot, a red-hot Ember lay beneath the surface of boiling water. It was the Heron's Heart. A brass-colored Frog swam happily in the boiling fluid as if it were a cool spring pond. Though it was submerged, the Ember still burned. Though it was boiled, the Frog still lived. This was the wonder of Miniver Elkin's study.

A full-length looking glass was draped by a sheet, and nearby sat a crib. In that crib, baby Clover chewed on a wooden spoon, occasionally pointing at her mother through the slats.

Constantine came in, handsome as a young cat, jet hair and velvet-trimmed coat. He said, "By my count, you haven't slept in three days."

"I'll sleep when I finish this experiment," Miniver answered, pulling a languid rabbit from the brass cage.

"You could make a mistake," Constantine said. "It isn't safe."

"My oddities and your plagues—we both take our risks." Miniver held the rabbit up so her husband could see its plump belly. "You praise the surgeons and chemists, but none of them do what I have done. This rabbit is alive. You can't deny it."

"It shouldn't be," Constantine said. He paced in a tight circle on the Persian rug.

Miniver clasped her husband's hand, stopping him. "During the war, you stanched the blood, but I saw the smiles on the politicians as they walked to church in their unstained silks, holding gilded canes. Wars are born in the hearts of men like that. They will never stop."

"I treat the body in front of me—"

"And you miss everyone else! The world suffers. How many elections, how many abolitionist meetings, how many clinics have we seen, and still: war, plague, slavery, corruption! And at the end, grinning death waiting to swallow all. Why should the innocent suffer generation after generation when we have the tools to change it?"

Constantine, his jaw clenched, gestured to the riot of equipment on the table. "But this alchemy . . . witchcraft. The audacity—"

"It was audacious to make a tea out of the foxglove flower."

Miniver's eyes pleaded with him to understand. "But in that poison was a secret cure for galloping hearts, which you use to save lives. Some audacious surgeon was the first to cut out a tumor, the first to inject medicine directly into the veins. It takes vision and courage to—"

"This is not medicine! You've already offended nature."

Baby Clover had dropped her spoon through the slats and whimpered, wanting it back.

"Oh, nature! Nature gave us cholera. Nature gave us measles. What do we owe nature?" Miniver was flushed, but she spoke slowly, clearly, as if to a child. "It took years for me to make the tiniest amount of Thread. The Pestle could cure illness, but I found the secret to magnifying its power. This rabbit cannot be killed by *any* means. I'm talking about the end of death, Constantine. I might not build the entire bridge, but someone must set the first stone."

"I can't talk to you when you're like this."

"You're not talking to me," Miniver said. "You're standing in my way."

Constantine watched her kneel to put the rabbit back in its cage.

"I worry, Miniver." He took a step toward her.

Miniver stood. Her face was determined, but her voice was gentle. "Didn't I worry when you rode through the battlefields? When you disappeared for weeks into Indian plague camps? But did I ever stand in your way?"

As they faced each other in silence, Clover warbled in her crib as if deciding between laughter and tears.

Constantine turned and left without another word, closing the door behind him.

The sound of the Pendulum filled the room. Miniver didn't return to work until she heard Constantine's horse galloping away. With a sigh, she picked up her journal and had just dipped her pen in the inkwell when the door opened again, startling her.

But it wasn't Constantine this time. It was a young man with a wild look in his eyes. He had a full head of hair and no hat. He wasn't twitching or scratching, but it was Willit Rummage.

Miniver was surprised. "It's late for a delivery."

"And yet the delivery is here," Willit said, holding out a wooden box with a broken seal. "Loyal Willit works day and night."

"You're drunk," Miniver said. As she reached for the box, Willit snatched it away as if he were teasing a child.

"Where is Constantine?" Miniver asked.

"Ridden off into the darkness. I'll bet he's gone to sleep with the injuns again."

"They have the pox," Miniver said. "He goes where there is need."

"What of my needs?"

"How much have you had to drink?"

"Only enough to give me the guts to say what's right." Willit opened the box and pulled out the Pistol. "And do what's right."

Miniver stood composed; the only sign of fear was the trembling of a muscle in her neck.

"I know what this is." Willit shook the Pistol. "I may not be learned, but I ain't dumb. The things I fetch for you are worth a pile of money."

"You are paid well to deliver my packages. It is not your business to open them or—"

"But I opened this one, didn't I?" Willit said. "I can't be your fetching man no more, knowing what I know. My heart has grander intentions. I aim to marry you, Miniver."

Miniver's chin lifted. "Shame on you! I am a married woman. My child is sleeping right there in that crib."

"Wake, children everywhere!" Willit shouted. "Wake! Your mothers are meddlers!" Willit knocked the handle of the gun along the rungs of the crib. "She's tinkering with things she ought not tinker with!"

"Hush! You're out of your mind," Miniver scolded.

"She tinkers with a man's heart!" Willit took a step toward Miniver, and she took two steps back. He bent down and took the rabbit from the cage. "Look here, children! She keeps the rabbit locked in its little jail, the poor thing. Have you got my heart in here as well? What is this?" Willit pulled a blue thread from the rabbit's ear.

Miniver screamed, but it was too late.

The rabbit shriveled in Willit's hand. In seconds it had become a lifeless husk of shedding fur, its ears stiffening to leather.

Baby Clover began to wail. Willit stared at the bundle of hide in his hands, the yellow teeth pointed as daggers. His voice sounded weary when he said, "Oh, Miniver."

"You've ruined years of work," Miniver said, her voice trembling. "But . . . we can discuss an increase in your pay—"

Now Willit pointed the Pistol directly at her and said, "Didn't you hear me? Grander ambitions!" He stuffed the dead rabbit into his jacket pocket.

Miniver swallowed. Then she said, "Perhaps I haven't treated you with the . . . regard you deserve. Naturally I owe you a bonus for your loyalty. Not just a bonus, but an oddity. A powerful one. A priceless one. It ought to belong to you." Miniver reached behind herself and found a battered Matchbox. She opened it and pulled out a single Match.

Willit squinted at it. "What does it do?"

"I'll show you." Miniver struck the Match on the table and disappeared.

Instantly, she reappeared behind him, snatched up a candlestick, and clubbed him so hard that the candlestick bent.

Willit fell to his knees, hollering, but he held on to the Pistol. He staggered up again, bleeding from the scalp, and grabbed the box of Matches. Miniver rushed at him, pushing him right through the stained-glass window. Willit fell two stories in a rainbow of glass.

Even as they heard the thud of his body on the ground, Miniver pulled Clover from the crib and threw open the door, starting for the stairs. At the bottom stood a hulking shadow.

Bolete hollered, "What's that commotion? Should I come up now?"

Miniver retreated back into the study and locked the door. She turned in three terrified circles, holding Clover to her chest. They were trapped.

From the street below, there was a shot, and the bullet lanced through the broken window. It looped about the room like a beam of light, smashing Miniver's experiments. Glass shattered, wood splintered. Miniver screamed and fell to the ground, covering Clover with her body as her life's work broke around her.

By the time the bullet had lodged itself in a table leg, the room was a disaster. Dark oils and strong-smelling fluids were spattered on the walls. The Pendulum was a ruined ring of tin. The

Frog hopped across the glass-strewn floor. Miniver was checking Clover for injuries when something volatile caught fire. The explosion blew Miniver to her belly and lit the walls.

The room was blazing. The curtains flapped like dragon wings. Miniver and Clover screamed. The air was an acrid haze, and the door was blocked by a burning bookshelf. Miniver huddled in the corner, trying to wrap Clover in her skirt to protect her from the smoke.

In the middle of the room, a whirlwind of smoke was gathering into the shape of the Heron. Miniver found the blacksmith's tongs in the wreckage and snatched the Ember up before the Heron could manifest. She thrust the Ember into the Teapot. A geyser of steam erupted. She tried to use the steam to extinguish the fire, but the room was already an inferno, blistering the wallpaper. There was no escape. Baby Clover screamed as if she were already burning.

Through the smoke and steam, Miniver saw something moving on the floor and grabbed it.

She waited for Clover to scream again. When she did, Miniver dropped the Frog into her daughter's mouth. With fierce resolve, she held the baby's jaw shut until Clover had swallowed it.

"*Hush, little baby,*" Miniver wept as she sang, "*don't you cry.*"

And when a wave of heat rolled toward them, scorching Miniver's face, baby Clover squirmed away and crawled through the flames, wailing but unburned. Miniver tried to follow, but the heat beat her back. Her hair caught fire, and she whirled in desperation. "Clover!"

Seeing no other exit, she ripped the sheet off the Mirror, revealing a reflection of her study before it had become an inferno, everything in its place and placid. There was a safe world waiting for her on the other side. She tried to find her daughter one last time, but her eyelashes singed and her skin blistered. In agony, Miniver dashed through the Mirror. But she was only halfway through that passage when another explosion shattered the glass. Miniver shattered with it, her body splintering. Two Minivers screamed. One burned. The other watched with wild eyes.

The Seamstress pulled off the Gloves. Clover was in the dim cavern of the present, with shriveled, shattered Miniver, both of them weeping.

Nessa stood by warily.

The vermin huddled, chirping uncertainly in the shadows.

"You saved me," Clover said to her mother. "The Frog protected me, but how did you . . . ?"

Miniver pulled her matted hair away from her neck. Through the shifting images, Clover saw a stitch of blue Thread through Miniver's earlobe. "We did what I had to do."

Clover hugged her mother again as they both shook. Through the willow frame of her mother's bones, Clover felt the broken heartbeat, sometimes faint, sometimes doubled, sometimes silent as a hollow tree.

Miniver hugged her daughter, and for a moment, Clover felt the undying strength of her mother's arms.

"It was grief that baffled us. We've been trying to find our way, trying to put the pieces back together, but . . . it was all tangled. We remembered that there was hope in the Frog . . . hope in the Frog, but . . . Where is the Frog?" She pulled back, her eyes lit with rage, the embers of that old fire. "Bring me the Frog! Bring me—"

The vermin tittered, roused to the command.

"It's me, Mother." Clover guided her mother's cheek until Miniver was seeing her again. "I'm right here."

"Oh dear . . . I'm sorry."

"No more vermin, Mother, please."

Miniver looked into the shadows where her creations twitched.

"Of course you are right. What do we need them for?" Miniver smiled. "Help us with this," she said, and the vermin rushed forward. "Not you," she said. "We're asking our daughter."

Clover and Nessa helped her dismantle the vermin manufactory, unstrapping the Churn from the table, winding the Thread into a ball, and sheathing the Shears.

Nessa pointed at the skein of Thread. "Isn't that what Auburn has been hunting for?"

With a surge of clarity, Miniver grabbed a lamp and tipped the burning oil into the basket of Thread herself. Years of work crackled brightly and was gone in seconds.

"We can't let them re-create the process," Clover said.

They continued disassembling the workshop. Miniver stopped occasionally, bent in pain or staring into the darkness with glimpses of horror, sorrow, and anger floating separately across her face.

"We burned to death," Miniver said. "We escaped unharmed. Which world is true? The Mirror wants us to forget. The shards cut us when we try to remember. But we found ways to remember you. We found ways to . . . persist."

Then, wanting to seize this moment of clarity, Clover heard herself ask the question behind all the others, the question that had pushed her to confront Smalt, pushed her across the Wine Marsh and up the crumbling mountain: "Did you love me?"

"Even when we forgot our own name," Miniver said, her eyes clearing. "Even when our mind scattered like a fallen wasp nest. We . . . I never stopped looking for you. I tried to tear this wretched world apart to find you."

Clover looked at the vermin, twitching and foul, and saw them, just briefly, as agents of love, misguided and toxic, but tireless.

"Father's love was like a cage. Yours looks like a pack of savage beasts."

"No family is perfect," Nessa said. "What is all that stuff in those other rooms?"

"Have we been introduced?" Miniver turned to Nessa with menace smoldering in her eyes.

"You didn't ask for an introduction when you stole my tooth," Nessa muttered, backing away.

"Nessa is a friend," Clover said.

"It was a milk tooth, wasn't it?" Miniver snapped. "Didn't it grow back?"

"No!" Nessa shouted.

"One of your vermin caused an accident," Clover said softly, "and killed Nessa's uncle, a good man whom she loved."

Miniver turned with sudden ferocity toward her vermin, who scattered into the darkness. Then she composed herself, brushing her hands down her front as if dusting flour from an apron. "How can you forgive something like that? Our nightmare spreads. There is no way to undo the things we've done. The other rooms hold oddities, Nessa. You must take something, a token of my regret. Any of my treasures are yours. Pets, fetch me a few."

Several vermin dashed into the tunnels, eager to please their mistress, and returned with broken items.

Miniver held up a cracked jug. "This is a milk pitcher that cannot hold milk! And here, a rare gem, a pair of spectacles that make vision worse!" She put the spectacles on. Her shattered eyes multiplied into stars. "And this beauty, the perfume bottle . . ."

"But those aren't oddities," Nessa said. "That's just junk."

The cracked bottle trembled in Miniver's hands. "Is it? Of

course it is. We get muddled, you see . . . We haven't slept since the fire. The Thread won't let us sleep."

Clover wished she could go back to that rose-lit room and save her mother, save them both. But there was no way to turn back time. Clover found the pocket watch in her bag and handed it over. "He kept this, Father did. Can you tell me why?"

Miniver held the timepiece with a trembling hand. "This was the first gift we gave him, while we were courting. Our handsome Constantine was always late. It made our father frown. We told Constantine, now you have the time, you have no excuses."

"*Celeritate functa*," Clover said. "Be prompt."

"He hadn't had it but three weeks before it got smashed during a ruckus with the Indians. It never worked again."

"He carried it until the day he died," Clover said. "He carried you too. He didn't know how to save you, but he never let you go. What happened after the fire?"

"It was like waking from a nightmare only to find you're still dreaming. We had wandered away from the flames. We were broken in two, one lost and one dying. So we took our own imperfect medicine. We went looking for you. Wandered. We made helpers. We only made them to find you, and to get ingredients for Thread to make more helpers . . . to find you . . . to find the Frog . . ."

"Not just that," Clover said softly. "You also made the Flea."

Miniver's face split into rage, then sorrow. "Yes, we made the Flea. For *him*. But we're too tired now for revenge."

Suddenly she went pale and toppled. Clover caught her. Miniver's face swarmed in the lantern light, confused.

"It's me. Clover. It's your daughter."

Relief brought Miniver's face together, and Clover saw joy

making her whole for just a moment before the pieces scattered again like minnows.

"I can't lose you again," Miniver said.

"We'll get you home," Clover said. "Start working on a cure."

"There is no cure. Look at us! It was only hunger to see you that kept us going. This is where we . . . where *I* want to stop, looking at you, my shining daughter."

"We'll find a cure—"

"No more experiments. No more mischief. I am tired, dear Clover. So tired. I finally have what I want; let me keep it. I have found my girl. "

From the Walnut shell in Clover's pocket came the sound of muffled explosions. Willit was still alive. He'd taken Bolete's half of the shell, and by the sounds of it, there was a battle brewing nearby.

"They are coming for the oddities," Clover said. "What can we do?"

"What is left to do? I have done it," Miniver said, slumping to the floor. "Oh, child, can't I sleep? Do me this favor, will you?"

Miniver lifted her hair again, revealing the strange earring made of blue Thread. "Can you get it for me? You've broken my fever, cleared my eyes. Smart and brave, marvelous girl. More than a mother deserves. I don't want to become . . . muddled again. I want to keep your face clearly in my mind."

Clover pinched the Thread between her fingers but couldn't make herself pull it. Her breath seized in her chest. "When we get you home . . ." She sobbed.

"My home is here." Miniver touched Clover's heart. "The Mirror will never let me go. The flames . . . the Thread will never. You must do this for me."

"I can't!" Clover's hand trembled.

"Set me free."

Then Constantine's steady hand was holding the Thread too, his silent strength supporting Clover. With one last sob, Clover leaned down and gave her mother a kiss on the forehead.

"Such a mess," Miniver said.

"Don't worry. We'll clean up," Clover said through her tears. "Rest now."

Clover pulled the Thread from Miniver's ear. The stitched body dissolved first, sloughing to ashes, and for a blessed moment, Miniver was singular, unburned and whole in her daughter's arms. Then she dissolved too, scattering like moonlight through a glass of water. Clover's arms dropped, empty, as shimmers of her mother lit the cavern like dandelion seeds in the wind.

CHAPTER 23

A MIRACLE OR A CURSE

Clover slumped on the cavern floor, and for a moment, everything was as silent as the heart of a mountain should be. Then the vermin, which had gone utterly still as Miniver dissolved, began to twitch and moan, grieving their mistress.

"Clover," Nessa said, her voice worried.

"On Sundays, Father and I ate supper with Widow Henshaw," Clover said, the memory pouring out of her with the tears. "They were forever discussing how to manage difficult pregnancies."

Nessa pulled her up, and Clover continued, "This one night, we'd eaten white-bean soup with salted pork, cornmeal fritters, mustard greens, and mulberry vinegar. I'd crawled under the table, stuffed and ready to fall asleep, and I heard the widow whisper, 'There could be a cure. If she's still alive in there somewhere.' And father said, 'I have saved what could be saved. I won't risk what's left.' I couldn't guess which patient they were talking about." Clover laughed, feeling delirious.

The vermin began to rustle, darting into the shadows with squawks and chirps.

"We have to go," Nessa said.

"Don't you see, though?" Clover said. "Father *did* know that Mother was the Seamstress."

"He should have told you."

"But the bliss of falling asleep to the crackle of the fire, the smell of the bread oven, the comforting voices around me. I felt safe! Father wasn't keeping me ignorant. He was keeping the horror out. He built that safety for me, and day after day, he fought for it."

Nessa pulled Clover toward the stairway that led to the main tunnel while the vermin began to writhe in the shadows like a gathering storm. The vermin cooed and wailed in the darkness.

"I understand now. I finally understand what happened to my family." Through the Walnut, the sounds of war grew louder as Clover dropped to her knees. The relief of finally knowing and the grief of losing her mother so soon after finding her was too much. She felt herself cracking, falling in several directions at once.

"You got to say goodbye," Nessa offered, shoving Clover's bag into her hands. "You set her soul to rest. No one else could have done that. Maybe that's why she was looking for you. But Clover, we have to go."

Clover's eyes were drawn to the worktable, the masterpiece of madness in disarray. She picked up the Pestle and examined it.

"My mother invented a process that reverses death."

"It makes *vermin*," Nessa said.

"It also made Susanna."

"We know what Auburn will do with it," Nessa said.

The thought of undead soldiers marching in an endless war got Clover to her feet. With the vermin moaning in the shadows and the rumbles of gunfire echoing above them, Clover and Nessa took the pieces of the laboratory in a hurry. They threw the oddities onto a dried bison pelt and dragged it back into the caverns. The orphaned fiends followed, their confused whispers growing.

As they passed through the storage chambers, Clover tossed oddities onto the heaps of junk, hoping to hide them among everyday things.

"Shouldn't you take some with you?" Nessa asked. "So no one can piece it together and start churning out vermin again?"

Clover agreed. She weighed each item in her hands, trying to imagine its power, remembering the disaster of the Ice Hook and of the Wineglass.

"Each one could be a miracle or a curse." Clover had to stop, her throat clenched around a sadness that seemed much older than she was.

"Whatever you do, do it quickly," Nessa said, peering into the darkness where the vermin shuddered. "I don't know what the vermin will do without her."

Clover wept as she threw the Churn and the Rolling Pin among the kitchen things. She wept as she threw the Hammer among the tools and put the Whisk in her bag. She wept as she wadded the Gloves into her pocket.

"I wish there was someone wise, someone good enough to make these decisions." But in the dim light there was only Clover and Nessa and the mute weight of the viper coiled around her arm.

Clover weighed the Pestle in her hand. The blue Powder it produced had saved her life, but it was also a crucial part of making vermin. Suddenly, an explosion rocked the mountain, knocking the oddity to the ground. The vermin rushed forward all at once, and Nessa screamed. But the beasts didn't attack; they ran right past, headed for the surface. Dust rained down upon them as Clover fell to her knees, searching for the Pestle.

"We have to go!" Nessa yanked Clover to her feet before she could find it. The two hurried for the entrance, trying to keep their footing in the scrabble of fur. Clover felt things falling from her bag as another explosion shook the earth. Clover's lungs vibrated as the mine trembled around them. The lantern dropped and broke—plunging them into darkness.

The vermin screeched and surged, knocking Clover off her feet. She tumbled, cracking her head against the cavern wall. She lost all sense of direction as the beasts trampled her.

"Where are you?" Nessa shouted over the thunder of the mine's slow collapse.

"Here!" Clover shouted desperately, not knowing where that was. "Nessa, here!" The riot of vermin suddenly coalesced under Clover, pressing closer, inflamed by the familiar timbre in her voice. Nessa's hands found Clover's just as the vermin lifted her in a crescendo of howls.

"Leave her alone, you mongrels!"

But Nessa was lifted too, still clutching Clover's arm, and both were carried on a tide of matted fur.

"Nessa, look, we've made it!" Clover shouted as they were ferried toward the glare of the sunlight.

At last they emerged at the bridge, stunned by light and deafening noise. The vermin kept running in a chaotic herd across the bridge, many falling into the void below.

The momentum carried the girls halfway across before the vermin abandoned them, leaving the girls gripping the planks and fraying ropes.

Clover, though, didn't slow down for long. She leaped from board to board toward the far side of the bridge, where the war had begun.

Rifles cracked, cannons thumped, the screams of dying men echoed through the trees. The fighters had dug in around the abandoned town, darkening the air with gun smoke. Hannibal's army, entrenched in the ditches on the eastern slope of Abbot's Highway, traded shots with the platoon of French soldiers who had apparently arrived early enough to occupy the ruins. Bricks burst into orange blooms where the bullets hit. A band of Sehanna fighters had assumed control of the wooded eastern slopes, cutting off any retreat toward Louisiana. Some of the copper smelting pans had been rolled forward as makeshift shields. Three nations had converged on Harper's Hope. The Seamstress's hoard had brought them all. The logic of war demanded a fight, here and now.

When Clover placed her feet on solid ground, she was stopped by the vision before her. This was what she had hoped to prevent: terrified young men, clinging to life, firing, reloading desperately, and firing again. Bodies littered the ground, sacrificed to the urgency of the battle.

Clover stood exposed and motionless, feeling as helpless as a baby in a crib. Then Nessa tackled Clover and dragged her behind a tree, bullets smacking into the bark around them.

"Is that as bad as it looks?" Nessa pointed toward the glowing haze of the mining town. There the Heron glided in bright swoops between the ruined buildings.

"The oddities have already been unleashed!" Clover wailed. Smoke blotted out the distance, but she could hear the screams of the Heron's prey.

Clover spotted Hannibal hopping from branch to branch in the nearby tree, shouting orders down to his men. Then Hannibal caught sight of Clover, and for a moment they regarded each other across the disastrous haze.

"He knows there's no way to recall the Heron," Clover moaned. "Oh, Hannibal, what have you done?"

"What is that?" Nessa pointed at another oddity making its way through the maelstrom: an armored Armadillo waddled in frightened circles near the entrance of the warehouse. When a bursting brick startled it, the Armadillo leaped into the air and curled into a tight ball. Immediately guns and bullets, cannonballs, and even belt buckles converged upon it. Anything iron within twenty yards was drawn by its powerful magnet. When it was a bristling ball of armaments, the Armadillo uncurled, shook off the scrap, and continued its terrified dash.

But the half-dozen men whom the Armadillo had disarmed didn't stop fighting. They ran at one another and fought fist and tooth.

"Look there!" Nessa shouted. A commander of Hannibal's regiment aimed Mr. Agate's Umbrella like a gun, but instead of bullets, a bolt of lightning arced across the field, splitting a boulder and shaking the mountain with its thunder.

"Whoever wins this battle," Clover whispered, "will march across the earth, if there's anything left of it."

"How can we stop them?" Nessa said. "Just us against all of that?"

Sweetwater's rattle rang in her ear, and Clover Constantinovna Elkin remembered that she was blood sister to a snake. She remembered that she was Miniver Elkin's daughter. She loaded the Pistol and closed her eyes. She gave the bullet directions and pulled the trigger.

With a crack, the bullet raced off, slamming into rifles, cannon flints, and quivers. The weapons it struck burst out of the fighters' hands as the bullet looped around the battlefield, quickly losing momentum. Clover reloaded and fired again. This time she aimed for the Umbrella and the powder kegs. The explosions knocked the wind out of her, but she did it again and again, forbidding the bullets to hit anything made of flesh. All around the mountainside, rifles exploded and arrows shattered.

But there were too many. The battalions had come with crates of munitions, knowing that this first battle might be the most important.

"You'll run out of bullets long before they do," Nessa said.

A Sehanna fighter picked up the bent Umbrella, and the scene was lit with another burst of ragged light. Clover's efforts only made the men load their rifles faster, frightened by the chaos.

"Even the poachers are here!" Nessa pointed to Willit's remaining bandits, some she'd never seen before, perched atop a crest of rock. They traded shots with Aaron Agate, dressed in his beaver-fur hat. A host of old Society members were with him, huddled in one of the ruined buildings, adding the smoke of their antique rifles to the storm.

The fighters dug in. With every passing second, the fever of war increased. "We'll make a dash for those boulders over there," Nessa said, giving Clover's arm a shake. "Stay close to the crevasse. They won't see us if—"

But Clover could only shake her head. She had been raised to heal bodies, to nurse them to health. This senseless violence shook her to the bone. With every explosion, a moan escaped her lips. Her jaws clenched so tightly she felt a tooth crack.

"Stop!" Clover screamed, but she hardly heard herself over the noise. A huge tree, broken by cannonballs and Heron's fire, shuddered and fell, tearing lesser trees down as it slammed into the earth.

"Stop!"

Clover heard the terrible howl of the Heron, getting hotter and stronger with everything it consumed.

With trembling hands, Clover lit a Match, and everything froze.

The mountain was suddenly silent as a winter night. The air was cluttered with debris; bullets, stopped midflight, hung like snowflakes, cannonballs like Christmas ornaments. Even the upturned beak of the Heron, huge in the distance, was still as a painted sunset.

Clover didn't know what to do. The quiet was such a relief that she almost wept. She wanted the Match to last forever, but it was already half-gone. She knew that as soon as it went out, the fighting would continue. And she only had four Matches left in the box.

She left Nessa behind and ran toward the nearest fighters, a row of French soldiers lying behind a bank of fallen brick. One squinted over his rifle sights, another grimaced as he urgently reloaded, yet they were all identical. Frozen as they were, Clover could see clearly the same grizzled face—thick eyebrows and slate gray eyes—repeated on each man. These were the notorious *accablant,* the relentless army Hannibal feared. Clover imagined a factory somewhere deep in Louisiana where a powerful oddity turned out copies of this soldier faster than a printing press. She tried to kick the rifles out of their hands, but the scene might as well have been carved in marble.

Clover clambered atop an overturned wagon, desperately searching for a solution. The Match was nearly out.

Looking away from the battle, scanning for a last-minute advantage, Clover found only trouble: Willit Rummage, still alive, was making a dash across the bridge. The Match had caught him at a precarious angle, leaning toward the mine.

Clover used the last of her time to dive back behind the tree trunk, close to Nessa. As the flame singed her fingertips, she shook it out, and the battle exploded around her.

"What did you do?" Nessa hollered.

But Clover ignored her and yelled into the Walnut instead.

"Don't go in there, Willit!" she said, watching the poacher helplessly as he made the last leaps across the gaps in the bridge and pulled himself to safety on the far side of the canyon.

Willit dashed into the mine. "Only a fool leaves empty-handed, and Willit Rummage is not a fool."

Seconds after his figure had disappeared into the gloom of the tunnel, a cannonball slammed into the cliff above. The stones came down over the entrance like a mouth closing, and Willit was swallowed inside.

CHAPTER 24

THE DAUGHTER OF TROUBLE

T he calamity paused for a moment as the fighters saw the mine entrance obliterated. But only seconds later, gunshots shook the air again. The battle would continue, even if the prize was out of reach.

The Heron moved in and out of the smoldering tree line, bringing a blistering heat. It towered above the soldiers who fled before it, its legs pillars of flame. Those it gobbled up turned to ash before they made it down the Heron's throat.

If the collapsing stones hadn't already crushed him, Willit would starve inside the mine. If anyone deserved to perish, it was Willit. But Clover couldn't stand to see another person die.

Sweetwater's rattle filled her head, drowning out even the roar of the cannon. She rose, hearing herself say, "Enough hiding . . ."

Nessa grabbed her arm. "What are you doing?"

"Enough secrets. Enough killing."

Clover shook Nessa off and strode forward.

Nessa hollered behind her, "Come back!"

Clover, backlit against the infernal gloaming of the wild-fire, walked directly into the middle of the battlefield, shouting, "Enough!"

She was exposed in the eye of the storm, the air around her glinting with shrapnel. Nessa came running after, plum-faced with fear but ready to tackle her crazed friend, when an explosion threw her to the ground.

A burning tree had fallen between them, spewing eddies of soot and embers. While Nessa coughed and cursed behind the wall of fire, Clover continued to march forward, all of the clamor and grief resolving into a single sound, as if every bullet and cannonball had struck a massive bell, and the bone-rattling knell came out as a single word:

ENOUGH.

· · · · · · · · · · ·

It was this moment that made Clover Elkin famous, that inspired songs about the doctor's daughter. Every newspaper would feature an illustration of her silhouetted in the middle of the battlefield. The fighters who survived would recall how they lowered their rifles when they saw the unsettling young woman, fearless in a storm of bullets.

The shooting stopped entirely when the horror of the Heron loomed up behind her like a demon from the molten core of the earth. Everyone saw it happen. With the last of the bullets melting into pewter mist against its plumage, the Heron snatched Clover up and swallowed her as if she were a tadpole. But the girl didn't burn. She tumbled down the throat and into the belly. She floated there, a fetal shadow in the white-hot blaze.

Then she grabbed the Ember Heart, gripping the source of

the inferno in her hand. The Heron let out a tortured wail, stagger-
ing as its furnace Heart smothered. As the living inferno sputtered
out, Clover dropped and landed in a crouch. She emerged from a
whirlwind of black smoke, still holding the Ember in her fist. It
must have been pure torture, but she held on to the Heron's Heart
as if it were a family heirloom. Witnesses would all swear that her
arm glowed red-hot. She was furious.

With rage enough to burn the world spreading into her, the
girl stood in the middle of the smoldering battlefield and screamed
at the fighters.

"Murderers! You want power? I am the only oddity that mat-
ters now. I am the daughter of trouble, with venom in my veins.
The Seamstress is dead and buried. Her methods destroyed. The
mine is collapsed. This mountain is a grave now. Leave it in peace.
There is nothing for you here but death."

This vision haunted everyone who saw it: the unearthly child
smoldering in the sudden silence. Even the rattlesnake around her
neck shone like molten bronze.

And then, as she shouted, "Go home while you still can!" the
vermin emerged from the trees and howled with her, a sound like
a hurricane wind.

Most fighters would say it was the forest fire or the slavering
mob of vermin that forced them to drop their weapons and retreat.
But a few honest men would admit that it was Clover who stopped
the battle. They saw in her a power greater than any oddity, greater
than any treaty or nation, a power that humbled them, that scared
them, that gave them hope.

· . · . · . · . · . ·

Clover's memories of that moment were as murky as a dream. She recalled the Heron's heat boiling her blood, pain turning to strength. She remembered the ash on the faces of the men running down the mountainside, vermin on their heels.

She remembered feeling Hannibal watching her from the highest branches of the remaining trees, like an angel scorned.

The surface of Salamander Lake was buckled and warped.

No one welcomed her home. Not even crickets or birds. The waterwheel was frozen in place. The silence was an accusation.

Clover dragged a long chain behind her. Attached to the end of it was a blackened iron box. She walked out across the frozen face of the ice, the box hissing behind her.

She found a particular point at the middle of the lake and knelt to open the box. The Heron's Heart tipped out and sputtered on the surface for a moment before melting a blue hole right through the ice. A steady column of steam came up through the vent as the Ember found its way to the bottom.

A moment later, a gush of water. Then another. The ice beneath her groaned and popped as Clover ran back to shore.

Somewhere below, the Ice Hook and the Ember were beginning their struggle. It would take days, maybe weeks before the ice was fully melted, but the Heron would never stalk the earth again. The ice and the fire would balance each other and return life to

Salamander Lake. Eventually, no one would know that such powerful oddities were down there, locked in an endless waltz.

As Clover crossed the empty village, she wondered how many other things were held together by hidden oddities. Was this universe just a foam floating on unseen forces?

But then, maybe a sunset was just a sunset. As her father had said, "A water pitcher that just holds water. A needle that just pulls thread."

The journal she'd taken from Mr. Agate's room was already ten years old, but it was more recent than any of Widow Henshaw's brittle issues. Clover was listed in it as "Unconfirmed . . . a Fireproof Child." But she was more than that now. She had been shaped not just by fire but by shadows and secrets, by hope and by love.

She walked to the mossy clearing of the graveyard. Her eyes welled up when she saw that they had given Constantine an honored position at the top of the little hill. Someone had even carved a soapstone marker that read:

Constantine Elkin
1780–1822
Doctor and Friend to All

Clover bowed her head, looking for the right words.

"They spent too much money on the stone," Constantine said.

Clover turned and saw her father's ghost clearly, the tapered beard, the sun-bleached rim of his hat, the smell of pine needles and smoked trout.

"I forgive you," Clover said.

"Forgive *me?*" There was the edge of a smile in his voice.

"I thought it was my fault," she said. "Then I thought it was your fault. I hated you for hiding the truth. For trying to control me. But now I understand what you were trying to protect me from. I know that everything you did . . . I know it was love."

Constantine looked at Clover, his expression a forlorn mixture of adoration and worry. He touched her cheek and said, "It holds hope."

"I broke my promise," Clover confessed. "I became a collector. It's messy and it's dangerous, but I didn't have much choice. I'm not the doctor you wanted me to be. But I tried to stop the bleeding. I stopped Smalt. I stopped the poachers, and I kept the worst from Auburn's hands. I faced the ghosts that haunted you." Clover wiped tears from her cheeks. "I'd been digging after the secrets you buried. I found myself. I found Mother. She loved you."

"What is to become of my remarkable Clover?" But it was clear in his voice that Constantine was no longer worried.

"I don't know, but my hands are steady. I have my own tools and I'm learning to use them. You can rest now."

He nodded, removing his hat and passing a hand through his hair as if a nap sounded like a good idea. And then he was gone.

Clover tugged the vial of dandelions from her neck and emptied the seeds upon her father's grave. The weeds would grow stubbornly, raggedly beautiful, and they would spread, generation after generation.

On her way to her house, Clover heard a chittering and flinched. But it wasn't a vermin in the trees; it was that grumpy squirrel, who'd somehow survived the unnatural winter despite a wounded leg. Its back paw was tangled in a length of fishing net. It huffed and barked at her, guarding its brittle kingdom even as Clover coaxed it down with a stale raisin bun from Widow Henshaw's cold kitchen.

Clover took her time, catching the squirrel in a laundry basket and holding its head firmly as she clipped the knot off its foot. It was furious, but its leg was already working better as it dashed back into the leafless canopy. After that, Clover chopped wood to replenish the pile behind the kitchen. It felt good to be solving small problems with nothing fancier that her own hands.

Of course, the rest of the surviving vermin were still out there somewhere. Clover wondered if they'd followed her at a distance, the poor, sleepless creatures lost now without their mistress. For lack of a better idea, she buried Smalt's Hat in a barrel of salt in the pantry, but she thought she could still hear it whispering.

One week later, when Nessa and Widow Henshaw arrived on the battered yellow wagon, the lake ice had broken into jade-colored bergs drifting on the warming water. Nessa waded upstream to find fry to restock the lake, while Widow Henshaw revived her spurned oven, humming as she fed it kindling.

A deep burn on Nessa's cheek, an injury she'd hardly noticed during the battle, was toughening into a pale scar despite the calendula and comfrey balm Clover applied. Nessa winced at the taste of the ginseng tonic Clover brewed but agreed it probably worked better than Bleakerman's.

Clover, for her part, spoke very little; the storm in her heart kept words from coming easily, but she laughed at Nessa's jokes, and she ate as if she'd never seen food before. She helped the widow cook huge meals, taking solace in the miracle of a well-stocked pantry.

On their second week together, Nessa played a tin whistle and sang experimental bits of a ballad about their adventures while Clover stirred a white-bean soup seasoned with smoked fish, rosemary, and pine nuts. Between songs, Widow Henshaw nudged the oven embers with a long stick, told stories about her days in the Society, and mused about reviving her old chapter. The soup had just been ladled into the bowls when they heard someone whistle from the bridge.

Clover leaped up, grabbing the Pistol from the battered medical bag, and ran to see who it was.

It wasn't poachers and it wasn't returning villagers. Margaret, the granddaughter of Yellow Mouse, was waiting on the bridge, attended by two runner-scouts. Margaret wore a beaded belt and the same scowl that Clover remembered.

Margaret lifted her hands to show that she wasn't holding a weapon.

"You dropped something," she said, opening the satchel on her hip. A little head poked out.

"Susanna!" Clover cried as the Doll leaped out and ran across the bridge, giving her leg a bruising hug. Clover picked her up and examined her. Susanna had been lovingly repaired with new hemp fabric. Her belly, well-stuffed with fresh wool, was now armored with stripes of red and yellow beads. She looked better than ever. Even her button eyes shone with beeswax polish.

Susanna spread her arms, proudly displaying her repairs. "Many stitches strong!"

"Of course you are!"

Margaret said, "The little monster insisted we bring her. She threw a tantrum. In fact, she threw a cannon."

"Did you throw a cannon?" Clover tickled Susanna, and the Doll grumbled, clambering roughly up onto Clover's shoulder. "Thank you for bringing her all this way," she said to Margaret.

Sehanna runners were famous for their endurance. The trip that had taken Clover a week might have taken Margaret only a few days, but it was still a considerable journey.

"You're easy to find." The way Margaret spoke, it sounded like a warning. "The war is still coming."

"I'll have no part in it," Clover said. She knew Margaret was right. Despite her best efforts, Clover had only postponed the hostilities.

Clover studied the visitors, wondering how Widow Henshaw would react if she invited Yellow Mouse's granddaughter in for soup. Something was troubling about Margaret's appearance, though Clover couldn't put her finger on it. The warrior wore the same enviable deerskin leggings and silver armbands. It was when Margaret turned to leave that Clover saw that the beads in her braids had been replaced with iridescent feathers. Clover felt Sweetwater's rattle twitch against her ribs. That was it. Even from a distance, Clover recognized those feathers.

They belonged to Hannibal.

But before Clover could say anything, Margaret and her lieutenants were gone, running swiftly down the road.

Clover considered running after them, demanding an explanation, but she was hesitant to cross the bridge. She was afraid that if she took one step from Salamander Lake, she'd be swept away by trouble again.

"Soup's getting cold," Nessa hollered, approaching the bridge. "Who was that, anyway?" Seeing Susanna on Clover's shoulder, Nessa stopped in her tracks and went pale. "Law and lye, not that thing again! Isn't the snake enough?"

Clover couldn't help but smile at the pout on Nessa's face. Clover put her arm around her friend's shoulder, and together the incorrigible group headed back to the warmth of the cottage, following the smell of the molasses-rye bread Widow Henshaw had just pulled, steaming, from the oven.

The Journal of Anomalous Objects

Notable American Artifacts, Persons, and Phenomena

Fifth Edition, 1813

Compiled and Edited by Ruth O. Yamada and Aaron Agate
Oddities denoted with †, having been in Miniver Elkin's collection,
were lost or destroyed in the fire of 1810.

◆ **Birdcage (see Canary)**

◆ **Canary, Fauna #FP5**, *Confirmed*
A brass-wire Birdcage, with a simple latch door. Upon placing one's head within the empty Birdcage, a person will see
through the Canary's eyes, no matter how far away the bird
wanders, to invigorating and disorienting effect.

◆ **Doll, AKA Susanna, Item #05**, *Confirmed*
A hand-sewn child's toy of cotton and faded yarn with button
eyes. The Doll is quick and extremely strong. The upper limit
of her strength has yet to be determined, but one editor of this
publication has seen her lift an anvil with ease. Her temper

makes her dangerous, though she can be mollified by the lullaby "Susanna, Don't Be Sore." She prefers to rest in dark nooks, such as cigar boxes or coffee tins, and is best left alone.

◆ **EMBER, AKA HERON'S HEART, ITEM #IEO32,** *Confirmed*
A hot coal the size of a dollar coin. A rare "Incarnate Elemental" object, the Ember never expires and cannot be extinguished by any means. It will ignite any flammable material it touches. When enough smoke has gathered, an explosion will produce an animated conflagration in the form of a Heron. It was previously catalogued as the "Phoenix," but ornithologists have since testified that the morphology of the bird is most similar to that of a blue heron. The Heron will always swallow the Ember first and then proceed on random and catastrophic wanderings, growing in size as it eats. It is responsible for the destruction of the entire Hawthorn Forest. It is an incredibly dangerous oddity that must be kept in a fireproof iron box, far from flammable materials.

◆ **FIDDLE, ITEM #O55,** *Unconfirmed*
A worn red-lacquered violin in the French style. The Fiddle, when played, is said to make anyone hearing it dance, against their will and without rest, until the music stops. This oddity has been described by people of dubious character, but reports of its existence persist.

◆ **FROG, FAUNA #F6,** *Confirmed†*
A small brass-colored tree frog. The Frog is unremarkable in

every way except that it is entirely immune to heat and fire. It has been known to swim happily in boiling oil. Tadpoles and minnows swimming near the Frog benefit from its effect, surviving similar insults until separated from the Frog.

◆ **GLOVES, ITEM #013,** *Confirmed†*
Pale-yellow calfskin long gloves of the type worn by ladies in spring. This pair of Gloves allows wearers to share thoughts, memories, and even dreams. If one user wears the right and the other user the left, they will be able to communicate in the most intimate manner no matter the distance between them. The effect is said to be quite pleasant.

◆ **HANNIBAL FURLONG (SEE ROOSTER)**

◆ **HAT (SEE SMALT), ITEM#AP29,** *Confirmed*
A light-blue silk Hat made in an outmoded colonial fashion. The Hat forces secrets out of anyone who looks into it. Its effect is irresistible and sickening. The secrets stored in the Hat can be retrieved at will by the user. The Hat has been classified as extremely toxic, having corroded the humanity of its longtime user, Smalt, who uses it to blackmail victims. Secrets have been known to leak from the Hat and move about of their own accord. By some accounts, Smalt has been in possession of the Hat for over a hundred years. The effects of the Hat have atrophied Smalt's body to an extremely frail state while somehow extending his lifespan unnaturally.

◆ **HERON'S HEART (SEE EMBER)**

- **HIERONYMUS K. WILLOW (SEE LONG COAT), WRAITH #M5**, *Confirmed*

A short, portly man, whose image wavers like a distant mirage. Willow is a reclusive being who vanishes when spoken to. Mr. Willow is often spotted stealing pies and pastries. His Long Coat seems to have rendered him intangible. Some describe him as "like a reflection on water" or "more shadow than man." Despite his girth, Willow seems to be suffering an insatiable hunger. He has also been accused of more serious crimes, ranging from poisoning wells to toppling church steeples, but it is hard to know what he is truly guilty of. When something unlucky happens, many people will say, "Willow did it."

- **ICE HOOK, ITEM #E07**, *Confirmed*

Curved steel tool with wooden handle. The Ice Hook is, itself, incredibly cold and will freeze any water it touches.

- **LONG COAT (SEE HIERONYMUS K. WILLOW), ITEM #AP42**, *Partially Confirmed*

A dark-gray woolen coat with an ermine collar. It is believed to be an oddity that gives its user the ability to move through shadows. Other theories posit that the Long Coat turns its user to smoke. Hieronymus K. Willow is said to use its power to steal food, traveling to distant locations instantly. Willow, however, is extremely antisocial, so this oddity has been particularly difficult to verify. The Long Coat seems to have made Willow insatiable and should be considered a toxic oddity.

♦ **MATCHBOX, MATCHES, ITEM #EO48,** *Confirmed*

A small wooden box, reddish in color, containing a number of sulfur Matches. The printed manufacturer's label is long since worn away and illegible. The Matches, when struck, stop time. So long as the Match burns, the user may move freely about a world completely frozen and immobile. A rare case of an oddity that degrades with use, the number of Matches seems limited. The box once held fifty Matches but as of this publication contains fewer than twenty. Some scholars speculate that the box itself is the oddity and will impart curious behavior to any Matches placed inside it. This has not been verified. The criminal Willit Rummage has been known to use the Matches to take victims by surprise. Rummage once sold a forgery of this oddity at auction for four hundred dollars. The buyer, not wanting to waste the matches, was not aware of the cheat for several months, by which time Rummage had fled the county.

♦ **MINER'S LETTUCE, FLORA #FL01,** *Partially Confirmed*

A weed looking like every other, in a small clay pot. One who eats even a single leaf from this plant will turn into an animal. Much is unknown about this oddity: whether one can choose which animal to turn into, whether the roots or flowers of the Miner's Lettuce have the same effect. Trusted Society member Kingsley Hook claimed to have witnessed his cousin eat a pinch and turn into a shrew. Shortly thereafter, Mr. Hook himself disappeared and is yet to be found. Mr. Hook's doors were found locked from the inside, and a barn owl was discovered roosting in his bookshelves. The owl flew away, but shrew bones were found in its nest. Anyone with any information about these events should write to the Society immediately. The particular effects of the Miner's Lettuce remain unstudied, as no safe test of its effects has been devised. Proposals to test the Miner's Lettuce on criminal convicts have been dismissed as inhumane.

◆ **MIRROR, ITEM #OO2**, *Confirmed†*

The poorly understood Mirror is both a portal to an identical world and a kind of Lethe. Those who enter forget. On September 17, 1789, Ephram Carter entered the Mirror with a rope tied around his waist and written notes to remind him of his purpose. However, upon crossing the threshold, he untied the rope immediately and wandered away. He spoke not a word, but his aggrieved assistant who held the rope on the other end reported that he looked happier in the Mirror than he had ever been on this side: "He seemed not to have forgotten this world, as much as to have remembered a better one. He moved with quick determination, as if called by a happy task, or a beloved's voice, just beyond the frame." No one who has entered the Mirror has ever returned. The Mirror never reflects the viewer herself. It presents an identical room but empty, as if waiting for guests. Collector and editor Ruth Yamada has offered this argument: "We know that everyone who enters the Mirror forgets themselves. But if they wander off into that twin reality and refuse to return, can we be certain that the world of the Mirror isn't a kind of heaven?"

♦ **MUSIC BOX, ITEM #O34,** *Partially Confirmed†*

A mother-of-pearl inlaid music box with a steel crank, in the Swiss style, playing a variation on Ober's Sonata in G. The Music Box is an item shrouded in much confusion. Although well-trusted Society members, including Miniver Elkin, Pierre Bertrand, and Kingsley Hook, have examined it at length, there is no clear consensus on its effects. Reports vary wildly, even from observers who witnessed the same demonstration. Some say the music from the Box induces a waking dream. Others say the music "rearranges reality." Some who heard the music suffered dramatic and permanent personality changes, while others claim to have "seen under the rug of creation itself." It is unclear if the Music Box affects the perceptions of witnesses or the world itself. Because of the uncertainty surrounding this object, it should be considered an object of moderate toxicity.

♦ **PESTLE, ITEM #O41,** *Confirmed†*

A ceramic pharmaceutical-grade mortar and Pestle. The Pestle can be used to grind human teeth into a blue Powder that is a powerful panacea, able to cure any ailment. It was this Powder that cured President Cooper of his typhoid fever and gout. Attempts to grind other items with the Pestle have resulted in nothing remarkable.

♦ **PHOENIX (SEE EMBER)**

♦ **PISTOL, ITEM #W17,** *Confirmed*

A single-shot handgun with a flint-strike hammer and walrus-ivory grip. The Pistol never misses its target. The user need only imagine the target before pulling the trigger, and the Pistol will send a bullet along a curved or even knotted trajectory if necessary. While the Pistol cannot miss a nearby target, those out of range will be spared, as the bullet cannot fly indefinitely. The Pistol will fire any bullet that fits its caliber.

◆ **POWDER (SEE PESTLE)**

◆ **ROOSTER, AKA HANNIBAL FURLONG, FAUNA #FP1**, *Confirmed*
A red leghorn cock. Sometimes referred to as the "bird that saved New Manchester," the Rooster is physically identical to any other bird of its pedigree, with the exception that it can talk and has the intelligence and personality of a grown man and proven tactical talents that led to US victories during the Louisiana War. The Rooster prefers to be addressed as Colonel Hannibal Furlong and, as a sentient being with its own agenda, is not subject to collection or study. The controversies over how to catalogue this rare living oddity have led to schisms within the Society, which will not be resolved in this publication.

◆ **SEAMSTRESS, AKA THE WITCH IN THE MOUNTAIN, WRAITH #P6**, *Confirmed*
A frail crone wearing rags and a necklace of human teeth, the Seamstress disturbs the vision of any witness, appearing as through a broken window, though some say she is sewn together like a quilt. The Seamstress, though called a witch, is presumably a human being in the grip of a savage oddity, just as Smalt is enthralled by the Hat and Hieronymus K.

Willow is subject to the Long Coat. She is said to have hoarded a large collection of oddities somewhere south of the Wine Marsh. Though the exact nature of these items is unclear, they have granted her the ability to reanimate creatures (see Vermin), which do her bidding. She has an unexplained craving for human teeth, and all children know that they should place lost teeth on the windowsill or risk the witch coming into their bedroom while they sleep. The Seamstress has been spotted in the Centurion Mountains, collecting dead-animal pelts and singing strange songs. The Seamstress has been blamed for the New Manchester fire that claimed the life of Miniver Elkin. Those events have led to increased secrecy and security around oddity collections.

♦ **SMALT (SEE HAT), WRAITH #P4,** *Confirmed*

A tall, very thin gentleman dressed in the elaborate fashion of the macaroni dandies. Smalt is a powerful manipulator of politics, using dirty secrets as currency. He has stationed messengers and lawyers in every major city under orders to deliver envelopes of secrets to the newspapers if Smalt suffers injury. Politicians have gone to great lengths to keep Smalt safe for fear that these secrets will come to public scrutiny. Smalt has been under the influence of the Hat for so long that even his body has withered, leaving him little more than a scarecrow. A carriage driver who once helped Smalt into his seat reported that he weighed "no more than a wet sock." Smalt survives entirely on a diet of white vinegar.

♦ **SUSANNA (SEE DOLL)**

- **TEAPOT, ITEM #092,** *Confirmed*
  A white china teapot with blue glazing. The Teapot will provide any amount of hot chamomile tea and has never been emptied.

- **THIMBLE, ITEM #0101,** *Partially Confirmed*
  A dimpled brass sewing Thimble. The Thimble, when worn in the usual manner, renders the user's body impervious to any kind of piercing. Needles, knives, and swords bounce harmlessly off anyone who wears the Thimble on their finger. Many believe that the Thimble would render the user bulletproof as well. This has not been confirmed, as a safe test of the theory has not yet been devised.

- **UMBRELLA, ITEM #AP13,** *Unconfirmed*
  Green silk over steel framework, with polished teak handle. The Umbrella is said to weather lightning strikes undamaged, protecting the user from even the most violent bolts. It may also store bolts indefinitely and then discharge them at the user's whim, which, if true, would make it a powerful and potentially dangerous object indeed. Previously catalogued as "confirmed" by Society member Thadeus Pendergrasse, the item is now of uncertain status. Tragically, Mr. Pendergrasse died of a lightning strike while holding a green umbrella. Whether he was holding a forgery or was mistaken about the power of the oddity entirely is uncertain. The Umbrella currently in Mr. X's collection is thought to be the genuine article but awaits confirmation. A safe test of the item has yet to be devised.

VERMIN (SEE SEAMSTRESS), FAUNA-PHENOMENON #FM3, *Confirmed*

Reanimated corpses of small animals, such as rats and raccoons, suspended on skeletons of twisted metal and miscellaneous materials, the vermin are autonomous creatures who serve their creator, the Seamstress. They are capable of speech but generally lurk about, spying or stealing objects for the Seamstress. They have been known to attack and should be considered extremely dangerous. Vermin should be utterly destroyed, preferably with fire, at every opportunity. The latest consensus is that vermin are not, themselves, oddities but are products of some unknown oddity used by the Seamstress. Their numbers have been increasing steadily over time and constitute a civic menace.

WINEGLASS, ITEM #067, *Confirmed*

A long-stemmed, blown wineglass. The Wineglass is perpetually full of red wine no matter how much has been drunk from it. Some members believe this glass fueled the debauches of certain Roman emperors. The Wineglass was lost in the Sojourner Valley, which has since become the Wine Marsh. Some say it was buried intentionally during the Louisiana War. If so, it is one of the first instances of an oddity used for purposes of war. The Wine Marsh grew relentlessly, causing panic that it would eventually drown the world. In 1809, the evaporation rate matched the pace of the Wineglass's outflow. The Wine Marsh is no longer expanding, but the Wineglass will likely never be recovered. Some members have suggested sinking explosives into the marsh in an attempt to shatter the Wineglass and drain the marsh. This is a controversial proposal.

ACKNOWLEDGMENTS

Without the support of the following people and institutions, this novel would not be what it is:

Beth Ryan, BREW Coffee and Beer House, Cadence Godwin, Catherine Armsden, Cheryl Klein, Dr. Crystal Feimster, David Goldstone, Davida Brown, Davon Godwin, Harold Brown, Karin Rytter, Laurie Fox, Nova Brown, the Sustainable Arts Foundation, Teagan White, Tony Guaraldi-Brown, Tonya Hersch, Ulli and Scott Klein of KLEINeFARM, and Yaddo.

I'm especially indebted to Melissa Michaud, Stephen Barr, and Susan Van Metre.

With sincere gratitude, I thank you all.

ABOUT THE AUTHOR

As a child, **ELI BROWN** thought he would have definitely befriended a sasquatch by now. His most recent novel, *Cinnamon and Gunpowder*, about a chef kidnapped by pirates, was a finalist for the California Book Award, a San Francisco Public Library One City One Book selection, and an NPR Book Concierge Great Read selection. Eli Brown lives with his family in California, where the squirrels bury acorns in his garden and the cats bury worse.